"You really do believe my brother was murdered?" Heather asked.

Tyler nodded. "I do. Whatever information he had found about the drug mastermind cost him his life."

And now put her and her son in danger.

She shook her head. "No, *you* cost him his life. You pushed him to do something he wasn't trained to do."

The sharp tip of her barb hit him squarely in the gut. "A fact I will have to live with," Tyler stated with more regret than she could possibly know. "Believe me, I wish I had done things differently."

Tyler had been doing his job. A job that wasn't finished. "If I am going to bring his murderers to justice, I need to find the notebook he told me he had."

She held his gaze. "That's why you broke into the house."

"I didn't break in. As I said, your brother gave me a key. He'd said if anything happened to him that I'd find what I needed here at the farm."

Well, something had happened. Something terrible. And he wasn't going to let *anything* happen to Heather and her boy.

Terri Reed's romance and romantic suspense novels have appeared on the *Publishers Weekly* top twenty-five and Nielsen BookScan top one hundred lists, and have been featured in *USA TODAY*, *Christian Fiction* magazine and *RT Book Reviews*. Her books have been finalists for the Romance Writers of America RITA® Award and the National Readers' Choice Award and finalists three times for the American Christian Fiction Writers Carol Award. Contact Terri at terrireed.com or PO Box 19555, Portland, OR 97224.

Maggie K. Black is an award-winning journalist and romantic suspense author with an insatiable love of traveling the world. She has lived in the American South, Europe and the Middle East. She now makes her home in Canada with her history-teacher husband, their two beautiful girls and a small but mighty dog. Maggie enjoys connecting with her readers at maggiekblack.com.

Murder Under the Mistletoe

Terri Reed

&

Christmas Blackout

Maggie K. Black

LOVE INSPIRED
INSPIRATIONAL ROMANCE

LOVE INSPIRED®

INSPIRATIONAL ROMANCE

Recycling programs
for this product may
not exist in your area.

ISBN-13: 978-1-335-42495-2

Murder Under the Mistletoe and Christmas Blackout

Copyright © 2021 by Harlequin Books S.A.

Murder Under the Mistletoe
First published in 2015. This edition published in 2021.
Copyright © 2015 by Terri Reed

Christmas Blackout
First published in 2015. This edition published in 2021.
Copyright © 2015 by Mags Storey

This edition published by arrangement with Harlequin Books S.A.

For questions and comments about the quality of this book, please contact us
at CustomerService@Harlequin.com.

Love Inspired
22 Adelaide St. West, 40th Floor
Toronto, Ontario M5H 4E3, Canada
www.Harlequin.com

Printed in U.S.A.

CONTENTS

MURDER UNDER THE MISTLETOE

Terri Reed

This book is dedicated to my family
for all the support and love you give me every day.
God blessed me greatly with a wonderful husband
and two fabulous kids.

Every good and perfect gift is from above,
coming down from the Father of the heavenly lights,
who does not change like shifting shadows.
—*James* 1:17

Chapter One

"Good night, sweet boy." Heather Larson-Randall leaned in to kiss her six-year-old son's forehead.

"Night, Mommy." Colin snuggled deeper beneath the thick comforter. He lay in the twin-size bed in the room that once had been Heather's.

Gone were the decorations of her adolescence—posters of the latest celebrity heartthrob and her 4-H ribbons and trophies. It had taken the past three days to transform the room in a superhero motif that would have made Ken, her late husband, proud.

A cold draft skated across the back of her neck. The late November night had grown chilly, but at least the northern Idaho rain had abated for now. The weatherman had predicted a drop in temperature over the next few days. Fitting for this year's Thanksgiving. She just needed to get through the day for Colin's sake. Then she could concentrate on Christmas.

Hopefully celebrating the birth of Jesus would take her mind off her brother's tragic death.

She also hoped they had snow by Christmas morning. Colin loved the snow. And, as always, her life's priority was Colin.

She moved to the bedroom door. The creak of the old farmhouse's hardwood floor beneath her feet followed each of her steps, echoing the hollow, lonely beat of her heart.

"Mommy?"

Pausing in the doorway with her hand hovering over the light switch, she smiled patiently at her son. Colin looked so much like Ken with his dark brown hair falling over one eye and his dimpled chin. She ached with love for her son and regret that he'd never know his father. "Yes, sweetie?"

Her late parents had taught her that replacing the word *what* with the more positive *yes* when talking to children created a strong, effective bond. The proof was in how close her family had been.

Colin's big blue-green eyes stared at her intently. "Do you think Uncle Seth is with Daddy and Grandma and Grandpa?"

The innocent question speared through her like a hot poker. She bit the inside of her cheek to keep the tears of grief at bay. Five years ago, just before Colin's first birthday, her husband had been killed while serving his country in Afghanistan, leaving Heather to raise their son alone. She'd made sure every day that Colin knew his father had loved him. Adding to her grief, her parents had been killed in a freak car accident when Colin was four.

Now, two years later and five days ago, she'd lost

her younger brother, Seth, to what appeared to be a cocaine overdose.

She struggled to comprehend how Seth had fallen back into using drugs after being clean the past couple of years. He'd had so much going for him. A fiancée he adored, half the tree farm and a bright future. She didn't know what had sent him running back to the abyss.

Placing one hand on her chest, she leaned against the doorjamb, needing the strength of her childhood home to keep her upright when the grief pressing down on her threatened to send her to the floor in a heap. "Yes, dear. I'm sure they are all together."

A familiar tide of anger washed over her. Anger at God for allowing the tragedies that had left her and Colin alone in the world. On the heels of the anger came a flood of guilt for blaming God. Sometimes it was hard to cling to her faith when the world tried to knock her down.

The cell phone in the pocket of her plush robe buzzed.

"I'll come back to check on you in a bit," she told Colin, then flipped off the light and stepped into the dimly lit hallway to answer the phone.

"Hello?"

"Your brother's death isn't what it seems," a rough, low voice said into her ear, sending a chill down her spine. "Leave the farm. It's not safe."

Her breath hitched; her mind reeled. "What? Who is this?"

The line beeped, then went silent.

A tremor from deep inside worked its way out of her. *Leave the farm. It's not safe.*

She put a hand on the wall to steady herself, feeling the familiar fuzzy velvet texture of the flock wallpaper. This couldn't be happening, not now with Seth's death hanging over her like a cloud of doom.

His death had been ruled an accidental overdose.

Even if she wanted to leave the farm, she and Colin had nowhere to go. The day she had learned of Seth's death, she'd given up her job and the apartment in Washington State to move back to Idaho.

Now the Christmas tree farm was her and Colin's only home. Their livelihood. Without the farm she wasn't sure what would happen to them.

Seeds of fear burrowed in her chest and took root. She quickly made her way downstairs, checking that the doors were securely locked. She peered out the front picture window. The full moon, big and round and shining brightly, bathed the sea of Douglas fir, grand fir and noble fir trees stretching over forty acres of land on the tree farm that had been in her family for three generations.

Long shadows obscured the front drive. The other work buildings on the farm were dark, as well. The small cabins that provided lodging for the seasonal employees couldn't be seen through the thick grove of trees, creating a sense of isolation that had never bothered her when she was growing up here.

But she'd never had a menacing phone call before now.

Suddenly movement on the fringe between the trees

and the wide expanse of lawn caught her eye. Then the shadow shifted and disappeared. Had she really seen something out there? Or was fear making her paranoid?

She yanked the curtains closed. Surely she was imagining things. Satisfied the house was locked up tight, she hurried back upstairs to the master bedroom that had once belonged to her parents and her grandparents before them. Though she'd replaced her parents' belongings with her own, she still considered the room theirs.

Sitting on the edge of the bed, she called the local sheriff's office and told the answering sergeant about the disturbing call. She couldn't be sure she'd seen anything in the shadows of the trees, so she kept that to herself. Because there was no immediate threat, the sergeant promised to send a deputy over in the morning.

Not at all reassured, she hung up and crawled into bed. She held her phone to her chest. Right now she wished she'd given in to Colin's pleas for a dog. Tomorrow she would go to the local animal shelter and find a nice big canine with a loud bark.

She leaned back against the pillows, her gaze landing on the picture of her parents hanging on the opposite wall. Her mother had been so beautiful and her father so handsome. But more important, they'd been great parents to her and Seth, providing a stable home and love. Lots of love.

The very things she wanted to give Colin.

Somehow none of that had been enough to keep Seth from turning to drugs. She didn't know what had driven him to seek the high of narcotics when he was younger. Or more recently. The not knowing ate at her. He'd refused to talk about the dark days of his addiction. Heather had hoped one day he'd realize she loved him no matter what.

Maybe if she'd stayed closer to home rather than leaving for college, Seth wouldn't have turned into a junkie. Maybe if she'd begged, Ken would have left the army. Maybe if she'd been with her parents that night, they wouldn't have died in that accident. Maybe, maybe, maybe.

She turned off the light and lay in the dark. She wanted to pray for God to protect them and lessen the burden of guilt she carried. But her prayers for Ken's safety had gone unanswered. Why would God listen to her now?

Her eyelids grew heavy. Her head bobbed as sleep's greedy hands pulled her into slumber.

A soft thud jolted her fully awake. Her heart nearly exploded with fright. She bolted from the bed and strained to listen.

Nothing.

Maybe it had been Colin getting up to use the bathroom. Yes, that had to be it. She sucked in air and slowly released her breath, working to calm her frantic pulse. She glanced at the clock. She'd slept for three hours.

After pulling on her robe, she padded quietly down the hall to check on her son. The bathroom was dark and empty. She moved on to his room. The moon's glow streamed through the open curtains, revealing

Colin fast asleep. She closed the door and waited. The house was silent now, yet the hairs on her nape rose and chills prickled her skin.

Cautiously, she moved to the top of the stairs and stared into darkness.

Was someone in the house?

Another noise jolted through her, making her tremble. She needed to call for help. As quietly as she could, she raced back to her bedroom and swiped the phone off the bed, then hurried into the hall and stood guard in front of Colin's door. She dialed and when the sergeant answered, she whispered, "This is Heather Randall again. There's someone in my house!"

"Are you sure?" the man asked. "Have you seen an intruder?"

"No, I heard a noise."

He sighed. "Sit tight. I'll send one of the deputies out."

Sit tight? It would take at least thirty minutes for a deputy to reach the farm from Bonners Ferry, the nearest town. Was she supposed to wait and see if the intruder decided to come upstairs? Then what? She had no weapon, no way to defend herself or Colin. She thanked the deputy anyway and hung up.

She couldn't sit there like some insipid victim. She crept slowly down the staircase, careful to avoid the spots that would creak. She knew every inch of this house, knew every board that would betray her presence, every piece of furniture to navigate around in the inky blackness. She made her way to the kitchen.

She glanced at the knife block with the razor-sharp

knife set. As tempting as it was to grab a knife to use as a weapon, she knew that wasn't a good choice. A knife could be too easily taken away and used against her. Instead, she moved to the stove.

Careful not to jostle the pans hanging over the range, she grabbed the largest cast-iron skillet. Her mother's favorite. Hefting the heavy pan in her hands like a baseball bat, she crept back to the stairs.

At the bottom step, she waited, listening.

All was quiet. She was being paranoid. The noises she'd heard had been the house settling for the night. All the doors and windows were locked up tight. The phone call had been a mean hoax, meant to frighten her.

Well, it had worked. Her hands tightened around the cold handle of the skillet. She placed one foot on the first step.

A soft knock at the back door echoed in the stillness of the house.

Abandoning the stairs, she pressed her back to the wall. Adjusting her grip more firmly on the skillet's sturdy handle, she inched toward the kitchen. She peered around the corner. The outline of a man shone through the curtained window on the back door.

She *had* seen someone creeping around outside. And now they wanted inside.

Who would come to the farmhouse in the middle of the night? Caution had her refrain from turning on the lights. If she didn't answer the door, would the person go away?

She hoped so.

The person knocked again, louder this time.

Maybe it was the sheriff's deputy. Right, one just happened to be close enough?

It was possible, she supposed. Wary, she approached the door and flipped on the outside porch light. But nothing happened. Great timing to have a burned-out lightbulb at the exact moment she needed the glow.

As indecision on what to do warred within her, the man outside turned the doorknob. She jumped back, prepared to use the skillet to defend herself.

She should retreat and wait upstairs as the sergeant had said. That would be the smart thing to do. But what if the intruder decided to break in? What if he got to her son before the police could arrive?

A surge of protectiveness coursed through her veins. Adrenaline shoved back the fear. She was alone. It was up to her to defend her house, her son. She stood her ground.

The unmistakable sound of a key sliding into the lock and the lock's tumblers turning ratcheted her tension.

She moved swiftly to press her back against the wall next to the door seconds before the door opened and the intruder stepped inside. A small beam of light glowed in the darkness as the man moved forward. Holding her breath, she knew she had the element of surprise on her side and one shot at felling the trespasser. She had to make it count.

Stepping carefully behind the figure, she raised the iron fry pan and swung.

* * *

The swoosh of moving air alerted DEA agent Tyler Griffin to an impending attack. He spun around, the penlight dropping to the ground, and raised an arm to deflect the blow. He was too late. Something hard and solid glanced off his elbow and connected with his head, sending pain shooting in all directions through his body.

The crack to his noggin sent him staggering backward until his back hit the dining room table. He toppled sideways into a sprawling heap on the floor. His elbow throbbed all the way to his shoulder.

He shook his head, trying to regain his equilibrium. He could barely make out the dark form of a body standing a few feet away. He wrenched his sidearm from the holster attached to his belt. "Halt! DEA!"

His shout didn't quite have the normal amount of punch it usually held.

The figure retreated a few steps.

Tyler blinked back the spots and aimed. His finger hovered near the trigger, but he couldn't keep his assailant in focus long enough to fire.

The sudden glare of the overhead light blinded him. With a sinking feeling, he realized he made an easy target if his assailant decided to finish him off. This wasn't the way he'd pictured his life ending.

But, then again, he wasn't in control of life's happenings. He'd learned that long ago. The best he could do was pray that if God wanted to take him now, that it was quick and painless.

"You're a cop?"

The distinctly female voice had him blinking rapidly to adjust to the light. He lowered his sidearm. His gaze fixed on the woman standing by the back door he'd just come through. She held a large black cast-iron skillet in her hands, looking as if she were ready to take another swing at his head.

He nearly laughed out loud. He'd allowed an assailant to get the drop on him. A woman with a frying pan, at that. Man, he must be suffering burnout.

He could only imagine the ribbing he'd suffer when his fellow agents found out he'd been clocked by a raven-haired beauty in a fuzzy yellow robe and… Were those toe socks?

Her tangle of thick ebony curls cascaded about her shoulders like a cloud, and the most amazing hazel eyes regarded him with stark fear. Her gaze moved to the gun in his hand, then back to meet his scrutiny.

Forcing himself to a sitting position, he reholstered his weapon and let his head sink into his hands with a groan. "You hit me."

"I'll do it again if you don't tell me who you are and what you're doing here and how you have a key to my house," she growled.

Feisty, considering he'd had her at gunpoint. Lifting his head, he started at the sight of his hands covered with blood. Apparently the knock over the head with the pan had broken the skin on his scalp. Hopefully, that was the only thing she'd broken.

He reached for his ID wallet and held it up for her to see. "Agent Tyler Griffin, DEA. You must be Heather."

One lip curled up. "Obviously." Her dark winged

brows dipped as she took a step closer to inspect his credentials. She danced back and frowned. "How do I know that's real, and how do you know my name?"

"It's real. You can check it out if you'd like." He held the leather case out for her to take. "There's a number on the card you can call."

"Throw it over."

Smart, too. He liked that. He tossed it so it landed at her feet. Keeping her focus on him, she picked the wallet up. Her straight white teeth tugged on her bottom lip. "You didn't answer me. How did you get a key, and how do you know who I am?"

"Your brother."

Her eyes narrowed. "What?"

"Seth gave me the key." Tyler probed the tender spot on his head. "He was working with us."

Disbelief skipped across her lovely face. "Right. Seth was working with the DEA? Why would he give you a key to the house?"

"Yes, he was working for us." He cringed. He loathed explaining why he had the key, but there was no help for it. He had to tell her. "He gave me the key in case anything happened to him."

"I don't believe you. The sheriff's on his way."

Perfect. Could this operation get any more complicated? They'd purposely kept the local law out of the loop in case there was corruption within the department. Tyler hadn't wanted to blow his confidential informant's identity.

He mentally snorted as the sharp blade of guilt

twisted in his gut. Seth's cover had been blown just the same.

"Look, call the number on the card. Then we'll talk."

"Put your gun on the floor and kick it over to me," she said, her eyes sparking with challenge and distrust.

"No way. That's not how this works." An agent never handed over his firearm. He stood. The world swam. His vision blurred. He reached out for the desk and missed.

He toppled face-first onto the floor and fell into darkness.

Oh, no. He'd passed out. Or had she killed him?

Horrified by either prospect, Heather remained rooted to the floor. Her first impulse was to help him. But the need to protect her son was a fierce force, urging her to turn tail and run, grab Colin and head for the car.

She couldn't leave the intruder lying there without making sure he wasn't dead. Or that he didn't die from the wound she'd given him. She would not feel guilty for clobbering him with the pan.

Stuffing his wallet into the deep pocket of her robe, she tentatively moved closer. Her foot bumped up against the gun holstered at his hip. Carefully, she slipped the weapon from the leather holster and clicked on the safety before tucking it into her pocket next to his ID.

Her muscles and nerves tensed, on high alert, ready to jump away if he so much as twitched. He didn't move. She laid two fingers against his neck. His pulse beat with a strong rhythm. *Good.* He wasn't dead, only unconscious.

Which wasn't good. She'd probably given him a concussion.

She gently turned him onto his back. He'd made an intimidating picture awake, but now with his features relaxed, she noticed the chiseled strength of his jaw, the angles and planes of his brow and cheekbones. *Handsome.* Though his eyelids were closed now, she'd noticed his striking blue eyes were the color of the sky on a clear day.

He had to be at least six feet tall. The black cargo pants and black long-sleeved T-shirt beneath the leather jacket showed off a well-conditioned physique. Was he really a drug enforcement agent? What did he mean, Seth had been working for them?

She grabbed a kitchen towel and used the material as a makeshift bandage for the laceration on his scalp. Then, after undoing the ties to the dining room chair cushion, she slid the cushion off the seat, gently lifted the injured, unconscious man's head and slipped the pillow beneath him. His eyelids popped open. Startled, she scuttled back and slipped a hand into her pocket to cradle the gun there.

Keeping a close watch on him, she called the number on the card placed opposite his badge inside the brown leather case and even though the man that answered identified himself as Deputy Director Moore, she asked, "How do I know you're who you say you are?"

The agent sat up and rubbed his head. She stared him down, and he met her gaze, waiting.

"Excuse me? Who is this?" Irritation threaded through the tone of the man on the other end of the line.

Not willing to give her name, she said, "I've a man here claiming he's a DEA agent and that you are his boss. But how do I know you two aren't in league together and this isn't some elaborate scam?"

"Madame, call this number." The man rattled off a ten-digit number. Thankful for the memorization skills she'd learned in college, she put the number to memory. "You can confirm for yourself who I am. Once you have, ring me back." The man hung up.

Still disbelieving, she input the number into the phone and waited a moment until a woman answered, "Department of Homeland Security, how may I direct your call?"

Surprised, she hesitated, then hung up. Was this for real? Homeland Security? No way.

She quickly called 411 and asked for the main number of the Department of Homeland Security. The automated voice gave her the same number that she'd just dialed.

Stunned but not quite ready to accept that the man sitting on the floor watching her was really law enforcement, she redialed the number for Homeland Security and asked to speak to Deputy Director Moore.

"The deputy director is not in at the moment. Would you care to leave a name and number for when he returns?"

Heather chewed on her bottom lip for a second before she said, "Uh, can you tell me if there is an agent name Tyler Griffin working for the DEA?"

"I'm not at liberty to give out that information. Did you want to leave a message for the deputy director?"

"No, that's okay." Heather hung up.

Tyler arched an eyebrow at her.

She narrowed her gaze and redialed Deputy Director Moore's direct line. He answered on the first ring.

The man confirmed his agent's identity. The relief was unexpected. At least she didn't have to fear the agent was there to hurt her.

"Let me speak to Agent Griffin," the gruff man on the phone demanded.

She squatted down next to Tyler and handed him the phone. "He wants to talk to you."

Tyler held the phone to his ear. "Griffin here."

He listened, his mouth pressing into a grim line. "Yes, sir. I understand, sir. The local sheriff is on his way here. Thank you, sir." He pressed the end button. "My boss will be in contact with the sheriff's department." He held out the phone. "Are you satisfied?"

"I suppose." Her fingers curled around the phone.

His hand clasped around her wrist.

She let out a little yelp and tried to break his hold. His grip was warm, tight, but not painful.

"Not so fast," he said. His intent gaze held her captive as surely as his hand. "I want my gun back."

Her heart beat wildly. "It's in my pocket." Why did she sound as if she'd run a marathon?

With his free hand, he reached into the pocket of

her robe, retrieved his weapon and jammed it into his holster.

"Uh, you can let go of me now." She stared at the point where his big hand circled her slender wrist. She had no doubt he could break her bones with a quick snap if he chose to.

He let go, holding his hands up, palms out. "Sorry."

"Tell me what you meant when you said my brother was working with you. And why did he think something would happen to him?"

Tyler scrubbed a hand over his jaw. "Your brother informed my office that your family's tree farm was being used to smuggle cocaine into Canada."

She dropped from a squat to her knees. "Cocaine?"

The official ruling in her brother's death flashed in her mind. Overdose of injectable cocaine. She'd had so much trouble accepting the coroner's findings. Seth had been belonephobic. He abhorred sharp objects, especially needles. He'd snorted, smoked and swallowed his drugs.

Plus he'd promised her he was clean. She'd believed him.

However, the sheriff hadn't believed her when she'd claimed Seth wouldn't have injected himself with drugs. She could tell the sheriff had thought she was fooling herself. He'd said junkies would do whatever they could for the high, even overcome a lifelong fear.

Without any evidence to the contrary, she'd had to come to terms with Seth's death as an accident. But now…?

"Someone here on the farm was involved in drug

smuggling?" It didn't make sense. "That can't be. Most of our employees have been with us for years. I trust them. I can't imagine any of them partaking in drugs, let alone using our farm for nefarious purposes."

"Not all of your employees are long-term, right? You do have some transient workers."

She chewed on the inside of her lip. An anxious flutter started low in her tummy. "True. We do have a few seasonal laborers who come in the fall and stay until Christmas day. Then they travel back to their homes. But those few have been coming for years, as well."

"You can't always predict what people will do if given the right motivation." He slowly stood.

His words sent a shiver of apprehension crawling across the nape of her neck. She rose to face him. "Where is the cocaine coming from?"

"We don't know the direct route, but we do know the source of the cocaine coming into the US is from Central America. There are many drug cartels in various countries south of the border infiltrating both the US and Canada. And more recently, Australia."

Her mouth went dry. "There's a drug cartel here?"

"Possibly." Tyler sank down on the dining room chair. "I'm working with IBETs—Integrated Border Enforcement Teams—we've been investigating rumors of drugs crossing the US–Canadian border for months. Two weeks ago Seth reached out to me and my team."

Pride filled Heather. She could only imagine how scary it had been for Seth to seek help. Going up against a drug cartel was no small feat.

"Apparently last year he'd needed some extra cash,"

Tyler continued. "He had allowed a shipment of co-caine to hitch a ride into Canada with a shipment of trees from your farm. He'd thought it was a onetime deal. But when they came back to him this year, he realized he'd gotten in over his head."

Heather silently groaned. One step forward, two steps back. Seth had always courted trouble with his decision making.

"We—" Tyler grimaced "—I convinced him to find out as much as he could and keep a record of everything he learned, including who, what, where and when."

Stunned, Heather rocked back on her heels. "Let me get this straight. My brother came to you with information about an illegal drug operation on our farm and you—" A cold sweat broke out on her skin. "He was spying for you?"

A grim expression stole over Tyler's face. "Yes."

Heather backed away. Her mind scrambled to make sense of what she was hearing. It was one thing for Seth to be a whistle-blower and another entirely for him to play the role of spy. "That was a dangerous thing for you to ask of him."

"Yes, it was."

She stilled as a thought burned through her brain. Her blood turned to ice. "He didn't die of an accidental overdose. Someone killed him."

"That's what I believe."

"He's dead because of you!"

Tyler closed his eyes. When he opened them, the bleakness in his gaze confirmed her accusation. "Yes."

Chapter Two

Tyler held Heather's gaze with what he hoped was dispassion and not the swirling maelstrom of guilt laying siege to his psyche. He wouldn't shirk the responsibility of Seth Larson's murder.

Despite Seth's past addictions, Tyler had sensed his sincere need to get out from under the thumb of the drug cartel. Though Tyler may not have injected Seth with the lethal dose of cocaine, he felt responsible. Tyler had no doubt that someone had found out that Seth was keeping an account of the illegal activities going on at the Larson family Christmas tree farm. And that someone then killed Seth. He gritted his teeth against the throbbing in his head.

Heather stared at him with wide eyes full of flashing anger. "How could you let this happen?"

It was a valid question. One he'd been asking himself for the past five days. One his superiors were asking, as well. "Your brother initially wanted us to raid the farm, but we didn't know who we were looking for and where the drugs were stashed. And Seth claimed he hadn't been privy to how the smuggling took place. At least at first. A raid too soon would have only shut down the operation here, not stopped the flow. We needed evidence. We needed facts. Still do. Seth began to gather intel and had thought he had enough to shut the ring down, but then he was killed."

Her eyes widened even more. "You really do believe he was murdered?"

"I do. Whatever information he had cost him his life." And now it put Seth's sister and nephew in danger. They weren't supposed to be here. Seth had said they lived in Washington State. And now, per Tyler's boss's mandate, Tyler and his team were to make sure the widow and her son were protected.

She shook her head. "No, *you* cost him his life. You pushed him to do something he wasn't trained to do."

The sharp tip of her barb hit him squarely in the gut. "A fact I will have to live with," Tyler stated with more regret than she could possibly know. This wasn't the first time an informant had lost his life. "But Seth got himself into this mess. Seth came to us. He knew the risks. Believe me—I wish I had done things differently."

If he could go back, he'd have extracted Seth a week ago. But Tyler had wanted more information. He'd wanted to cut off the head of the ring, not just pull in a few low-level minions. So he'd pushed Seth to keep up the pretense of going along with the drug-smuggling scheme until he knew the identity of the mastermind behind the illegal operation.

Tyler had been doing his job. A job that wasn't finished. "If I am going to bring his murderers to justice, I need to find the notebook he told me he had."

"That's why you broke into the house."

"I didn't break in. As I said, Seth gave me a key. He'd said if anything happened to him that I'd find what I needed here at the farm. I didn't mean to scare you. I had thought you and your son lived in Washington and would have returned there after Seth's burial. Otherwise I would have arranged to meet you away from the farm."

A contemplative expression crossed her face. "Ah. That's why Seth offered to pay for our plane tickets to Florida for the upcoming holiday—so we wouldn't come here." A sad light entered her eyes. "My late husband's parents live in a nursing facility there. Seth had insisted we should spend Thanksgiving with the Randalls. I declined Seth's offer." She gave a little shrug. "The Randalls barely know us, and we wouldn't be able to stay with them. I didn't want to spend the holiday in a motel."

Her words resonated with him. He spent most holidays in motels or on stakeouts. It was a lonely way to celebrate.

"And now we'll be spending the holiday here alone, without Seth."

Guilt burned at her words. He had nothing to say to soothe her hurt.

Visibly pulling herself together, she asked crisply, "What does this notebook look like?"

"I wish I knew. All Seth had told me was to get the

notebook if anything happened to him." Tyler planted his feet beneath him and slowly rose. The world tilted. He swayed. He braced his feet wide, forcing back the dim shadows creeping in at the edges of his mind.

Heather rushed forward to steady him. "Take it easy. You probably have a concussion. You should go to urgent care. You might need stitches."

"I'm not going anywhere until I find what I came for." But he would lean on her for the moment, to keep from embarrassing himself again by falling flat on his face a second time. "You know how to handle a frying pan."

"If I'd had Ken's service weapon handy, I'd have used that," she retorted drily. "But it's locked in a safety deposit box at the bank in town."

He slanted her a glance. "What were you thinking to begin with? You shouldn't have confronted an intruder. You could have been seriously wounded or killed."

From the background search he'd done on Seth and his family, Tyler knew Heather's husband had been killed in action and they had a young child, who he assumed was upstairs at this very minute unaware of the danger that could have befallen his mother.

She paled and squared her shoulders. "I had to protect my child. My husband taught me how to take care of myself. I know how to shoot a gun. I know enough self-defense to break a stranglehold. And, as you said, I know how to wield a frying pan."

He couldn't help the little burst of admiration for the gutsy lady.

Slowly she extracted herself from his side. She

moved away when it became apparent he was going to stay upright.

"You're still bleeding," she said. "Come along and let me take care of your head." She turned and walked away.

He followed Heather to a large mudroom just off the kitchen, where he washed his hands while Heather grabbed a first aid kit from the cabinet over the washing machine and set it on the counter beside the washbasin. Next she dragged a chair in from the dining room.

He looked at the sturdy lattice-back chair with the pale yellow seat cushion. "I don't want to ruin any more of your cushions."

She found three towels in a drawer and brought them over. After laying one across the chair, she pushed on his shoulder. "Sit. I can't work with you standing."

Even sitting, he was as tall as her petite frame. She stood in front of him. The scent of her skin, a mix of soap and vanilla, teased his senses. Her face was a study in concentration as she unwound the cloth she'd fastened around his head.

"This is going to hurt," she warned as she dabbed him with a cotton ball soaked in antiseptic.

The biting pain made him wince. When she finished, he sighed with relief.

"I think I can use butterfly bandages to close up the wound." She worked with quick efficiency. "Why come at night? Why not come in the daylight with a search warrant?"

"Because I didn't want to alert the bad guys that

we're onto them. I was hoping to get in and out un-noticed."

She made a delicate-sounding snort. "But if you'd found the notebook, would its contents be admissible as evidence?"

"Yes, it would. The person, or persons, involved in the drug ring have no reasonable expectation of privacy on your farm, even if they are staying in one of the cabins. You're the only one who would be exempt from the rule because you're the owner. But you're not involved, so that point is moot."

"How can you be sure I'm not?"

"Seth was adamant you weren't. Plus, I did a background check on you. You're clean. I have no reason to believe you're tangled up in this mess." Could he be mistaken? His gut tightened. "You aren't, right?"

The corners of her mouth quirked, and she shook her head. "I'm not."

The last bit of doubt drained away. "Good."

"You don't even know what you're looking for," she said.

"True. But I'm sure I'll know it when I see it."

She frowned, her brow creasing. "Are you the one who called me?"

He cocked his head. "No, I never called you."

"Well, someone did, and they seemed to share your thought that Seth's death wasn't just an overdose."

A spike of concern sent his blood pressure soaring. "What did the caller say?"

"That my brother's death was more than it seemed and I should leave the farm because it's not safe."

Dread punched him in the stomach. "When was this?"

"A few hours ago."

His head pounded a rapid staccato. "All the more reason for me to find the book quickly. We need to put a stop to this fast before anyone else gets hurt."

She stepped back and put the first aid kit away, then tossed the soiled towels into the washing machine. "I'll help you look for the notebook, but first you need some fluids. Follow me."

Bemused by her take-charge attitude, he allowed her to lead him out of the mudroom. She stopped in the kitchen and turned on the light over the sink. A large butcher block served as a center island. Long wooden counters and blond oak cabinets with glass doors gave the place a homey feel. The appliances were older but clean. Blue-and-yellow gingham curtains hung over the window behind the sink. The place had a cozy feel that was foreign to Tyler.

She took a tall glass from a cupboard, filled it with tap water and handed it to him. "Drink."

"Aye, aye, Captain." He took the glass and drank the cool liquid.

She dug into a drawer and came up with two over-the-counter painkillers. "Here, these should help."

"Thanks." He popped the tablets and swallowed them with another large gulp of water. When he was finished, he set the glass on the large center island. "Let's check your brother's room."

In Seth's room they worked in silence, rummaging through drawers, checking under the mattress, under the bed. In the closet, inside the crawl space in the closet floor. Their search resulted in nothing but frustration.

Fisting his hands, Tyler glanced around the tidy room, taking in the tall dresser standing in the corner, the desk and chair placed beneath the window and the long twin bed covered in a geometric-patterned quilt.

Seth had told Tyler he'd kept the journal on the farm; it stood to reason it was in this room. There were many places to hide a notebook in the large farmhouse, but which nook or cranny had Seth used?

Tyler's head throbbed and so did his heart. He couldn't change the past, only hope he could affect the future. Wasn't that what his gran always told him?

Next they tackled the living area. It was a large great room that flowed into the dining area with the kitchen around the corner to form an L shape. Tyler searched the well-worn leather couches, while Heather checked the bookshelf, taking the books down, inspecting them and then piling them on the floor.

Tyler even checked under the large throw rug covering the hardwood in the living room. No secret compartments. No secret hiding places. He moved on to the dining room while Heather continued her slow but steady pace through the bookshelf.

The large rectangular table had no drawers or hidden slots in which to stash a notebook.

"Mommy?" A small boy stood at the bottom of the stairs staring at Tyler with wide eyes beneath a fringe of dark brown bangs. He wore footie pajamas with rockets all over them. A plush dinosaur dangled from one tiny hand.

Tyler untucked his shirt and quickly pulled it over his hip holster, hoping the boy hadn't noticed his firearm. No need to frighten the child.

"Colin, honey." Heather rushed to her son's side. "What are you doing up?"

Keeping his eyes on Tyler, the child said, "I heard a noise."

She picked him up, hugging him close. "It was just me and…" She looked at Tyler as if she weren't sure how to introduce him.

Tyler stepped closer. "I'm Tyler. A friend of your uncle Seth."

"Uncle Seth is with Daddy now," Colin replied gravely.

"Yes, he is," Tyler said. He gave the boy a sad smile. "I'm sure they are both watching over you and your mommy."

Colin scrunched up his nose. "What happened to your head?"

Heather grimaced.

"I had an accident," Tyler said, touching the bandage on his head. "With a frying pan."

Heather's eyes widened, and a pink blush stained her cheeks. He grinned at her. She flushed a deeper shade of red.

The boy snuggled into the crook of his mother's neck. She kissed the top of his head. The sight of Heather and her son made a touching picture. Tyler's chest grew tight.

"I'll be right back," Heather said and carried Colin upstairs.

Something shifted and constricted inside Tyler as he watched them go. Heather's love for her son was obvious in the tender way she treated him. Tyler had never known that kind of love.

Certainly not from his mother. She'd been too busy scoring her next high or lost in a haze of drugs to bother with affection. Her only son had been a means to gain the weekly welfare check, nothing more.

After Heather and her son disappeared from Tyler's sight, an unfamiliar ache of longing lingered. He wasn't even sure what he longed for, but he was determined to keep Heather and her son safe.

He could only pray he didn't fail them like he had Seth.

Heather tucked Colin back into bed. "You need your sleep, big guy. Tomorrow we're helping Rob change out the village lights."

Rob Zane lived in one of the houses on the property. Her parents had offered him the job of caretaker for the farm's Christmas Village after he'd recovered from a house fire that had taken his own family nearly fifteen years earlier. A fire that some whispered he'd started. Her parents had stood by him through the arson investigation. And even though the fire had been deemed an accident, many in the area weren't convinced. He'd been kind and generous to her family in return for her parents' loyalty.

"And the decorations," Colin said, the thrum of excitement in his tone. "Rob said I could help him with Santa's house."

"That will be fun." This coming weekend they would open the farm up to the public to come enjoy the village and sleigh rides and to cut their own trees to take home. But first Heather had to get through Thanksgiving. The day wouldn't be anything like she'd hoped, but she'd do her best to make it special for Colin, despite her sorrow over her brother's death. *Murder.* She shuddered.

Careful to keep her expression from betraying the quiver of fear, she kissed Colin's forehead. "You need to get some sleep so you're bright-eyed and bushy-tailed tomorrow."

"I don't have a tail, Mommy," Colin admonished her with a grin.

She laughed, thankful for his sweet innocence, and smoothed back a lock of hair, her chest crowding with a mother's love. "No, you don't, sweetie."

Heather left Colin's room and ducked into her own bedroom to change into comfortable sweatpants and a pullover hoodie. When she went back downstairs, she found Tyler had turned off all the lights except one lamp by the couch.

He stood looking at the family photos lining the mantel with his back to her. His feet were braced apart. He had wide shoulders and a slim waist. He clenched and unclenched his hands at his sides. With anger? Frustration? Perhaps both. The bandage she'd put on his head glowed in bright contrast to his short-cropped dark hair.

Part of her was so angry with Tyler for putting Seth in danger. And yet she was angry with Seth for not telling her what was going on and getting himself involved in something so dangerous. She might have been able to help him. Or at the very least talk some sense into him.

Tyler turned around. She glimpsed the tortured expression on his handsome face before he quickly settled his features into a shuttered look that hardened the line of his jaw. She resisted the empathy flooding her veins. What did he have to be tortured about? It was her brother who'd died because Tyler and his team couldn't protect him.

Could she trust him to protect her and Colin?

What choice did she have but to put her life and that of her child into his keeping? "The only way you'll get access to the farm is if you're here on my say-so."

He narrowed his eyes. "Meaning?"

"That we do this my way."

"What's your way?"

"I'll hire you as the new foreman to take over for Seth. That way you could stay on the farm. I assume you have your team nearby. They could hire on as part of our seasonal labor." They hadn't hired enough people, and she hadn't been able to think about the shortage the past few days as she dealt first with Seth's death, then his burial.

He cocked his head to the side and appeared to consider her offer. "Only problem is I know nothing about tree farming. Anyone would see right through that."

She thought for a moment. "An investor?"

"A business partner," he countered.

"That would work. Then we'll scour the farm until we discover where my brother hid the book."

"Sounds like a great plan." Tyler held out his hand. "Partners."

After a brief hesitation—did she really want to partner with this man?—she slipped her hand into his larger one and repeated the word, answering her own question. "Partners."

His fingers curled over hers, causing a riot of sparks to shoot up her arm. Disconcerted by the odd effect of his touch, she extracted her hand. "I'll make the arrangements in the morning."

He held her gaze. "I'd appreciate it. I'll help you put the bookshelf back together."

She glanced at the stacks of books on the floor. "I'll take you up on the offer." Only because she knew she wouldn't get any sleep now anyway, not because she felt safer with him here.

Needing the calming properties of some herbal tea, she asked, "Would you like some tea?"

"Sure. I'll try some."

They moved into the kitchen. After taking two mugs from the cupboard, she dropped an herbal tea bag into each mug. Then she set the electric kettle to boil. "How are they smuggling the cocaine? And how do we stop it?"

"I don't know." Tyler leaned against the counter. "I'm confident Seth's notes will give us all the necessary details."

She poured hot water in the mugs, then slid one to

him. "Hopefully this nightmare will end soon so no one else will pay the price Seth did."

Unable to continue looking at him, she stared out the window over the sink. The back of the house faced the large horse barn to the left. And farther out to the right was the processing yard where the cut trees were fed into balers and stacked, ready to be loaded onto trucks for transport.

Within the next few days, hundreds of trees would leave the farm on trucks bound for destinations all over the country and up into Canada. Not to mention all the townsfolk who would come out to take a tree home and visit the Christmas Village, eat homemade donuts, drink hot cocoa and take a sleigh ride. The busyness would take her mind off her grief. But with so many people on the property, would the danger increase?

A shadow flickered near one of the balers and stole her breath. She leaned forward, straining to see. Was she imagining the movement? She'd dismissed what she'd seen earlier as paranoia, but now...

"Heather, what is it?"

No. She hadn't imagined what she'd seen. There was definitely someone skulking around the balers. The hairs on the back of her neck rose. "Someone is out there."

Chapter Three

Adrenaline saturated Tyler's veins at the prospect of an intruder lurking outside Heather's farmhouse. He quickly set his mug down and gripped Heather by the elbow to draw her away from the window. "Turn all the lights off and go upstairs. Don't come down until I tell you it's clear."

She blinked up at him with wide, stunned eyes. "What are you going to do?"

"Find out what's going on." Maybe this was his chance to capture those involved in the drug ring. If he could catch them in the act of hiding the drugs, then Heather and her son would be safe and he could move on to the next assignment. This one had grown exponentially more problematic. He'd rather be chasing down drug-pushing thugs than dealing with a protective mom.

He released Heather's elbow and sent her up the stairs. Once she reached the top landing, he slipped out the back door, leading with his gun in a two-handed grip. The moon provided enough light for him to navigate his way through the yard toward the three hulking pieces of machinery where Heather said she'd seen someone. He paused with his back against the side of a baler and listened.

A breeze had kicked up, and it rustled through the trees. The howl of some creature sent a shiver down Tyler's spine. Too close for his peace of mind. Had it been a wild animal Heather had seen?

Noise near the barn drew his attention. The barn's door sliding open and then closing?

He ran in a low crouch toward the large structure. Pressing his back against the side of the barn, he peered around the edge. No one there. From inside the barn, one of the draft horses used to pull the sleigh nickered. Inching his way to the barn door, he kept an eye out for any signs of life.

He eased the barn door open as soundlessly as he could. The pungent scent of hay and horse made his nose twitch. He ducked inside and hid in a pocket of shadow, waiting, listening.

A horse whinnied. The sound of metal scraping against metal raised the fine hairs on Tyler's arm. The scuff of a shoe on the dirt floor jolted through him. There was definitely someone in the barn.

Keeping low, he crept toward the rear part of the barn, where a pen had been constructed to house the smaller animals of the farm's petting zoo. He bumped into a pail, momentarily losing his balance in the dark. The noise spooked the horse to his left. Tyler reached out for the edge of the stall to steady himself just as someone bolted past him for the barn door.

"Hey!" Tyler shouted, barely making out the silhouette of a man as he yanked the door open wider and ran through.

Tyler chased after him. He caught a fleeting glimpse of the dark figure disappearing into the inky shadows of the tree crop. For a moment Tyler contemplated giving pursuit, but the prospect of getting lost among the hundreds of trees disabused him of that thought. Heather and her son needed Tyler to stand guard, in case the man decided to approach the house from another direction.

After shutting the barn door, Tyler retraced his steps to the back of the farmhouse and entered the back door. He threw the bolt into place.

"What did you see?" Heather's whispered question brought him up short. He spun around and could just barely make out her form. She stood in the archway of the kitchen, the frying pan clutched in her hands.

Achingly familiar with the damage the utensil could inflict, he kept his distance. "Someone was in the barn. They ran away when they realized I was there."

"I can't believe how paranoid I'm being," she said, laying the frying pan on the counter. "It was probably one of the farm employees checking on the barn animals. He's probably calling the police on you as we speak."

Following Heather into the living room, Tyler said, "Maybe." But he wasn't so sure. If it had been an employee who had every right to be there, why hadn't he confronted Tyler? "But you did receive a threatening phone call, right? Your paranoia is appropriate."

She blew out a breath. "You're right." She turned on a table lamp before picking up several books and arranging them in the bookcase.

"You can go on to bed and get some sleep," he told her. "I'll take care of this while I stand watch."

She made a face. "I won't get any sleep, so I might as well tackle this now."

He didn't blame her. She'd had a scary night, and there was a stranger in her house. He grabbed some books and handed them to her so she could place them on the shelf.

"Do you have a wife? Kids?"

The question punched him in the gut, stirring up an old dream that he knew would never happen for him. "No. I'm not husband material, let alone father material."

"Why would you say that?"

Aware of her curious glances, he kept his attention on the book in his hands. "I don't lead the kind of life that lends itself to settling down in one place for very long."

"Surely you must have a home somewhere."

He had an apartment where he stored his few belongings, but he wouldn't call the place homey. Not anything close to what she meant. "Los Angeles."

"Parents? Siblings?"

He arched an eyebrow. "Do you always grill your guests like this?"

She matched his arched eyebrow with one of her

own. "You aren't a guest. You came uninvited into my house, my life. I think I can ask you all the questions I want."

Liking her spunk, he said, "Touché." He handed her a book. "In answer to your question, no. I'm alone in the world, and I like it that way."

He wouldn't mention that deep inside, in places he'd rather ignore, the acute emptiness of his life pressed in on him like a boulder that wouldn't budge.

Placing the last book onto the shelf, he cleared his throat and wished he could clear away his thoughts as easily. He sat in the wingback chair by the front door and stretched his legs out in front of him. "Now, if you don't mind, I'd like to get some rest."

He closed his eyes, hopefully putting an end to her curiosity. Not that he was about to sleep, not when the danger plaguing the farm could strike at any moment. On any undercover assignment or stakeout, one learned how to rest while still staying alert.

For a moment she was silent. Then he thought he heard a little huff of exasperation as she moved to the couch. A moment later the light winked out. He smiled in the dark.

Rest, my eye! Heather shifted on the leather couch. She was certain the man sitting across the darkened room had no intention of sleeping. He'd just wanted to stop her questions, which only made her more curious about him. What made a man like Tyler go into law enforcement? Why the drug enforcement agency? Why was he alone in the world?

If not for Colin, she'd be alone in the world, too.

The familiar ache of loneliness camped out in her chest. She missed her husband. Missed having someone she could count on to always have her back, to hold her when the world became too much.

In the years since his death, she'd had to learn to be strong on her own. For Colin. For herself.

Had Tyler lost someone, too? Was that the hurt she sensed in him?

The trill of her cell phone startled her. She flinched and quickly dug it out of the pocket of her sweatpants.

"Put it on speaker." Tyler's voice came to her in the dark.

Remembering the last call, she really wanted to ignore it, but burying her head in the sand wasn't smart. She needed to face this head-on. She pressed the answer button and then the speaker icon. "Hello."

"I told you once," said a muffled male voice. "You need to leave the farm. Do it now! It's not safe for you here." The caller hung up after the last word.

Alarm wormed its way through her, making her tremble.

Tyler moved to sit beside her. "Turn on the light."

With shaky hands, she groped for the switch. She turned the table lamp on and was grateful when the light dispelled the gloom.

Tyler was on his phone. "Hey, I need a call traced now." He held out his hand for her phone. She set it in his palm. He quickly rattled off her phone number to whomever was on the other side of his phone conversation. "The caller ID comes up blocked. I need to know where the call originated and if the phone can be tracked." He cupped a hand over the phone's microphone. "This will take a few minutes."

Heather drew her knees to her chest as they waited. The tick of her mother's grandfather clock sitting on the mantel seemed extraordinarily loud.

She knew the moment they had an answer by the troubled look on Tyler's face. Her blood ran cold in her veins. As soon as he hung up, she asked, "What happened? Were they able to trace the call?"

"They were able to triangulate the approximate location." He laid her phone on the couch. "The call originated from somewhere here on the farm."

Her stomach sank. Betrayal swamped her. She'd stepped into a surreal world where she had no idea what was what. Not only had her brother *not* trusted her enough to tell her what was going on, but someone on the farm wanted her gone.

"Once the guys and I have secured our covers, you and Colin should leave."

She let out a mirthless laugh. "We have nowhere else to go."

"Your in-laws?"

"I told you—they're in an assisted-living facility in Florida."

"A friend? Seth's fiancée?"

Her shoulders sagged. "My life revolves around the farm and Colin now. There's no one who I'd feel comfortable asking to stay with, especially with Thanksgiving coming up. As for Olivia, I'd rather keep her out of this. She's grieving. She doesn't need to know about Seth's troubles."

"Maybe she already knows?"

Heather shook her head. "Liv is as uptight as they come. No way would she have let Seth get away with what he was doing." She shrugged. "Besides, when I talked to her at Seth's funeral, she said she was going to visit her folks in California for the holiday."

Tyler laid his hand on her arm. "Don't worry, Heather. I'm not going to let anything happen to you or your son."

As much as she wanted to believe him, she knew that life could turn on a dime. A life, any life, could be snuffed out as quickly and as silently as a candle's flame.

The next morning dawned with a cloudless blue sky bathing the living room in soft light. Heather rubbed her stiff neck and glanced at the time on her phone. Early still. The farm employees wouldn't start their day for another couple of hours. *Good.* She needed some time to figure out how she was going to explain why she'd formed a partnership. She'd just buried her brother.

The thought brought the ache of loss to the forefront of her mind, diminishing the physical pain of stiff muscles from falling asleep sitting upright on the couch, her feet tucked beneath her. With a little start, she realized Tyler had spread the blanket that had hung on the back of the couch over her while she slept.

She was touched by Tyler's thoughtfulness, and her

gaze landed on the man sleeping in the chair across the room. After the second menacing phone call, he'd double-checked that all the windows and doors were locked. He'd taken her rolling pin and placed it into the channel of the windowsill in Seth's room, saying the window would be too easy to jimmy open.

Now his eyes were closed, his legs spread out in front of him and his arms hugged a pillow to his chest like a favored toy. For some reason the sight stirred something inside her, something she hadn't felt in a long time and refused to feel now. Not for this man. Not for any man. She'd had her one true love.

In the light of day, Tyler was even more of a presence than he'd been last night. His day's growth of beard darkened his jaw, emphasizing the contours of his face. Dark circles rimmed his eyes beneath the splay of long lashes resting against his cheeks.

Despite her anger at Agent Tyler Griffin, she appreciated that he accepted the responsibility for her brother's murder. He didn't make excuses, but he'd pushed her brother to risk his life, a means to an end. He'd put his mission before her brother's safety.

Ken had been like that. Quick to assume responsibility. Always putting the military before his family. She hated the little whisper of bitterness that floated at the edges of her mind. She'd admired Ken's dedication at first but came to resent it in time.

It had been five years since he'd left on that final mission, promising to return soon. And not a moment went by when she didn't hope there'd been some mistake and he'd come home to her and Colin.

Ken had been the love of her life. She doubted she'd ever find anyone she could love like that again. The thought filled her with a stinging emptiness.

One of Tyler's eyes popped open. Caught staring, she felt a heated flush creep up her neck. She took that as her cue to stand and divert her attention, which was hard to do considering every fiber of her being was aware of the man stirring in the chair. Plus the last thing she wanted was for him to think she was interested in him in any way.

The sooner they found Seth's journal, the quicker Tyler would be gone from her life and she could grieve in peace without worrying about drug lords and murderers.

Tyler sat up and tucked his sidearm back into its holster. He met her gaze. "G'morning."

"Morning," she replied and stretched out the kinks from the awkward position she'd maintained through the night. She went to the front window and pulled the curtains back all the way. The view of the acres of trees stretching out in all directions usually brought her a nostalgic sense of pride. This morning however, she felt only anxious.

Someone living on the farm had probably killed her brother.

And threatened her.

Who?

She clenched her fists at her sides. A sense of betrayal wrapped around her, making her pulse pound.

The quick footsteps of her son racing down the stairs

forced back the tide of anger. She rounded the couch and caught him in her arms.

Lifting him high, she said, "Whoa, slow down, little man."

He stared at her with frightened eyes. "You weren't in your room."

She hugged him to her chest, sensing his unspoken fear that she, too, would go away. "I'm right here, buddy."

Colin pulled back and leaned to peer around her shoulder. "Good morning, Mr. Tyler. Are you having breakfast with us?" Colin asked.

Heather's heart hiccupped. Her son was so accepting, so trusting. She prayed he never lost that ability.

"Not today, buddy. But thank you for asking me."

Heather met Tyler's gaze. He clearly wanted to talk to her. She ruffled Colin's hair. "How about pancakes?"

Colin let out a whoop. "Pancakes!"

The second she set him on his feet, he was off at a mad dash to the dining room. The sound of a chair being dragged across the hardwood floor to the kitchen counter filled the house. A cupboard banged open. She tensed, hoping the glass bowl she imagined Colin reaching for didn't slip from his hands and break on the counter.

Tyler came to stand beside her. Her senses flared as waves of heat coming off him warmed her chilled limbs.

"I take it pancakes are a special treat?"

Tyler's low voice washed over her, making her pulse

spike. Uncomfortable with her reaction to him, she stepped away. "Yes. Pancakes are a special treat."

One corner of Tyler's mouth curved upward, making him look boyish and roguish at the same time. "I'd love a rain check."

Words stuck in her throat. She nodded.

"I'm going to retrieve my truck," he said, keeping his voice low so Colin wouldn't hear him, which she appreciated. "I left it out on the shoulder of Johnstone Lane. I'll return with my colleagues Blake and Nathanial."

"Sounds like a good plan," she replied. "We'll be okay." She hoped.

"Let me program my number into your phone," he said. "Just in case. The guys aren't staying far away. We'll be back within the hour."

As she watched him punching his numbers into her phone, she had the strangest urge to plead with him not to go. She lifted her chin in determination. She would not let fear rule her life.

Tyler hesitated, suddenly loath to leave Heather and Colin, even for as long as it would take him to get his truck, go to the motel to retrieve his travel bag and the guys and then drive back here. He had a sneaking suspicion that the reason he didn't want to leave was much more complex than he wanted to admit.

This whole assignment had become extremely unpredictable. Heather and her son were distractions he couldn't afford, yet he had to stick close. To protect them.

Yeah, that was right. Wanting to stick close to the stunning widow had nothing to do with the fact he found Heather appealing.

He couldn't forget his primary objective was to bring down the drug ring and discover the identity of the mastermind. Not yearn for the dark-haired beauty.

Stalling, he found the restroom and freshened up as much as he could. But he wished he had his to-go bag handy. The stubble on his face itched. He stepped into the living room and made a decision.

Making sure his sidearm was concealed beneath his shirt, he entered the kitchen and stopped in his tracks. Colin stood on a chair pushed up to the counter. Heather was pouring milk into the measuring cup Colin held over a large bowl. The domestic scene looked like something one would see in a greeting card. Tenderness flooded his system.

"That's enough, Mommy," Colin exclaimed, then dumped the milk into the bowl.

Heather set the milk carton aside and handed him an egg. "You remember how to crack this?"

"Yes, I can do it myself," Colin insisted, snatching the egg from her hand.

Heather met Tyler's gaze over Colin's head. "Honey, I'll be right back. Try not to let any of the shells get into the mix."

Heather moved to stand in front of Tyler. She'd tied her dark hair back with a ribbon. White flour dusted her cheek. She looked so pretty and so fragile. The oversize sweats she wore hid her feminine form, but her beauty went deeper than her skin. It was in the gentle way she related to her son, in the way she'd taken care of Tyler's injury. An injury she'd inflicted out of fear and the need to protect her child.

Beneath that soft female exterior was a strong and brave woman.

"Is something the matter?"

"No, everything's good." He was quick to assure her. "I was thinking I'd have the guys pick up my truck and head on over here. If you're okay with that plan."

The relieved smile she flashed hit him square in the chest.

"Of course it's okay. That would be great. We'll make plenty of pancakes."

Fifteen minutes later, Heather's dining room was filled with three large men and one small boy who stared at the newcomers with awe as they ate pancake after pancake. She'd made a triple batch of pancake batter, fried up three pounds of bacon and made a gallon of orange juice. Though it had been years, she remembered what it was like to cook for hungry men. Ken had brought home his army buddies often to their small duplex on the Joint Base Lewis-McChord in Tacoma, Washington.

Heather didn't blame Colin for being mesmerized. She'd forgotten what it was like to be around men like these. Hard men. Men who not only faced danger but sought it out.

She'd thought Tyler intimidating on his own. Flanked by his fellow team members, she pitied anyone who would take on this trio.

US Immigration and Customs Enforcement agent Blake Fallon's hard features could cut diamonds out of stone. Though she doubted the stoic man realized how his penetrating dark gaze softened when he answered Colin's many questions in the subtle accent of the Southern states.

The other man, Canadian Customs Border Patrol agent Nathanial Longhorn, was charm personified. His comments made Colin giggle in a way usually reserved for silly cartoons. But there was a lethal grace to the man that made Heather suspect he was the type of guy one wouldn't want to cross.

"That was delicious." Tyler tilted his chair back on two legs and smiled at her across the table.

His praise brought heat to her cheeks.

"Thank you, Mrs. Randall," Blake said. His deep voice rumbled from his chest. "It's been a while since we've had a decent meal."

"Hey, now," Nathanial said. "My cooking's not that bad."

Blake raised an eyebrow. "Says you."

"You make a mean hot dog," Tyler quipped.

Heather couldn't help but laugh at the ribbing between the men.

"I will admit these pancakes were out of this world," Nathanial stated, then eyed Heather. "There was a touch of vanilla and something else…"

"It's a family recipe," she said. "Highly guarded."

He grinned. "Ha! A challenge. I'll ferret out the secret."

The front legs of Tyler's chair dropped to the floor.

Tension radiated off him in waves as he shot to his feet. "Someone's here."

A knock at the back door punctuated his words.

Wow, how'd he know that?

"Rob!" Colin cried, jumping out of his chair and racing to the door.

"Colin, wait!" Heather hurried after him.

Nathanial snagged Colin by the waist and lifted him off his feet. "Slow up there, speedy."

Heather hadn't even seen the man rise out of his seat, let alone beat her son to the door. He carried him to the living room. Within seconds, Nathanial had her son laughing hysterically as the man acted out a story.

Tyler moved to her side while Blake disappeared from the room like a puff of smoke.

Heather frowned at Tyler. "It's Rob Zane. He's a longtime employee."

No doubt he suspected Rob was in on the drug ring, but, then again, she figured Tyler would suspect everyone on the farm.

She hated the thought that one of the farm's employees could be involved in smuggling drugs and threatening her, let alone her brother's death.

Especially the man her parents had trusted completely. She wasn't about to drag Rob into the danger surrounding the farm.

Unless he was already mixed up in it.

The thought shook her to the core.

No. She wouldn't, couldn't, believe such a thing. Despite how uncomfortable he made her feel at times, Rob was a God-fearing man. Or at least he had been once. He'd been a friend of her parents for as long as she could remember. Despite the unsubstantiated suspicions that he'd been responsible for the fire that had claimed his family, he deserved the benefit of the doubt from Heather. Didn't he?

"Heather?" Rob called, sounding worried.

"I have to answer the door," she said to Tyler. "My parents trust him."

Though his expression wasn't pleased, Tyler gave her a sharp nod. His hand rested on his holstered weapon.

Heather opened the door. "Rob, we weren't expecting you this early."

He tried to peer around her. "I wanted to make sure you were all right."

Was his concern real or a ploy to garner her trust? She stared at the man who'd become a surrogate grandfather to Colin after her parents were killed and searched for the answer to her question. In all honesty, she didn't know that much about Rob, but she had always trusted him with her son whenever they'd come home for a visit.

Now she wasn't sure who she could trust.

Chapter Four

"I thought I saw someone through the window, and I wanted to make sure you were all right," Rob said.

Tyler tensed, and his "something's hinky" senses went wild. Rob had been watching the house? Why?

Needing to establish his cover sooner rather than later, Tyler stepped out from behind the door. The man standing on the other side of the door was average in height and build with blond hair. He wore corduroy pants and a thick jean jacket over a black turtleneck and he leaned heavily on a cane.

Horrible scars twisted the flesh of his hands and one side of his face. Empathy crimped Tyler's gut. He'd read in the dossier about the tragedy the man had suffered, but seeing the evidence… Tyler could only imagine the agony Rob had endured, both physically and emotionally. Enough to need illegal drugs to dull the pain?

"Robbie!" Colin reentered the kitchen at a run and charged at them. Afraid the boy would bowl

Rob over—he appeared unsteady on his cane—Tyler snagged Colin with one arm and lifted him to settle him on his hip. Glancing over his shoulder, Tyler saw Nathanial slip out the front door on Blake's heels.

"Mr. Tyler, this is Mr. Robbie. He takes care of the Christmas Village." Colin patted Tyler's chest, having no idea of the turmoil he was causing inside Tyler. Holding the boy in his arms as if he were the child's parent made Tyler's heart ache in ways he'd never experienced. "Mr. Tyler's a friend of—"

"Mine," Heather interjected, cutting off her son's words. "My new business partner, to be exact."

Appreciating Heather's quick thinking, Tyler held out his hand to the other man. "Hello, Rob. I'm Tyler."

The man's shrewd gaze bounced between Tyler and Heather and back again. After a long moment, Rob grasped Tyler's hand. "Tyler, nice to meet you."

"Likewise."

"Partner?" Rob released Tyler's hand to stare at Heather.

A slight grimace pulled at the corners of her mouth. "Uh, yes."

They hadn't had time to come up with a proper explanation, so Tyler had to wing it. "I'm here to help Heather at this difficult time. More in a business advisory capacity than an operational partner."

"Ah." Obviously troubled, Rob slanted one brow upward at Heather. "I'm glad to see you're all right. Since you have company, I'll make myself scarce. When you're ready, I'll be in the village."

"Me, too!" Colin cried, launching himself toward Rob. Tyler held on fast.

"We will go to the village after you're dressed." Heather lifted Colin out of Tyler's arms and set the boy's feet on the floor. As soon as he touched down, he darted off, running through the kitchen. The echo of his feet pounding up the stairs rang through the house.

Rob's deep chuckle drew Tyler's attention.

"That child never walks. He always runs." Rob shifted on his cane with a wince.

"So I've noticed," Tyler confessed.

"We'll come help in the village a little later," Heather told Rob.

He nodded and turned to leave, but he drew up short at the sight of Blake and Nathanial standing side by side at the end of the walkway.

Tyler had to admit they made a daunting pair. Big and brawny, the two men blocked the path. Tyler cut Heather a pointed look.

Understanding widened her eyes, and she nodded. "I forgot to mention," she said, drawing Rob's attention back to her. "I hired two more hands since we're short-staffed." She motioned to the two men. "This is Blake and Nathanial."

Nathanial stepped forward and gave Rob a charming smile. "Hello. I'm Nathanial. It's nice to be working with you."

Rob shook his hand without comment.

Blake remained stoic as he shook Rob's hand. "Blake."

"Nice to meet you both," Rob murmured.

"Rob, would you show the men to the empty cabin?" Heather asked. "And then introduce them to Don." To Tyler she said, "He's our unofficial foreman now that Seth is gone." Her voice broke as she said her brother's name. Tyler felt the stab of her grief like a sharp-tipped knife to the chest.

Rob nodded. "Of course. This way." He hobbled away from the house.

Blake saluted Tyler. He inclined his head, acknowledging the agent's communication. Their undercover operation was under way.

Shutting the door, Tyler said, "I'll join the guys later."

"The cabin's barely big enough for two," she said. "I was thinking you'd be more comfortable in the carriage house. It's where we keep the sleigh. There's an upstairs apartment with running water and a kitchenette."

He'd seen the detached garage last night. Staying there would allow him to be close enough to quickly reach her and Colin if they needed him. "That would work."

Colin rushed back to the kitchen and skidded to a stop beside Tyler. "Where's Rob?"

Colin had pulled on a pair of sweatpants that were inside out and backward with the tag sticking out like a flag. He'd missed a few buttons on the plaid flannel shirt, no doubt in too much of a hurry to be careful. Tyler pressed his lips together to keep from smiling.

Heather bent down to talk to him. "He's showing Blake and Nathanial to their cabin."

"But we were going to decorate and change the lightbulbs at the village," Colin complained.

"And we will. Later." Heather rose and began clearing the table. She moved with fluid grace like a dancer. Tyler wondered if she had some training. She carried herself with an elegance that fascinated him.

Colin tugged on Tyler's hand, drawing his attention away from Heather.

"Are you coming to the village with us?" Colin craned his neck to look up at Tyler.

Swallowing back the tenderness swamping him at having the boy's hand clutching his, Tyler said, "We should help your mother clean up."

"Okay." Colin let go of his hand to grab a plate and then danced away from the dining table.

"Carefully," Heather called just as the clatter of the plate hitting the sink mocked her warning. She cringed.

"Sorry." Colin raced back to Tyler's side. "I cleaned up. Can we go now? I want to help decorate."

"There's more to do, honey," Heather said to Colin.

Needing to appease his curiosity, Tyler finally asked, "What's the Christmas Village?"

Heather smiled at Tyler as she washed a dish. "Exactly what it sounds like. We have a gift shop, bakery, a toy shop, a model train depot and, of course, Santa's house."

"And the nativity! With baby Jesus and real animals," Colin piped up as he stood on a chair to reach the empty bacon plate.

Tyler rushed to steady the chair before it tipped over. "Well, I definitely want to see this place."

There was a lot about this farm he couldn't wait to see. But, he reminded himself not for the first time, he wasn't here on a social visit. He needed to stay focused on the objective. Protect Heather and her son while finding Seth's killer and stopping the drug flow in and out of the farm. And that big Christmas Village meant lots of places to hide a journal.

Colin hopped down and took the plate to his mother.

"Did you brush your teeth?" she asked him.

He scuffed the toe in the hardwood floor. "No."

"Upstairs, buddy," Heather directed Colin. "Sixty seconds, uppers and lowers."

Colin huffed out a frustrated-sounding breath and took off like a rocket, disappearing up the staircase. It was a surprise his socked feet didn't slip out from beneath him.

Tyler picked up a towel and dried the dishes Heather set on the drain board. "So tell me about Rob." Though he'd read the dossier on the employee, he wanted to hear the man's history from Heather.

"He's been a part of our family since I was a kid. He served on the worship team at church. My mom was one of the singers on the team." She sighed, a sad sound that made Tyler's chest ache. "There was a house fire fifteen years ago. The ceiling fell on him, breaking his leg in multiple places. His wife and infant son didn't survive the flames."

Empathy twisted in Tyler's gut. "That's awful. Did they discover the cause of the fire?"

Tyler had read the police report and knew Rob was suspected of purposely starting the flames that had engulfed his house and killed his wife and son. But Tyler wanted to hear Heather's take on the tragedy.

"A plastic bag too close to a space heater. A tragic accident." She wiped her hands on a dish towel and stared out the little window over the sink.

A motor started up, though Tyler couldn't see the machinery. Outside the farm was stirring.

"He and his wife were very active in our church," Heather continued. "But after the fire he had a crisis of faith."

"It's hard to go through something like that and not wonder where God was." Tyler understood questioning God in such dire circumstances. He'd done his fair share of asking God *why* when he was a kid. Why wasn't Tyler important enough to keep his mother from using drugs? Why was he taken away from his grandparents? Why wasn't there enough food to eat?

If not for his grandparents' steadfast faith, Tyler doubted he'd have any faith now.

Heather turned to study him. "You believe in God?"

"Yes. Though it's hard at times in this line of work to not question God."

"You must see the worst in humanity."

"My fair share, anyway. But without faith, I don't know that I could do this job. I have to believe that people can be redeemed, saved from their own folly." Unfortunately, his mother hadn't wanted to give up her addiction. Not for him, not for God. "That is, if they choose to," he amended. "Not everyone does."

A thoughtful expression settled on her face. "After Rob recovered and was released from the hospital, my parents brought him to live here. He's been the care-taker of the village ever since. He likes to do something different every year so people will return. Colin's fascinated with the whole thing, just as Seth and I were as kids."

"It sounds special."

"Very special," she said. "We open for business the day after Thanksgiving. I usually look forward to the first day of the season." Her shoulders sagged. "But with Seth gone…"

She was hurting, and there was nothing Tyler could do to ease her pain except find the people responsible for her brother's death. To do that he had to find the journal. Her words sank in, and alarm bells went off in his head. "Wait a sec. You mean you still plan to open the farm for business?"

Lifting her chin, she met his gaze with a direct look. "Yes, I do. We have trees that are being harvested as we speak. There are people counting on us for their paycheck."

He shook his head. "Opening up the farm to strangers is asking for trouble."

Her eyes narrowed. "But you and your men will be here, right?"

"Yes. But that's not the point."

"Then what is the point?"

"That anyone coming or going from the farm would have access to whoever is peddling the drugs, and we'd have no way of watching every person."

"Then we both better pray you find the drugs before 9:00 a.m. on Friday morning."

Beautiful and stubborn. A potent combination. "Heather, be reasonable. Last night someone called and threatened you."

She scrunched up her nose in a cute way that distracted him for a moment. "You know, it was more of a warning than a threat. But now that you're here, Colin and I will be safe."

Tyler scrubbed a hand over his jaw. How was he going to convince her that she needed to postpone opening day of the Christmas tree farm? He understood her obligations to the employees. He weighed his options. If he shut the farm down to search for the journal, they potentially could lose the opportunity to catch the drug traffickers. If he let things unfold organically while searching covertly, then he and the guys had a better chance of apprehending the culprits.

"You have to promise me you'll be careful," he said.

Her smile was victorious. "Of course."

A chime filled the house in the tune of "Jingle Bells." Tyler cringed. "What is that?"

"The front doorbell." Heather headed for the living room.

Tyler caught her by the arm. "Another unexpected guest?"

She shrugged. "People come and go all the time."

Not liking the sound of that, Tyler took a position next to Heather out of direct sight of the door, then gave her a nod.

She opened the door and was nearly bowled over as a woman barged past her.

Tyler tucked Heather protectively behind him.

The woman stopped in the living room with her back to them and put her face in her hands and sobbed. She was petite, with shoulder-length blond hair and a bright pink coat wrapped around her slight frame.

Heather skirted out from behind him to gather the other woman in her arms. Tyler got antsy looking at the two women. Was a cry fest about to ensue?

"I know, Liv," cooed Heather with a soft soothing tone. "I know."

"I just can't believe he's gone," the woman said, her voice muffled by her manicured hands.

Ah, this must be Seth's fiancée. Seth had mentioned her, saying she was the reason he stayed clean. And why he couldn't continue letting the drugs go through the farm. They were getting married, and he hadn't wanted to do anything that would jeopardize their future. Unfortunately, doing the right thing had had dire consequences for Seth. Guilt bubbled inside Tyler.

Liv's sobs subsided, and she lifted her tear-streaked face. "I'm sorry. I didn't realize how hard coming here would be."

Heather patted her shoulder. Her pretty hazel eyes darkened with sadness. "It's okay, Liv. It's hard for me, too."

Glancing around, Liv asked, "Where's Colin? I could use a hug from him."

"He's upstairs brushing his teeth."

Disappointment marched across Liv's face before she turned her dark-eyed gaze on Tyler. Something close to wariness flashed in her eyes and echoed in her voice. "Who are you?"

"A friend," Heather said before he could reply. "Tyler Griffin. This is Olivia Dorsett, Seth's fiancée."

Liv sniffled and didn't extend her hand. "Nice to meet you, Tyler." She turned to Heather and dropped her voice a little. "I didn't know you were dating anyone."

"We're not dating," Tyler said firmly. "We're business partners."

Liv's eyes widened. Was that disapproval? "I see." She dug in her purse for a tissue and blew her nose.

"Liv, why are you here?" Heather asked gently. "I thought you were going to visit your family in California."

She sniffed again. "I couldn't face all their sympathy, so I canceled the trip."

So Liv was in town? An idea formed in Tyler's mind.

Liv dug into her purse and produced a brochure. "Besides, I wanted to talk to you about a memorial service for Seth. Mr. Sanders at the mortuary recommended it as a way for people to say goodbye."

Heather paled. Her hand shook as she took the flyer from Liv. "I— That would be nice, Liv. I'm sure Seth would have liked a memorial in his honor."

"I thought so, too. I mean, the graveside service was nice and all, but so few people were there." She gave a wobbly smile. "I was thinking it would be nice to have it here in the barn. Maybe light the big Christmas tree in his honor."

"Yes. That sounds lovely. Seth loved Christmas." Heather clutched the brochure to her, crumpling the edges. "Liv, did you ever see Seth writing in a journal or notebook?"

Good question! Tyler shot an approving glance at Heather before turning his attention back to Liv.

She cocked her head to the side and frowned. "I don't recall him keeping any kind of journal or diary. Why?"

Tyler tensed. Would Heather reveal the situation to this woman? He hoped not.

"He kept one when we were kids," Heather said. "I wasn't sure if he still did. Maybe it would provide us with a clue as to why…"

Liv teared up. "As to why he overdosed. I'll look in the townhouse. He'd started moving things over in preparation. I guess I should bring his boxes back." She dug into her purse and pulled out her smartphone. She fiddled with it for a second, frowned and then said, "I've been in such a fog I forgot I have an errand to run. I should go. I'll call you later to talk more about the memorial."

"Maybe we can plan the memorial closer to Christmas," Heather said, walking toward the front door and opening it. "I don't think I can handle it emotionally right now."

Seeing an opportunity to send Heather and her son somewhere safer, Tyler gave voice to his idea. "Heather, you and Colin should go spend some time with Liv. It might be helpful for you to be together at this difficult time."

Heather shot him a sharp glance.

"Oh, normally I'd love that," Liv said quickly. "But

the place is a mess. I'm a mess. It wouldn't be comfortable for you or Colin. Now, I really must go." Liv gave Heather a hug and hurried out the door.

Heather shut the door and leaned against it for a moment before straightening and squaring her shoulders. "I need to check on Colin," she said in a choked voice before she spun around and left the room.

Tyler ached for her loss and wished there was something he could do to comfort her. The only thing he had to give her was bringing her brother's murderer to justice. He went to the kitchen and poured himself more coffee, then called his boss to report in. Just as he hung up, Heather and Colin came back into the kitchen, both wearing warm coats. Heather had changed into jeans and a cream-colored cable-knit sweater.

Heather held out a shearling-lined brown corduroy jacket. Her eyes were red, no doubt from crying. But she held her chin high and regarded him with a steady gaze. He admired her fortitude. "It's brisk out, and that leather jacket of yours won't cut it. We're expecting a cold front in the next few days."

Grateful for her thoughtfulness, he took the jacket and slipped it on. It fit as if made for him. He didn't think it had been Seth's since he was shorter and stockier than Tyler. Her dad's? Or her late husband's? Mentally shrugging, he figured it didn't matter either way. He appreciated her consideration. "Thank you."

They headed out the back door. Colin ran ahead, his little legs pumping fast and his arms swinging wildly. Ah, to be that young and carefree, full of excitement for the world. Tyler couldn't remember ever being that untroubled. His youth had been spent shuffled back and forth between his mom and grandparents and sometimes even children's protective services. He'd been scared most of the time, but it had also made him tough. He could handle all that life threw at him. Yet he hoped little Colin never had to face any more hardships than what had already touched his young life.

"Not so far ahead of me, Colin," Heather called out. There was a definite tremor of concern in her tone.

Keeping his gaze on the child, Tyler said, "I'll make sure nothing happens to either of you."

She slanted him a quick glance, which he caught in his peripheral vision.

"I was thinking about getting a dog as a defense against strangers."

The not-so-subtle barb made him wince and smile at the same time. She didn't fully trust him. Not that he blamed her. He'd failed with her brother. He was determined not to fail again.

"Mommy, can I please go to the village?" Colin asked for the umpteenth time.

Heather gripped his hand, reluctant to let him roam too far from her. "We'll head there next."

They were showing Tyler the harvesting of the Douglas fir trees. The morning temperature hadn't increased much since they'd left the house. Heather tucked her free hand into her parka pocket. Her feet were beginning to ache. She wasn't used to this much walking. The job she'd left to return home had been a desk job as a receptionist for a mortgage broker. Her boots were rubbing, and her legs were tired. Showing Tyler the lay of the farm had taken longer than she'd expected because Tyler asked so many questions and wanted introductions to every worker.

Having him practically attached to her hip was wreaking havoc with her senses. Every time he bumped into her or touched his hand to her elbow, sparks shot out from the point of contact, making her face heat up. She tried to ignore the reaction, telling herself she was being silly. She was reacting to the possible danger, not to Tyler.

With each employee they encountered on the farm, she searched for some clue to indicate malicious intent. But try as she might to find something or someone suspicious, she only found the same people who had worked for the Larson tree farm every holiday season for years.

Though she had moved away at age eighteen, she'd always returned for opening weekend. She knew and trusted these people. Or she had trusted them until yesterday when the world she'd thought she'd known went spinning out of control like a child's toy top by the appearance of the man standing at her side.

She amended that thought. It wasn't fair to blame everything on Tyler. Her brother had started this mess by allowing a drug cartel to use their family's farm to move illegal narcotics. Every time she thought about what Seth had done and the danger he'd put himself and everyone else in, anger flooded her system until she thought she might drown. Seth had made so many impulsive, irresponsible decisions in his life. And his last one had been a whopper.

A choice that had rippling consequences.

Not only had Seth been murdered; now she and Colin were potentially in danger.

And the only defense she and her son had were three men, albeit well-trained ones. She sent up a silent prayer that Tyler and his IBETs colleagues would be enough to keep her and her son safe.

They stopped near a flatbed truck loaded down with a mound of trees that had been through the baler, a machine that wrapped the trees in twine so they could be more easily transported. The trees were then stacked and chained in place.

Colin broke free and ran a few paces away. He squatted down to poke at something on the ground. "Mommy, it's a roly-poly bug."

She smiled, thankful he still found things like bugs interesting. "Don't squish it."

His brows puckered. "I wouldn't do that!"

"Are all the trees transported like this?" Tyler asked, studying the flatbed, drawing her attention away from her son.

"When the delivery location is within the state." Gesturing to the larger refrigerated box trucks a few yards away, she said, "These trucks are used for longer hauls to other states—and into Canada." A lightbulb went off in her head. "Do you think the drugs were smuggled in these vehicles?"

"I was wondering the same thing," Tyler said with

a speculative gleam in his eyes. "Have you ever been inside one of these trucks?"

'No, I've never had a reason to. Seth handled all of that."

"I think I need to inspect these trucks," Tyler said.

Before she could respond, the loud rattle of a chain releasing from its mooring rent the air.

"Watch out!" someone cried.

Chapter Five

Heather had no time to process the sharp cry of warning before a hard body rammed into her, lifting her off the ground, sending them both flying out of the path of an avalanche of trees spilling from the flatbed and landing in the spot where she had just stood.

Heart hammering, Heather scrambled to her knees, her gaze going to the mound of trees. Her mouth dropped open. She could have been crushed.

"Are you okay?" Tyler gripped her by the shoulders, forcing her to look at him. His bright blue eyes were filled with anxiety. "Did I hurt you?"

He'd tackled her to prevent her from being flattened by the trees. He'd saved her life.

Colin!

Her attention whipped to her son. He sat a few feet away with his arms wrapped around his knees, his eyes round.

"Heather?" Tyler persisted.

She put a hand on Tyler's arm. "I'm okay thanks

to your quick reaction." Gratitude flooded her. He'd acted swiftly, without thought to himself. That kind of selfless act touched her deeply and dissolved any lingering anger.

He nodded, expression grim. He helped her to her feet. Colin jumped up and ran to her, colliding with her legs and nearly knocking her back to the ground. His arms wrapped around her and held on tight. Her heart swelled with love for her son.

"You two stay put while I figure out what happened." Tyler went to the truck to inspect the chains that had held the trees in place.

Heather gathered Colin in her arms. He clung to her, putting his head on her shoulder. She hugged him, savoring the moment while her pulse still zinged at a rapid clip.

A dozen men crowded around them, asking if they were hurt. Suddenly feeling vulnerable and claustrophobic with so many people pressing in on her and Colin, Heather said, "Please, everyone, we're okay. Give us some breathing room."

"Come on, guys, let's give Mrs. Randall space," said Don Kline. Don was one of the farm's longest-employed workers. He had been the unofficial foreman since Seth's death. Don was in his late sixties with a shock of white hair and wide girth that made him the perfect choice to play Santa during the holiday season. He wore navy coveralls, work boots and thick gloves and a worried scowl on his weathered face.

Heather grasped his offered hand. The work gloves

were rough against her palm as he drew her and Colin farther away from the scene of the accident.

"Mommy, Mr. Tyler saved you." Awe filled Colin's voice.

She patted his back while her gaze sought out Tyler. He and Blake were conferring near the trailer bed. Tenderness choked her. "Yes. Yes, he did, honey."

She thanked God above for Tyler's quick action. If he hadn't reacted as quickly as he had, she'd have been seriously injured or killed. A quiver of fear raced through her. Had it been an accident? Or something more sinister?

Tyler joined them. "Someone cut the chain holding the trees in place."

Alarm tightened Heather's neck muscles. Someone deliberately tried to hurt her? *No.* That couldn't be.

There was no way anyone could have predicted she'd be standing in that spot at that exact moment. But then why would someone sabotage the flatbed's chain in the first place?

She tried to remember who had been standing on the other side of the truck from her. But she hadn't noticed. Her focus had been on Tyler, on the connection sparking between them. Further proof of how foolish it would be for her to allow him past her defenses. She'd almost been killed by her inattention. And if Colin had been standing there... She shuddered.

Don frowned. "Are you sure? Why would someone do that?"

Tyler placed his arm around Heather. This time she

edged closer to him, grateful for his steady presence. "Have you had any other trouble on the farm?"

Don's bushy white eyebrows twitched. "No, not really. Well, other than poor Seth's death."

The reminder of her brother's murder made her hug Colin tighter.

Tension radiated off Tyler, adding to her already tightly strung nerves.

"What do you mean by 'not really'?" Tyler asked. "Has something else happened?"

Don rubbed a hand over his jaw. "Earlier this month we had a shipment of fertilizer go missing. That's never happened in the nearly forty years I've been here."

Tyler's fingers flexed against her shoulder where his hand rested. "How much fertilizer are we talking about?"

"Four hundred pounds." He waved his hand toward the acres of small, medium-size and large trees. "We have a great deal of ground to cover."

"That's not good." She watched news reports on the television; she knew fertilizer was a component used to make bombs. Her stomach roiled. She shifted Colin to the side. "Why didn't I know about this?"

Don grimaced. "Seth said he'd take care of it. Another order appeared within a few days. I assumed it had been some sort of mix-up."

Her stomach dropped. Had Seth provided some terrorist faction with the means to create an explosive device? *Oh, Seth, what were you thinking?*

Tyler nudged her. "I need to make a phone call."

A cold numbness washed over her as they walked

back toward the farmhouse. As soon as they were far enough out of hearing distance of the employees, Tyler paused and withdrew his cell phone from his cargo pants.

Heather strode away with Colin, not wanting him to hear the details of Tyler's call. Undoubtedly, he was calling his boss or some other law enforcement person who dealt with terrorists and bombs. She shivered and set Colin down. Holding on to his hand, she pointed out the different types of trees.

"I know, Mommy," he said. "Uncle Seth explained that each has its own uniqueness."

"Did he?" She was glad Colin would have good memories of her brother. "Did he tell you that he and I helped plant most of the trees?"

"Uncle Seth said for every tree that is cut down, we replant two."

"That's right. And see on this stump how there's still a live branch? In twenty years, the tree will have grown and be ready to harvest again. We have to be good stewards of the gifts God has given us." This land, this farm, was her family's legacy. She had to protect it for her son.

Tyler walked over. His troubled expression didn't bode well. "I informed my boss," he whispered. "ATF will look into the missing fertilizer."

"Will more agents arrive, wanting access to the farm?" she whispered back.

"Not unless they have intel that can link the farm to a terrorist cell." She wasn't sure if she was relieved or more terrified.

"It's not polite to whisper," Colin scolded them with a scowl.

Heather bit back a surprised laugh. "You're right, honey. It's not. But sometimes grown-ups have to talk about issues that aren't meant for little boys."

His face brightened. "Like my Christmas present?"

This time the laugh escaped. "Definitely like Christmas presents."

"That's not just for adults," Colin said. "Uncle Seth and I whispered about your present."

Her pulse accelerated. She shared a startled glance with Tyler. "What is it?"

Colin tsked. "I can't tell you, Mommy. It's a surprise."

Tyler hooked his thumbs into his belt loops. "You can tell me. I'm really good at keeping secrets."

Colin's face scrunched up as he debated. Finally, he nodded and crooked his finger at Tyler. Tyler knelt down so that Colin could whisper in his ear. The dark shade of their hair was so close in color it was hard to distinguish where one stopped and the other started.

Heather held her breath as an ache deep inside came to life. Seeing them together like that brought home how much Colin was missing out on by not having a father in his life.

She had to be both mother and dad. The load of responsibility weighed heavily on her shoulders, but she gladly, and lovingly, bore the burden. She would do whatever it took to make sure her son grew into a responsible, worthwhile man.

When Colin was done, he stepped back with a grin.

"Well done," Tyler said and high-fived her son before standing.

Dying of curiosity, Heather stared at Tyler, willing him to spill the beans. Anticipation tensed her shoulder muscles and chased away the numbness. What had Seth left her? Could it be the journal?

He winked. "It's a good present. Perfect for a six-year-old to give his mother."

She let out a breath as the tension left her body. Obviously not Seth's journal. "I'll have to wait for Christmas morning, then."

"Are we ready to see the Christmas Village?" Tyler asked.

"Yeah!" Colin jumped up and down and clapped his hands.

Tyler's deep chuckle caught Heather off guard. The sound was rich and warm and something she wanted to hear again.

"Lead the way, little buddy," Tyler said.

Colin raced away.

"Hey! No!" Concern arched through her.

Tyler caught her hand in his. "Come on, Mom. We have to catch up."

Stunned, it took a second to comprehend what he meant, and then he tugged on her hand and she had no choice but to break into a jog to maintain pace with him. They had to increase their combined speed to keep Colin in sight. It felt good to move, to exercise her legs, her lungs and her heart. As if running could distance her from the mess her brother had left behind.

The cool air swept over her face, ruffling her hair

and making her feel alive in a way she hadn't in a long while. By the time they made it to the other side of the property where the Christmas Village sat off the main highway, giving the public easy access to the wide gravel parking lot, she was winded but exhilarated, as well.

Seeing the village stirred a nostalgic sense of well-being. She'd loved this place as a kid. Who was she kidding? She still did, even with danger looming over her like a gloomy cloud.

A high arch structure built by her great-grandfather marked the entrance to the village. Fresh green garland snaked around the arch. Embedded in the greenery were tiny white lights. A big gold satin bow with long tails graced the top of the arch.

Inside the village, constructed to replicate an Old West town, employees worked to prepare for opening day. The various storefront facades were in varying stages of decorating with gold ribbons, gold ornaments of different sizes and gold garland mixed with greenery around the wood railing of the ramps that allowed for wheelchair access.

It seemed this year Rob was going for a golden Christmas theme. She couldn't wait to see what he did with the sleigh. Would he paint it gold? She remembered one year when he'd done a white-and-blue Christmas theme, he'd painted the sleigh blue and hung white lights on it.

Coming to a halt, Heather put her hand over her racing heart. "I haven't run that far in ages."

Tyler grinned, knocking what little breath remained in her lungs out with a one-two punch.

"Whew!" Tyler said. "Is your son training for a long-distance race?"

Catching her breath, she forced her attention to where Colin was talking with Rob outside the bakery shop. "He has a lot of energy—that's for sure."

"He's a good kid."

"Thank you."

"You're a good mom. It shows in Colin."

His comment raised her curiosity. "Have you had much experience with kids?"

He let out a small scoffing laugh. "Not to speak of. But I've seen enough unruly children in public places to spot a genuinely well-behaved kid when I see one. And I would hazard a guess that has a great deal to do with parenting."

"The old nurture versus nature debate, huh?"

"I don't know. But I have to believe that having a parent who loves and cares for their child the way you do Colin, that he's bound to turn out well."

"You must have had good parents, then," she said. "You turned out well."

He blanched. "No. I didn't."

Did he mean he didn't have good parents or that he hadn't turned out well? Or both?

Did she really want to know? Somehow, getting close enough for him to share his history with her scared her. She wasn't looking to get emotionally involved with this man. He was here for a purpose. And it wasn't to comfort her lonely heart. It was to protect her and her son's life. And bust a drug ring. She would do well to remember that despite how much the thought of comfort from him appealed to her. She shoved her hands into the pockets of her red parka.

She had to stop this nonsense and focus on her priority. Her son. "I believe that having a relationship with God is what makes the difference. He is, after all, the ultimate Father."

One side of his mouth slanted upward. "You're right."

They joined Rob and Colin. The delicious aroma of cinnamon and vanilla wafted out of the bakery building. Heather's mouth watered. "Ohhh, Mrs. Theid is making sweet rolls."

"Can I get one?" Colin danced on his toes.

"Me, too," Tyler said, giving Colin another high five.

Amusement danced in Rob's eyes. "I told Colin he'd have to ask you."

Colin and Tyler both gave her a beseeching smile that melted her insides like warm butter on a sweet roll. "Pastries for lunch?"

"Pleeeeeease," Colin said with a wide smile that showed all his little teeth.

Rob chuckled. "How can you resist that face?"

"Right," Tyler chimed in with a big toothy grin of his own. "How can you resist?"

Unable to deny them the treat, she relented with a laugh. "All right. But we've got to head back to the house for some real lunch. A healthy lunch."

"Aww, we just got here," Colin protested.

"Let's not push it, buddy," Tyler said, holding out his hand to Colin. "Let's get a treat." He looked at Heather expectantly. "You coming?"

"I'll be right there," she assured him. "Mrs. Theid was one of my mother's best friends. I should come in and say hello." But she didn't move. Maybe it was because the thought of going inside the bakery with Tyler and Colin as if they were a family unit left her mouth dry and tore a chunk out of her heart.

Tyler hesitated, clearly torn between wanting to stay close to her and wanting to fulfill his word to her son. Tyler was a good man. She'd only had a few hours on which to base her assessment, but so far he'd proven he was a man of honor and integrity. A man worth taking a second look at. But she wasn't looking, not once, not twice.

Colin tugged on his hand, practically dragging Tyler through the bakery door.

Seeing the two walking into the shop hand in hand made her insides melt all over again. She wished she could bottle up this time and keep it for darker days when she and Colin needed a little pick-me-up.

"He seems like a decent guy," Rob said, reminding her she wasn't alone.

"Yes. He does."

And that was a problem.

One she didn't know how to solve. But it was clear she was going to have to guard her heart if she hoped to get through this unscathed. She'd lost her one true love. She had no intention of putting herself at risk again.

Shifting her focus to the village decorations, she said, "Gold this year. I like it."

"It seemed appropriate since this is the golden anniversary of the farm's Christmas Village."

A fist-size knot tightened in her chest. Of course it was. If she'd been paying attention, she'd have remembered. Every Christmas season her parents had been marking off the countdown to the anniversary. Her great-grandparents had bought the farm nearly eighty years ago but waited until their own children were grown and had their own lives before building the village and opening it up to the public.

Touched by his observance of the date, she said with honest gratitude, "Thank you, Rob, for remembering."

"Of course. You are very important to me."

Swallowing back the unease itching its way up her throat, she replied, "Our family is grateful for all you do."

She stared at his scarred face, battling the suspicions rearing within her mind. Was he involved with the drug smuggling? Or was he innocent?

Seth had looked to Rob as a surrogate father. Did she dare take a chance on asking Rob about the journal? Would she be tipping off the bad guys? Where had Rob been standing when the chain on the trees let loose? Had Rob been involved with Seth's death? Was Colin safe with Rob around? Colin looked up to Rob. It would tear him up to discover the man was in any way responsible for Seth's death. And her parents had trusted him...

She looked away from Rob to gaze over the village.

She recognized every face. Year after year these same people journeyed to the tree farm to help make Christmas bright for others. Yes, they were paid, but each one enjoyed their time here enough to return. She'd never worried about her or Colin's safety here on the farm before. But now she stared at each person and questioned whether they were really what they seemed. Any one of these employees could be involved in the drug-smuggling ring. Involved in Seth's death.

A throbbing headache pounded behind her eyes, and her stomach burned with agitation. She didn't know how long she could handle the dread that seemed to have taken up residence inside her. She prayed it wouldn't have to be long and that she and Colin would make it through alive. With their hearts intact.

The cute little bakery was bigger on the inside than Tyler had expected with a full kitchen, large ovens, a few tables and chairs. And the most decadent-looking array of pastries and candies Tyler had seen in a long time.

Before they were served, he called Nathanial and asked him to bring the truck around. Tyler didn't think any of them were up for the hike back.

The woman behind the counter, Mrs. Theid, boasted that all her treats were homemade. She'd been working for the Larsons since before she was married, and she'd just celebrated her thirty-third anniversary.

Tyler hadn't been free to ask too many questions with Colin next to him. But what he did learn made him realize there were more people involved in the

Larson Christmas tree farm than he'd first thought. Which meant more suspects to cull through.

Tyler followed Colin out of the bakery, their hands filled with large gooey sweet rolls dripping with icing. One look at Heather's face had concern crowding out his enjoyment of the pastry in his hand. He cocked his head as he studied Heather. Her face had lost some of the color she'd had from their run. And her lips where pressed tightly together, her eyes troubled. "You okay?"

Her smile looked forced. "Yes. Though I'd like to head back now. I'm tired."

"I called Nathanial and asked him to bring my truck around to pick us up."

"You did?" Heather's eyes brightened. "That was thoughtful of you."

As if on cue, a horn honked. Nathanial waved from the driver's seat of Tyler's large black truck with an extended cab.

Colin's face scrunched up, but Heather held up a hand before he could protest. "We will return to help later. I promise."

Colin huffed and then chomped on the roll, apparently satisfied with her words. Tyler liked that she was firm yet kind with the boy. So different from the way his mother and his grandparents had treated him. He'd dealt with both extremes. His mother had been harsh, sometimes mean when she was coming down off a high, whereas his grandparents had been overindulgent with their affection and praise.

They climbed into the cab of the truck.

"You didn't bring me one of those?" Nathanial

groused good-naturedly, eyeing the remnants of their pastries.

"Wouldn't want to ruin your figure," Tyler shot back, then finished off his pastries with a flourish.

Nathanial grinned as he drove. "You got that right. Too bad you can't say the same for yourself."

Tyler chuckled. He liked the Canadian. They'd only worked together a handful of times, but Tyler could count on Nathanial to have his back.

Glancing over his shoulder at Heather, who stared out the side window with a pensive look on her face, Tyler wondered what Rob had said to upset her. He still hadn't made up his mind about Rob. He seemed to genuinely care for Heather and Colin, but there was something off with the guy. And that bugged Tyler.

When they reached the house, Tyler climbed out and opened the rear cab door for Heather. Nathanial did the same for Colin.

"I need a moment with Nathanial," he told Heather as she climbed out. "You and Colin wait for me on the porch, okay?"

She nodded, but he wasn't sure she really heard him. He snagged her elbow. "What's wrong?"

Her brows knit together. "Everything. I hate this. I hate not trusting the people working on the farm. I hate the fear that something bad will happen to me or Colin."

Hurting for her, he brushed back strands of dark hair that clung to her cheek. "I know. I wish you weren't going through this. But we'll get to the bottom of this— I promise."

For a long moment she stared at him, her eyes so forlorn and vulnerable. He fought the need to take her in his arms and assure her all would be well. But he didn't. Couldn't. Letting this assignment become any more personal than it already had was a bad idea.

His boss had commanded him to stick close to the widow and her son, to protect them. Not so he could fall for the beautiful lady and her adorable kid. He ignored the little whisper inside his head that told him he was fast on his way to falling and there wasn't a safety net to catch him.

Man, he needed to get his head in the game and out of the clouds. There was no possible future in letting himself become emotionally attached to this woman.

Yet, holding her gaze, with the strong pull of attraction weakening his resolve, he found all he wanted to do was gather her to him and kiss her.

The sound of Colin's feet pounding up the porch stairs broke through the moment. He stepped back, thankful for the reprieve. "I need to talk to Nathanial."

She nodded and walked away.

Forcing himself to not watch her, Tyler came around the front of the truck to where Nathanial leaned against the grill.

"We have a problem," Tyler told Nathanial. "There are more employees—"

"Tyler!"

Heather's frantic cry from inside the house sent Tyler's pulse skittering.

Chapter Six

Heart flooding with adrenaline, Tyler raced inside the Larson farmhouse with his hand on his weapon and a prayer on his lips. He had asked Heather to stay on the porch and wait for him, but she'd gone ahead and entered the house unaccompanied.

He shouldn't have let her get out of arm's reach. That was unprofessional and plain stupid. If she ended up hurt because he'd made an error, he'd never forgive himself. He already carried enough guilt for not having extracted Seth before his duplicity was discovered.

Tyler raced into the living room, while Nathanial hurried past him to clear the kitchen. The place had been ransacked. Tyler surveyed the destruction for half a second. The books they had painstakingly gone through the night before and arranged on the shelves were now littering the floor in a haphazard fashion. Throw rugs had been lifted and carelessly deposited in a heap in the corner. Couch cushions had been slashed, the stuffing spilling out. The side tables turned over. The lamp smashed.

"Heather!"

"Here." Her voice came from down the hallway on the ground floor.

He rushed to her side outside her brother's room. She held Colin in her arms, his face buried in her neck. "Are you hurt?"

She shook her head but shock clouded her eyes. "Someone…"

He followed her gaze into Seth's bedroom. Here the damage was more vicious. The dresser had been toppled. The mattress pulled from the frame. The floorboards ripped up. Clothes stripped off the hangers and shredded. The senselessness of the carnage appeared personal, as if the perpetrators had been taking out their aggression on Seth's belongings.

Gripping her elbow, Tyler led Heather back to the living room. They met Nathanial at the bottom of the stairs.

"The kitchen and the rooms upstairs have been searched," Nathanial said in a tone filled with anger.

Colin whispered something into Heather's ear. She nodded and set him down. He ran to the bathroom and shut the door behind him.

"Do you think whoever did this was looking for the journal?" Heather asked.

"I think that's exactly what it means." Tyler had to admit he hoped that the extent of the ransacking was a sign the bad guys didn't have the notebook. But it also meant Seth's murderer knew about the records he was keeping. "When we searched we didn't see any signs of loose boards or hidden compartments in the furniture."

"I wish Seth had told you exactly where he'd hidden the notebook," Heather said in a strained voice. "It could be anywhere on the farm."

Tyler didn't like hearing the miserable tone. He wouldn't let her give up. "And we will find it."

"I hope so," she said with a weary sigh. "We need to call the police."

Tyler exchanged a glance with Nathanial. "Bringing in local law enforcement could jeopardize our investigation by spooking the people we're trying to catch."

Heather arched an eyebrow. "Won't it seem suspicious if I don't call the police? We know whoever did this is working for or with the drug cartel and is probably keeping an eye on me and the house. If the police never show, they'll know and wonder why not."

"True. We need to act as if we aren't aware of the drug ring." Tyler took out his phone and called the Bonners Ferry sheriff's department. They promised a deputy would be out to take their statements for a report.

Tyler knew the procedure. They would take print samples and look for trace evidence. All standard and necessary. However, Tyler held little hope that the perp would leave behind anything incriminating. Not when they'd been so careful committing Seth's murder and making it look like an accidental overdose.

"I need to make sure nothing of value was taken," Heather said as Colin came out of the bathroom and clung to her leg, his eyes wide.

Kneeling down so he could be at eye level with

Colin, Tyler said, "I know you're scared, but I won't let anything bad happen to you." So many bad things had happened to them already. Tyler would do everything he could to make her and Colin's world better. Safer. He gestured to the living room and the damage. "This can all be fixed."

Colin straightened. "I'll help."

Tyler put his hand on the boy's thin shoulder. "You can certainly help once the police have done their thing."

They waited out front for the sheriff's deputy to arrive. As it turned out, Sheriff Paul Rodriguez came out to the farm along with a crime scene unit. He took their statements and waited while Tyler and Colin helped her straighten up the mess left by the intruder. She'd found nothing of value missing.

The sheriff pulled Tyler aside. "I've spoken with your boss, Agent Griffin. If there's anything the Boundary County sheriff's office can do to assist in your investigation, you let us know."

"Thank you, sir." Tyler shook his head. "I appreciate the offer." And he was surprised. He was glad the situation hadn't turned into a turf war. Sometimes the local law got a bit prickly when any of the federal agencies came into their territory working a case.

After the sheriff and the crime scene unit left, Tyler crouched next to Colin. "Let's get that healthy lunch your mother was talking about so we have fuel in our bellies to get the job done."

With a solemnness that tore at Tyler's heart, Colin

nodded and tugged on Heather's hand. "Come on, Mommy. We need fuel."

Tyler rose. The gratitude in Heather's hazel eyes gripped him by the throat. She smiled and mouthed, *Thank you.*

Forcing himself to stay on task, he turned to Nathanial and gestured toward the living room. "Can you deal with this?"

"Yep. Nothing a little duct tape can't fix," Nathanial said. "I have some in my to-go bag."

Not taking the time to ask the Canadian why he traveled with duct tape, Tyler ushered mother and son into the kitchen. Drawers had been removed from their railings; cupboard doors were open and the shelves empty. Dishes were knocked haphazardly on the counter and floor. Fortunately, several had escaped damage.

Without comment, Heather picked up the silverware drawer and threaded the roller on the slide frame to put the drawer back into place. Tyler caught Colin's eye and pointed to the pots on the floor. The boy immediately replaced the pots and pans to their rightful cabinet, while Tyler tackled putting the dishes in their proper place. Once the kitchen was in working order, Heather shooed Tyler from the room.

"Go help Nathanial," she said. "Colin and I have this."

Sensing her need for space, he agreed. "I'll be in the next room if you need anything."

She smiled her thanks, but her eyes glittered suspiciously. Struggling to maintain his focus and pushing back the urge to pull her into his arms, he turned and left the kitchen.

He joined Nathanial in the living room. He was working on restuffing the couch cushions and securing the insides with long strips of silver duct tape.

"The lady okay?" Nathanial asked.

Tyler gathered books and replaced them on the bookshelf. "Rattled."

"The good news is, whoever did this won't be looking here again," Nathanial stated. "The bad news is they will be looking elsewhere on the farm."

"We have to get to Seth Larson's notebook before they do." Tyler's fingers flexed around the thick book in his hand. "I wish I knew who 'they' were. The farm employs nearly a hundred people, way more than I originally estimated."

"We start taking names and running them." Nathanial righted an end table and lamp. "Something will pop."

Finished with the bookshelves, Tyler repositioned the throw rugs on the hardwood floor. "We need to search the grounds. How many cabins are there?"

"I counted six plus another small house where the tightlipped Rob lives."

"It might be worth checking that the cabins and Rob's place haven't suffered the same fate as the farmhouse."

"Right." Nathanial tipped his chin. "You got this?"

"I've got this." Tyler would put everything back in place, sure. But he wouldn't be able to make this right for Heather until they found that journal. Everything rested on the notebook Seth had hidden. Where was it? And why were the bad guys one step ahead of him? If he failed to catch them…

The fear of failing Heather burrowed in deep, making him even more determined to protect her and her son.

Later that evening, after restoring Colin's room to its original form, Heather put Colin down to bed earlier than usual. The day had taken an emotional toll on them both.

She was thankful her bedroom hadn't suffered the same degree of assault that Seth's room had. Had the intruder assumed Seth wouldn't hide the journal where Heather might stumble upon it? The thought that whoever had done this knew her family so well made her skin crawl.

She'd had to bag up Seth's ruined clothes. No sense in putting them back in the drawers or on the hangers in the closet. Thankfully the bedding had been spared.

The living room looked almost normal. She'd have to replace the lamp, but that was easy enough. The cushions now had duct tape on one side. She appreciated the men's attempt to patch things together. But nothing could change the fact that her brother was dead and bad people were roaming her family's farm.

After kissing Colin good-night, she headed downstairs. Tyler sat at the kitchen table with a laptop and a printed list of the farm's employees he'd obtained from Payroll, which she'd given him access to. She stood in the shadows, watching him work. His broad shoulders were hunched, his fingers pecked at the keys and his focus darted back and forth between the computer screen and the list of names on the sheets of paper at his side.

Two days' worth of stubble darkened the contours of his strong jaw. The planes and angles of his face were deepened by the play of light from the drop-down light fixture hanging over his head. It was strange to have him in her house, underfoot. Despite the chaos of her home being ransacked and the stress of knowing someone on the farm had killed her brother and was using the farm to peddle drugs, she had every faith that Tyler would keep her and Colin safe. He had a way of making them both feel cared for.

But Tyler was only here temporarily. She would do well to remember that. Soon he would be gone, and her life would return to...what it was before he'd shown up. She could hardly remember what that felt like despite it being less than twenty-four hours ago. She had to guard against letting Tyler break into her heart.

He glanced up and smiled, knocking the breath from her lungs. "Colin settled in for the night?"

She was glad he couldn't see the heat in her cheeks. "For now." With a deep breath, she pulled back the attraction zinging through her blood and walked briskly into the kitchen. "I'm making tea. Would you like some? Or would you rather have coffee?"

"Coffee, thank you." Tyler rose and stretched to his full height. Heather was momentarily dazed as she watched, appreciating his trim muscular frame. When he moved to lean against the kitchen counter, she quickly busied herself with the coffeemaker and the electric kettle.

"How are you doing?" he asked.

Her first thought was to prevaricate. Tell him she was just dandy. But she was far from all right. She was freaked out by the danger, attracted like crazy to him and totally irritated by the circumstances she'd found herself in.

All control of her life seemed to have run out the door. She was on the edge and not sure how much more she could take. But she had to hold it together. *Be strong.* Colin needed her to be strong. "I'm hanging in there."

Needing to redirect his interest away from her, she asked, "Have you made any discoveries?" He'd told her he wanted to check the employees against the National Crime Information Center's database.

"So far I'm not finding anything to indicate who might be working with the drug cartel."

"That's good, I guess." She set the kettle to boil for her tea, then readied a coffee mug. "If I hadn't received that phone call and someone hadn't trashed my house, I would question whether or not Seth had really helped smuggle drugs using our farm. We saw no sign of drugs today. And I'm assuming your men didn't either."

"No, they didn't. But that doesn't mean anything. It's been my experience that those in the drug trade are crafty. They know how to hide their stash from even experienced agents."

"What about dogs?" She grabbed two mugs from the cupboard and dropped an herbal teabag in one.

"Couldn't you bring in a K-9 unit to sniff out the nar-cotics?"

"We could and may if we don't find anything soon. But once we do that, our cover will be blown and we can kiss any chance of shutting the pipeline down goodbye."

"And you won't settle for the minions," she said, re-membering what he'd said the night before. She poured hot water into her mug. "You want the head bad guy."

He inclined his head. "That's the goal."

She admired his dedication even as she prayed his quest to take down the drug cartel didn't harm her or her son. She prepared his coffee and slid the cup to him. "How long have you been with the DEA?"

"Eight years." His hand wrapped around the hot mug. "I applied to become an agent right out of col-lege."

He'd started out young. "Did you always want to go into law enforcement?"

"Yes." He sipped the black liquid, apparently imper-vious to the heat causing steam to rise in the cool air.

She waited, using her own heated mug to warm her hands. When he didn't elaborate, she asked, "What drew you to the drug enforcement agency?"

He stared into his cup. For a long moment, he was silent.

She told herself to stop pressing. Learning more about him may appease her curiosity, but it would also endear him to her even more than he already was, and that wasn't a good plan.

"My mom was an addict," he finally confessed. "The drugs killed her."

"I'm so sorry."

No wonder he'd followed the path he had. His relentless pursuit of those who imported and exported the poison that had destroyed his mother made sense now. And it formed a bond between them. One she couldn't undo with the knowledge that drove him. They both had lost people they loved. She'd lost Seth to drugs, just as Tyler had lost his mother. But bonds of grief weren't enough to build a future on, not that she was looking to build anything with Tyler.

He shrugged. "Nothing for you to be sorry about."

His nonchalance didn't fool her. She knew the heartache of watching someone battle an addiction. And lose. As much as Seth had wanted to be clean and stay clean, he'd still found a way to let drugs kill him. "How about your father?"

He gave her a rueful smile. "Don't know him. Mom never said who he was, and when I asked, she'd get mad so I stopped asking. Even my grandparents didn't know who he was."

Empathy gripped her heart again. That had to be tough on a boy. At least Colin knew his father had loved him and had died a hero.

Tyler was a hero, too. He was driven by a need to rid the world of the drugs that had robbed him of his mom. Just as drugs had robbed her of Seth.

The flash of headlights sweeping across the kitchen window sent a jolt through her system. She wasn't expecting anyone at this late an hour.

Tyler set his mug down. With a hand on the weapon at his side, he moved to the kitchen door and looked out the window. "It's Liv." He hid his sidearm beneath his black T-shirt.

Surprised Olivia had returned, Heather moved to open the door as Liv stepped up to knock. Liv's gaze widened slightly when she saw Tyler. He moved to the dining table to close his laptop and gathered the papers to stuff into his leather backpack.

Unmistakable curiosity gleamed in Liv's eyes. "I'm sorry, is this a bad time?"

"No," Heather said. "Not at all. Come in."

Liv had changed into black leggings tucked inside tall black boots. She slipped out of her classy black-and-white houndstooth wool coat. Beneath she had on a knee-length sheath dress. She looked elegant and smart. Heather wished she'd changed out of her grubby jeans and sweater into something more... She mentally snorted. *Stop it.* It didn't matter how she looked. She wasn't trying to gain anyone's attention, and she certainly couldn't compete with Liv when it came to fashion.

"What's brought you out here so late in the evening?" Heather asked.

"I was going stir-crazy in my apartment," Liv explained. "I needed to get out. And next thing I knew, I was here. I hope it's okay. I should have called first."

"It's fine," Heather assured her. "We were wrapping up anyway."

Liv bit her lip, uncertainty lighting up her eyes. "I was thinking about what Tyler said this morning about

staying together to help each other through our loss."
Her voice broke on the word. "I was hoping you'd let
me stay here. I don't have to be back to work until Friday afternoon. I just can't be in the apartment anymore."

Sympathetic to Liv's grief, Heather debated the wis-
dom of inviting her to stay. But short of telling her
about the drug ring, Heather couldn't really say no.
"I'll make up—" Heather swallowed back the sudden
lump of sorrow "—Seth's bed for you."

Relief swept over Liv's face. "Thank you. I'll go
get my bag."

Liv left the room and went out the back door.

Tyler scoffed. "She packed a bag."

Heather was perplexed, too. But then again, she'd
never really understood Liv. Heather had been looking
forward to getting to know her better and to calling
her sister. An ache throbbed in Heather's chest. She'd
never have a sister now.

Liv returned with a large designer bag in tow. "I
was also hoping you'd have some childhood photos
of Seth," she said as she dragged her bag all the way
inside. "I'd like to get started on a memorial board."

Heather gritted her teeth. She'd thought she'd been
clear that morning she wasn't up for tackling a memorial for Seth. "Yes, we have photos. They're stored in
the attic. But, Liv, I'm not ready to do this."

"I will take care of it," Liv said as tears welled. She
blinked several times, visibly gathering her composure.
"I need the closure. Point me in the right direction, and
I'll find what we need."

Closure. Heather wouldn't have closure until she knew who'd killed her brother. But she couldn't tell Liv that. "I'll show you where they are." She turned to Tyler. "The key to the carriage apartment is under the doormat. We keep the place stocked, so it should be ready to go."

He held her gaze. "You'll call me if you need anything?"

"Of course," she assured him. He'd programed his number into her cell phone already and had made her promise to keep the phone on her person at all times.

"Where's Colin?" Liv asked.

"In bed," Heather replied. "We had a big day."

Disappointment dampened the other woman's expression. "I didn't get to see him this morning either. I could really use one of his hugs."

Heather had no words for Liv. She wasn't about to tell the woman to go wake Colin.

"I'll check in with you later," Tyler said, throwing his backpack over his shoulder. "Nice to see you again, Liv."

"And you," Liv replied politely.

Once Tyler left the house, the exhaustion that Heather had kept at bay threatened to send her to her knees. But Liv was staring at her expectantly, so Heather bolstered her stamina. She would get through this. She sent up a silent prayer for God's strength. "Follow me."

A few hours later, with the kitchen table covered in Heather's and Seth's childhood photos, Heather accepted a second cup of tea from Liv, who'd taken it upon herself to boil more water and scramble some eggs for them both. Once they'd brought the boxes of pictures down from the attic, Heather had intended to walk away and leave Liv to her project, but for some macabre reason, Heather needed to see the photos, even though the memories created pain deep in her core.

"These photos are wonderful," Liv said as she took her seat next to Heather. "I so wish I could have met your parents. They seem like the best."

"They were." Heather picked up a family photo taken at Christmas Heather's freshman year of high school. Seth was so young and gangly in the photo. Heather had thought herself so trendy in her skinny jeans, cropped cardigan and slipper boots that were comfortable but not functional. Her parents had looked so happy, so alive.

Her heart pulsed with anguish. She missed them so much. They'd been so caring and supportive. Of both her and Seth. She remembered how proud her father was to walk her down the aisle when she married Ken. And she also remembered her father's tears at Ken's military funeral.

Heather hadn't cried until the folded flag had been placed in her hands. Then the numbness had broken. Her mother had held her in her arms. That moment was imprinted on Heather's heart like a scar.

To hide the tears burning behind her eyes from Liv, she sipped from her tea.

"I love this picture of Seth." Liv held up a photo from his high school graduation.

Heather remembered that night. After the ceremony,

Seth had taken off. Her parents had been frantic when he hadn't returned. And when he did show up three days later, he was high and combative. Her parents had hidden the incident from her. Like so many other times.

It wasn't until after Ken died that her parents had confessed that Seth was in a bad way. Heather had been grieving her husband but had come home to talk some sense into Seth. He'd tuned her out. She'd gone back to Washington, only returning for holidays and then after the tragic car accident two years ago that had claimed her parents' lives.

Pressure built within Heather. Suddenly nauseated, she quickly rose. "I need some fresh air."

She stumbled out to the porch, down the stairs and hurried around the side of the house where she dry heaved into the barren rosebushes.

Wrapping her arms around her middle, more to keep herself from breaking into a million pieces than from the cold, she walked away from the house to the lone lodge pole tree in the backyard. At the base of the tree was a bench where her father would often sit to whittle.

She sank down on the bench. Snow flurries swirled in the air, but she hardly noticed or cared. All that had happened over the past week crashed in on her. Everything hurt. The first tear slid slowly down her cheek. The rest came out in gushing sobs. Dropping her face into her hands, she let loose the grief she'd bottled up inside.

The snap of a branch blasted through her sorrow. With dawning horror, she realized how foolish she'd been to leave the safety of the house. She jumped to her feet. In her peripheral vision she saw movement. Panicked, she ran and prayed she made the safety of the house in time.

Chapter Seven

"Heather!" Tyler called out in a hushed tone as he caught up to her and gripped her elbow to stop her from running away.

Heather froze, her body rigid.

"Tyler!" She whirled to confront him. The shadows concealed her expression, but moonlight glistened on the flakes of snow landing in her dark hair, creating little sparks that matched the anger in her tone. "You scared me."

Contrite, he rubbed his hands up and down her arms. "Sorry. I didn't mean to."

She let out a trembling breath. "What are you doing out here?"

"I was walking the perimeter and I saw you come outside." He wished he could see her face. "Are you ill?"

"No." The stiffness left her body. Her shoulders slumped, and her voice quivered. "Just overwhelmed."

Hurting for her, he led her back to the bench and

eased them both down to sit side by side. He shed his jacket and draped it over her shoulders, keeping his arm loosely around her. The frigid night air seeped through his T-shirt. "You shouldn't have come outside alone."

"I know. I wasn't thinking." She sat with her spine straight as if to avoid leaning too much on him. She tried so hard to be independent. Was that why he felt such an insane desire to ease her load, to take care of her?

Needing a distraction from his thoughts, he changed the subject. "It must have been hard to look at pictures of your past," he said softly. His fingertips drew small circles on her biceps.

"Yes." She sniffled.

He tensed, unsure how to deal with a crying woman. Then something his grandmother said came to mind. "It's okay to cry. My gran always told me crying was the heart's way of letting out the bad stuff to make room for the good stuff."

"She sounds like a smart woman."

"Gran was my rock. She'd held me together so many times as a kid."

"Was?"

Sorrow pinched his heart. "She and Gramps are gone now."

A shudder worked through Heather. He pulled her close. Alarm bells went off in his head, but he ignored them. She needed comfort right now, and he knew she wouldn't ask for it. It was the least he could offer her, considering he'd scared her. Not to mention upset her life even more than it had been by revealing her brother's less than honorable actions. Holding her now had nothing to do with opening up to her earlier, revealing his private pain. He wasn't sure why he'd done that. Maybe because of all the people in his life, she'd be the one to understand. She, too, had been touched by drug addiction. A bond shared was a powerful thing indeed.

For a moment she resisted, and then she melted into his arms. Her silent tears soaked through his T-shirt where her cheek rested against his chest. For a long moment he held her as she cried. Her tears didn't scare him as he'd thought they would. He doubted she'd let very many people see her break down before. For some reason that made his ego puff up for a moment.

But then reality dawned, and he squashed his inflated ego. Comforting her wasn't about him. She was so busy being strong for her son, for Liv, for her employees. That she felt safe enough with him to lower her defenses only told him how much she needed to let loose. Bottling up all the emotion couldn't be good for her or her son.

That was all that mattered.

She shivered and burrowed in closer. "It's snowing."

The flakes were bigger now and sticking to the ground.

"Come on—let's get you inside," he said as he pulled her to her feet. After he tucked her in close to his body, they walked across the lawn, leaving a trail of footsteps in their wake. Side by side they climbed the stairs to the back porch. She hesitated at the door. He gave her a questioning look.

"Thank you," she said softly, laying both of her

hands on his chest, covering the stain of her tears. The warmth of her touch sank through him, heating his heart, making it feel full. Complete…

"You're welcome." Gazing into her lovely eyes, so pretty with specks of gold and green. They made him think of picnics and warm, lazy days. His gaze dropped to her mouth. Full lips, red from the cold. Such a pretty mouth. So kissable.

She glanced up and then made a small noise of dismay before stepping back. He followed her gaze to the sprig of mistletoe hanging from the eave above him.

Without another word, she opened the door and stepped inside, leaving the door open for him. Disappointment engulfed him. He scrubbed a hand over his whiskered jaw and called himself a jerk for thinking about kissing her when she'd been so upset. But the reality was he wanted to kiss the lovely Heather, and he'd be kidding himself if he denied that fact. And if she hadn't retreated when she had, he might have weakened and given in to the temptation to kiss her.

He filled his lungs with the fresh, freezing air to cool down his blood and calm his racing heart.

Why was it every time he was around Heather, he lost focus on the job?

His fascination with her had to stop.

Now.

Though he knew he should return to the carriage house over the detached garage and create some distance between himself and Heather, he didn't feel right deserting her when she was so upset. That was all. So instead of beating a hasty retreat he entered the farmhouse and shut the door behind him. Warmth from the central heating chased away the chill from outside. Heather stood at the kitchen counter sipping from a mug, her gaze everywhere but on him. Liv sat at the dining table, surrounded by photographs.

Liv glanced inquisitively from him to Heather and back.

But she didn't comment.

"I'm going to check on Colin," Heather said before hurrying from the room.

Rising from her seat at the table, Liv speared him with a hard look that was so different from the mushy mess she'd been earlier. "What are your intentions toward Heather?"

Taken aback by both the question and that Liv was taking it on herself to be Heather's champion, he sought for a neutral tone as he answered. "We're friends. Business partners. Nothing more."

She pointed one red-tipped nail at him. "Don't play with her affections. She's been through enough trauma in her life."

Half offended and half pleased by her concern for Heather, he said, "I wouldn't dream of hurting Heather. Or Colin."

"You better not," Liv stated in a firm tone that didn't quite match his perception of her. "I'll be watching you."

He suppressed a chuckle. "It's good to know you're watching out for her best interest."

Liv nodded. "I am. I was going to be her sister, you

know." She moved back to the table. "Just because Seth is gone doesn't mean I should stop caring about Heather and Colin."

"Of course not." Tyler stepped to the table and stared at the images spread out before him. Heather had been a cute kid and a pretty teen. The happy pictures of her family seared him clean through. She deserved to be happy again. She and Colin deserved so much more than a man like him. Not that he was asking to be their man. But seeing these images brought home how very different their lives had been and how different their futures were.

And how a relationship with Heather was an impossible dream. A dream he needed to put out of his mind.

When Heather returned a few moments later to report Colin was still fast asleep, Tyler took his leave.

"Good night, ladies." He shut the door behind him and made his way back to the carriage house. He paused at the top of the stairs leading to the apartment door. His gaze swept across the view of the house, the work buildings and rows and rows of trees. All was peaceful, quiet. But for how long?

At some point the people responsible for Seth's death would surface with their drugs. And when that time came, he and the team would be ready. He could only hope it happened before all his defenses crumbled and he allowed the sweet and tempting Heather to breech the barricades of his heart. He could still feel the heat of her touch. He put his hand over his heart as if doing so would be enough to block Heather from getting inside.

* * *

The next morning, Heather had her emotions back under control. She was so embarrassed about her sob-fest last night. Thankfully, poor Tyler had endured her tears, and for that she was grateful. But he wasn't here to be her shoulder to cry on. He was here to bring down a drug ring and find her brother's killer.

That was reason enough to keep a firm rein on her control and not give in to the need to lean on Tyler, to long for his kisses. And, oh, boy, did she. When they'd been standing there at her back door, the tenderness in his eyes had melted her heart into a puddle, and for a moment she'd been on the verge of rising on tiptoe to close the gap between them. But then she'd spied the green mistletoe with the red ribbon hanging overhead and reality slapped her upside the head.

Kissing him wasn't something she could allow. Not now, not ever. She had to think of Colin. She had to maintain control of her emotions to be everything her son needed despite how good it had felt to release her anguish. She'd kept all her suffering locked up inside, thinking it would make her strong. Letting it out had had the desired effect. She was infused with renewed strength, energy.

Tyler's words floated through her mind, and she smiled. She liked the idea of relinquishing the bad to make room for the good. She could use some good right about now.

But freeing her inner torment hadn't quelled her queasy stomach. This morning was not much better.

She prayed she wasn't getting sick. The last thing she needed was to be laid up with the flu.

After dressing, she checked Colin's room, but he wasn't there. A bubble of concern stirred her nausea. Clamping her lips together, she hurried downstairs to find Colin and Liv sitting on the couch watching a kid's show with the volume low. Relief swept through her like a clean wave, but it did nothing to quell her upset stomach.

"Mommy!" Colin cried when he noticed her. He jumped up and raced into her waiting arms.

She swung him up and kissed him noisily, loving his laughter.

Liv walked past them into the kitchen. "I'll make French toast. Anybody want some?"

"Me!" Colin pushed at Heather's arms. She released him, and he ran into the kitchen.

Following at a more sedate pace, Heather noticed the dining table had been cleared except for a stack of photos and a large three-sided display board.

A knock at the back door drew her attention. She pushed the curtain aside and wasn't surprised to see Tyler. Sunlight bathed him in a soft glow. He'd shaved and changed into jeans and a plaid button-down shirt beneath Seth's old shearling jacket. Her heart did a little jig in her chest. Remembering what a mess she'd been last night raised her blood pressure.

Stifling the urge to do an about-face and head out the front door, she opened the back door instead and stepped aside so he could enter. "Good morning."

Though he smiled, there was a determination in his eyes that hadn't been there yesterday. "Morning."

"Mr. Tyler!" Colin ran straight at him.

Tyler lifted him high and then set him on his feet. "Little man, how are you today?"

"Good. Aunt Liv is making French toast."

The shock of hearing her son call Liv *Aunt* reverberated through Heather and dislodged a shard of grief to pierce her heart. She supposed there was no harm in Colin referring to Liv with the familial title. If Seth had lived, Liv would have been Colin's aunt.

"Would you like to join us?" Liv called out from the kitchen. "There's plenty."

At his questioning glance, Heather nodded her encouragement.

"Sure, I'd love that," he said to Liv, but his attention remained on Heather.

Suddenly hot, she tugged at the collar of her sweater.

"It's beautiful outside." He shed the jacket and hung it on the back of a chair. "The layer of snow makes everything look so pristine."

"Hopefully it won't melt." Like she was doing beneath his heated gaze.

Heather escaped into the kitchen to gather plates and utensils. She set the table, skirting around Tyler but pausing slightly to inhale his aftershave. A woodsy scent that brought to mind cozy nights curled up on the couch by the hearth. Her mouth went dry.

"Sit down," Liv ordered. "Breakfast is served." She carried in a plate piled with thick slices of egg-dipped bread that had been cooked to golden brown on both sides.

Heather hadn't expected to have much of an appetite, but she easily ate two pieces. Liv kept up a running dialogue of stories about her clientele at the beauty salon she owned. When they were done, Tyler helped Heather clear the table.

"Liv, we've got this," he said when Liv followed them into the kitchen.

Apparently he wanted to talk to Heather alone. She hoped he didn't bring up last night. She owed him an apology. However, she had no desire to talk about her mini-breakdown.

A frown puckered Liv's perfectly plucked eyebrows. "Are you sure?"

"Yes," Tyler said. To Heather he said, "I'll wash—you dry."

Heather opened a drawer and took out a clean dish towel. "Sounds good."

Liv shrugged and left the room.

As soon as the other woman was out of earshot, Heather said, "Sorry about last night."

He scrubbed a dish. "No worries." He handed her the plate. "I've been thinking." He lowered his voice. "What if Seth stashed the notebook in the Christmas Village?"

Placing the dried plate in the cupboard, she contemplated Tyler's question. "He might have. Though there would be a greater possibility of discovery by just about anyone."

"Not if he disguised the journal," Tyler countered.

"I remember peering into a couple of storefronts that had bookshelves."

Why hadn't she thought of that? "I think you're onto something there. I remember once he hid a book that my parents disapproved of in the tailor shop."

"There you go."

"I did promise Colin we could help Rob some more today."

"That would be the perfect cover for looking around," Tyler said in an accent that made her think of Inspector Clouseau from the Pink Panther movies.

She smiled but didn't dare try an accent. "Yes, it would."

He waggled his eyebrows. "Then it's a plan."

She laughed, liking his playful side. They finished cleaning up the breakfast dishes, and then she got Colin ready to go outside.

Knowing the polite thing to do was invite Liv, Heather asked, "Would you care to join us?"

Liv waved her hand and sat at the dining table again. "I'm going to work on the memorial board." She picked up the stack of photos and laid them out on the table.

Afraid she'd tear up again, Heather turned away from the pictures. With Colin between them, she and Tyler walked across the property, through the trees and past the cabins to the Christmas Village.

Most of the decorations had been finished the day before. A few employees swept the wooden walkways. Others had put down sand to smooth out the graveled ground. Today the petting zoo was being assembled. At the back of the large pen where the animals would roam free was a large-scale nativity scene with mannequin Joseph, Mary and baby Jesus in a manger. A large star hung over the baby from a pole that had been attached to the back of the pen.

"You go all out here," Tyler commented.

"We do," she agreed.

Rob was standing with a man Heather didn't recognize near the Toy Shoppe. The outside of the shop had been painted red with white trim. Two large windows flanked the door. In one window an array of china dolls stared out at them with unblinking eyes. The other window had various-sized stuffed teddy bears and an assorted display of old-fashioned toys made from wood, some of which her father had crafted.

As Heather, Tyler and Colin approached, Rob broke off his conversation with the young man, saying, "We'll discuss this more later."

The young man nodded and sauntered away.

Colin tugged his hand loose from Heather's to run to Rob. The older man ruffled his hair.

Exchanging a curious glance with Tyler, Heather asked Rob, "What was that about?" Her gaze strayed to the man heading out of the village.

"That is Paul Ambrose," Rob said. "Dean Ambrose's kid."

Though she recognized the name, she couldn't put a face to it.

"Dean usually drives the sleigh," Rob supplied. "But he's having some health issues, and Paul has volunteered to take his father's place."

"That's kind of him," Heather said. "Does he know how to drive the sleigh?"

Rob shrugged. "Better than I do." He shifted on his cane. "We're almost ready here."

"Yesterday I didn't get a chance to show Tyler the different buildings." She gestured to the toy shop. "Is it unlocked?"

"It's not." Rob held out a ring of keys. "The red key opens that door."

"Who, besides you, has keys to the buildings?" Tyler asked.

"Seth had a set." Rob frowned. "Not sure where they ended up."

"I didn't see them in his room," Heather said. "Could they be in the barn?"

Rob shook his head. "I didn't see them in the tack room or any of the stalls."

She unlocked the door and pushed it open. Inside the air was musty and stale. A layer of dust coated everything.

"Look, Mommy, my old tricycle!" Colin sat on the blue trike, his long legs scrunched up to his chin, and rode forward a few inches.

"Hey, buddy, why don't we take that outside," Tyler said.

Colin jumped up to drag the trike to the door. Tyler helped him get it outside.

Grateful to Tyler for his care of her son, Heather stepped past a rocking horse to the workbench made to look as if the toy maker were in the process of building a dollhouse. The dust here had been disturbed as if someone had laid something across the bench. Behind the half-made dollhouse she found a leather-bound book.

Excitement accelerated her breathing. Could this be Seth's mysterious journal? She opened the book to find it was a ledger with the farm's payables and receivables for the past two years.

The corner of a white envelope sticking out from inside a small cubbyhole in the workbench caught her attention. She tugged the envelope out and found more than a dozen similar envelopes. Curious, she opened one and found an overdue bill dated last month. Her heart beat a frantic tune as she opened each envelope. They were all overdue bills. Some so past overdue that a collection agency had sent notices.

Her stomach sank. She began to understand. So this was why Seth had gone into business with a drug cartel. But why hadn't he told her the farm wasn't making a profit? And how long had this been going on?

Tucking the envelopes into her coat pocket and clutching the ledger under her arm, she went outside to find Tyler. He leaned against the railing, encouraging Colin as he rode the tricycle up and down the walkways, his little legs pumping as fast as he could. The tenderness on Tyler's face stopped her breath.

The man might claim to not have any experience with children, but he obviously had a soft spot for them. Or at least for Colin. An ache of longing hit her so hard she fell back a step from the blow.

She wanted Colin to have a father. She wanted a

husband to call her own. She wanted what she'd lost when Ken died.

Guilt for even contemplating replacing Ken in her heart, in her son's heart, charged through her, setting her nerves on a sharp edge. She fought the urge to steady herself with a hand on the building's outside wall. She had to get a firm handle on her feelings. Right now.

Tyler looked her way. She prayed he didn't notice she was upset. Squaring her shoulders and lifting her chin, she repaired the crumbling shield around her heart as best she could. She had too many other things to worry about right now. She didn't want to have to deal with her uncooperative heart craving something she couldn't allow herself to have.

"What's that?" Tyler said, his gaze on the book in her hands.

His eager tone propelled her to his side. "It's the farm's accounting records."

"Oh." There was no mistaking the disappointment in the word.

"I need to go into town and reconcile the farm's finances." She pulled the envelopes of unpaid bills from her jacket pocket. "Seth wasn't paying the bills. I have no idea where the farm stands financially."

"Does your family have a safe-deposit box where Seth might have hidden the journal?"

"I don't know. My parents never mentioned one."

"Any chance your brother might have opened one?"

She shrugged. "If he did, he never told me about it.

But, then again, there seems to be a great deal he never shared with me."

It hurt to realize how little she actually knew of Seth's life and the secrets he kept. Secrets that put them all in jeopardy.

And had put her on a collision course with a wonderful man who had her emotions spinning out of control and made her long for things that could never be.

Chapter Eight

"I can't believe Seth did this." Heather clutched the leather-bound ledger with the farm's bank records inside to her as Tyler started up the engine of his truck. She sat in the passenger seat and stared out the window at the passing scenery. Her stomach hurt; so did her heart.

She and Tyler had just come from the bank in Bonners Ferry where they'd gone over the farm's financials with the bank manager and were now on their way back home. She'd left Colin with Liv. Blake and Nathanial had promised to keep an eye on the house, so Heather wouldn't worry.

But *worry* was such a mild word for how she felt now that she'd learned Seth had put the farm in a precarious financial situation. He'd siphoned a good portion of the farm's income to purchase personal big-ticket items. The new car that Olivia drove, the down payment on the town house he had intended to share with Liv once they married and the beautiful diamond engagement ring that Liv wore. Not to mention the deposit on a honeymoon package to the Cayman Islands.

"It seems your brother had made more than a few bad decisions," Tyler commented, taking the turn off the highway onto the road leading to the tree farm.

"Understatement of the millennium. Bad decisions and lying to me. When I asked Seth about Liv's ring, he claimed he'd been saving up. I had no idea he had paid for her car or the town house. I wrongly assumed those were Liv's expenses." Her fingers tightened around the ledger. "If we don't turn a profit this season, I don't know what will happen to the farm. To Colin and me."

The thought of losing her family home was like a physical blow. The nausea she'd been trying to ignore for the past several hours intensified. She swallowed several times to keep bile from burning her throat.

Up ahead the Christmas Village came into view. So festive and inviting. It was late enough in the day that most of the employees who didn't live on the farm had left for the day and wouldn't return until Friday morning when the farm opened to the public.

Tomorrow was Thanksgiving.

She let out a groan.

Tyler shot her a glance. "What's up?"

"I didn't get a turkey. Or anything else, for that matter. And Thanksgiving is tomorrow. I always fix a meal for the staff who stay behind." She sighed. "My grandmother and mom both did. Now I've dropped the ball."

He reached over and took her hand. "I'll take care of it."

His big warm hand engulfed hers, offering comfort

and protection. She wanted to lean on this man. To let him shoulder some of her burdens, her concerns. It had been so long since she'd had someone to share her load with that the weight of her troubles threatened to bury her. But it would be selfish of her to slough off her duties and obligations. Wouldn't it?

Not to mention dangerous. She couldn't let herself become too dependent on him; doing so would only lead to more heartache when he left.

"I can't ask you to do that," she said, withdrawing her hand from his. "I'll have the grocery store deliver what we'll need for tomorrow's feast." It would cost twice as much, but what choice did she have?

"Seriously, let the guys and me take care of everything." He brought the truck to a halt at the back steps of the farmhouse. "You've enough to contend with right now."

"You're sweet to want to help," she said. "But I don't think catering a meal for my employees is in your job description."

"But it is." He cut the engine and swiveled to face her. "This will give us a good opportunity to interact with the employees. And while they are all gathered eating, Blake and Nathanial can search the farm without prying eyes."

He made a good case. But… "Letting you take over doesn't sit well."

"Why not?"

"I don't like the fact that I'm losing control of my life." And her heart if she wasn't careful. Two good reasons to say no to his proposal.

"You can supervise," he said with a smile that had her heart fluttering.

Maybe that would work. And truthfully, the thought of putting together a Thanksgiving dinner completely overwhelmed her given what had gone on in the past few days. She was spent. Besides, as he'd said, it would be good for the investigation, and the sooner the investigation was over, the sooner her life would go back to normal. Whatever normal was anymore.

As much as it galled her to hand this over to him, doing so would be for the best all around. "That would be fine. Thank you." She dropped her gaze to the ledger in her lap. "What am I going to say to Liv? Seth spent money that wasn't his to spend. Liv will have to give up the town house and the car at the very least."

"You'll find the right words when the time is right." Tyler lifted her chin with a finger, forcing her to meet his gaze. "You are not alone in this, Heather. I'm here to help you. But more importantly, God is with you."

How did Tyler do that? He understood what she was feeling when she hadn't even admitted to herself how alone and lonely she felt. A chunk of her heart melted.

But Tyler was temporary. When this was over, he'd leave. And she and Colin would have to learn to live without him or anyone else. It would be just the two of them against the world.

She didn't want to think about that yet. Didn't have the mental fortitude just now. For the time being she was grateful to have Tyler's stable and calm company. Tyler and his team, that was.

They left the truck and entered the house. Colin

and Liv were seated at the dining table playing Candy Land. Seeing them together brought a pang of sorrow. Liv doted on Colin and would have made a wonderful aunt.

"Mommy, I'm winning," Colin boasted with a big grin.

A rush of love infused Heather, taming the worries about the farm's financial situation. As long as her son was safe and healthy, nothing else really mattered. Tyler was right—God would protect them and provide for them. She couldn't let circumstance diminish her faith.

Her faith was stronger than that. She only hoped she was stronger than her attraction to Tyler.

Nathanial rubbed his hands together. "A real American Thanksgiving dinner."

The Canadian's enthusiasm brought a smile to Tyler's lips. He sat on a rickety chair inside the cabin in which the two IBETs members were staying in.

Two extra-long twin beds took up half the space, while a small table, chairs and kitchenette took up the rest. A community restroom with showers was a few paces outside the door.

Heather was right when she'd said the cabin would barely be big enough for the two men. Since Liv was there with Heather and Colin, Tyler had risked taking fifteen minutes to update the guys on the situation and asking for their help in providing a Thanksgiving feast for the dozen or so people who would remain on the tree farm tomorrow. "You up for the challenge?"

"Better believe it." Nathanial's lit-up expression reminded Tyler of a kid in a candy store. "Would we be having the marshmallow yam dish? I had that once years ago." He smacked his lips. "Yum, yum."

"You mean sweet potato pie," Blake drawled, letting his Southern twang out in all its glory. "I will make my mama's recipe. There's nothing better."

"As long as there's turkey and gravy, I'm sure everyone will be happy." Tyler opened his wallet and thumbed out several large bills. "This should cover the expense."

Blake took the money, then eyed him with concern. "You're getting invested in this woman and her problems."

He clearly wasn't referring to the case in his hands. Tyler wouldn't deny the statement. Instead he deflected the comment. "I'm invested in seeing this assignment through. If that means paying for a fancy meal cooked by you two, then so be it."

"Be careful, bro," Blake said with a dose of censure in his tone. "Someone's gonna get hurt. They always do."

Tyler studied the other man. "You speaking from experience?"

Blake's jaw hardened. "This isn't about me. That kid's growing attached to you. Not to mention the mom."

Guilt scratched at Tyler's conscience. "I'm not making promises I can't keep. I've been straight with Heather. She understands the priority is bringing down the drug ring."

"And finding her brother's killer," Blake stated.

"Yes, that, too." Though Tyler was positive they were one and the same.

"To that end," Nathanial interjected, "the trucks are scheduled to leave tomorrow, late afternoon. If we're going to find out how the drugs are being smuggled out, we have a very short window of time."

"True." Tyler rose. "So here's the plan. One of you goes into town and does the shopping. While you're there, look into Liv's town house. Find out who holds the loan. Heather's going to need that down payment back."

Blake wagged his head. "Man, what are you doing? That isn't our business."

"Technically, no, it's not, but—"

"But nothing," Blake cut him off.

Nathanial held up a hand. "Time out. I'll head to town." He pointed at Blake. "You make a shopping list." Nathanial opened the cabin door. "Tyler, you get back to the lady and her son. You were tasked with their protection. We'll do our part."

Thankful for Nathanial's level head, Tyler rose. "I appreciate it."

He left the cabin, but Blake's words hounded him all the way back to the farmhouse. After checking in on Heather and Colin, seeing that they were safe, Tyler headed to the carriage house to ponder how he'd let himself get so involved in Heather's well-being, not just physically keeping her safe, but her emotional well-being. He really needed to put the kibosh on the latter because it was wreaking havoc with *his* emotional well-being.

Blake was right. Any way Tyler played it, someone was going to get hurt. Letting himself care too much would jeopardize his judgment, not to mention set him up for disappointment. Or worse, he would end up disappointing Heather and her son.

He needed to distance himself from the mother and child. Though he couldn't physically distance himself, he could be more detached, more professional.

That meant no more hanging around her for the sake of being near her, no more touching her and definitely no more thoughts of kissing her.

Unfortunately, he had a feeling detachment would be a harder battle to win than bringing down a drug cartel.

While Nathanial stayed at the farmhouse with the ladies talking turkey and desserts, Tyler and Blake took advantage of the cover of night to inspect the refrigerated trucks. Tyler knew the Canadian would protect Heather, Liv and Colin. He was a good guy, trustworthy. Yet Tyler couldn't ignore the bits of jealousy that clung to him as he and Blake made their way to the loaded trucks by the light of the moon.

"You take that one," Blake said, pointing to the first truck. "I'll take the other one."

Tyler acknowledged Blake with a thumbs-up, though he wasn't sure the other agent could see him. Starting with the cab, Tyler inspected the inside compartment, checking the obvious places first like the glove box, under the seats, in the door panels and in the sleeping bunk behind the captain's chairs. He pried off the door panels, felt around the headliner and checked under the mats for secret cubbyholes. Nothing.

Using his penlight, he checked the engine, the body panels, the chassis and differential for signs of tampering. No scratch marks, no uneven alignment.

Frustrated by the lack of evidence, he figured the concealed drugs must be inside the refrigerated truck with the Christmas trees. He opened the back doors. A foul odor emanated from inside the box. He faced a mound of trees wrapped in thin netting to condense the size of the trees while protecting them from damage during transport. There had to be at least a hundred trees filling the whole box.

Great. He'd have to unload all the trees to search inside for a hidden compartment.

He grasped the end of the closest tree and tugged. The whole stack shifted. Concerned the whole lot would come shooting out, he let go. His hand came away with a sticky residue that smelled so bad his eyes watered. "What in the world?"

He shone his penlight on the tree and inspected the stem. A thin cut circled the trunk about a half inch from the butt end.

"Find anything?" Blake asked as he approached.

"Something odd." Tyler showed Blake the tree trunk.

"That is odd. And smelly." Blake leaned closer. "Hmm, deer urine."

Tyler cringed. "Yuck. Did you come across something worth mentioning?"

"Nope. That truck hasn't been filled with trees yet. I couldn't find any hidey-holes for drugs inside or outside."

Disappointed, Tyler shut the box door. "I want Heather to take a look at this tree. And I need to wash my hand."

"I second that."

When they reached the farmhouse, pie prep was in full swing. Tyler stopped in the doorway. "Heather, can I see you for a moment?"

They stepped out onto the back porch.

Heather's nose wrinkled. "What have you been doing?"

"Apparently a deer used a tree before it was cut down." He hid his hand behind his back, but that did nothing to alleviate the smell.

"Ugh. We do have a whitetail deer herd that comes through when the weather turns cold. You really should go scrub your hand. Deer carry some nasty diseases."

"I don't want to smell up your house," he said.

"I'll be right back." Heather hurried inside. A few minutes later she returned with a wet, soapy washcloth, a dry towel and a dish of water.

Taking the washcloth, he wiped his hand, then rinsed in the water she held. Using the towel, he said, "Thank you. That's much better."

"If I were you, I'd do another scrub at the sink."

"I will, thanks."

She set the bowl aside on the wooden porch. "What did you find?"

"Nothing. Or maybe something. I need you to look at a tree in one of the trucks."

"Let me grab my coat." She gathered the soiled cloths and bowl, then headed back inside. When she returned, she'd put on her red parka. She handed him a pair of work gloves. "So you don't get smelly again."

Her thoughtfulness touched him. The moon's glow illuminated the night enough for them to walk side by side to the box truck. He pulled on the gloves and opened the door.

"Whew!" Heather pinched her nose. "Wow, I never realized how stinky the trees could be."

With his gloved hand, he grasped the tree with the cut. Shining his penlight on the trunk, he asked, "Is this normal?"

"No. That's odd. Does the cut go all the way through?"

"Good question." He tugged, and it loosened. Slowly, he pulled and twisted until the very end of the trunk popped off like a cork. "Well, what do we have here?"

Stuffed inside the hollowed-out trunk was a package wrapped up airtight in plastic and duct tape.

"Is that cocaine?"

"I'd say yes." He stuffed the package back inside and jammed the butt back on.

"Hey, what are you doing?" Heather asked. "I thought you wanted to find the drugs so you could bust the ring. Aren't you going to confiscate it?"

He pushed the tree back into place. "Not yet. We don't know who put it there or when or if that's the only tree. The other truck has yet to be loaded. We'll need to catch them in the act."

Heather sighed. "When will this be over?"

Giving in to his need to reassure her, he put his arm around her shoulders and hustled her back to the house. "Not long now. Do you know where that truck is headed?"

"Not offhand, but I'm sure Don will have the itinerary."

"Can you get a hold of him and ask?"

"Sure. Though what reason do I give him for asking? I've never been involved in that part of the farm."

"Just say you're curious. Or better yet, your new business partner is curious."

"Right. My business partner." He heard a smile in her voice. "I can do that."

They went inside where it was warm and smelled like cinnamon and vanilla.

Heather slipped upstairs to make her call. Tyler joined Colin in the living room to watch a holiday cartoon. Taking a seat on the couch, he looked at the television and said, "Hey, I remember this from when I was a kid."

Colin got up from the floor where he'd been lying on his belly and climbed onto the couch right next to Tyler. "It's my favorite."

Affection flooded Tyler as the boy snuggled against his side. Colin was so trusting and innocent. Blake's words came screaming back to Tyler.

Someone's gonna get hurt. They always do.

That kid's growing attached to you.

The last thing he wanted to do was harm this boy in any way. But for the life of him, Tyler couldn't push the child away, nor did he want to move away from him. Sitting like this was so foreign yet so comfortable and natural.

Heather returned a few moments later and stopped in the archway to the living room. Tyler locked gazes with her. The tenderness in her eyes and the small smile on her lips had his heart thumping in his chest. It wasn't good to get her hopes up, either.

He wasn't father material. He didn't know how to relate to children, and he didn't know how to parent. He had no role model to fall back on. Though he'd had his grandparents, they had overcompensated for their daughter's failings by being lenient with him, making his time with them seem more like a vacation than an actual home.

Regretfully, he extracted himself from Colin. Heather gestured to the front door. They stepped outside.

Brimming with excitement, she said, "The one already loaded is headed for Calgary. The other is headed east."

"Okay, now we're getting somewhere." Anticipation revved through his veins. "Who's driving the trucks?"

"Don said he was going to assign drivers to the trucks tomorrow. He said he has three volunteers to drive the one across the border. And another three volunteers to drive the other truck."

Tyler stroked his jaw, contemplating the implications. "Six drivers willing to transport the trees. Question is do they know the drugs are inside the trees? I want those six names."

"The thing is we give bonuses to the drivers on Thanksgiving and Christmas Eve. So they may be eager for the bonus rather than having anything to do with the drugs."

That poked a little hole in his hope that one of the six would be the guilty party he sought. Still, they were closer to their objective than they had been. At least now they could confirm that Seth had been telling the truth. They'd found the drugs in the tree. How many more trees held packages of cocaine?

If they could only find the journal, then they could end this for all their sakes.

"Do we have info on the company taking possession of the trees in Canada?"

She handed him a piece of paper. "Don gave me names and contact info."

"Good. I'll pass this on to my boss."

Before he could step down the front stairs, Heather placed her hand on his arm. "Thank you, Tyler."

"I'm doing my job, Heather. Nothing more." He deliberately infused an impersonal tone into his voice.

Hurt bloomed in her eyes, and the look instantly tore at him. He wanted nothing more than to take her in his arms and soothe her worries away. But that would be a mistake.

He wasn't there to play house, and she needed to understand that reality. So did he. He was there on a mission, and he would leave when the mission was accomplished. Tyler couldn't let his feelings for the pretty widow derail this operation by letting things become personal.

He couldn't lose his focus. If he let down his guard, he might miss something that could blow this case wide-open. He had to stop letting Heather and Colin be a distraction to his end goal.

With a quick nod, he hurried to the carriage house for privacy to call his boss, who was excited by the new development. "You've done well, Agent Griffin. Now we need to catch these smugglers in the act."

"We'll sit on the trucks tonight," Tyler assured him. "When the second truck is loaded in the morning, we'll round up the employees. They won't have any choice but to cooperate. Then Blake and I will drive the drugs north. I'd like to leave Nathanial here as protection for the Larson-Randall family."

"Sounds like a plan," Granger said. "I'll coordinate with the Royal Canadian Mounted Police and be ready to move in once the trees are delivered."

"Great. Thank you, sir," Tyler said before hanging up.

When he returned to the farmhouse, he drew Heather into the hall and whispered, "Can you have Liv take Colin upstairs without raising any questions?"

Concern darkened her eyes. "Yes, what's up?"

"I need to talk to you and the guys, privately."

Though he could see she wanted more information, she pressed her lips together and strode back into the kitchen where Liv, Nathanial and Blake were busy cooking. The place was a disaster zone.

"Liv, would you be willing to take Colin up and get him ready for bed?" Heather asked.

"Of course." Liv dropped the dough she was kneading onto the wooden cutting board, whipped off her apron and washed her hands before hurrying from the room.

"You didn't have to ask her twice," Nathanial observed.

"She loves Colin," Heather said. Turning to Tyler, she put her hands on her hips. "So tell us. What's the plan?"

He quickly outlined what he and Granger had decided.

Heather frowned. "You're leaving?"

He didn't like the guilt clawing up his neck, but there was no help for it. He had a job to do. "After the feast tomorrow. I promised we'd help you with that."

"Hey, I'll be here," Nathanial said. "Once these lugs leave."

She sent him a polite smile. "That'd be great."

When she swept past Tyler, she shot him a half bewildered, half hurt look that constricted his chest. In her eyes he was letting her down. And that realization hit him harder than the knowledge that he'd let things get too personal between them and that it had to stop.

Chapter Nine

Heather paced her darkened bedroom Thanksgiving eve. The house was quiet. Colin slept soundly in his bed, and Liv was asleep in Seth's room. Heather had been surprised by how well Liv was holding up. After her initial tears, Liv had been energetic in helping the guys prepare for the Thanksgiving feast. She'd bathed Colin and put him to bed after reading him several stories.

Heather was thankful Colin liked Liv, but she couldn't help worry that one day Liv would move on with her life and leave them behind. It seemed everyone left her behind. Ken, her parents, Seth. Now Tyler.

He, too, was leaving. It would be too much to hope that he'd be the one to return her truck. Most likely he'd stay to wrap up his investigation by arresting whoever took possession of the drugs.

She'd known he would eventually leave, but she'd thought, hoped, he'd stay long enough to see that she and Colin were safe and the drug smugglers were no longer a threat. He'd promised he would. Apparently, his promise wasn't something she could count on.

And it wasn't that she didn't trust the other man, Nathanial. She did. It was just that… She couldn't put to words the reason why Tyler leaving so soon felt like he was abandoning her. Them.

She let out a frustrated breath, irritated at herself for being so foolish. He was only doing his job. His promise was to protect her, and if leaving was his way of doing that, then she needed to buck up and deal with his absence. Yes, Tyler leaving was for the best; she'd begun to rely on him too much, to look forward to seeing him and wanting to share her thoughts with him. Things she'd missed since Ken's death.

Pushing back the curtain, Heather peered out at the farm. Another layer of snow had fallen to make the world outside bright with the moon's light reflecting off the white powder. She couldn't see Tyler or the others. The guys had left the house an hour ago. Heather had heard them talking about staking out the trucks in the hope that whoever had put the drugs in the harvested trees would come out to check on their stash. If they caught someone, then what?

Would that be the end of it?

She prayed so.

Her breath fogged the window. It was cold out there.

She left her room and silently made her way downstairs to the kitchen. She didn't dare let her mind question what she was doing as she made three thermoses of hot cocoa. With the thermoses in hand, she hesitated. How did she get them to the guys? She couldn't very well go marching across the farm calling out their names.

She figured Tyler would be positioned in a spot where he could watch the truck and the house. Or at least one of the men would be. She hoped.

After putting on her parka, she slipped out the front door, carrying the hot thermoses. She stood in the shadows, unwilling to venture farther into the moonlight. For a long moment she waited. Then, feeling silly, she shook her head at her own ridiculousness. Even if Tyler could see her, he wouldn't break cover to retrieve hot chocolate.

She reached for the doorknob, intending to go back inside where it was warm and no one could see her embarrassment.

"Heather?" Tyler's whisper floated in the air.

She froze for a long moment, and then slowly turned to find Tyler standing at the bottom of the stairs. She recognized the set of his shoulders and the way he stood with his legs braced slightly apart. Her heart thumped. She was glad he couldn't see her face because she was sure her cheeks were bright red.

"I made you hot chocolate." She held up the thermoses. "And some for the guys."

He vaulted up the stairs to stand beside her. Though it was too dark to see his expression, she could feel his energy swirling around her, stirring up her senses.

"That was sweet of you," he whispered. "You really should go back inside."

"I wanted to apologize."

"For?" He'd moved so close his breath tickled her ear.

Her mouth went suddenly dry. She forced her words past her parched throat. "For not being gracious earlier. You're doing your job, which is to stop the drug ring. Of course you should go with the trees and drugs to Canada."

After taking the thermoses from her, he set them down on the porch, then took her hand and led her to the stairs. They sat on the top one.

"I've decided I'll be staying here with Nathanial."

She tamped down the spurt of joy filling her. "But who will drive the second truck?"

"Unless something changes tonight, only the one truck has trees filled with contraband. We'll put a tracker on the other truck to monitor it in case it makes any unscheduled stops, and we'll inspect the truck when it returns, but for now we only need one driver."

"I'm glad you're staying."

"Me, too."

She bit her bottom lip to keep from asking him why he wanted to stay.

"Even if we stop this shipment of drugs, it won't shut down the cartel. We need your brother's journal."

Of course. He was staying for Seth's notebook, not for her. That made sense. Then why did knowing she wasn't the reason he was staying sting so badly?

"Tomorrow we can search more of the village," she whispered, thankful her tone didn't reveal her upset. "Seth hid the bills in one of the shops. Stands to reason he probably hid the journal in one, as well."

Tyler suddenly stood up. "I'll be right there." He

pulled Heather to her feet. "You need to go inside and lock the door."

Confused and scared, she asked, "What's happening? Who are you talking to?"

"Someone's approaching the trucks."

She glanced out at the rows of trees. The trucks weren't visible. "How do you know that?"

"I have a com device in my ear," Tyler explained. His hand grasped hers and tugged her toward the door. "Go inside and stay away from the windows."

She moved quickly, slipping inside and closing the door. With shaky fingers she slid the lock into place and said a prayer of safety for Tyler. And the others, too, of course.

Slipping on his night vision goggles, Tyler made his way through the dark toward where the trucks were parked. He'd been surprised when he'd seen Heather step outside the front door. She'd stood in the shadows of the eaves for such a long moment he'd been concerned something was wrong. He'd been hiding where he could watch the house and the path leading to the trucks, while Blake and Nathanial had taken positions closer to the trucks.

She'd made hot chocolate. That was so thoughtful of her, a little inconvenient considering they were in the middle of a stakeout, but thoughtful just the same. She was a generous, compassionate woman. One he was finding hard to resist.

Holding her in his arms while she'd cried had nearly torn his heart apart. He hated that she hurt so badly.

She'd suffered so many traumas and yet she willingly took care of everyone else. His admiration and respect for her swelled inside of him.

He'd made her a promise that he'd protect her and Colin. He intended to see that through. Making the decision to stay hadn't come lightly. There was still a chance the empty truck would be a viable way to get a lead on the drug cartel. But Tyler's commitment to finding Seth's journal and protecting Heather and her son outweighed the slim chance that the second truck would bear any fruit. He'd called his boss back, and he'd agreed that it was more important for Tyler and Nathanial to remain at the tree farm.

The communication device in his ear crackled. Then Nathanial's voice came through clearly. "Tyler, heads up. The unidentified subject has veered away from the trucks and is making his way toward the house."

The news sent a burst of alarm into Tyler's midsection. "Copy that."

He ducked behind the nearest bushy tree since there was no way he'd make it back to his position in time to stop the guy's advance. Tyler waited, calming his breath and slowing his heart rate, preparing to take the guy down before he got anywhere close to the house.

All was quiet. No nocturnal noises from beast or fowl. *Wait.* The faint rustling of feet slogging through the newly fallen snow reached Tyler. He estimated the intruder was ten feet to his right.

Staying low in case the guy had his own set of night vision goggles, Tyler moved around the backside of the tree, the pine needles tickling his nose. He saw a figure pass by. Sure enough the man had on a pair of night goggles, and he carried a gun in his hand.

Fearing for Heather, Colin and Liv's safety, Tyler knew he couldn't let the man reach the house. As soon as the man broke the tree line and started across the wide expanse of lawn, Tyler rushed at him, driving his shoulder into the man's back, wrapping his arms around the intruder and letting momentum carry them both down to the snowy ground.

"Tyler!" Blake's voice blasted in Tyler's ear. "On my way."

"I can handle this," Tyler huffed out as he and the intruder scuffled for control of the gun, rolling across the wet, cold ground, trading punches and exerting energy in an effort to subdue each other. Moonlight glinted on the ring the guy wore on his middle finger seconds before he landed a hard right cross. Tyler absorbed the blow and, with a deep growl, threw an uppercut and a quick jab aimed for the bridge of the man's nose. He heard the crunch of cartilage breaking, giving Tyler the momentary advantage, which he capitalized on by knocking the gun from the man's hand. It went sliding away.

Lights flooded the yard.

The intruder let out a roar of pain and twisted away from the bright glow of the house's floodlights. Momentarily blinded, Tyler ripped off his night vision goggles with one hand while the other hand grasped the man's jacket. The man had also taken off his goggles and was working to dislodge Tyler's hold.

The door opened, and Heather ran out, hefting a large shotgun. Her red jacket made her a visible target.

Momentarily distracted by the sight, Tyler lost his grip on the assailant. He wiggled away, jumped to his feet and took off at a dead run for the rows of trees.

"He's making a break for it. Southwest of the house through the trees," Tyler said. "I'm securing the house."

"On it," Nathanial said.

"I'm holding my position watching the truck," Blake declared. "This could have just been a distraction."

Agreeing with his colleagues, Tyler moved with purpose to the house. Heather held the shotgun with the barrel pointed downward. The light from the wall fixtures slashed across her anxious face. "He's getting away."

"Nathanial's on his tail."

Her brow was furrowed with worry. "You're hurt."

Ignoring her statement and the pain from where the guy had sent his fist into Tyler's jaw, Tyler wrapped his hand around the long barrel of the shotgun. "Where on earth did you get this?"

"When I was searching for Seth's notebook, I came across my dad's stash of firearms in a safe at the back of the downstairs closet. I had no idea they were there. I wasn't expecting another attack on the house, but I got it out anyway." She shrugged. "I'm glad I didn't need it. And frankly I'm not sure it's loaded. But it looks intimidating."

"And dangerous." Taking the shotgun from her hands, he ushered her inside. "Though I admire your tenacity and bravery, don't ever do that again. Next time I tell you to stay out of sight, you need to stay out of sight."

Her mouth lifted on one side. "You didn't say stay out of sight. You said stay away from the windows."

"Really? You're going to quibble with me on this?"

She shook her head. "No quibbling here. Come into the laundry room and let me take care of the cut on your chin."

Exasperated yet glad she was safe, he followed her to the small laundry room. She dragged a stool out of the corner. "Sit."

He sat down. "It's not that bad."

With an arched eyebrow, she countered, "You haven't seen it."

Rising, he faced the mirror over the sink. A deep slash cut into the skin on his jawline and extended over his chin. "The guy had a ring on."

"Could you identify the ring or the man?" She dabbed his cut with an alcohol swab.

He gritted his teeth against the sting. "Not the ring. The guy's face seemed vaguely familiar, but I only caught a glimpse of him without his goggles on."

She used butterfly bandages to close the wound. "Familiar, huh? That doesn't bode well."

"No, it doesn't."

"What do you think he was after?" Heather met his gaze.

Her green-tinted eyes were round. She was so close. All he'd have to do was lean toward her a fraction of an inch, and their lips would touch. He held himself still by sheer force of will. "Not sure." His voice cracked.

That hadn't happened since he was a teen. But considering he felt like a love-starved teen with hormones racing through his blood, he shouldn't have been surprised. He strove to keep his tone even. "I can only guess that his intention was to see if you knew where Seth's journal was."

She licked her lips. He tracked the moment with his gaze.

"I hope your team catches him," she said, her voice breathless.

Was she struggling with the same attraction that had him in a stranglehold?

"Oh, my." Liv stood in the doorway.

Tyler jerked his gaze away from Heather at the exact moment that she broke contact, as well. Heat clawed up his throat and settled in his face.

Liv's gaze narrowed. "What happened? I heard noises."

Heather backed away from him. "Tyler stopped a trespasser."

"Are we safe?" Liv's expression showed panic.

Tyler stood. "Yes. Everyone is safe." He turned to Heather. "I'll call the local police and loop them in."

She gave him a faint smile. "Thank you."

He slipped past Liv and headed down the hall, thankful not to have succumbed to the temptation to kiss Heather. The last thing either of them needed was Liv witnessing an error in judgment. Especially after he'd assured Liv his intentions toward Heather were purely platonic.

But whether he liked it or not, his feelings for the

widow were far from platonic. And that made everything much more complicated.

And if there was one thing he didn't want, it was complications.

"Are you all right?"

Liv's worried expression had Heather blowing out a shaky breath. "Yes. Kind of. I mean, no."

She was scared, freaked out and way too aware of how close she'd just come to kissing Tyler. He'd saved her life twice and that of her family. She shuddered to think what would have happened had the man with the gun slipped past Tyler and broke into her house.

"It was a good thing Tyler was around," Liv said. "Though what was he doing outside, anyway?"

Heather shrugged. "I guess he couldn't sleep and decided to take a walk."

"Hmm. Well, it worked out for us, didn't it?"

Heather put away the first aid kit. "It did, indeed."

"So he's your business partner?" Liv's smirk grated on Heather's nerves.

"Yes," she affirmed in as neutral a tone as she could muster.

"How long have you two known each other?"

"A while." That was vague enough, wasn't it? The last thing she needed was for Liv to prod too deeply into Tyler's cover. Heather yawned. It started out as a fake, but it turned into a real one. "I'm done in."

A knowing look in Liv's gaze made Heather want to squirm. There was no way Liv could guess Tyler's true purpose on the farm. But she'd witnessed the sizzling attraction between Heather and Tyler when she'd walked into the laundry room, much to Heather's chagrin.

"Good night again," Liv said and strode out of the laundry room.

Once she was alone, Heather sat on the stool for a moment and lifted a prayer of thanks to God for protection and for Tyler and his team.

She heard voices coming from the living room. She hurried down the hall to find Nathanial and Blake had joined Tyler. All three men were dressed in dark clothes. They kept their voices low.

"Guy had an ATV stashed in the trees," Nathanial said. "He was prepared for a quick getaway. I tracked the ATV to the road and then lost him. I'll go back out there in the morning and see if I can distinguish his trail."

"Too bad he got away," Blake said. "I'd like to know what he was doing here and who he's working for."

"Wouldn't we all," Tyler commented, frustration evident in his tone.

"I found his gun," Blake said. "An MP9. Slick. I bagged it and will send it in for printing."

Heather had no idea what type of gun that was, but Tyler looked pleased.

"At least that's a start," Tyler said. "You two head on back to the truck, though I doubt we'll see any more action. I'll stand guard here, just in case."

Heather didn't like the "just in case" scenarios playing through her mind. Just in case the intruder tried to break in again. Just in case he brought buddies with him. Just in case Tyler and his team weren't successful a second time around.

When the two men vacated the house, leaving her and Tyler in the living room, she felt a strange sense of déjà vu. Had it really been only two nights ago he'd entered her life? It seemed like a lifetime.

Strange how easily she'd let him into the very fabric of her life. And she was afraid she was letting him into her heart, as well.

Time to retreat. Yet she couldn't make her feet move. Truth was she didn't want to leave the living room. She didn't want to leave Tyler's side. For that reason alone, she forced herself to say good-night and hurried upstairs.

She'd escaped his presence. But she was pretty sure she wouldn't escape her growing feelings for him quite so easily.

Tyler sat in the darkened living room, his weapon at the ready on his knee. He hated that he'd allowed himself to be distracted by Heather and let the man with the gun escape. It had been a rookie move.

And a testament to how deeply he'd gotten in over his head with the lovely Heather. He'd let her get under his skin, into his mind and definitely into his heart.

He needed this assignment to end so he could move on to a safe one. Safer for his heart, anyway.

There was no way he could let himself believe he had a future with Heather and her adorable son. He wasn't cut out to be a dad, and he wasn't the settle-in-one-place kind of guy. He didn't know how to do domestic. He knew undercover work. He knew taking down bad guys. But being someone's husband, some kid's father? No way.

Yet he couldn't deny that being with Heather and Colin filled him with cravings for a life he'd never known. Would probably never know. He knew better than to say never, but he couldn't envision any other life than the one he led now where he moved from one assignment to another all over the continent. It worked for him. Even if at times it was lonely.

The hours ticked by as the sun slowly made its rise on the eastern horizon. Just as dawn broke, there was a rattle at the front doorknob. Tyler bolted for the door. He unlocked it, grasped the handle and swung the door open in one swift movement. He caught the would-be intruder unaware. A large-framed man tumbled into Tyler, knocking him back several steps. The stench of alcohol hit Tyler in the face like a brick wall. "Whew!"

The intruder wasn't the man Tyler had grappled with the night before. This man was built like a tank with dark hair and a weather-beaten complexion as if he spent his days in the sun without UV protection. Tyler recognized him as one of the men who worked with the trees.

He pushed at Tyler, squirming to get free and yelled, "Mrs. Randall!"

"Whoa! Dude." Tyler wrenched the guy's beefy arm behind his back, whirled him around and drove him face-first into the couch.

"No, you don't understand." The man's slurred

words were muffled by the couch cushion. "Mrs. Randall is in trouble. I need to warn her."

Feet pounded down the stairs. Heather skidded to a halt. She wore the same sweats outfit she'd worn the other day. Her hair was messy from sleep, and surprise and panic warred in her eyes. "Ernesto?"

"What's going on?" Liv's sleepy voice cut through the air. She walked out wearing a pink silky robe over a long matching gown and fuzzy pink slippers.

Tyler yanked Ernesto upright. "What do you need to warn Heather about?"

He wobbled on his feet. His gaze darted around until it latched onto Heather. "There are bad people here. You can't trust anyone."

Chapter Ten

Heather's heart jumped into her throat. Morning sunlight flooded through the window and open door along with a chill from the cold air temperature outside. Tyler had Ernesto's hands jerked tight behind his back. She reached out a hand to Ernesto. "What do you mean bad people? Who can't I trust?"

Liv made a derisive noise. "He's drunk or high." She marched closer to stare the man in the eye. "He's just trying to make trouble. Or scare you." She shook a finger at the man. "Why would you do this?"

Ernesto's face paled. He whipped his gaze to Heather. "You must call the police."

"You bet we will." Liv reached inside the pocket of her silk wrap for her phone. Within seconds she had the sheriff's department on the line. "This is Liv Dorsett. I'm at the Larson tree farm. We've captured an intruder. You need to come take this crazy man away."

"I'll take Ernesto outside." Tyler gave Heather a look that she interpreted to mean he'd question Ernesto without an audience. He propelled the other man out the front door.

Heather was torn between wanting to hear what Ernesto had to say and needing to keep Liv from following Tyler and finding out that Tyler was more than he claimed.

As Liv headed for the door, Heather made her decision and snagged Liv's hand. "I'm so glad you're here. This is such a nightmare."

Liv frowned at the closed front door, and something dark crossed her face. Heather chalked it up to the fright and anger about the invasion. She felt the same sense of fear and vulnerability. But not because of Ernesto. He couldn't possibly be a part of the drug ring. She'd known him and his family her whole life.

"It's a good thing your boyfriend was here to intercept that lunatic," Liv said. "Who knows what he might have done?"

Heather froze. Remembering the pulse of attraction last night as she'd tended to Tyler's chin, Heather's face flamed. She should have known Liv wouldn't believe her when she insisted she and Tyler weren't romantically involved. "Tyler is not my boyfriend, but, yes, it was good that he was here." Confusion swirled through her. Had Ernesto been the one to call her the other night, advising her to leave the farm? "Ernesto and his brother, Sal, have been with the farm for longer than I can remember. He was trying to warn me, not threaten me."

"Right. You believed him?" Liv flicked her blond hair. "That whole bit about bad people and not trusting anyone was probably his way of weaseling out of a breaking and entering charge."

At one time, Heather might have agreed, but with all that had happened, she knew the man hadn't been fabricating a plausible excuse. He knew something. Something about the drugs and Seth's death. Heather had confidence that Tyler would find out exactly what. In the meantime, Heather's job was to keep Liv and Colin in the dark about the danger. She didn't want to upset either one of them. Liv's grief was still so raw, and Colin was too young to be burdened with the truth.

Heather glanced at the wall clock. It was a quarter after eight in the morning. "The sheriff will be here soon," Heather pointed out, gesturing to Liv's silky pink robe over the matching nightgown. She hoped Liv would get the hint that she needed to change out of her pajamas. Heather had pulled on sweats when she'd heard the commotion, and though she wasn't dressed fashionably, she was presentable. But she did need to do something with her hair and brush her teeth.

Liv's eyes widened, and she let out a little yelp of dismay. "I better change." She hurried out of the living room and down the hall, disappearing into Seth's room.

Heather took the opportunity to duck out the front door. Ernesto sat on the stairs, his head in his hands. Tyler, Blake and Nathanial conversed a few feet away. Taking advantage of the moment, Heather sat down beside Ernesto.

"Ernesto, who are the bad people?"

His head snapped up. His dark eyes grew round.

"Oh, Mrs. Randall, I'm so sorry. I don't know what I was thinking to come here like this. I meant no harm."

She smiled at him, willing him to stop dodging her question. "I'm sure you didn't. But what did you mean?"

"No, no. I am drunk." He smiled crookedly. "I need to go to jail."

"Are you the one who called me the other night telling me to leave the farm?"

He shook his head. The pleading expression in his gaze tugged at her. "Not me, but that's good advice. You should leave before something bad happens."

"What do you know about Seth's death?" she pressed in frustration.

The sound of a siren sent birds flying from the perfectly conical sheared Douglas fir trees closest to the snow-covered lawn.

Ernesto lurched to his feet and practically ran to the sheriff before the man had even brought his silver SUV to a halt. Tyler strode over to the vehicle as the sheriff got out. The three men conversed, and then the sheriff opened the back door for Ernesto to climb inside the vehicle. Heather watched the sheriff and Ernesto drive away with annoyance pounding at her temples. She hoped Tyler had been able to extract some information from Ernesto. She'd failed miserably convincing him to talk.

She approached Tyler where he stood with Blake and Nathanial. When she stopped beside Tyler, the other two men strode away.

"Well, what did Ernesto tell you?"

Tyler shook his head. "Nothing other than he wanted to go to jail. He said he'd be safe there."

A fissure of fear bubbled to the surface. "That doesn't sound good. He wouldn't answer my questions. This is all so…so… Argh."

She couldn't find words to express how upsetting and irritating and frightening this situation was for her. She'd come to the farm hoping, needing, a peaceful place to raise her son. There was nothing peaceful about having her brother murdered, drugs planted inside her Christmas trees, threats and warnings, people sneaking around at night. It was as if she'd stepped into a horror flick. At least there weren't psychos running around with chain saws. Though, she supposed that was possible because there were several chain saws on the farm. She shivered at the thought.

Cupping her elbow, Tyler urged her back to the house. "No, it doesn't sound good. Nothing about this sounds good."

Liv came out of the house as they reached the top step. She was dressed in dark skinny jeans tucked into her tall black boots and her pink coat was buttoned up. She slung her purse over her shoulder and held her phone in her right hand. Clearly she planned to leave.

"Where are you going?" Heather paused on the stairs with Tyler beside her. She didn't recall Liv saying she had somewhere to be on Thanksgiving.

Wrinkling her nose, Liv said, "I completely forgot I'd promised one of my clients I'd do her hair in an updo for her family Thanksgiving dinner." Liv hurried down the steps. "I'll stop by the grocery store on the way back and pick up a few things we're missing for our feast."

The thought of Liv's extravagant tastes sent a shudder through Heather. "There's something we need to talk about," Heather blurted. She didn't want to burden Liv with the sad state of the farm's finances, but she also didn't want Liv spending money when she may need to be saving it for herself.

Liv halted and spun around, sending her loose blond hair swirling. Cocking her head, she blinked at Heather. "Can it wait?"

Heather chewed the inside of her lip. Guilt ate at her for not being able to spit out what she needed to say.

"You can do this." Tyler leaned in close and whispered in her ear. "She's an adult. She can handle it."

Freaked out by the fact that he could tell what she was thinking, she slanted him a glance. He arched an eyebrow. *Okay.* Shaking off his uncanny ability to read her mind, Heather walked back down the stairs and gathered Liv's free hand in hers. "I don't want you spending your money on the farm."

A crease appeared between Liv's eyebrows. She opened her mouth to undoubtedly protest, but Heather rushed on to say, "Seth wasn't managing the farm's money well. He used the farm's income that should have been for paying bills to buy personal items."

At least Seth had been responsible enough to make payroll. Heather hadn't taken a salary from the farm, since she had no part in running the business. She'd assumed it would be her retirement nest egg.

Liv convulsed as if Heather had sent a bolt of electricity through her. "What are you saying?"

Though Heather had to get the issue out into the open, she still cringed as she explained. "Seth used funds that weren't his to buy your car. And the down payment on the town house…"

For a moment Heather feared Liv would either pass out or get sick. Her eyes went wide, her jaw dropped open.

Liv lifted their joined hands. Her diamond ring glinted in the sunlight. "This, too?"

With everything in her, Heather wanted to say no and let Liv keep the memento of Seth's love, but she couldn't lie to her. "I'm afraid so."

Liv pulled free of Heather's hand and slipped the ring off her finger. She handed the gold-and-diamond engagement ring to Heather. Her hand shook; her face paled. "Here. I can't do anything about the car or the town house right now, but next week…"

Tears burned the backs of Heather's eyes. She hated hurting Liv like this. But this was Seth's fault. A simmering anger boiled inside. "That will be soon enough." She held the ring out. "If you want to wear this until next week, you can."

Liv's sad smile wobbled. "No. I would have to take it off eventually. Might as well be today." With a small cry of distress, she hurried to where she'd parked her new luxury sedan and drove away.

Heather clutched the ring in her hand and pressed

her fist against her heart. "Oh, Seth. You hurt so many people."

Sensing Tyler behind her, she didn't resist when he put his arms around her and pulled her close. She needed his strength at the moment. Her throat worked, but she couldn't thank him.

Slowly, he turned her to face him. With his hands on her shoulders, he dipped his head to meet her gaze. "You did the right thing by telling her."

"I know." She sighed. "But it doesn't make it hurt any less."

He rubbed her arms. "We have a Thanksgiving feast to get ready."

She appreciated his attempt to distract her. "Yes. We do." She stepped back and regained her composure. "I'm going to wake Colin and get him ready." She slipped the ring in her pocket. "Then we'll have to grab tables and chairs out of the barn's attic."

A loud explosion rent the air. The earth shook.

Startled, Heather jumped and collided with Tyler. He held her tightly against him. She grabbed his arm as an anchor as her mind tried to make sense of what was happening. A black plume of smoke billowed from behind the building that housed the farm's machinery.

Stricken, she met Tyler's gaze. "Oh, no! The propane tank!"

Flames shot toward the sky. Even though the wave of heat made sweat break out on her brow, the dawning horror sweeping through her froze her blood. "There are gas tanks inside the building. If the fire reaches it—"

She broke free of Tyler's arms and ran toward the fire.

Tyler caught her about the waist and hauled her off her feet. "No." He swung around to face the house and carried her to the porch.

Beating at his arms, she cried, "We have to move the equipment out."

"Someone will." He set her down but kept a firm hand on her arm. "But not you."

His cell phone buzzed. He yanked it from his pants pocket. "Yeah?… I see it. I'll call nine-one-one. Heather says there are gas tanks inside the building… Roger that." He clicked off, then dialed the emergency number and quickly explained the situation. When he hung up, he turned his grim gaze on Heather. "Blake and Nathanial will do what they can to keep the fire contained until the fire department arrives."

"This wasn't an accident, was it?"

"I seriously doubt it."

Her hands fisted. "We should help them."

"It's too dangerous. I promised you I wouldn't let anything happen to you or Colin, and I mean to keep that promise."

She shook her head. "But you can't make that kind of promise." Her gaze went to the rising black smoke. "Bad things happen despite how much we pray and hope they won't." Tears blurred her vision. "Ken promised he'd come home, but he couldn't have predicted his helicopter would crash." She turned her gaze to Tyler. "Any more than you can guarantee whoever is trying to hurt the farm, hurt me, won't succeed. Life is random. Unpredictable. And scary."

Taking her in his arms, he held her close. His heart beat a frantic tune in her ear. "You're right. I can't anticipate every scenario, control every moment, but I can promise I will do everything humanly possible to keep you and Colin safe. The rest I have to trust to God."

His words reverberated through her. Trusting God. She did. But yet there was a small part of her that held back. Anger reared up, demanding to be acknowledged. "I'm so mad. Mad at Seth. Mad at the person doing this. Mad at God."

But not Tyler. She'd let go of her initial anger at him for using Seth because ultimately the responsibility of all this lay on Seth. And he'd paid a steep price for his actions.

Tyler pulled back to look into her face. "It's okay to be mad, but your feelings shouldn't dictate your trust of God. God is the same yesterday, today and tomorrow. His love and faithfulness never changes."

She really wanted to believe him. But at the moment it felt as though God were far away.

Behind her, the front door opened and Colin raced out to latch onto her leg. "Mommy? What's happening?"

She disentangled herself from Tyler and bent to pick up Colin. "Something caught on fire."

As her employees raced to help, she did a mental head count to make sure everyone was accounted for. Thankfully everyone was.

It seemed like an eternity before the distinct sound of a fire engine approaching drew her attention. "Hurry, hurry," she muttered.

Colin pointed toward the drive. "Look, a fire truck."

Hugging her son close, Heather was grateful Colin was more interested in the truck than the fire.

The three of them watched the six firemen disappear behind the building to extinguish the flames. Colin was awed by the whole process. Heather had to admit she was pretty wowed, as well. She had no idea they used foam to put out this kind of gas fire. She'd never seen firefighters in action in real life. While some of the firemen worked at extinguishing the propane fire, others hosed down the outside wall of the machinery building with water to keep the building cool so there'd be no secondary fires. When the fire was finally out, Heather, Tyler and Colin thanked the firemen. The captain even let Colin climb inside the truck and sit behind the wheel.

Blake and Nathanial joined Tyler and Heather. Both men were covered with soot, their faces streaked with black ashes.

"The fire investigator will be here later to take a look at the scene," the captain told them. His curious gaze landed on Blake and Nathanial. "You two did a good job of isolating the flames."

The two men looked almost embarrassed. Heather hid a grin. She was thankful she could smile now that the catastrophe had been averted. Though the air still reeked of the residual propane that had burned and smoke created a haze that she hoped would dissipate by tomorrow when they opened for business. Fortunately, the Christmas Village was on the far side of the property and was accessed by a different entrance.

"Captain, would you and your men like to stay for Thanksgiving dinner?"

"That's kind of you to offer, Mrs. Randall, but we're set with our own feast waiting back at the station house," he replied, then plopped his hat on his head. "Happy Thanksgiving." He held up a finger and made a circular motion. "Let's round up and hit the road."

The six firefighters climbed aboard the truck and waved as the red engine backed out of the driveway and then drove away, back to Bonners Ferry.

As soon as the truck was out of sight, Heather looked at Blake and Nathanial. "Thank you both for… everything."

"Just doing our job," Blake stated with a cryptic look at Tyler.

Nathanial flashed a grin. "We weren't going to let a fire ruin our feast."

"Speaking of which," Heather said. "I can take it from here. You need to clean up and meet back here at two. We'll eat at three."

Blake gave a single nod before turning on his work boot heel and striding away.

Nathanial shook his head at his coworker's retreating back. "He's not one for too many words." He smiled again at Heather. "We'll be back to help set up." He saluted Tyler, then jogged away to catch up to Blake.

Heather caught Tyler's gaze. "I don't know what I

would have done if you and your team hadn't shown up when you did."

For that she would thank God every day. Even when Tyler left, she'd know she'd been changed by his presence. For the better.

Tyler was so proud of the way Heather managed to keep a positive attitude as she tirelessly served the twelve men in her employ who didn't have family in the area to go to for the holiday meal. Ernesto wasn't among them. Nor did he recognize the face of the man he'd wrestled with last night. The one wearing the ring Tyler's face had become well acquainted with.

They'd set up another long table connecting end to end with the farmhouse's dining room table. The turkey was moist and delicious, the side dishes mouthwatering and the pumpkin pie sweet. After the excitement of the fire, which Liv seemed convinced was a terrible accident, everyone, including Blake, Nathanial and Liv, seemed to be having a good time. Conversations and banter filled the house. Colin couldn't sit still. He bounced from person to person, retelling how the firefighters had put out the flames and declaring he wanted to be a firefighter when he grew up.

Sitting back, watching the festivities, Tyler knew a contentment he'd never experienced before. To be a part of a family-type gathering was something new for him. Oh, his grandparents had tried to make the few holidays he'd been able to spend with them homey, but it hadn't been like this, noisy and festive and full of cheer. His grandparents had been somber people with quiet voices, but they had been filled with love for each other. And love for Tyler.

As an adult he always volunteered for an assignment on Thanksgiving and Christmas. Better to let those with families have the time off. He'd never minded missing out on something he never had to begin with. But he was glad that today he hadn't had to miss out. This could be his one and only opportunity to experience a real family-style Thanksgiving feast with people he would like to call friends.

That was, if he weren't so aware that besides his team members, Heather, Liv and Colin, any one of the others could be involved in murder and part of a drug ring. Kind of put a damper on things. But for the moment, Heather and Colin were safe and clearly enjoying themselves. He'd take it. As a memory to cherish.

Colin climbed onto Tyler's lap. "Mr. Tyler, what are you thankful for?"

Tyler tweaked the boy's nose. "I'm thankful for Christmas trees."

A big grin spread over Colin's face. "Me, too!" He rubbed his hands together. "I can't wait for Christmas."

"Hear, hear," someone said.

Tyler met Heather's gaze over the top of Colin's head. The gentle affection in her eyes and the small pleased smile playing at the corner of her mouth hit him like a ton of bricks. Momentarily stunned, he realized the war within himself to keep his defenses from crumbling was in full battle mode. Uneasy concern slipped into his psyche like a sliver festering beneath a fingernail. Yet he found he didn't want to fight it. He wanted to embrace this new and wonderful occurrence.

Blake scooted his chair away from the table and cleared his throat. Tyler's focus snapped to him. Blake jerked his head toward the door before he left the table and exited the room.

Nathanial scooped up a roll and popped it into his mouth before following Blake.

Tyler sighed, reining in the wayward emotions that would only lead down a path he really had no business traveling. The fun and games were over. Time for Blake to leave with the truck full of trees stashed with cocaine.

Setting Colin back on the floor, Tyler ruffled the boy's hair. "Gotta see Blake off."

Heather came over and took Colin's hand. "Come on, sweetie. Time to start cleaning up."

At her cue, the men rose, clearing their plates and the serving dishes from the tables.

"Colin, let's wash the dishes together," Liv called from the doorway to the kitchen.

Heather let of his hand. Colin ran to help Liv.

"He's a great kid," Tyler told her as they moved to the entryway. "You've done such a good job with him."

She beamed. "He is great." Her smile dimmed, and she lowered her voice. "So it begins?"

He knew she referred to the sting operation that the IBETs were orchestrating on the tree farm in Canada that would be receiving the illegal drugs. That was if the trees cleared customs. Seeing how well they'd hidden the drugs and concealed the scent, Tyler didn't doubt the truck would be waved through this time. But after that, never again. The IBETs director would make sure every border crossing was aware of the sneaky way the drugs were being smuggled.

Rob hobbled over to join them. "It's fortuitous of your friend to have family up north. I appreciate him volunteering to drive the truck across the border."

Wary of Rob's intentions, Tyler shrugged. "Yes, it is."

"Is it his parents that live near Calgary?"

Remembering the cover story they'd devised, Tyler shook his head. "No. Cousins."

Rob raised his eyebrows. "Ah, right."

"Rob, would you mind going over tomorrow's schedule with me one more time?" Heather asked, drawing the older man's attention away from Tyler.

Bless her. Tyler would have to thank her later for giving him the perfect opportunity to slip out the door.

Blake and Nathanial were waiting at the edge of the driveway.

"Everything is in place," Blake said. "Border Patrol agent Jeff Steele is meeting me at the Eastport–Kingsgate crossing."

"Good." Tyler liked Steele. He was a stand-up guy. They'd worked together on a few assignments. Though Tyler hadn't been on the assignment where Steele had met his wife, Dr. Tessa Cleary, Tyler had met the red-headed fish biologist at their wedding. He'd liked her. And Tyler had to admit he'd been slightly envious.

The thought of having someone to spend the rest of his life with tied Tyler up in knots. An image of

Heather danced through his mind, and his mouth went dry. The battle he'd been fighting seemed to lean toward disaster. He was in real jeopardy of falling hard for this woman.

He gave himself a mental shake to dislodge the image. Not meant for him. What did he have to offer Heather and Colin? Nothing. With determination, he told himself to stop longing for what would never be and put his mind on the job that needed to be finished.

Chapter Eleven

After the Thanksgiving dishes were cleaned and put away, and the guests had dispersed, Heather took a moment to sit down on the couch with Colin tucked beside her in the same position she'd seen Tyler with Colin earlier.

Seeing them together had brought an ache of loss for all that Ken had missed and for Colin not knowing his father. And for what couldn't be with Tyler.

He'd made it clear he wanted no part of being a family. He'd made the statement he wasn't father material, but he was so wrong. He related well to Colin, playing with and teasing her son. Encouraging him on his trike and being content to sit with Colin watching a kids' show. Tyler would be an excellent father.

She wished she could tell him that, but she wouldn't. She wouldn't make his eventual leaving any more difficult by pointing out that he wasn't being honest with himself. That denying his own abilities and worth was keeping him from potentially finding the beauty of a family. Of love.

Not that she'd fallen for him.

Okay, maybe a bit, if she was honest with herself. But she couldn't let affection for him make her vulnerable to hurt, not if she hoped to survive his leaving.

Liv came into the room carrying a mug. "I made you a cup of tea."

"Thank you." Heather accepted the cup and wrapped her hands around it, letting the heat warm her. The calming scent of chamomile rose with the steam. She took a sip, warm but not too hot to drink. It felt good going down, but after a bit she realized the tea didn't agree with her tummy.

She set the half-empty mug on the coffee table. She was obviously too upset to drink anything. She'd barely eaten as it was, and the little she did manage to get down hadn't wanted to stay down. All the stress lately had really done a number on her digestion.

A few minutes later, Liv returned to the living room and sat on the recliner. She had a small leather book in her hands.

Heather's heart bumped against her ribs. Was that Seth's journal? "Liv, what do you have there?"

Liv held it up with a sad smile. "I found this in one of the boxes Seth had moved into the town house's garage."

Heather's mouth went dry. She placed a hand over her roiling stomach. "Have you read it?"

Liv shook her head. "Just the first page." Tears gathered in her eyes. "I couldn't bring myself to read any more."

Needing to get the book to Tyler, Heather extracted herself from Colin and rose. For a moment the room tilted. She braced her feet apart, chiding herself for getting up too quickly.

Colin jumped to his feet. "Mommy, can I have a snack?"

"Of course."

Colin raced into the kitchen.

As Heather made her way to Liv's side, she struggled to keep the dizziness from overcoming her. She didn't have a cold, so she wasn't sure why her equilibrium was off. "May I see the book?"

Liv handed the notebook over. "If you discover why he—" she lowered her voice to a whisper "—started using again, you'll let me know?"

Grateful for her consideration of Colin, Heather touched Liv's shoulder. "Of course."

Liv's mouth twisted. "I hope it wasn't because of me."

Seeing the hurt on Liv's face, Heather crouched down and took her hand. "Liv, you aren't to blame. Seth loved you. His death—" She clamped her lips together to keep from spilling out the truth.

Once Tyler arrested the person responsible for Seth's death, then Heather would reveal the whole story to Liv. But until then it would be wiser, safer, to keep Liv in the dark. "Please, don't think that you had anything to do with his death."

"I keep wondering if I wasn't enough for him." She

darted a glance at Colin as he skipped back into the living room with a bowl of animal crackers. Liv's face softened with love, but her eyes were sad as she looked back at Heather. "I was so looking forward to being a part of your family."

"You'll always be a part of our lives," Heather assured her and meant it. Spending this time with Liv had given Heather a chance to get to know her better. Heather liked how generous and caring Liv was to both her and Colin. Which only made the loss of Liv becoming Heather's sister-in-law more distressing.

Liv squeezed her hand. "Thank you for saying so." She released Heather's hand and stood. "I'm going to go lie down. It's been an emotional day."

Heather understood the feeling. She'd like nothing more than to crawl beneath her covers and forget the past few weeks. But hiding from reality wasn't her style. With the notebook in hand, she went to the kitchen and called Tyler.

He answered on the first ring.

"Are you okay?" he asked.

She leaned on the counter. For some reason her legs were wobbly. Her head had stopped spinning though. That was good. "Yes. Liv found a small journal in Seth's things at the town house."

"I'll be right over," he said and hung up.

Heather waited for him at the back door. When she heard his boots on the stairs, she opened the door. "Blake and the truck are gone?"

"Yes. I was headed over here when you called."

His grim expression caused a riot of anxiety inside her. "What's wrong?"

"The other truck is missing."

"How can that be?" She knew Tyler had held on to the keys for both trucks and replaced the padlock on the refrigerated boxes.

"Someone else had a set of keys."

She groaned. "Seth's missing keys."

He nodded. "The new padlock had been cut off by bolt cutters."

Her stomach sank. "That's weird. Why would someone take an empty truck?"

"No clue. Though I plan to question Rob and Don. See if either of them have an explanation for the missing truck. Last I'd heard the trip east had been canceled."

She wanted to come to her employees' defense, but she just couldn't be sure of their innocence. Ernesto's warning not to trust anyone rang through her mind.

"But the good news is we'd set up a surveillance camera," Tyler informed her. "I've sent the picture of the guy who stole the truck to my boss. He'll run it and see if we can get an ID on him. Thankfully he's not one of your employees. He doesn't match any of the IDs we have already on file. And all law enforcement agencies will be looking for the truck." He gestured to the book in her hands. "That's the notebook?"

She handed it to him. "I haven't looked at it. I wanted to wait for you."

"Let's sit, and we can read it together," he said.

After checking that Colin was occupied with one of

his favorite animated movies, Heather and Tyler sat at the dining table. Tyler cracked the book open.

Heather read the date of the first entry with surprise. "He started this when he was in high school."

They flipped through the pages. As Heather read the words written in her brother's neat and precise handwriting, sadness descended on her like a heavy cloak. The picture unfolding on the pages chronicled Seth's downward spiral into drugs. He'd started using to fit in with a certain crowd of kids. Kids he felt accepted him for who he was, which didn't make sense to Heather. If he'd felt the need to adopt a drug habit to fit in, then those kids hadn't truly accepted him. Acceptance came with no conditions. She wished she'd been around to explain that to him.

The deeper they went in the book, the sadder and angrier Heather became. Seth talked about the drugs and his dependence on them. He talked of the rehab centers their parents had dragged him to. If only he'd been able to get clean and stay clean. It wasn't until after their parents' fatal car accident that he'd been able to conquer the addiction.

He talked of meeting Liv in his last rehab center. Stunned, Heather met Tyler's gaze. "I didn't know that she had an addiction."

Tyler's eyes were soft with compassion. "Seth writes that she successfully kicked her habit. He clearly admired and respected her as well as loved her."

Grief ravaged Heather's heart. "Liv needs to read this. She thinks maybe he started using again because of her." Heather lowered her voice. "It was all I could do not to tell her the truth."

Tyler covered her hand with his. "You'll be able to soon."

Taking comfort from his touch, she continued to read. The words on the pages didn't make sense. Seth wrote that he felt guilty for their parents' death. Why? Farther down the page she had her answer. She read the entry with dawning horror.

Seth had been driving the car. He'd caused the accident that had taken her parents' lives. "No. This can't be true."

"You didn't know?"

Tyler's question pierced her to the quick. "No. Seth never said a word. I never dug into the accident. I took what I was told at face value. Dad lost control of the car and hit a tree, killing them both."

"There's nothing about it in the police report," Tyler admitted softly.

Her vision was blurry with tears. "You read the police report?"

"As part of my investigation. The report cited your dad as the driver. Seth had pulled your parents out of the car before emergency vehicles could arrive."

"So Seth lied to the police, too." She pinched the bridge of her nose. When would this madness end?

"If what he writes here is true, then, yes, he did."

"How could this happen?" She spread her hands out. "What made Seth into this person?" Blame clawed at her throat. "I let him down. I let my parents down. If I'd been a better sister—"

"No."

The sharpness in Tyler's tone startled her.

"You are not at fault for your brother's choices. He was an adult, capable of knowing right from wrong. As much as you'd like to believe you're in control, you're not. Only God has that kind of power, but He gives each of us free will to decide our own fates."

Tyler touched her cheek, his fingers so gentle and warm. Tears filled her eyes. He was right, of course. Berating herself for something she had no control over was a waste of time and energy. She wasn't a martyr. Releasing the burden of regret that she hadn't been there to help her brother and her parents wouldn't come easily, but acknowledging the need to was a start.

She forced back her tears. Her gaze dropped to the book. She didn't want to read any more about Seth and his lies. She wanted to know about the drugs. Nothing mattered except making the farm safe for Colin. For herself.

Flipping through the pages, she skimmed the words for anything that would tell them who on the farm was responsible for the drug trafficking. But there was nothing. The journal ended without providing any clues.

"Ugh!" She slammed the book shut. "This is useless."

Tyler put his hand on her shoulder. "Heather, we'll find the right notebook. It has to be here on the farm somewhere."

"But where?"

"We haven't completed our search of the village."

"True." There was still a chance they would find the incriminating evidence Tyler would need to bring down the drug smugglers and put an end to her brother's deceit. And then Tyler would no longer have a reason to stay.

There was nothing she could do about the fact that Tyler was leaving.

The next morning, Tyler stood at Heather's back door. She'd invited him for breakfast with her, Colin and Liv before heading over to the Christmas Village to open for the public. As an added precaution, Tyler had arranged for a couple of sheriff's deputies to have a presence at the village today. Tyler and the guys could have eyes on every person and every nook and cranny, so the added security for Heather and Colin was more than welcome. Last night, after the disappointment of realizing that the notebook Liv had found wasn't the one they needed, he and Heather had made a plan to spend the day in the village and covertly search for Seth's missing journal.

He could only imagine how shocking it had been for Heather to learn the truth that Seth had been the one driving when their parents were killed. It had taken all Tyler's self-control not to pull her into his arms.

He wanted to soothe her hurt, protect her from the painful reality that her brother hadn't been the man she'd thought he was. Instead of an embrace, he'd settled for touching her shoulder.

Even that simple, innocent touch created sparks and

fueled his yearning to be the one to comfort her. As more than an assignment. As more than a friend.

What was wrong with him?

He knew better than to become emotionally involved. *Right.* He mentally snorted. His head may know, but his heart wasn't cooperating. Time to backpedal and gain some much-needed distance. Both physically and emotionally.

He turned to go, and the door opened.

"Mr. Tyler!" Colin ran full speed at him.

Tyler caught the child and lifted him high in the air. Colin's laugh settled in Tyler's chest. Tyler realized with a heavy sigh he would miss the boy. Setting Colin back on his feet, Tyler found Heather watching him with a look that made emotion clog his throat. There was tenderness in her gaze but also resignation, as if she, too, were aware how brief this time together would be.

Despite his mental lashing for letting his emotions off leash, it made him sad to think of the day when he'd no longer be at the farm. But he wanted that day to come because it would mean Heather and Colin were no longer in danger. There was no room for sentiment here. Only action.

"Eggs?" Liv called from where she stood at the stove.

Though he had no appetite—his stomach was tied up in knots from his conflicting thoughts—he nodded. It would be out of character and draw unwanted attention if he refused. He only wished he could hide the truth from himself as easily. "Please. Thank you."

Colin climbed off a chair at the table and dragged the chair next to him closer. "Sit here, Mr. Tyler."

Unable to refuse the kid, Tyler sat down. Heather brought over a mug of coffee for him. "Thank you."

She smiled, though her eyes didn't sparkle. He missed seeing the sparkle.

"You're welcome," Heather managed to say without her voice trembling with suppressed emotions. "As soon as we're done with breakfast, we need to hurry to the village. The gate opens at nine."

That gave them a little under an hour to eat and hoof it across the property.

After they ate and cleaned up the breakfast dishes, Liv announced she was going into town. "I have clients," she explained before heading out the door.

Once Heather had Colin dressed and ready to go, they made the trek to the Christmas Village, which was abuzz with activity. She was grateful to see two of Boundary County's sheriff deputies walking around, keeping an eye on things. Tyler had mentioned he'd asked for the help. She hoped their day was quiet and boring.

She waved to Deputy Daniel Potter. They'd gone to high school together. He nodded a greeting.

The Thanksgiving snowstorm had left a nice layer of white powder on the rooftops, but the sidewalks had been cleared. The graveled lot in the middle of the village showed faint tracks of the large gold-gilded horse-drawn sleigh that waited near the bakery. A man dressed in a Santa suit stood in front of a building labeled Santa's House and waved at them.

"Santa!" Colin cried and ran for the man.

"That's Don," Heather explained.

"Now's a good time to ask about the missing truck."

Heather shielded her eyes from the morning sun as they strode over to where the bearded man in the red suit had bent down to hand Colin a candy cane.

When Don straightened, Heather put her hand on her son's shoulder. Noticing Deputy Potter, she waved him over and introduced him to Tyler, Don and Colin. "Daniel and I were in the same grade growing up. He married one of my high school friends."

Daniel grinned at her. "Betsy says hi. She and the kids are planning to come out on Sunday after church."

"Wonderful." Sensing Tyler's impatience to talk to Don, Heather said, "Colin, do you want to see if Mrs. Theid needs more help?"

"Yes!"

Daniel stepped forward. "Would you like me to take him to the bakery?"

Grateful for the offer, she said, "That would be fabulous. Thank you."

"Sure thing." Daniel directed his attention to Colin. "Lead the way, young man."

"Thanks, Santa, for the candy cane." Colin raced away, and Daniel hurried after him.

Heather appreciated that Colin had his own deputy sheriff watching over him.

As soon as Colin was out of earshot, Tyler faced Don. "One of the refrigerated trucks went missing last night. What do you know about that?"

Behind his white bead, Don frowned. "It's not missing. The truck headed east to bring back a load of imported trees from Canada's northeast region." He turned his gaze to Heather. "Didn't Seth tell you this?"

Heather frowned. "I knew the truck was headed east, but since trees were never loaded into it, I assumed that meant it wasn't going to be used. Seth never mentioned anything about importing trees." Of course there seemed to be a great number of things her brother had neglected to share with her. So why was she surprised? "When did this start?"

"We tried it last year as an experiment," Don answered. "And it went so well that Seth had arranged for another load this year."

"Why would you import trees when you grow trees?" Tyler asked. The whole thing sounded suspicious.

"Because we don't grow balsam fir, which is pretty popular, as it turns out. I think it's the novelty of having something different." Don shrugged. "The balsams grow in the northeastern part of the United States and Canada. Seth found a grower willing to bring the trees halfway. The trees in the shipment coming in are already spoken for. When the truck rolls back in on Saturday, there will be a line of folks coming from as far away as California waiting to pick up their tree."

That definitely set Tyler's senses on alert. He'd make sure to get a look at the trees that came back. "Can you get me the contact info for the supplier of these balsam trees?"

"Sure. I won't have time until noon when I take my lunch." Don's gaze moved past them to the front gate.

"Oops," he said. "I better get to my post. It looks like the gate's opening."

"Thank you, Don," Heather said. When he'd gone inside, she turned to Tyler. "I need to check on Colin and then the front to make sure everything is running smoothly." She shook her head with self-mockery. "I shouldn't worry. Everyone here knows what they're doing."

"It's okay to be concerned, considering what's happened this week." Tyler didn't blame Heather for expecting the worst. One of these people could potentially be Seth's killer. And was definitely involved with the illegal drugs stuffed inside the Christmas trees headed to Calgary.

At the bakery, they found Colin wearing a small apron and kneading pastry dough. Mrs. Theid was in the process of putting out a batch of warm scones and cinnamon rolls in the display case. Deputy Potter had taken up a position near the door where he could keep an eye on Colin and on the activities outside.

Heather put her hand to the mouth. Her face had gone white.

Concerned, he touched her elbow. "Are you okay?"

"I need fresh air." She hurried outside.

Tyler followed her. She gulped air as if she were oxygen deprived.

"What's going on?"

"The smell of the grease was too much for me," she explained.

The only aroma he'd smelled was the cinnamon rolls.

They walked to the front gate where Rob oversaw the admittance box. A line had formed of people eager to come and see the Christmas Village. Heather asked if the attendants needed anything. They assured her they had everything under control.

"Come on," she said to Tyler. "Let's pretend for a few moments we're tourists."

He smiled, glad to see the color back in her pretty face. "Okay. Take me on a tour of the village."

She led him through the gift shop, where they sold handcrafted items from local artisans as well as an assortment of different types of ornaments. Christmas carols played from speakers mounted in the corner. Heather sang along for a moment, her voice clear and melodic. She encouraged him to sing, so he added his baritone voice to hers. Their two voices melded well together. They were compatible in so many ways. He shook off the wayward thought and stopped singing.

"I doubt Seth would hide the journal in a place where it could be accidentally found by anyone in the shop," he whispered to Heather.

With a nod, she thanked the carolers. She and Tyler moved on to the train depot, where a modular train set was on display. He enjoyed the excitement in Heather's tone as she explained how the set had been collected and built by her grandfather. Tyler had to force himself to remember why they were in the train depot building.

After covertly searching the building and not finding the notebook, they continued on their way. Heather linked her arm through his as they made their way down one side of the little make-believe town. Tyler couldn't stop himself from enjoying the closeness even as he began to despair they'd never find Seth's journal.

Plus, the place was now packed. Tyler hadn't expected the village to be so popular. Families, young couples, older couples all filed in to pass some time in the village, buying gifts in the gift shop, eating pastries or sipping hot cocoa, before heading to either the precut tree lot or to hike through the rows of trees to cut their own.

Keeping Heather close to his side, he moved through the crowds until they came to a stop outside a petting pen where the mannequin nativity scene was lighted from the back, making the figurines glow. Children petted the goats, sheep, a small donkey and some rabbits. The snow turned dirty beneath the animals' hoofs and children's feet.

"I don't remember rabbits in the story of baby Jesus's birth," he commented to Heather.

She laughed. "We make do with what we have. One year when I was a kid, my dad put ducks in the pen. He'd found them wandering on the property, so he cared for them and they stayed for a long time. Then one day they flew away."

He chuckled. "That must have been disappointing."

She shook her head. "They were free to go. But we decided it would be best to keep grounded animals from then on."

Staring into her beautiful eyes, Tyler felt grounded, anchored in a way he'd not thought possible.

"Tyler!" Nathanial waved them over to where he

stood by the precut trees, which had been wrapped in plastic netting.

He was grateful for the excuse to dispel the disconcerting sensation. No matter how much he liked and admired and respected this woman, he eventually had to walk away. That was the nature of his job. The nature of his life.

They joined Nathanial. "What's up?" Tyler asked.

"I just heard from Blake. The sting was a bust."

Not the news Tyler wanted to hear. "What happened?"

"When they arrived at the location where they were to drop off the trees, they were told to take them back. They wouldn't take possession of them."

"Do you think they found out it was a sting?" Heather asked.

Tyler ran a hand through his hair. "If so, how? We've been careful here. I don't think anyone suspects we're law enforcement."

"Maybe, maybe not," Nathanial said. "I did overhear a couple of the guys talking about a shipment they were expecting. When I asked what they meant, they clammed up."

"We just learned that the missing truck isn't exactly missing," Tyler said. "A shipment of trees coming from the northeast part of Canada will be arriving sometime tomorrow. Don said he'd get me the info at noon."

Heather touched Tyler's arm. "It's a quarter to noon. I should get Colin back to the house for lunch and a nap."

"I'll escort you," Nathanial offered. "While Tyler talks with Don."

It was logical for the other man to take Heather and Colin back to the house and stay with them as protection, yet Tyler didn't want to let Heather out of his sight. But he couldn't very well protest. He had a job to do. It would be strange and suspicious for Nathanial to get the information from Don.

And right now, he had to focus on his job.

"As soon as I'm done talking with Don, I'll come back to the house," Tyler promised.

Heather smiled. "We'll be fine."

Of course they would be. Nathanial would keep them safe. As he watched them walk toward the bakery, Tyler couldn't deny he was falling for the beautiful widow despite knowing he shouldn't. He had nothing to offer her. Nothing but love.

He snorted. What did he know of love?

Nothing. Nothing at all. And he didn't see that changing anytime soon.

Heather had to pry Colin from the bakery. "Come on, sweetie. It's time to have lunch."

"But I'm not hungry, and I'm helping customers," Colin declared.

Bending down so they were eye to eye, Heather said, "Sweetheart, we are going now. If you want to come back this afternoon, you need to cooperate now. It's your choice."

His bottom lip stuck out. "Fine. I'll cooperate."

She took him by the hand, and they met Nathanial on the wooden sidewalk.

"I thought we'd ride back to the house in the truck," Nathanial said.

Grateful for his thoughtfulness, Heather smiled. "That's a good idea. I need to touch base with Rob first and let him know I'll be at the house if he needs anything."

They found Rob in Santa's House. He'd put on the Santa outfit so that Don could take a break. A line of children and parents waited along the sidewalk to get their pictures taken with Santa. Two women dressed in green elf costumes played Santa's helpers. One controlled the line while the other manned the camera.

Colin slipped inside and ran straight for Rob, beating out a little girl of about four.

Heather rushed to pluck Colin up and held him on her hip. "Honey, there's a line. You'll get your chance to have your picture taken with Santa later."

"Ah, man," Colin groused.

To Rob, Heather said, "I'm taking him to the house. If you need anything, call."

"You aren't going alone, are you?" Rob rose from the large chair.

Uneasy with his concern, she replied, "No. Nathanial is taking us over."

He settled back onto the chair. "Good. You shouldn't be alone."

Not sure what to make of his words, she turned to go and noticed the supply closet door had a shiny new padlock on it.

"Rob, when did you put the lock on the closet?"

"I didn't," he replied. "I thought you had."

"No, I didn't."

"Then Seth must have."

Could this be where he had hidden his journal? She remembered seeing a set of small keys in his desk drawer when she was searching his room for the notebook. Could those keys fit the padlock? Would they find the answers to his death behind the door?

She hurried from the building. She couldn't wait to tell Tyler.

Chapter Twelve

"Finish your mac and cheese, sweetie. Then we can head back over to the village." Heather rose from the table with her own plate and took it to the sink. Through the window over the sink she saw Nathanial walk by. She'd invited him in for lunch, but the man had politely declined, saying he wanted to stand guard outside. Walking the perimeter, as Tyler had called it.

She smiled at the thought of Tyler. This morning, strolling through the Christmas Village together, arm in arm, had filled her with a serenity she hadn't felt in a long time. She had to fight against wishing the contentment would last. She had to stop letting herself hope for something with Tyler that wasn't going to happen. For now she'd appreciate his presence. His and his crew's, that was.

Admittedly, she was grateful for the time alone with her son. It seemed in the past few days there had been little opportunity for some one-on-one time with Colin. He'd talked nonstop from the moment they'd entered the house. It seemed he, too, was taken with Tyler and Nathanial. But what boy wouldn't be when he had no father figure in his life?

Maybe she was doing her son a disservice by not seeking companionship and love again.

The thought slid through her, stirring up yearnings she'd thought she'd suppressed. But only now did she realize they had been bubbling in her subconscious for days.

Yearnings for someone to share her burdens and her joys with. Someone to teach her son how to be a man. Someone to love and cherish her, to make her feel wanted and beautiful.

The way Tyler did.

But Tyler couldn't be that man. Even if she really wanted him to be. He didn't want a family. He was married to his job. End of story. And she needed to keep herself in check if she didn't want to end up brokenhearted when he left.

And the sooner they found Seth's journal, the sooner she could get on with her life. Alone. But safe.

After setting her dish in the dishwasher, she made a beeline for Seth's room. She knocked just in case Liv had returned, though Heather hadn't seen her car in the driveway. Hesitating for the briefest moment, she pushed open the door. After the break-in, she and Tyler had restored the room as much as they could, but it was still a blow to see the bed rumpled just like Seth would always leave his bed. But then Liv's clothes strewn over the chair in the corner and hanging in the closet reminded Heather that Seth was gone.

She hastened to the desk and paused as her attention landed on the stack of photos waiting to be attached to the large three-sided poster board that was now tucked away between the bed and the desk. The photo showed Seth mugging for the camera wearing a jersey with the Steelheads logo of the Idaho minor-league ice hockey team he followed. He'd loved the sport of ice hockey and had played for a while in his teens, but then drugs had put a damper on things and he'd quit.

"Oh, Seth." Heather heaved a disappointed, sad sigh that vibrated through her and made tears well.

Blinking quickly to rid herself of the waterworks, she opened the top dresser drawer. When she'd returned the contents after the intruder had dumped them on the floor, she hadn't take time to arrange anything, so she had to wade through the jumble of pens, paperclips, packs of chewing gum and other miscellaneous things that had found their way inside.

She found the two tiny keys she'd noticed earlier fastened together with a ring. She'd shut the drawer and turned to go when her gaze snagged on a small clear vial filled with white powder on the floor under the desk.

She picked it up. Was this cocaine? Had the intruder left it behind? Heather hadn't recalled seeing it when they had searched the room for the journal or when they'd cleaned up the mess left after the break-in. But maybe it was Seth's? Or had Liv brought this into Heather's house? Heather hated to even contemplate the idea. Was Liv using again? Had Seth's death led Liv back down a destructive path?

"Oh, please no, Lord." Unfortunately, she couldn't shake the thought that Liv was back to her old ways. Another more horrifying thought ricocheted through Heather's mind. Was Liv involved in the drug trafficking?

No. Heather refused to believe that Liv was complicit in something illegal. She had a thriving hair salon to protect. And she certainly wouldn't have killed Seth. She'd loved him too much. But that loss could have sent her running for something to dull the pain.

Tucking the petite bottle into her pocket, she left the room. She could be totally jumping to conclusions. Heather didn't know how to tell if the powder was cocaine or something less sinister. For all she knew, the vial could contain a sleep aid.

She'd ask Tyler and see what he thought. Later tonight she could broach the subject of the vial and its contents with Liv. And if the bottle was filled with cocaine, she'd hopefully be able to convince Liv not to destroy the life she'd built by using again. And Heather was sure Tyler would want to know who her supplier was.

Heather refused to believe the worst of Liv. Not when they were just starting to get to know each other.

When they were ready to leave the house, Nathanial drove them back to the Christmas Village.

"Can I go back to the bakery?" Colin hopped from foot to foot, clearly anxious to help Mrs. Theid again.

Heather had a feeling it was the free pastries and ice cream that he wanted. But she didn't want to burden Mrs. Theid, and she didn't like the idea of Colin not being protected.

"I'll ask the deputy to keep an eye on him," Nathanial offered, somehow sensing her hesitation.

How could she refuse? "I'm okay with you helping out Mrs. Theid, but only one treat."

His little face scrunched up in protest.

Heather arched an eyebrow.

Colin heaved a sigh that made his shoulders droop for a moment. "Fine. One treat." Then he was off, running for the bakery. Heather followed him while Nathanial found Deputy Potter and sent him to the bakery.

After thanking Daniel and making sure Colin wasn't bothering the baker, Heather took a turn at the front gate for a couple of hours. A prickly current of awareness announced Tyler's presence when he relived Nathanial as her shadow.

She put Tyler to work handing out the brochures and giving directions to the trees. When there was a lull, she grabbed the vial from her coat pocket and called to Tyler. He stepped over, and she took his hand, slipping the vial into his palm. "I found this in Seth's room."

He gave her a quizzical look. "When?"

"This morning."

She could see the questions churning in his eyes as he tucked the vial into a pocket, but there was no time for more conversation. The time passed quickly as more visitors arrived and the excitement of the Christmas season settled inside Heather. Despite the dangers, they would soon be celebrating Jesus's birthday.

When the next person scheduled to man the entrance arrived, Heather and Tyler made their way to the gift shop, where she would relieve the woman behind the counter.

Tyler patted the pocket where he'd stashed the vial. "This wasn't in Seth's room when we searched it or after the break-in. I would have noticed."

"I know," Heather admitted. "Do you think it's—" she lowered her voice "—cocaine?"

"I won't know for sure until I test it." He opened the gift shop door for her.

As she passed him, she said, "I hope it's not."

He nodded in understanding.

Heather settled behind the cash register. After about ten minutes in the gift store, it was clear Tyler was uncomfortable as he fidgeted and tried to find a spot out of the way among the ornaments and knickknacks. There were a few scary moments when she thought he'd knock over a display as he tried to stay out of the way of the customers. Taking pity on him, she said, "I'm fine." She held up her phone. "I have you on speed dial."

He gave her a lopsided grin that did funny things to her insides. "Thanks. I'll be right outside."

A few hours later, the gift shop quieted down. She'd ended up staying even after her employee returned because there were so many customers waiting to be helped. It was nearly closing time. She debated gathering Colin from the bakery but decided to wait a little longer when she spotted Tyler and Rob deep in conversation by the puppet playhouse. At the moment the puppets were gone, but the puppeteers did two shows a day, one in the morning and one in the afternoon. As a kid she'd been fascinated by the handmade puppets.

She stepped up, and the men stopped talking. "Sorry to interrupt."

"Not at all," Rob said. "We were just discussing the finer points of physical therapy."

She slanted her gaze to Tyler. "I didn't know you'd ever had PT." In fact there was a great deal she didn't know about Tyler. And wouldn't learn because they weren't in a relationship. A stab of regret reverberated through her, but she steadfastly ignored it. She had to remember that there was no future for her and Tyler.

"I was stabbed with a hunting knife in the thigh a few years ago," Tyler explained. "Thankfully, no arteries were nicked, and the blade missed the bone. But it took a good six months before I was able to walk without limping. But my PT wasn't nearly as involved as Rob's."

She wondered if the incident had occurred while he was on the job. Most likely. "You were fortunate." So was Rob, but she could never bring herself to broach the topic of the tragedy that had taken his family and left him scarred.

Tyler's cell phone rang. "Excuse me." He walked a few paces away as he answered.

Heather watched him for a moment. She'd known he had a dangerous job, but for some reason the reality hadn't sunk in until now. What was it about alpha males willing to put their own lives at risk for others that drew her in like a bee to a picnic? The thought knocked her back a step. Ken's job had been dangerous just like Tyler's. The connection couldn't be ignored. And one more reason why she couldn't let herself fully fall for the handsome DEA agent. She never wanted to go through that kind of loss again.

"You like him," Rob stated, his voice gruff.

Yes. She couldn't lie to herself. She more than liked Tyler. Alarm fluttered through her.

But she was unwilling to engage in a conversation with Rob about her affection for the DEA agent. Instead she held up the two keys. "Let's see if these fit the padlock."

Rob inclined his head. "After you."

She motioned to Tyler, letting him know where she was going, then walked with purpose to Santa's House. The line had thinned; she'd bring Colin over for his picture with Santa after looking in the supply closet to see if Seth's journal was hidden there.

She and Rob slipped inside the house. Thankfully, the big chair Santa sat in hid her and Rob from the camera's lens as the last of the visitors had their picture taken with Santa. She fit the tiny key in the lock. It worked.

Pleased, she undid the padlock and cracked open the door to peer inside. The interior was dark. She groped for the chain that would turn on the single overhead light. Her finger curled around the chain and she tugged. Light dispersed the shadows. The closet had been emptied of the supplies it was supposed to hold. Instead, there was a small desk and a chair. A black book sat on the desk.

"Apparently Seth made himself a private little office," Rob observed.

Excitement revved through Heather's blood as she fingered the black book. This had to be Seth's journal. He'd made himself a small refuge where he could make notes on all he had learned about the illegal drug operation. Heather picked up the book and thumbed through the pages, seeing names and dates and other notations. She wasn't sure what they meant, but she knew she'd found Seth's elusive notebook.

Closing the book and hugging it to her body, she quickly locked the closet back up; then she and Rob went outside. Heather wanted to show Tyler the book right away, but he was still talking on his cell. His gaze met her across the expanse separating them. She patted the book. He gave a thumbs-up sign, then held up a finger, which she figured meant he needed a few more minutes on his call.

Rob's eyes narrowed, making the puckered scars on his face appear molten. "What did you find?"

"Another of Seth's journals." Though it was technically true, she couldn't divulge the uniqueness of this particular notebook. "Did you know he kept journals since he was very young?"

"No, I didn't know."

"Liv found one from his high school years in his things at her town house," Heather said. "Did you know that Seth was driving the car when my parents died?"

Something flashed in Rob eyes. Fear? Dismay? Guilt?

Heather couldn't be sure. Rob seemed to be struggling with some inner conflict.

"Rob?"

Finally he looked up. His twisted and scarred face was awash with regret. "Seth confided in me not long after he was released from the hospital."

Seth had suffered minor injuries. She'd never thought to question why he hadn't been more banged up. The grief of losing her parents, after suffering the loss of Ken, had been almost more than she could bear. Those first few months were a fog. She'd cried herself to sleep many nights.

She pinned Rob with a direct look. "Why didn't you tell anyone?"

"It wasn't my secret to tell." Rob shifted on his cane. "Heather?"

At the sound of her name, Heather turned around to find Liv hurrying toward her. Heather wished she'd thought to hide the book beneath her coat. Hugging it protectively, she smiled as Liv came to a halt in front of her. "Hi, Liv. How was your day?"

Liv's focus was riveted to the book. "What's that?"

"Oh, nothing much. Just a book," Heather said, not wanting to get into a discussion that might lead to revealing what was going on at the tree farm.

"Is it another of Seth's journals?" Liv lifted her gaze.

The hard coldness in her eyes confused Heather. She sought for some way to answer the direct question without lying. Seeing no other option, she said, "Yes, but it's not a personal journal. It's a ledger of farm transactions."

"I want to see it," Liv said and grabbed for the book.

Stunned, Heather tightened her hold on the journal. No way was she giving it up after all the time and energy, not to mention pain, she and Tyler had gone through to find it. Besides, what would Liv want with the book? "Liv, please. This isn't for you."

Liv tugged and twisted. "Give it to me."

"Olivia! Stop." Heather didn't know how else to respond to Liv's childish behavior.

"I want that journal!" Liv raked her fingernails across Heather's knuckle.

"Owww," Heather cried, involuntarily loosening her hold on the book. "Liv, what's gotten into you?"

Rob reached for Liv's arm. "Miss Dorsett, you need to let go."

With Rob's help, Heather regained her grip on the book and wrenched it away from Liv. "Olivia, why are you doing this? What does this book mean to you?"

Rob grabbed Liv again when she raised her arm as if to hit Heather. Liv let out a growl of pure rage and pushed Rob, hard enough that he stumbled to the ground on his unsteady leg. Then Liv ran toward the parking lot, her boots kicking up gravel in her wake.

Heather helped Rob to his feet. After assuring herself he was unhurt, she stared after Liv. She'd parked her car just outside the gate. Her sedan shot forward, spitting gravel as she took off at a fast speed down the village's long drive. Then she hooked a right, tires squealing on the pavement, and disappeared from sight.

"That was so weird," Heather said. "I've never seen her act so…"

"Crazy?" Rob supplied.

"Exactly."

The sound of pounding feet drew her attention. Tyler and Nathanial ran over to Heather and Rob. "What was that about?" Tyler asked, his eyes dark with concern.

Heather shook her head. Her hand stung where Liv had gouged her. "I think Seth's death is catching up to Liv and making her act out of character. She's usually so composed and elegant."

"She was pretty desperate to get her hands on the book Heather found in the closet," Rob stated. "I don't think it was grief driving her."

Heather stared at Rob. What was he saying? Did he know what the journal contained? Did Liv?

Tyler noticed the book pressed to her chest. "Is that…?"

She said in an even tone, "One of Seth's notebooks."

Understanding and excitement built in his gaze. "Okay. Well, let's get you back to the farmhouse so you can read it."

"Heather, wait." Rob assessed Tyler. "You're not her business partner, are you? You're some sort of law enforcement. DEA?"

Heather's breath hitched. How did he know? Her attention flew to Tyler. The tense line of his jaw hardened his features, and the dangerous glint in his eyes made her want to step back.

"What makes you think that?" he asked.

Tyler's voice was quiet, and yet the sharp, jagged tone sent a shiver down Heather's spine. She'd never seen him like this. This was the cop who brought down drug dealers for a living.

"I'm observant." Rob leaned on his cane. "I've noted you snooping around, asking questions. And if I have, so have others."

"Others like who?"

Heather was glad Tyler asked the question because she wanted to know, as well.

Rob glanced around. "Not here. Let's take this discussion to someplace more private." Rob hobbled away toward the back of the buildings, where there was a small outer building used by the employees during their breaks and lunches. Nathanial was on Rob's heels within seconds.

"Heather, you should stay," Tyler said, holding out his hand for the book. "If this is some sort of trap, I don't want you anywhere near."

Hanging on to the book, Heather shook her head. "No way. I'm not letting this book out of my sight until I've looked through it." She lifted her chin. "Besides, you and Nathanial will protect me."

His mouth pressed into a thin line. "Fine."

She had to double her steps to keep up with his long stride as they made their way to the break house, as the employees affectionately called it. Heather followed Tyler inside and shut the door behind her.

Though it was only the four of them inside the building, Rob pinned her with a direct look and spoke in a low voice. "Do you believe your brother overdosed?"

She inhaled sharply at the question. Her gaze sought

Tyler's, but his focus was trained on Rob. She licked her lips and shook her head. "No. I don't."

"He didn't," Rob said with certainty. "I can't prove it, but Seth was in trouble."

She nodded, aware that Tyler's hand rested on the butt of his weapon beneath his shirt and jacket. "What do you know?" she asked Rob.

"I know the people behind his death are ruthless," he answered.

"Do you know who *they* are?" Tyler practically barked at Rob.

"A few months before Seth's death he confessed to me that he'd allowed himself to be roped into permitting the farm to be used by a very vicious drug cartel. He was scared and wanted out but didn't know how to get out from under the bad deal he'd made."

Since it seemed Rob wanted to address only her, Heather asked the question Rob had ignored. "Do you know who on the farm is working for the cartel?"

"I have a few suspicions," he admitted. "But nothing concrete. I didn't want to get involved." He turned to Tyler. "That's why I implored Seth to contact the drug enforcement agency."

A muscle in Tyler's jaw twitched.

"Why didn't you contact the police?" Nathanial asked.

Rob shrugged. "I'm not very popular around here. People believe that I murdered my wife and son. I didn't want to draw any more attention to myself."

Pity stirred in Heather, but she couldn't stop a spurt of anger, as well. If Rob had taken a chance and called the authorities, maybe Seth would be alive. And probably in jail.

"I tried to warn you, Heather," Rob said. "When you returned home, I knew you were in danger."

"You're the one who called?"

He nodded. "Yes." His face twisted. "I'm sorry I didn't do more to help Seth."

Finding compassion within her, she said, "He did listen to you. He called the DEA." She put the book she held on the table. "And he kept records."

"So you two are with the DEA," Rob said.

"I'm DEA. Nathanial is with the Canadian Customs Border Patrol."

"And the other one? Blake?"

Tyler raked a hand through his hair. "ICE."

"I thought so. It seemed a little too coincidental that he had family to visit in Canada."

The excuse Blake used as to why he wanted to drive the refrigerated truck across the border. Unfortunately, their hopes of catching the people waiting for the drugs hadn't panned out. Hopefully they'd find what they needed to take the drug cartel down in the notebook. Heather sat at the table with the journal in front of her. Tyler dragged a chair over to sit next to her. Nathanial leaned over Tyler's shoulder while Rob hung back.

"I should leave you to your investigation," Rob said.

Tyler and Nathanial exchanged a look rife with meaning. Heather supposed the men still didn't trust Rob and were afraid he'd either skip out or tell someone they'd found the book.

"For now, we'd like you to stay," Nathanial said in

a tone that left little doubt his words were a command and not a request.

Rob nodded but stayed far back as if getting too close to the book might somehow taint him.

Opening the book, Heather stared at Seth's neat script.

"Look at this." Tyler pointed to the notes. "Seth got names, dates and times. This is great."

Heather wished she could share in his enthusiasm. But seeing the evidence that Seth died to keep hidden only filled her with sadness.

"This is bigger than we thought," Nathanial pointed out. "Look at this. He names the suppliers in California who are bringing in the cocaine from Mexico."

"And here." Tyler's voice echoed with excitement. "He gives the name and location of the Canadian buyer of the farm's drug-stuffed Christmas trees."

"And look at this." Nathanial pointed to another notation. "Now we know what will be coming in with the balsam fir trees. OxyContin. Didn't Don say that buyers from as far away as California would be picking up their trees?"

"Yes, he did," Tyler said. "We need to bring Don in for questioning." Tyler took a small notebook out of his back pocket and ripped out a page, then twisted in his seat to look at Rob. "I want you to make a list of anyone you suspect might be a part of the drug-smuggling ring."

"Sure, I can do that," Rob said and moved to the other side of the table. He took a pen out of his shirt's breast pocket.

Heather turned the page and froze. The words written there jumped at her. Seth had named Olivia Dorsett, his fiancée, as the US contact for the Mexican drug cartel. Heather's jaw dropped open. *No way. This can't be true.*

Tyler's hand covered hers. "That's unexpected."

But was it? Liv and Seth had met in rehab. She'd ingratiated herself into their family. She probably had seen a perfect opportunity to manipulate Seth into using the farm as cover for the drug cartel. Had she even loved Seth?

Heather's nausea came back full force. She jammed her hands into her pockets to keep from showing how shaky they were. Her fingers flexed, then fisted. A terrifying thought screamed through her brain. Had Liv somehow orchestrated Seth's overdose? Her breath stalled. Spots danced at the edges of her mind.

"I'll let the bosses know," Nathanial said and walked out with his cell in his hand.

Tyler closed the book and put his hand on her shoulder. "Breathe."

Forcing air into her lungs, Heather tried to grapple with the revelations, but her mind didn't want to believe it. "I want to go back up to the house."

"Of course." Tyler helped her to her feet. "We'll stop by the bakery and pick up Colin. He was having a blast when I checked in on him. They were making marzipan."

Before they left the break house, Tyler took the page filled with names from Rob. "Thank you for this. And for trying to protect Heather."

Rob's mouth twisted. "The Larsons are as close to family as I'll ever have."

His words filled Heather with tenderness. She laid a hand over his. "Thank you."

"I'd do anything for you and Colin," Rob said in a voice thick with emotion. "Your parents believed in me when no one else would. I owe them so much."

She nodded. Anxious to get Colin and go back to the house, she left the break house at a brisk walk. The gates were closed and only a few stragglers remained. She entered the bakery with Tyler close behind her.

The bakery was empty.

A tight fist of anxiety slammed into Heather's gut. "Where? Oh, no. Where's my son?"

A banging came from the back of the building. Tyler ran forward. The storage closet where Mrs. Theid kept her supplies was closed, the door locked. From inside, they could hear Mrs. Theid and Deputy Potter.

Tyler broke the lock and opened the door. "What happened?"

Mrs. Theid bustled over to Heather. "It was awful. Seth's fiancée and a nasty man came in with a gun and forced us into the closet."

"Colin?" Tyler asked the question that was lodged in Heather's throat.

Deputy Potter's grim expression didn't bode well. "They took him."

Heather's world shifted. Her knees buckled. Tyler caught her.

Her worst nightmare hadn't prepared her for the searing agony slashing through her. "Liv has my son."

Chapter Thirteen

Tyler held on to Heather and slowly eased into one of the bakery chairs. Deputy Potter was already on Tyler's phone calling in the kidnapping. The distress of learning that Liv had taken off with Colin swept through Tyler.

He hadn't seen that one coming. Liv had snowed them all with her very convincing act of the grieving fiancée. To think she was the one to orchestrate bringing the drugs into the state of Idaho and using the Larson Christmas tree farm as a way to smuggle illegal substances across the Canadian border boggled the mind. Tyler had to give Seth credit for going against the woman he'd loved by being willing to bring down the cartel. But why hadn't Seth told Tyler Liv was involved? Had he hoped by keeping her part in the drug cartel secret that somehow the authorities wouldn't find out she was in league with the ring and would therefore avoid prosecution?

Tyler crouched down next to Heather and smoothed

back a lock of dark hair that had covered her face. Her knuckles turned white with the grip she had on Seth's journal. Her face lost all color, and her breathing was rapid. Shock was setting in. He had to bring her out of it. "Heather, honey, look at me."

She took an audible breath. Fury deepened the color of her eyes. "She has my baby," she ground out. "We have to find her. Now."

Not shock. Fury. A mother's fury. His surprise rapidly morphed into admiration at the fire he saw, hot enough to bring back the color to her face. She was a strong, capable woman with a fierce love for her son. She was a fighter. Good for her. "We will." He almost added *I promise* but they'd already had that conversation. So instead he said, "We'll do everything humanly possible to find Colin. You have to trust me and God."

"I'll try." She stood. "Maybe they're at the house."

He doubted it, but the house was as good a place to start as any.

He escorted her out of the bakery.

Nathanial was finishing up a call and loped over. "The boss is coordinating with the local law and putting out a be-on-the-lookout for Liv."

"She took Colin," Tyler informed him.

Nathanial bared his teeth, a clear sign of his anger. "If she hurts a hair on the child's head…"

"Stand in line," Tyler replied. "We'll make the farmhouse our base of operation."

"Let's go." Nathanial stalked toward where he'd parked the truck.

Tyler and Heather were quick on his heels. Heather

slid into the backseat. She was a bundle of nerves if the restless way she tapped her foot and drummed her fingers on her knees were any indication. Not that Tyler blamed her at all. Colin was Heather's world. And she'd trusted Liv. They'd all trusted Liv.

Liv had a lot to answer for. Not only the drug smuggling and Seth's death, but why blow up the propane tank? Why send an armed thug to the house? What was her endgame? Tyler wanted answers. But they had to find her first.

Please, Lord, don't let Liv hurt Colin. Help us find him. Tyler silently prayed the litany over and over again as Nathanial drove them to the farmhouse.

Now Tyler understood why the sting operation in Canada went belly-up. Liv had warned her people there.

Had she also killed Seth by overdosing him with cocaine?

Heather had mentioned Seth had a phobia of needles. It was logical to assume that Liv had somehow incapacitated Seth and then injected him with the drug. Cold-blooded murder.

He fisted his hands with anger at himself for not picking up on Liv's duplicity.

Now the contents of the vial Heather had found took on an even more sinister meaning. The test kit he carried in his travel bag had ruled out cocaine or heroine. He would need to send the vial out for further testing to confirm his suspicion that the white powder inside could possibly be toxic. Considering how Heather had been feeling the past few days, he suspected that Liv had been giving Heather small amounts. Not enough to kill her quickly, just enough to wreak havoc with her system. The question was why?

Dusk bathed the world in shadows and gloom. The snow that had glistened in the light of day had turned icy with the evening temperature dropping. As soon as Nathanial brought the truck to a halt, Heather jumped out. She ran inside, calling Colin's name.

She'd left the journal on the seat. Tyler grabbed it and handed it off to Nathanial. "Can you make a copy?"

"Yep."

Tyler followed Heather inside, dreading the disappointment he knew would come when she realized Liv and Colin weren't there.

He found her in Colin's bedroom. She stood in the middle of the room holding his plush dinosaur. His bed was messy, toys littered the floor and his baby shampoo smell lingered in the air. Tyler's chest tightened.

It tore him up inside to see the distress in her eyes.

"She took some clothes, but she forgot his favorite toy." She took a deep shuddering breath. "Surely she won't hurt him." Tears glittered. "Right?"

Tyler gathered her in his arms. She stiffened and then melted into his embrace, sliding an arm around his waist and laying her cheek against his chest. Tenderness flooded him. He smoothed a hand down her back and wished he had some reassuring words. But he didn't.

Lord, how do I help her?

He breathed in the fresh vanilla scent of her dark hair and closed his eyes. "Please, dear Father in heaven, we pray for protection over Colin. And for help in finding him. We know we can't do this on our own power but by Your might. We ask this in Your precious son's name, amen."

"Amen." Heather lifted her tear-streaked face. "Thank you. I couldn't—" She extracted herself from his arms, lifted her chin and visibly gathered her composure. "How do we track down Liv and bring Colin home?"

That was a question he didn't have a ready answer for. But he made a silent vow to do whatever it took to find her son and reunite him with Heather. He would do anything to make her happy, to take the anguish out of her beautiful eyes.

Heather paced the dining room as Nathanial and Tyler worked at finding Colin. Both men had phones to their ears and each had a laptop computer open on the dining room table. Tyler had shared that Sheriff Rodriquez had gone to Liv's town house, but she wasn't there. The place had looked as if she'd hurriedly packed up her belongings and fled. The sheriff assured Tyler he'd have an officer watch the place in case Liv showed up.

Though Heather wasn't sure who Tyler and Nathanial were talking to now, she could hear the agitation in Tyler's voice. He was as scared for Colin as she was. And knowing that he cared for her son filled her with affection. But she couldn't shake the sinking sensation that Liv and Colin could be in Canada by now or halfway to Mexico.

This waiting and wondering and not being able to do anything was driving her crazy. Her mind kept playing horrible scenarios like an animation flip book. In each image Colin was scared or hurt and crying for her.

No. No. No. Liv may have betrayed her trust, but Heather couldn't believe that Liv would hurt Colin. But why had she taken him? And where?

To give her hands something to do, she went into the kitchen and made a pot of coffee. She pulled out deli meat and cheeses from the crisper in the refrigerator. Though her hands shook, she set out a snack tray with crackers. Then she began to clean the sink, scrubbing and scrubbing and praying and praying.

Her cell phone rang, making her jump. She quickly grabbed the device from her pocket. The identification bar at the top blocked the caller ID. She answered. "Hello?"

"Don't say a word," Liv's voice spoke into Heather's ear. "If you want to see your son again, don't let your boyfriend the cop know you're talking to me."

Heather's fingers tightened around the phone. She turned away from Tyler. Her first instinct was to do as Liv required of her. But she wasn't good at deception. Hated to be dishonest. Yet her son's life hung in the balance. For Colin she'd walk on hot coals if she had to. Anything for her son.

If she didn't do as Liv demanded, there was a risk she'd never see Colin again. Liv hadn't been bluffing.

Heather's mind told her to go along with Liv, to do as she was told. She had to save her son.

But her heart, her soul, begged her to reconsider.

To offer the sacrifice of faith to God. She had to let go of her need to control and trust that God would bring Colin home safely.

Deep inside she knew she couldn't trust Liv.

Tyler had asked her to trust him. He'd said she needed to trust God.

She knew Tyler would comb the earth to find her son.

To do this alone would be foolish. She could end up dead; then Colin wouldn't have anyone to love him.

She met Tyler's questioning gaze across the island counter. She mouthed, *It's Liv.*

He stepped closer and mouthed back, *Speaker.*

Forcing herself to remain calm, she pressed the Speaker button so Tyler and Nathanial could listen. Then into the phone she said, "Hi, Marge, it's been a long time." She hoped Liv bought her pretense of talking to the wife of one of Ken's best friends. "What's up?"

"Listen carefully," Liv said. "In two hours, bring Seth's notebook to this address." She rattled off a street address.

Trembling, Heather fumbled to find a pen and paper in the kitchen utility drawer. Tyler appeared at her side and handed her his pen and notebook. She wrote down the address.

"Come alone," Liv continued. "Or you'll never see your boy again." She hung up.

Heather met Tyler's gaze. "She told me not to tell you. She knows you're law enforcement."

Surprise flared for a moment, then tenderness softened his features. "Thank you for trusting me."

Assured she'd done the right thing, she said, "If I don't show up, I'll never see Colin again."

"That's not going to happen." He pulled her to him and held her tight. "We'll figure this out." He lifted her chin with a finger. "We will get Colin back."

He sounded so sure, so confident. She wanted to believe him. She had to believe him. Believe in him. Otherwise, her life was over. She tugged his face to hers. "I know you will."

Then she kissed him with every ounce of love she could pour into him as if somehow she could give him the power to be the hero she needed.

Deeply touched by Heather's confession, her trust and her kiss, Tyler eased his mouth away and touched his forehead to hers. His breath came in sporadic spurts. Now was not the time to examine why she'd kissed him or what the kiss meant. They had a child to rescue.

With that thought firmly in place, he asked her, "Do you know this address?"

"No." Heather sank onto a chair as if her legs could no longer hold her. "I think it's out by the Boundary County airport off Highway 2."

"Let's call the locals and get some eyes on the place," Tyler said. "They can form a perimeter."

"I mapped it," Nathanial said, pointing to his computer screen. "She's right. It's very close to the airport. Liv must have an exit strategy."

"Call the airport and tell them to ground all planes," Tyler instructed. Seeing how distraught Heather was made him concerned. He needed her to be strong now. "Heather, this is what we're going to do."

She gave him her attention, her hazel eyes wide with fear, but there was enough of the fire left to keep her going. She may have been knocked back a step or two, but she wasn't giving in to despair. He was proud of her. And when the time was right, he'd tell her so.

"You'll drive while Nathanial and I hide in the back-seat," he said. "As soon as we're close, we'll jump out and come the rest of the way on foot. You will give Liv the book in exchange for Colin. Once you have him in your grasp, we'll step in and arrest her and her thug."

"That sounds so easy," she said with a faint twist of her lips.

"It won't be. I'm sure Liv will have lookouts antici-pating a trap. But we have darkness on our side and night vision goggles so we'll see them even if they see us. It will give us the opportunity to deal with any threats," he assured her. Though the thought of send-ing her into a dangerous situation by herself made him break out in a cold sweat.

She must have sensed his inner turmoil because she grasped his hand. "You asked me to trust God, remember?"

"Yeah."

"You need to, as well."

He couldn't refute her statement. "You're right." He lifted her hand and kissed her knuckles. Then he turned to Nathanial. "Can you outfit Heather with coms?"

"You bet," he replied. "Come on over here, Heather. I've got just the thing for a pretty lady like you."

Tyler shook his head at his team member's perpetual charm.

While they were busy wiring Heather with communications so they could hear her and she could hear them, Tyler made plans to make sure Liv and her cohorts wouldn't get away.

He had the feeling there was so much more on the line than he'd ever believed possible.

Heather eased the car to a halt at the entrance of a scrap metal junkyard. She consulted the address Liv had given her just to be sure she was at the right place. She was. "Okay, guys, this is odd."

She'd let the two men out about a half mile back. They were traveling by foot through fields and woods as the crow flew to the drop-off location Liv had specified. The thing Nathanial had stuck in her ear crackled; then Tyler's voice filled her head.

"What's up?"

"It's a scrap metal junkyard."

"That's interesting," Nathanial stated. "We'll be there in two minutes."

"What should I do?" she asked.

Tyler spoke, "Go on in. Park near any light that you can find."

"Okay." She stepped on the gas and rolled into the junkyard. She parked beneath a telephone pole that also served as a light source. The place looked deserted. "I don't see anyone."

"Get out and hold up the journal," Tyler instructed.

Taking a fortifying breath, she popped open her door and stepped out of the car, holding Seth's notebook up high.

From the shadows, Liv emerged with a tall muscled man who held a gun to her son's head. Colin's little face was tearstained, his lip quivering. The overhead lamplight reflected off the ring on the man's hand. Heather swallowed her panic.

To hide the fact she was speaking, she put a hand to her mouth as if to cover a gasp of fear she didn't need to fake. "Here she comes," she said. "The thug's got a gun on Colin."

Tyler's voice helped to calm her nerves. "Steady now. Don't give her the book until you have Colin by your side."

Taking a steadying breath and exhaling to keep from giving in to the urge to rip Liv's hair from her scalp, Heather said in a loud voice, "Here's the book. Send Colin to me, and you can have it."

Liv walked forward until she stood a few feet away. "You surprise me, Heather. I figured you'd bring your cop boyfriend." Her eyes glinted with malice. "I guess you aren't as perfect and smart as Seth boasted you were."

"I'm far from perfect, Liv." Heather's gaze lingered on Colin. He was shivering uncontrollably. "Let's get this done. It's cold out here."

Liv held out her manicured hand.

Heather did the same, while keeping the journal tucked at her side. "Give me my son."

Liv harrumphed and gestured for her sidekick to release Colin, who ran full speed for Heather. Needing both hands to gather him close, Heather tossed the notebook at Liv, who fumbled with it. Heather knelt down and hugged Colin to her in a fierce grip. She had her baby back. Nothing else in the world mattered.

"Thank you, Heather," Liv said. "It really is too bad Seth had to go and grow a conscience. I was really looking forward to being a part of your family."

Heather shot her a glare.

Liv shrugged and turned to walk away. "Shoot them both," she said over her shoulder.

Terror streaked through Heather. She pushed Colin behind her and shielded him with her body as the man aimed his weapon at her heart.

Chapter Fourteen

Hiding behind the stripped-down shell of what used to be a luxury sedan, Tyler's stomach dropped. Liv had just instructed her goon to shoot Heather and Colin. Tyler couldn't let that happen.

The primal instinct to protect the woman and child he loved roared through him.

With a guttural growl, he charged at the thug holding the gun, tackling him before he could pull the trigger. Knocking the goon down to the hard-packed ground, Tyler wrenched the gun from the man and tossed it aside.

This was the same man Tyler had wrestled with before. But this time, nothing could distract Tyler.

His focus had narrowed. Rage infused his body. Adrenaline pumped through his veins as he grappled for dominance over the thug. Landing a hard blow upside the guy's head, Tyler gained the advantage.

Straddling the man, Tyler delivered blow after blow. No one hurt the people he loved.

Strong arms wrapped around Tyler and lifted him off the now-unmoving thug.

"Stand down, Agent Griffin."

Nathanial's hard voice penetrated through the fog of fury that had overcome Tyler. He froze, then tapped Nathanial's arm, giving him the signal to release his hold. Nathanial let go and stepped back.

Tyler gathered his control. His chest heaved from the exertion. His heart continued to beat in a sporadic tempo while the adrenaline rush eased, allowing his sanity to return. He held up a hand to Nathanial to let him know he had his self-control back.

"Thanks," he said gruffly to his fellow IBETs member. If Nathanial hadn't pulled him off the thug when he had, Tyler wasn't sure he would have stopped pummeling the guy. "Cuff him."

Nathanial gave a sharp nod, then removed a set of plastic zip ties from his pocket. He flipped the now-moaning goon onto his stomach and tied his wrists and his ankles together.

With his head now clear, Tyler hustled to where Heather, holding Colin, stood. He hated that she'd seen him lose control like that. He never lost control. But he'd never had to defend someone he loved before. This was unfamiliar and scary territory.

"Thank you," Heather said as she threw her free arm around him. "I thought we were going to die."

He gathered them both within his embrace. "I promised you I'd protect you. I always keep my promises."

Heather rose on tiptoe and placed a gentle kiss on his lips. "I know."

His heart squeezed tight. He wanted to bury his hands in her hair and kiss her with all the love he felt, but there was still something he needed to do. "I've got to find Liv."

Heather's eyes rounded. "The journal, too!"

He urged them over to her car. "Get inside, lock the doors and stay down. I'm going after Liv."

Heather placed her hand on his chest. "Don't get yourself killed."

He covered her hand. "I won't. Now inside."

After they were both safely in the car with the doors locked, he withdrew his sidearm and hurried in the direction Liv had disappeared. Once he cleared the light, he pulled the night vision goggles that hung around his neck up so he could proceed into the inky blackness of the junkyard. He moved steadily, searching for any sign of Liv. Toward the back of the junkyard was a mechanic's bay. Light flickered from inside.

Flipping down the night vision goggles, Tyler approached the closed side door. Without hesitation, he kicked the door in, then immediately crouched, making himself a smaller target in case Liv or whoever else was inside took a shot at him.

He rushed into the workshop. In the center was a large metal barrel on fire and Liv was ripping pages from the journal to use as fodder for the flames.

"Liv, it's over," he said as he advanced on her with his weapon aimed at her head. He stayed alert in case another goon was waiting to ambush him.

Seeing him, she tossed the rest of the book in the

flames and then gloated, "All your evidence is up in smoke."

"I don't need that book to make sure you end up in jail for a very long time," he countered as he continued to close the distance between them.

"What kind of cop are you?" she asked as she backed away. She jammed her hands into the pockets of her pink coat.

"Show me your hands!"

"Now, now," she said. "No need to be rude." She withdrew her hands. "You didn't answer my question. Are you FBI, ATF, DEA?"

Not willing to give her the satisfaction of guessing which agency he was with, he said, "It doesn't matter who I work for. What matters is you're going to jail."

Her mouth stretched in a feral grin. "What makes you think you can make any charges stick?"

Behind her, Nathanial entered through another door and slowly moved toward Liv. Wanting to see if he could get more information from her, he gestured for Nathanial to hold up. "Look, tell me who you're working for."

She snorted. "I don't know what you're talking about."

He didn't quibble by arguing with her. She obviously assumed that by destroying the book Heather had given her, they had no information on the drug cartel and no way to connect her to the smuggling ring. He decided to ask something else that was bothering him. "Why were you poisoning Heather?"

"Who says I was?"

"We found the vial of poison," he told her. From behind Liv, Nathanial was ready to apprehend her and gave him a questioning look. Tyler lifted his hand in a subtle gesture to wait. He wanted answers. "You weren't trying to kill her. So I can only guess you wanted her sick enough that she'd have to rely on you."

The way Liv twitched made Tyler believe his guess had hit the mark. "You're the sick one." He tipped his chin, giving Nathanial the go-ahead.

Nathanial holstered his weapon. Then in one fluid motion, he grabbed Liv from behind before she even had time to squawk a protest. The stunned surprise on her face was priceless. While Nathanial quickly secured her wrists behind her back, Tyler recited her Miranda rights.

Together, they escorted her to the main entrance of the junkyard where sheriff's deputies and Bonners Ferry police officers waited for them. The thug was already confined in the back of a cruiser.

As Tyler and Nathanial approached with their suspect in tow, Heather ran from where she'd been talking to the sheriff. Tyler sought out Colin. He was with Deputy Potter.

Heather skidded to a halt in front of Liv. "Liv, why? We trusted you."

Liv's lip curled. "Your mistake. Not mine."

Anger flinted in Heather's eyes, making the green and gold flecks spark. "Where's Seth's journal?"

"Up in flames." Liv's smug tone grated on Tyler's nerves.

Seeing the disappointment marching across Heather's

face prompted him to say, "Really, Liv? Did you really think we'd be foolish enough to hand over Seth's journal without making a copy?"

Liv blanched. She bared her teeth at him. "A copy won't hold up in court."

"Maybe not," he said with a shrug. "But that's not something we have to worry about since you burned the copy and we still have the original."

She hissed at him.

"Tell me what happened to my brother," Heather demanded.

"I'm not telling you anything." Liv yanked her gaze back to Tyler. "I want a lawyer."

She was playing this smart. They had her dead to rights with the information in Seth's notebook. "Take her away," Tyler said to the approaching sheriff.

"Please, Liv." Heather blocked their path. "Did Seth really overdose or did you kill him?"

Liv lifted her chin but remained mute.

Heather fisted her hands. "You may think you're clever. But my brother was more so."

Liv sneered. "He was a lapdog, making promises he couldn't keep. He'd have lost the farm if I hadn't bailed him out." She made a disgusted sound. "Get out of my way."

Tyler tugged Heather aside and wrapped an arm around her waist. "Let it go for now," he told her as they watched the sheriff escort Liv to his car, put her in the backseat and shut the door. "We'll eventually get the truth from her. Especially if she makes a deal."

"I guess it's over, then," she said, leaning into him.

"Not quite. There's still the matter of who was working with her on the farm," Tyler said, figuring it was better to let her know what was coming next. She had to be ready to face the fact that another person or persons that she knew and trusted had betrayed her and her brother.

Her weary gaze met his. "Can that wait until morning?"

"I wish it could, but as soon as news gets out that we've arrested Liv, her associates on the farm are going to disappear."

"I understand," she said. "And then what?"

Staring into her beautiful face, he wanted to tell her that he loved her and never wanted to leave her side, but the words stuck in his throat. He couldn't make her any promises. He didn't think he was cut out for a settled domestic life on the farm. He had no skills other than being a cop. And he would never put her and Colin through the agony of disappointment if he couldn't cut it as a father and husband. So instead he said, "With Seth's journal we'll be able to track down the cartel in the US and on both sides of our borders."

"Do you have to go?" The pleading in her eyes shredded his emotions. "Can't someone else do that?"

He shook his head. "I started this—I need to finish it."

No matter how much he wanted to stay and be the man she needed, he couldn't because he wasn't that man. She needed someone who'd be content working the Christmas tree farm year-round. A man who'd know how to parent a little boy. A man who'd know how to be a good husband to Heather.

Tyler had to seal away his feelings for the widow and son or he might do something foolish and throw caution to the wind and stay.

"What's all this?" From the backseat of her car where she sat with Colin asleep at her side, Heather gaped as they pulled up to the tree farm. The place was ablaze with freestanding lights and a sea of uniformed law enforcement officers was everywhere along with the farm's employees.

Tyler brought the car to a halt at the back of the house. Beside him Nathanial jumped out and hustled around to the front of the house where all the action was going on.

Tyler twisted around to face Heather. "A full-scale investigation is under way. My IBETs taskforce leader is here, along with ATF, ICE, RCMP, DEA and most likely the FBI."

Her head spun with all the acronyms. That was a lot of manpower.

"I told you we would be looking for Liv's cohorts. Seth's journal gave initials and a few names. But for their operation to have worked, more than a few people were involved. And with the added detail of the fertilizer gone missing, we have to do our due diligence. If a terrorist cell is involved under the disguise of a drug cartel, we need to find out."

The heaviness of distress pressed on her chest. "This

keeps going from bad to worse. I'm still struggling to wrap my brain around what Liv did."

Tyler reached over the front seat and took her hand. Their palms fit neatly together. She entwined her fingers through his, wishing she'd never have to let go. But the reality was she'd have to. His job wasn't over. He would follow the trail of the drug cartel, or terrorist cell, or whatever it happened to be. His dedication to serve his country and the people was admirable. Yet she couldn't stop the selfish desire to ask him to give that up and stay with her and Colin. She wouldn't ask, though. For the same reason she'd never asked Ken to give up the military. She never wanted to be the reason they walked away from what they felt called to do. That would only lead to resentment and bitterness down the road. It was better for her, for Colin, to keep her feelings to herself. She smoothed a hand over Colin's dark hair.

"I can only imagine how disappointed and hurt and even angry you are at Liv," Tyler said, drawing her focus back to him. "What she has done is beyond betrayal." He squeezed her hand. "I hope you'll find it in your heart to forgive her."

Taken aback by his words, Heather tried to tug her hand out of his, wanting to break the connection between them. He wouldn't let go. "How can you ask me to forgive her? She used my brother and probably murdered him. She kidnapped my son and would have had us killed if not for you."

"I know it sounds too hard to forgive," Tyler said. "But if you don't forgive her, the anger you feel will turn to bitterness and hate. And that will poison you far worse and faster than the stuff she was giving you."

Heather stared at the night sky. She knew deep in her soul that God would want her to forgive Liv and all of those involved.

But how? Her spirit cried out to God. Aloud she said, "How do I do that?"

Tyler let go of her hand. Startled, she watched him climb out of the car and come around to the back passenger door. He opened it and then crouched next to her and reclaimed her hand. "It's a choice you have to make. Evil is like a cancer. It ravages hearts, minds and souls. Yes, she chose her actions and will pay the price here on earth. But you don't need to pay the price along with her."

He reached up to wipe away a tear. She hadn't even realized she was crying.

She knew the Bible talked of forgiving those who wronged us. Tyler had asked her to trust God. She would have to trust God to help her learn to forgive, as well. She reached to touch Tyler's face. Her emotions swelled to the point where she couldn't contain them any longer. Taking a leap of faith like she'd never taken before, she said, "I love you, Tyler Griffin."

Tyler closed his eyes for the briefest of moments, but she'd seen the stricken expression before his shuttered gaze came back to meet hers.

A knife of pain twisted in her heart, but she wouldn't regret telling him. She dropped her hand. "It's okay if you don't feel the same. I understand." She gave him a smile that wobbled despite her attempt to keep it from doing so. "You've made an impact on my life. And on Colin's."

"And you both have made an impact on me."

He tipped his chin toward Colin. "Let's get you and this little guy in the house. I'm sure you must be exhausted, too."

She was, but doubted she'd sleep soundly again for a long time. She unbuckled Colin's seat belt.

"Here," Tyler said. "Let me carry him in."

Grateful for the offer, she scooted out of the car and allowed him to scoop Colin up into his arms and carry him inside to his bed. She followed them.

As Tyler covered Colin with his comforter, she whispered, "Will you stay long enough to say goodbye to him?"

Tyler put his arm around her waist and led her into the hall. "I'll be leaving early in the morning. If he's up, I'll definitely say goodbye to the little man."

"Thank you."

He hesitated as if he wanted to say something. Then a resigned, stoic expression settled on his handsome face. "Try to rest. I'll keep everyone out of your hair until morning. Then you'll be asked questions." He tucked a lock of her hair back behind her ear, his fingers gently caressing the line of her jaw before his hand fell back to his side. "Just tell them what you know. This should wrap up pretty quickly once everyone has been interviewed."

"How will you get anyone to confess to helping Liv?"

One side of his mouth lifted. "The journal will be a

powerful motivator. My boss has already agreed that we give everyone an opportunity to come clean for a reduced sentence."

She let out a weary sigh. "I hope they will cooperate."

"It will all work out," Tyler assured her. "By late afternoon tomorrow, your life will resume, and you can move forward."

"But without knowing what really happened to Seth." That burned inside her like a lit match.

"Be patient," he said. "As soon as Liv breaks, and she will—they always do—I'll send word."

Be patient. That would be a test. "I should let you get to it, then."

"Yes. I'll see you in the morning." He left, his footsteps echoing in the quiet house.

Heather made herself crawl into bed. She did need rest. Tomorrow would be grueling. In so many ways. Sleep came quickly, and so did the morning.

The aroma of fresh-brewed coffee wafted upstairs, stirring her awake. She dressed, choosing a pair of stretch jeans in a dark wash, a green sweater that she knew brought out the green in her eyes and short boots. She combed her hair into bouncy waves and put on just the barest hint of mascara and lip gloss. If she had to say goodbye to Tyler, she wanted him to remember her like this and not in her baggy sweats. She checked on Colin. He was still fast asleep. She headed downstairs and found Tyler sitting at the dining table with a cup of coffee.

He rose as she entered. The appreciation in his gaze

brought heat to her cheeks. "Hope you don't mind, but I helped myself to some coffee."

Her heart thumped. He looked so handsome in his cargo pants and black T-shirt. His dark hair was damp from a recent shower and his jaw clean-shaven. She could smell the spicy aftershave he used. She imprinted the scent in her mind. "Not at all."

"I hung Seth's coat in the hall closet."

"Thank you."

"Crime scene techs will need to collect Liv's things that she left in Seth's room."

"Okay."

"Is Colin still sleeping?"

Hoping her son wouldn't feel the disappointment of Tyler leaving as keenly as she did, she said, "I'll tell him you said goodbye."

An awkward silence descended between them.

Finally, he held out his hand. She grasped it like a lifeline.

"I have to go now," he said.

Her heart cried out, *No!* She put on a brave smile. "I'll walk you out."

He opened the front door, and they stepped out onto the porch. He drew her close and pointed up to the sprig of mistletoe hanging over their heads.

This time she didn't run away. She wasn't sure if she moved first or if he did, but they met in a fiery kiss that curled her toes and left her breathless.

Uncertainty shone in his eyes. "I'll keep in touch, okay?"

She wasn't sure she could stand the torture of hearing from him without being able to see him. "Would you like to spend Christmas here? We'd love to have you."

A pained expression crossed his features. "As much as I'd like to say yes, I have no idea where I'll be at Christmas. I can't make any promises to you, Heather."

Though he didn't say it, she heard the unspoken *Not now, not ever.*

Needing to be strong for him and herself, she stepped out of his embrace. She had to send him on his way and make sure he didn't see how torn up inside she was. Forcing her voice to an even tone, she said, "Then I wish you well, Agent Tyler Griffin."

"Goodbye, Heather."

He walked away, taking her heart with him.

Chapter Fifteen

Tyler hunkered down inside the small confines of a battered surveillance van. He was parked in an alley outside of the known hangout of a major drug dealer, a nightclub in central Los Angles.

It had been nearly a month since he'd left Idaho; following the information in Seth Larson's journal had led to a successful closure to the case. The IBETs force had confiscated thousands of dollars' worth of cocaine, made multiple arrests, closed off this particular Mexican pipeline of illegal drugs both in the US and Canada.

The Mexican authorities were cracking down on the members of the drug cartel's operatives that the Border Service had shared with them.

It was Christmas Eve, and as he had for every major holiday, with the exception of the wonderful Thanksgiving he'd spent at the Larson Christmas tree farm with Heather and Colin, Tyler had volunteered for tonight's assignment. Doing so meant another man could spend the time with his family.

Never before had Tyler begrudged his career choice. Never before had he felt restless on a stakeout with questions bombarding him. Had he done the right thing by not telling Heather he reciprocated her love? He'd walked away, allowing her to believe he didn't love her. Which was so not the truth. He loved her. Loved her in a way he had never loved anyone else. Sure, he'd dated and he'd had relationships, but he'd always bailed when things became too emotional. Too complicated.

Just as he had with Heather.

He was an idiot. He didn't want to be here tonight. Or tomorrow on Christmas Day, if the drug deal that the information grid indicated went down.

"We've got a live bogey coming your way," the voice of his fellow DEA agent, Paul Summers, came over the radio. Paul was in another vehicle on the main thoroughfare with a clear view of the alley entrance.

Tyler snapped to alertness. Through the dingy front windshield of the van, he saw a figure scurrying down the alley. "On it."

He grabbed the camera and snapped pictures. He couldn't move in until he saw an exchange of drugs. And if the deal went down inside, he'd have to wait for the players to leave before busting them.

"What's happening?" Paul asked, his voice sounding a bit garbled. Probably from the cheeseburger dinner Paul always had on stakeouts. The man lived on fast food.

"Not much," Tyler replied. Weary, he set the camera aside to take a swig of water.

"Well, I wish they'd get on with it," Paul groused. "My old joints are getting stiff sitting here."

Like him, Paul was single and worked the holidays. Paul was fifteen years Tyler's senior.

It occurred to Tyler in a brief moment of clarity that with the way things were going, he would be Paul in fifteen years. Alone and sitting in a too-small car on Christmas Eve waiting for some criminal element to make his day.

"I'm done," he said aloud. He didn't want this life anymore. He wanted to be with Heather and Colin. Though he knew they were doing all right without him. He'd kept tabs via Deputy Potter, who had agreed to regularly check in at the farm. But Tyler needed Heather and Colin in his life. He loved them both and wanted nothing more than to spend Christmas with them.

"What's that?" Paul asked.

Tyler watched the suspect enter the building, the door closing firmly behind him. "Tonight's stakeout is a dud. Guy disappeared inside. I'm calling it."

Meaning he was packing up shop and would hand the case over to someone else. For Tyler tonight was the beginning of what he hoped would be a wonderful life.

"Mommy!" Colin jumped onto Heather's bed, waking her from a sound sleep. She sat up to smile at him. He was dressed in his rocket pj's, his dinosaur hung from his hand and his little face was lit up like a Fourth of July sparkler. "It's Christmas morning! Happy Birthday, Jesus!"

"Yes, it sure is." Instead of pretending that Santa was real and leaving presents under the tree, she'd taught Colin that the giving of gifts to each other was an expression of love, following God's example of giving humanity Jesus. "Shall we sing happy birthday to Jesus?"

"Not without the cake!"

They'd baked a carrot cake with cream cheese frosting, Colin's favorite. They would put candles on it and blow them out together.

"Okay, sweetie, give Mommy just a minute to wake up."

"Can I go look at the presents?"

She smiled as love crowded her chest. "Yes. After you brush your teeth."

"I already did." He crawled over to her and breathed his minty breath in her face. "Smell."

She laughed and hugged him tight. "Okay, smart boy. You can go downstairs. Just don't open any presents until I get there."

"I won't." Colin bounced off the bed and ran out of the room. His feet pounding down the stairs reverberated through the house.

Heather flopped back for a moment. She hadn't been sleeping well this past month. Nightmares of Liv and her thug disturbed her rest. Many times in the middle of the night Heather would reach out, calling Tyler's name, and she'd awaken knowing he wasn't there. She hadn't heard from him since a week after arresting Liv.

He'd called to tell her that Liv had cracked, like he'd predicted. She'd admitted to injecting Seth with a lethal amount of cocaine. She'd also stated she'd wanted Heather sick so that she could ingratiate herself more firmly on the farm.

It had been so good yet so distressing to hear Tyler's voice. She'd wanted to beg him to come back. She hadn't. He had a life that didn't include her and her son. End of story.

But today she wouldn't think about the heartache that throbbed within her chest. Today she'd concentrate on her son. She threw back the covers and changed from her pajamas into her comfy sweats. She swept her hair up into a loose ponytail and brushed her teeth.

The tune of "Jingle Bells" filled the house.

She groaned. Who would be coming to visit on Christmas morning? She wasn't expecting anyone. She padded downstairs in time to see Colin streaking across the hardwood floor toward the front door.

"Colin, no." She hurried down the last few stairs and rounded the corner just as Colin yanked open the door.

Tyler stood on the other side of the threshold, looking so handsome in pressed khaki slacks, a button-down shirt beneath a down jacket. He held a bag of presents in one hand and a bouquet of red and white roses in the other. His gaze collided with her, knocking the breath from her lungs and sending her senses reeling. He was here. Really here. She pinched herself to make sure she wasn't dreaming.

"Mr. Tyler!" Colin cried and flung himself at Tyler's legs, hugging him tightly.

Stunned, Heather moved to him. She blinked back the tears burning her eyes.

"What are you doing here?"

He gave her a lopsided grin. "There's nowhere on earth I'd rather be on Christmas than here with you two." He held out the flowers.

She took them and buried her nose in the fragrant blooms to hide her confusion and delight.

"Hey, squirt." Tyler easily lifted Colin with one arm. "I missed you."

Colin flung his arms around Tyler's neck. "We missed you."

Heather met Tyler's gaze. He arched an eyebrow. "Is that so?"

"Yes. We missed you."

His smile could have lit up all the United States. "Good."

Setting Colin down, Tyler entered the house and shut the door.

"Are those for us?" Colin asked, pointing to the bag of presents.

"They are." He handed Colin the bag. "Can you put them under the tree?"

Colin grabbed the bag and dragged it into the living room where their large Douglas fir, decorated with a ton of ornaments and multicolored lights, stood in front of the living room window.

Tyler closed the distance between him and Heather. Though he didn't touch her, his gaze was a soft caress that sent a delicious shiver down her spine.

"I love you, Heather Larson-Randall. And I want to spend the rest of my life with you, if you'll have me."

"What about your career?" Surely he wasn't leaving law enforcement for her. She couldn't allow that because one day he might come to resent her for it.

"Seems the sheriff's department is in need of someone with my experience and background."

Overcome with joy, she circled her free arm around his neck and pulled him closer. "Yes. Oh, yes, I'll have you. I love you." She pressed her lips to his in a soul-searing kiss.

"Hey, you're not under the mistletoe," Colin chided.

They broke the kiss with laughter filling their hearts.

Colin bounced on his feet. "Can we open presents now?"

Filled with love and gratitude, Heather thanked God for giving her the best gift ever—a wonderful son and a man to love for eternity.

* * * * *

CHRISTMAS BLACKOUT

Maggie K. Black

For my strong, brave and beautiful girls.
You are what makes Christmas special.

I will lead the blind by ways they have not known,
along unfamiliar paths I will guide them; I will turn
the darkness into light before them and make the
rough places smooth. These are the things I will do;
I will not forsake them.

—*Isaiah* 42:16

Chapter One

Benjamin Duff gripped the steering wheel with both hands and tried to turn into the skid. It was too late. Pelting sleet and freezing rain had turned the southern Ontario back road into a treacherous mess of slush and ice. The storm had picked up quickly. He'd been just a fraction of a second too late in catching the change of traction from paved road to country lane.

Now his pickup truck was spinning.

Benjamin held on tight as the world flew past the windshield in a blur of gray and white.

Trees. Snow. Sky.

Lord, please keep us safe.

The truck gave a final rotation and came to a stop.

He looked out. Branches, heavy with snow, buffeted against the driver's-side door. The truck was now pointed back the way he'd come, but he'd somehow managed to stay out of the roadside ditch. He rested his forehead on the steering wheel and let out a long breath. "Thank You, God."

The hospital room where he'd spent so many months in traction as a teenager flashed through his mind. It would be sixteen years this February since a terrible snowmobile accident had taken a friend's life and left fifteen-year-old Benjamin with a body so broken that doctors didn't know at first if he'd ever walk again. Since then, he'd built a successful business as an extreme sports instructor and even used the lingering notoriety as a platform to teach thousands of young people about outdoor safety and living life to the fullest.

Now his business was successfully sold. He was just three days away from catching a Christmas night flight to Australia, to pick up the boat he'd saved his entire life for. First he'd embark on a year long sailing voyage for charity. Then he'd use his new boat to start his own Pacific charter service.

Life on the open waters meant that finally he'd be living somewhere he could escape the long shadow the accident had cast over his life.

Yet here, in an instant, he'd been reminded of just how easily everything could be taken away again.

Not that that he'd ever forgotten.

A soft whimper came from the passenger seat.

"I'm sorry, Harry." Benjamin slid one hand into the dog's thick fur. He scratched the young black-and-white husky on the back of the neck, just where the seat belt clipped into his safety harness. "Don't worry. We're almost there. Piper's bed-and-breakfast is only a few minutes away."

I hope.

He eased the truck back onto the road and kept driving. He'd met Piper Lawrence during the summer, when the spunky brunette had walked into his sports shop. Truth be told, they'd barely kept in touch since then and he didn't know her all *that* well. But he knew she had a bed-and-breakfast, on a huge property on the edge of Lake Erie. While Harry was a pretty good dog he sure wasn't suited for life on a sailboat, so he'd asked Piper if she'd be interested in giving him a new permanent home. She'd said yes.

But the weather forecast was pretty much as bad as the holidays could be. His deep blue eyes glanced at the console clock. It was quarter to four. It was a seven-hour drive from here back to his sister's place on Manitoulin Island, the home he had shared with her. At this rate, he'd be driving well into the night.

"See, dog, Meg and Jack are getting married on Christmas Eve, which is the day after tomorrow." Maybe talking out loud would calm both the husky and himself. "Sounds like your Christmas will be exciting, too. Our friend Piper is hosting a huge Christmas Eve thing."

Our friend Piper. He scratched his trim brown beard. Why did it feel weird to call Piper Lawrence a "friend"? But he couldn't think of a better term to call her. The second to last week of August, he'd just looked up over the counter one day and saw Piper there in the doorway. A mess of tumbling dark hair, plaid shirt worn over jean shorts, sparkling eyes behind huge, round glasses. The dog had charged her instantly, tail wagging. Puppy love at first sight.

She'd had just four days on the island and only been there to escort her aunt. But there'd been this glint in her eyes that told him she could use an adventure. So, he'd done his best to find her one. Together they'd gone hiking, boating, parasailing and waterskiing. Sure seemed like a friendship. Good one, too. But then, when they'd gone out for dinner her last night on the island, somehow everything had gone from comfortable to awkward between them, and he still didn't know why.

"But when it was time to find you a new home, she was the first one I emailed." Benjamin ran one hand through Harry's fur. "Living all by herself, taking care of a bunch of strangers, Piper could use a guard dog, I figured."

He dialed her on his cell phone, which was mounted on the dashboard. The hands-free earpiece was clipped to the corner of his tuque.

"Hello?" Piper's voice filled the car.

Something about her voice always reminded him of salted caramel. Sweet and light on the surface, yet down-to-earth and gritty at the same time.

"Hey. It's me. Benjamin. I'm sorry. I'm running a bit late."

"A bit? I expected you hours ago." Her tone was somewhere between frustrated and worried. Whatever the tension was between them, this probably wouldn't help.

"Yeah, I'm really sorry. Had a lot of goodbyes to get through and you're my last stop—"

"Hang on. The signal's patchy. I'm just carrying

some Christmas decorations down to the barn. I was going to wait until after you'd left. But I didn't expect you to be so late and now the storm is getting worse." There was the crunch of footsteps. He heard the sound of a door creaking and the dull sound of stomping. "Now when—"

A loud bang shook the air.

He heard the clatter of her cell phone hitting the floor.

Then the muffled sound of someone screaming.

"Piper? Piper! Hey? You okay?"

The phone went dead.

A shiver shot down his spine. He hit Redial. The call didn't go through.

The dog growled.

"Don't worry. She probably just got startled by something and dropped her phone."

He hoped. He prayed. Eighteen months ago, a serial killer had targeted his sister, Meg. It's what had brought her and her fiancé, Jack, together. Ever since, every unexplained footstep had sounded just a little more ominous.

Benjamin's headlights flickered over a wooden sign for The Downs Bed-and-Breakfast. The house lay straight ahead. A smaller sign advertised Christmas Eve at The Downs and Barn. He followed the arrow and pulled a sharp right and found himself driving down a slope toward the barn where he'd find Piper. "See, we're here."

The truck jolted over uneven ground. The twisting lane dipped even steeper. Wet snow pelted verti-

cally across the windshield like Impressionistic paint
strokes. When the trees parted, he spotted a large
wooden barn at the bottom of the hill. The frozen surface of Lake Erie spread out behind it. He hit the brakes
but the truck kept inching forward slowly. The hill
was in desperate need of both plowing and sanding.
Even with snow tires it might've been better to wait
for Piper at the house.

He tried the phone one more time. Still, no answer.

Below, the barn door opened and someone walked
out. Didn't look like Piper. No, this was a big, wide,
grizzly bear of a man. The man was dragging something behind him. He hoisted it onto his shoulders, took
a few shaky steps across the snow and then dropped it.

Not it. *Her*.

The man was dragging a woman's body out onto
the lake.

Benjamin's heart stopped cold.

She started thrashing, flailing and kicking out
against her attacker.

Piper!

Piper was fighting for her life down on that ice.

And he was too far away to save her.

Ice smacked hard against Piper Lawrence's body,
jolting her into consciousness. She opened her eyes but
couldn't see anything. She tried to turn her head and
felt the rough sting of burlap on her cheek. Her glasses
were gone. Someone had pulled a feed sack over her
head. She tried to scream but the string around her
neck choked the air in her throat. Her hands were tied

together in front of her at the wrists by the very same string now looped around her neck. She could barely move her arms without choking.

Lord, please save me.

A hand grabbed her ankle, pulling her backward. She twisted around, flailing from one side to the other as she tried to wrench her leg from his grasp. He laughed. It was an ugly sound that filled her veins with dread. She kicked back hard and made contact. The man swore and let go.

She dragged herself to her feet. She was running blind. Desperately her fingers pulled at the string around her neck as freezing rain smacked her body.

Disjointed memories filtered through her fear like pieces of a nightmare. She'd walked into the barn carrying a box of decorations. She'd been talking to Benjamin on the phone. Someone in a ski mask had rushed her in the darkness and thrown her against the wall. It was all a blank after that, until the moment he'd dropped her in the snow.

Please, Lord. Help Benjamin realize something's wrong and come looking for me. He's the only person who even knows I'm here.

She could hear her attacker behind her, muttering curses and gasping for breath. She stumbled up the snowbank and struggled to run, but the two feet of snow was coated in half an inch of ice. She managed to take three steps on the slippery surface before her foot plunged into snow up to her knee. She yanked her leg back and lost her boot in the snow. *No!* She dropped to her hands and knees, and dug for her boot. Her fingers brushed the cuff. She tugged it out and put it back on.

But she was too late. Her attacker tackled her from behind.

He pressed a knee into her back and spoke in her ear, his voice deep and as rough as sandpaper. "Tell me where Charlotte Finn is and I'll let you go."

Charlotte Finn? Her head swam. Charlotte was the history student Piper had briefly shared an apartment with in college six years ago. She hadn't seen the snobby, slender blonde since Charlotte had asked if she could come visit The Downs for Christmas that year—and then robbed them.

"I don't know." She shook her head. "Honestly, I don't."

"You're lying." He flipped her over and pushed her back into the snow.

She tried to yell, but her voice broke. "I have no idea where Charlotte is!"

Piper kicked him hard with both legs. He grunted and fell off her. She struggled to her feet and kept running. The string around her neck had loosened just enough for her to see a couple of inches under the bag and to gulp in a deep, pain-filled breath. She felt her shins smack against something—the barn steps. She found the railing and then ran her gloved hands along it. The old rotting wood was a mess of splinters and nails. If she could just loop the string around her wrists on something sharp, she might be able to snap herself free.

"I know she's here." Footsteps landed hard behind her. "You're going to tell me where she is."

He grabbed her jacket and yanked her around. For a split second she could see his wrist—the blurry lines of a bear tattoo and the word *Kodiak*. He grabbed ahold of the string around her neck and yanked her back hard, cutting off her windpipe. Pain shot through her lungs. Her hands tore free of their bonds and she clutched at her throat.

She couldn't breathe.

"I'm not playing around." He choked her harder. "Charlotte's here. Somewhere. You think you're helping her out by hiding her and lying to me? I got too much on the line to let this go and if I've got to murder all her friends to make her show herself, I will. So, you're to tell me where she is. Right now. Or I will kill you."

There was the metallic clink of a butterfly knife. Then she felt the tip of the blade pushing through the bag and into the back of her neck.

Oh God, help me. Please.

A horn split the air. The loud, insistent blare sounded as if someone was leaning on it with their full weight. Her attacker swore and shoved her off the steps. She fell into the snow and gasped as air filled her lungs again. The honking grew louder. Then she heard a man shouting, but she couldn't make out the words.

There was the long, painful screech of brakes.

Then a deafening, splintering crunch.

Chapter Two

The side of the old wooden barn rushed up toward the windshield. Benjamin yanked the steering wheel hard to the left and prayed for just enough traction to avoid ramming straight through it. He spun and barely cleared the corner. But the brick chimney wasn't so fortunate. The truck crashed through the chimney sideways. Bricks rained down onto the hood, cracks spreading across the windshield like sudden frost.

The seat belt snapped him back against the seat.

He gasped in a breath. Well, that was either the bravest or the most foolish thing he'd ever done. His attempt at a steady but fast descent down the hill had turned into more of a slide than he'd wanted. But it was more than worth the risk if it meant saving Piper's life.

Where is she now? Is she all right?

At least he'd thought to let the dog out before attempting the hill.

Benjamin yanked open the driver's door and leaped out into the snow, throwing the door closed behind him.

The windshield exploded, showering the inside of the truck with glass.

He cupped his gloved hands around his mouth. "Piper! Shout if you can hear me!"

He yanked his hat down farther, wrapped his scarf twice around his face and pushed his way through the snow.

A huge man dashed around the corner and froze. A battered black winter coat hid his form and a black ski mask covered his face. But Benjamin could clearly see the knife clenched in his outstretched hand. Benjamin leaped for it, forcing the masked man's arm into the air as he wrenched the weapon from his grasp. The masked man punched out hard, catching him in the jaw.

Benjamin stumbled back. But he managed to keep hold of the attacker's knife.

The man gave up and bolted for the tree line. The urge to chase after him surged through Benjamin. But finding Piper was all that mattered now.

"Hey, Piper!" He ran around the side of the barn. "Piper! Where are you?"

No answer but the howl of the wind and the ice pellets smacking the ground.

Then he saw her. Facedown in a heavy snowbank beside the barn stairs. He ran for her, slid one strong arm under her and pulled her to her feet. When he saw the bag tied over her head, his throat tightened so he couldn't even speak. He unwrapped the string from around her neck as quickly as he dared and pulled the sack off her head.

His gaze fell on Piper's face. Chestnut hair fell loose

around her shoulders. Her huge, dark eyes looked up into his. She gasped in a deep breath.

Then she punched him squarely in the gut. And ran.

Benjamin felt the air rush from his lungs. "Piper... Wait..." His winded chest struggled for breath. "It's okay! It's me—"

"Benjamin?" She turned back. Sleet poured down her slender frame. Her eyes scrunched as if trying to focus.

He realized she wasn't wearing her glasses and could barely see without them.

"Yeah, Piper," he said softly, yanking off his hat and scarf. "It's okay. It's me. Benjamin."

"Thank God!" A smile crossed her lips as her eyes rose upward in prayer. Then her gaze turned back to his. "I'm so glad you're here."

He crossed the snow toward her, feeling that odd lump in his throat grow even bigger.

Piper had been the first person to really call him "Benjamin." She'd known exactly who he was the moment they met. Most Ontarians between the ages of thirteen and twenty-eight seemed to, thanks to a particularly horrendous documentary about his accident that was regularly shown in high school assemblies. But in that moment, when she'd been play-fighting with the dog in the entrance to his store and he'd rushed over to greet her, she'd stretched out her hand and said, "Do you prefer Benji or Benjamin?" As if the fact that his sister, his friends and every single news outlet still referred to him by his childhood nickname hadn't settled the matter. It was the most rebelliously thoughtful question he'd ever been asked.

"It's okay. You're safe now." He pulled off his gloves and let his bare fingers brush her hair. "Are you okay?"

"Yeah, I'm okay." She grabbed his left hand and held it tightly. Somehow her voice managed to sound a bit stronger than his. "What happened to the guy who attacked me?"

"Gone." His eyes glanced toward the empty tree line. "He ran."

"What did he look like?"

"Tall. Heavyset. Black ski mask. Tattoo on his wrist but I couldn't make it out."

"It was a bear," she said, "and the word *Kodiak*. But I have no idea who he was. He said he was looking for someone I used to know, a woman named Charlotte. But I haven't seen her in years."

She didn't move. Neither did he. They both just stood there, knee-deep in ice and snow, with sleet smacking against their bodies and their hands holding on to each other. Her face was turned up toward his, her cheeks flushed. *She's beyond beautiful.* The thought hit him from out of the blue. There was a quality to her that defied his ability to find adjectives to describe her. He wanted to pull her close, wrap both arms around her and shield her body from the storm.

But he'd never hugged Piper before. Sure, they'd hung out as pals. Great pals. Which was different than a hugging kind of friendship.

Her free hand brushed his beard, as if to double-check he was really there. "But how about you? Are you okay? Where's the dog? I thought I heard something crash into the barn."

"Don't worry. Everything's fine." He pulled her hand away from his face, stepped back and held both her hands together in front of him at arm's length, with what he hoped felt like a reassuring squeeze. "I let the dog out at the top of the hill so he's probably racing through the trees right now. My truck is mostly okay. I didn't spin out of control so much as do a fast and calculated skid." Because, in that second, it was a choice between watching her die from a distance or getting down the hill fast enough to save her. "Now, we need to call the police. My cell phone can't get a signal."

"Mine might. I dropped it in the barn. Plus, that's where I lost my glasses. My vision's pretty blurry without them."

He stretched out his arm to guide her up the stairs. Instead, she let go and started walking. He followed her into the barn. The smell of old wood and hay filled his senses. Lights flickered to life above them, revealing rows of stacked chairs, folding tables and boxes of Christmas decorations. A loft lay on one side, with bales of hay tucked underneath. He spotted a fireplace against the far wall, but it was entirely cemented up on the inside and probably hadn't been used in decades. At least he hadn't driven into the chimney of a working fireplace. Something crunched under his foot. He bent down and picked up the remains of a blue-and-silver decoration.

"Watch your step. He jumped me the moment I

stepped in the door." She started feeling around on the floor. He unzipped his ski jacket and knelt down beside her. The wind howled, shaking the door in its door frame. "I hit my head and lost consciousness. I never even saw it coming."

All the more reason to be thankful he was leaving Harry behind as a guard dog. "Isn't it a bit late to be down here all by yourself?"

"I've been walking down the hill to the barn, alone, ever since I was a kid." She rolled her eyes. "Even before Uncle Des put the path and lights in. Which I think he only did because Aunt Cass was worried I'd break my neck running through the trees in the dark."

"You used to live with them, right?"

"Yeah. The Downs is theirs and I run it for them. They've had to temporarily move in to a retirement building in town because of health problems." She sighed and sat back on her heels. "Found my phone. Parts of it, anyway."

He looked down at the pieces in her hand. It looked as if someone had stomped on it. Glancing behind her, he spotted her glasses. He carefully bent them back into shape and cleaned them on the corner of his shirt before handing them to her. "Here you go. Now, what kind of security do you have if he comes back?"

"Just the usual locks on the doors and windows." She slid her glasses on. Then she grabbed a box of Christmas things from the floor and carried it across the barn, scooping stray decorations off the floor as she went. "I have three guests at The Downs right now, so I won't be alone. But there's absolutely no reason for anyone to come back here looking for Charlotte. If she was in trouble I'm the last person she'd go to for help. We weren't even friends."

She set the box down beside a pile of other ones. "Charlotte was just my arrogant, former roommate. Six years ago, she talked me into letting her come stay at The Downs by telling me she could prove it had some hidden, rum-running past and had been used as a speakeasy during Prohibition. But she was probably just using me to get a break from her abusive, controlling ex-boyfriend. He was some nasty piece of work."

"Nasty enough to threaten to kill you in order to find her six years later?" he asked.

"I don't know." Piper shrugged. "I never met him. She called him Alpha—like the head of an animal pack. He called her constantly, expected her to drop everything and run to him, and sometimes sent really creepy presents like dead flowers. But he was also really financially generous when he wanted to be. Rich and twisted. Even if this Kodiak guy isn't Alpha, he could be a sign her taste in men hasn't changed." She crossed the barn toward him. "But either way, any sympathy I had for her disappeared the moment she repaid our kindness by robbing The Downs, smashing years' worth of handmade Christmas decorations into tiny pieces and knocking our tree through the front window—"

The door slammed shut so hard the whole barn shook.

The lights went out.

* * *

Her heart was beating so hard she was almost afraid Benjamin could hear it. He'd thrown his arms around her and now the warmth of his chest was pressed up against hers, the strength of his arms wrapped around her shoulders. Right then she needed it. She could barely keep her knees from buckling.

"Hey, it's okay." She forced herself to step back out of his arms. "It's probably just the wind coupled with some ice on the power lines."

"Maybe it's nothing. But maybe it's something." Benjamin's hand slid down her arm and squeezed hers. "Either way, get behind me and stay close."

Tempting. But no. She'd spent way too long trying to rid herself of the dizzying butterflies that soared through her veins whenever Benjamin was near. She wasn't about to lose her head now. Sure, back on the island last summer she'd thought their relationship was heading somewhere romantic. Right up until he'd taken her out to dinner her last night on the island only to blindside her with the news that he was determined to remain a commitment-free bachelor for the rest of his life.

"Power goes out around here all the time in the winter." She pulled her fingers out of his grip. "It usually comes right back within minutes. But even if it is someone dangerous, I'm going to meet it head-on."

Benjamin didn't step back. "Look, Piper. I know you're plenty strong—"

"Yes, I am. Just because one thug managed to get the jump on me doesn't suddenly mean I'm helpless."

She sounded more defensive than she meant to. But the fact that Benjamin was probably pretty used to taking charge in bad situations didn't mean she was some damsel in distress, counting on a handsome man to save her. Especially not the kind of a man who was in a hurry to leave. "Don't forget, I was a pretty fierce hockey player and not half-bad at mixed martial arts, too. Both times I took out guys every bit as big as Kodiak."

The only reason she didn't compete nationally was the cost of the training and the time she'd be away from The Downs, where she was needed to help run the place.

"I remember." His voice dropped. "But I nearly lost my sister, Meg, to the Raincoat Killer last year. I'd never forgive myself if anything happened to you. Not when there was a chance that I could've stepped up and done something to protect you."

The lights flickered on again. There was the furious yip of barking and the scramble of paws. Piper flung the barn door open, then dropped to one knee as Harry bolted through. She buried her face in the husky's soft fur. "Hey there, guard dog. Welcome to The Downs."

Benjamin looked out. "Well, if there was anyone there, Harry frightened them off."

"Thanks for bringing him down. I think he's exactly what I need around this place." She gripped the dog's collar and stood. Time for her to call the police and for Benjamin to get back on the road.

"I'm going to miss him like crazy." Benjamin followed her out of the barn. "But sadly, once I'm on my boat, I've got no room for Harry."

Or a relationship. Or a family. Or emotional complications of any kind.

He'd told her so that last night on the island. It didn't matter what kind of fireworks that man set off inside her chest, Benjamin couldn't even commit to a dog.

They rounded the corner and Piper gasped—his truck was a mess of scrunched metal and broken glass. "I thought you said everything was okay."

The chimney had a huge chunk missing from one side. Bricks dented the hood of his large black pickup. Yes, she'd heard the sound of a collision. But he'd been so reassuring she'd just trusted him when he told her everything was okay.

"The truck will be fine," he said. "A new side panel and a fresh windshield and it'll be good to go. I'm really sorry about the chimney. Hopefully it's nothing a good masonry job won't fix. I'd offer to do it myself if it wasn't knee-deep in snow and I didn't have places to be. I just hope it won't be a problem for your Christmas Eve shindig."

"It's more than a shindig." She took a deep breath and reminded herself that none of this was Benjamin's fault, and that he was even more inconvenienced than she was. "It's called Christmas Eve at The Downs. The purpose is to provide a really awesome potluck dinner and carol singing for people in the community who have nowhere else to go. Aunt Cass started it twenty-five years ago. This is the first year I'm managing it on my own. The barn's really old and I really should have gotten a new roof put on it this year. But the priority has been saving up to renovate the bed-and-breakfast."

The sooner she could get Uncle Des and Aunt Cass out of that awful seniors' residence the better.

"*Torchlight News* did a big article on your renovation plans, right?" Benjamin asked. "Because your house was declared a heritage site of historical value, you needed to apply to get special permission?" He brushed the glass off the driver's seat and climbed in.

"Yup. The Downs is over a hundred years old. We're pretty isolated, so there are rumors that during American Prohibition, people used to sneak across the lake and fill their boats up with bottles of illegal rum out of this very barn. Some even say there was a full-fledged speakeasy lounge with drinks and music running in The Downs. All these people would supposedly boat across the lake and sneak up through our woods in their finest evening wear. But no one's ever found any evidence. Not even so much as an empty rum bottle or lost earring in the trees. Trust me, I looked."

As a little girl she'd combed The Downs for some hidden stash of jewelry or money. As an adult, she'd be happy to just see The Downs increase in value enough they could get a loan to cover renovations.

Benjamin pulled the truck back. The corner of the hood was crumpled and the whole right side was dented. But still the engine ran smoothly and the air bag hadn't deployed.

"We've got a really good mechanic here in town," she said. "He'll be able to get you fixed up in no time."

He ran one hand through his dark mop of hair.

"There's a wedding rehearsal tomorrow afternoon and I'm also supposed to be fitted for a tuxedo. But I can't exactly drive without a windshield."

Before she could respond, she saw a shadow move through the distant trees. A shiver ran down her spine. Was someone watching them? But when she looked again, it was gone. Which probably meant her imagination was now playing tricks on her.

"Well, looks like I'm not going anywhere fast." Benjamin yanked a vintage red hockey bag out of the backseat. "You got room at The Downs for one more?"

Chapter Three

To his surprise, Piper blinked. Her hand rose to her lips as if his question had somehow caught her off guard. "Oh. Sure. Of course. I've only got three guests staying right now. I can definitely house one more."

Okay, and what was he missing now? It had seemed like a pretty straightforward thing to ask. After all, she ran a bed-and-breakfast, and it was unlikely a mechanic would get him back on the road before morning. He turned off the truck and climbed out. "Well, as long as it's no problem and won't cause you any extra trouble."

"No, no trouble at all." She wasn't meeting his eye. "It's the least I can do, considering you probably saved my life."

Alrighty, then. Benjamin yanked a tarp out of the backseat and began tying it down over the missing windshield to keep the worst of the snow out. Truth be told, he'd feel a whole lot better staying close by in case Kodiak was still lurking around. Something told him that memory of Piper down in the snow with a bag over her head would haunt his nightmares for a long time. There was a tug on the tarp. He looked up. Piper had grabbed the other side and was tying it down on the passenger side.

Her eyes cut to the National Hockey League team logo on his bag. A smile curved on her lips. "You're just lucky you saved my life before I remembered you supported our hockey rivals in Montreal."

He chuckled. Yeah, he hadn't forgotten just how passionate she was about cheering on Toronto. "Well, as long as you don't high stick me, I promise to leave all conversations about Stanley Cup history at the door."

She rolled her eyes. They started up the steep, narrow path through the trees. Harry ran beside them for a while then disappeared on ahead. Benjamin tried to hitch his duffel bag higher on his shoulder and just barely managed to keep from knocking into her.

"That's a pretty big bag for visiting a few friends," she said. "I thought you believed in traveling light."

"I do." He swung it around to the other shoulder. "Actually, this is everything I'm taking with me to Australia. Passport, airline ticket, travel money—if it's crossing the world with me, it's in here."

The sun had set behind the snow. Motion sensor lights wound through the trees ahead of them, flickering on as they neared. He reached the top of the hill and looked out. Snow-covered trees flowed down the slope behind them, spreading all the way out over the lake. It was breathtaking.

"On a clearer day, you can see the American shoreline," Piper said. "Uncle Des and Aunt Cass married in the south of England. He had what he thought was a temporary job at a company in Niagara and they moved out here. Aunt Cass named The Downs after the South Downs, this range of hills near the village she's from. They got the property in a foreclosure sale actually. Took them years to sort through all the junk the previous owners left behind."

"But sadly no illegal rum in the cellar or stacks of secret cash in the wardrobe?"

She shook her head. "Nope."

He turned toward the house. The Downs was three stories tall, with lead piping on the windows, peaked roofs and shuttered doors opening onto small balconies. Christmas lights wrapped around the windows and balconies, and looped around the fire escape that ran all the way from the ground floor to a round window high in the roof peak. "So this would be your fairy-tale castle?"

She stopped walking. "What did you just say?"

"I seem to remember you telling me that you were born in England, too, but that you and your mom moved here to live when you were really little. So, you used to pretend you were secretly an English princess and The Downs was your castle."

She paused for a moment then shook her head. "I can't believe I told you that."

If anything, she sounded disappointed with herself. But why? They'd talked for hours during those four days last summer. She'd told him all sorts of things about herself. He in turn had confessed stuff about himself that nobody else knew. Like how he'd decided he was never going to have a wife or family.

"I was one when I moved in here actually," she said. "We were pretty broke. My father left us a couple of weeks before Christmas and my mom had no way to pay the rent without him. The British expression is 'he did a runner,' so for the longest time I thought he'd literally leaped out a window and ran. Our flight landed Christmas Eve. We were the first two wanderers to be welcomed at Christmas Eve at The Downs."

He followed Piper past a towering woodpile, through a small back door and into the garage. His eyes ran over racks of ice-hockey equipment. A kayak, canoe and two surfboards lay on beams above their heads, and there was camping equipment on wall shelves. Steel-toed hiking boots hung on a peg by the door, next to two pairs of boxing gloves, some climbing gear and what looked like a heavy wool cloak. All of the gear looked high quality, well loved and as if it hadn't been touched in ages.

"So, if you keep the bed-and-breakfast open over Christmas, when do you take your own holidays?"

"I don't really." She pulled off her coat, then pushed her foggy glasses up onto the top of her head. "The Downs is open and running 365 days a year."

Okay, he heard what she was saying, but there was something wrong with this picture. They were standing in a garage surrounded by incredible sports equipment. Sure, living in the Niagara region meant she could probably get in a bit of skating or cross-country skiing. But there were only so many times a person could hit the same patch of earth before wanting to try something new. And she could hardly surf or camp without taking a day off.

"Yes, but the whole reason we met is because you were on holiday on Manitoulin Island this past summer—"

"No, I was on the island for four days while my uncle was here helping movers pack up their things so they could move into the seniors' home. My aunt's health is poor, and a friend of hers who lived on the island invited her to stay for a few days. She wasn't able to make the trip alone so I went with her." She shrugged. "I'm going to need to run this place nonstop at capacity if I have any hope of starting the renovations by this summer. Even once they're done, my uncle and aunt are going to need me around on a daily basis. Like I said, they have health problems."

"Okay, but what kind of health problems?"

"My uncle has arthritis in his hands and arms. Not too bad, but he's also seventy-two. My aunt's a lot younger but she has mobility problems. She needs help doing things and getting places." She wiped her glasses on her shirt and then slid them back on. But she still wasn't looking at him. "If it's okay with you, I'd rather not go into it right now."

He ran his hand through his hair. Why did it feel as if this conversation was one wrong sentence away from turning into an argument? His sister's anxiety disorder had kept him from pursuing his own dreams for way too long, so he should be the last person to judge anyone else's commitment to family. It was definitely time for a subject change. He looked around the garage and spotted a small tractor by the wall with a snowplow on the front. "Nice piece of machinery. I'm guessing you clear your own snow?"

"Always. I also rake my own leaves in the fall and mow my own lawn in the summer."

"Well, how about I plow the driveway and hill, while you call the police?"

She opened the kitchen door, pulled a key chain off the wall and tossed it to him. "Thanks. I'm also going to call my uncle and aunt, and the mechanic about your truck."

"Great. Tell him I have insurance but I'm happy to pay out of pocket if that speeds things up. Anything I can do to get out of here faster."

"Will do." She walked into the kitchen.

Benjamin opened the garage door and stared out at the dark, snowy night. What was it with Piper? There was this weird tension between them that he couldn't get his head around.

He'd told himself that when the time came to leave Canada, he'd do his best to make peace with everyone he left behind. But how could he make peace with Piper if he didn't even know what he'd done wrong?

The steady clacking sound of fingers on a type-writer echoed through The Downs, like some kind of robust combination of music and water torture. Tobias Kasper wrote books on tactical warfare and was the kind of guest who treated the entirety of The Downs as an extension of his suite. Right now, the short, rotund middle-aged man sat in the middle of the living room, sporting a paisley bow tie and the kind of vest that some people called a waistcoat. He was pounding the keys of a machine that had to be at least sixty years old.

Piper nodded to him politely and closed the kitchen door. The Downs's galley kitchen was much smaller than she would've liked, while the living room was huge, with an old brick fireplace and a huge wooden staircase leading to a sweeping second-floor balcony. When it came time to renovate, they'd be knocking down the wall between the two rooms. But right now, she was thankful for something to muffle the noise.

Her nerves were frayed enough as it was. She'd thought her heart was going to leap into her throat when Benjamin asked if he could take a suite for the night, and it finally hit her that he'd be staying around a little while longer. Benjamin had absolutely no idea the effect he had on her. And he was never going to know.

The phone began to ring. Piper was about to let it ring through to the answering machine, when her gaze caught the name on the display: Silver Halls Retirement Home. She grabbed the phone. "Hello?"

"Piper, honey?" It was Aunt Cass.

Piper smiled. "Hi, Aunt Cass. I see you finally managed to get a turn on the landline phone."

Laughter trickled down the line. "I was about to use my cell phone. But your uncle started going on about saving minutes and I didn't know if you'd gotten my text."

Piper's sparkling, vibrant, sixty-three year old aunt

was nine years younger than Piper's uncle, and so very young at heart. Aunt Cass hadn't wanted to do anything even close to retire when persistent, unexplained numbness in her legs and then her arms forced her and Uncle Des to move out of The Downs into the only available rental place in town where everything was accessible on the ground floor.

"I've got an appointment for more tests at the hospital in Niagara Falls on January 12," her aunt informed her.

Piper grabbed a pen and wrote it on the calendar. "No problem. I'll be able to drive you."

What kind of health problems? Benjamin had asked the question so casually, as if the answer was as simple as a sprained ankle or chicken pox. It had taken everything inside her not to groan, "We don't know! That's the problem!" She wasn't even sure when her aunt's limbs first stopped cooperating with her brain, like a frustrated marionette with intermittent strings. But after sudden numbness in her legs sent Aunt Cass tumbling down the stairs into the living room last summer, a broken arm and nasty bruises had woken them all up to the reality that their lives were going to change. Since then it had been a string of doctors, tests and possible diagnoses like amyotrophic lateral sclerosis, multiple sclerosis, Parkinson's disease. And prayers. Lots of prayers.

Piper ran her hand along her neck. It was tender. Now she was about to tell them something that would make life even more complicated than it already was.

"Now, Aunt Cass, please don't worry, but I was just... accosted by a trespasser down by the barn."

"Desmond! Get your coat!"

"No, wait! It's okay." Piper waved her aunt down, even though she couldn't see her through the phone. "He's gone and I'm fine! I am going to call the police and file a report, but he was just looking for Charlotte Finn."

"The sad, blonde girl who liked puzzle books?"

Trust her aunt to remember Charlotte as the girl who was sad and liked puzzles, as opposed to the one who'd smashed every single one of Aunt Cass's cherished handmade nativity figures on the fireplace mantel. "Yes, her. I haven't seen her or heard from her in years, and I told him so."

"Was it her young man?" Suddenly Uncle Des was on the line and Piper realized her aunt must be holding the phone up between them.

"I don't know," Piper said. "I never met him."

"Tall. Big shoulders. Young lad."

"You met Alpha?" Piper blinked. "Six years since she robbed us and you never told me that!"

"Didn't know who the guy was. Just saw her smooching someone in the woods out my window one night when I was locking up. Told her to knock it off and come inside. He ran off and I never saw his face. I didn't think it was anybody's business. But I gave the police a description then and I'm happy to do so again now."

"You come by tomorrow and fill us in," Aunt Cass said. "In the meantime, you might want to see if Dominic Bravo wants to rent a suite. You remember him? From youth group?"

"Yeah, of course I do." Dominic was a great guy. Sure, the former high school athlete was pretty quiet and shy, and floundered in school. But when Charlotte's robbery rampage had included knocking Piper unconscious, Dominic had been the one who'd realized Piper was in trouble and had come to find her. "Didn't even realize he was back in town."

"He's back in town for a few weeks studying for the police academy. His grandmother says he's staying with his sister and all her little ones right now, sleeping on their pullout couch."

"Good for him! My friend Benjamin is taking the final suite for tonight, but I'll keep Dominic in mind. Speaking of which, I really must call the police now. I'll come by and see you tomorrow."

She said her goodbyes and hung up the phone. When she heard a floorboard creak behind her, she turned. Tobias was standing in the doorway, leaning on his cane. As far as she could tell the cane was simply part of his eccentric style and fashion sense, as opposed to something he actually needed to walk.

"I'm sorry," he said, "I couldn't help but overhear. You have a problem with intruders?"

Piper stepped back. She hadn't even thought through how she was going to tell Tobias and her other two guests about what had happened with Kodiak. "Yes, I was just about to call the police. Then I thought I'd call you, Gavin and Trisha together in the living room to update you all."

He ran one hand through his salt-and-pepper hair. "You know, rumor has it that back in World War II, the enemy used the most inventive booby traps against the Allies, including exploding soap, oil paintings and chocolate. It's all about thinking like a predator, Piper."

"How interesting." She smiled politely. "But I'm sure if we do beef up security we'll find something a little less dramatic." A building as old as The Downs tended to attract a lot of quirky folk, but exploding chocolate was definitely a new one. "Speaking of history, have you ever heard the rumor that The Downs used to be used in alcohol smuggling?"

"Oh, my expertise is in warfare, not local history." Tobias shook his head. "But, I'd have thought most of the action took place closer to either Michigan or New York. This stretch of Lake Erie was supposed to be fairly uninteresting."

Downright boring is the way she'd have been tempted to describe it, if it wasn't for Charlotte bringing unwanted chaos to her door.

The next couple of hours passed in a blur. Cops came to take their statements. A tow truck took Benjamin's vehicle to the garage. She called her other two guests, married lawyers Gavin and Trisha, but only got their voice mail. Tobias typed though it all.

And Benjamin…

She leaned back on the couch and looked down at her tea. Benjamin had been everywhere at once, plowing the drive, sanding the steps as the freezing rain continued to fall, taking coats as people came in and giving them back as they left again. He'd even found his own linens and made his own bed when she pointed him in the direction of his suite.

Before she knew it, the clock struck eleven.

"Why don't you have a Christmas tree?" Benjamin's voice cut through her thoughts.

She looked up and only then realized that they were now alone in the living room. "I put so much work into decorating the barn, I didn't really plan to do anything for inside the house. I'm going to cut down a tree for the barn tomorrow."

The fire dimmed in the hearth. Benjamin added some kindling, then got down on his stomach and blew on the flame. The dog promptly laid his head on top of him. *Don't let yourself get too comfortable, pup. He's not staying long.*

"How did everything go when you called your sister?" she asked.

"Okay." He sat up and the dog moved with him. "But she sounded really stressed. I should be there making things easier for her, not adding to her problems. It's bad enough I'm the guy who triggered her anxiety disorder to begin with by some stupid snowmobile accident. I don't want to be the guy who makes her relapse right before her wedding."

There was a bitter edge to his voice that she wasn't used to hearing, almost as if he was simultaneously talking and smacking himself on the back of the head.

"I get that." She leaned forward. "But don't beat yourself up. You saved my life from a violent creep today. And that snowmobile accident happened way back when you were a kid."

"I was fifteen." He turned back to the fire. "I was old enough to know better."

Piper pressed her lips together. Benjamin had been driving underage, on a highway, without a license and without a helmet. Those were a lot of mistakes to go through life hanging over his head. The older friend he'd been snowmobiling with hadn't even survived the crash and the media coverage had been harsh and relentless. Long before she'd met Benjamin, she'd known exactly who he was—her generation's poster child for foolishness.

"Well, I'm going to sleep." Benjamin stood. "I've got a long drive tomorrow."

"Good night." She started up the stairs shortly after she'd taken care of the fire. The Downs had three unique guest suites on the second floor, but her room was up another flight of stairs in a large loft space with slanted ceilings and round windows.

When she opened the door that led to a flight of stairs to her loft, she felt fur brush past her ankles, then Harry bounded onto her bed under the eaves. She snapped her fingers and pointed to the stairs. "Sorry, dog. I need to sleep. I can't afford to be woken up in the middle of the night just because you feel like wandering."

The husky gave her a pointed look with sky-blue eyes that looked like his owner's. What had she been thinking inviting a constant reminder of Benjamin to move into her home?

"Tell you what. I'll get a doggie door installed soon. Okay?" She let him down and locked the door behind him. Then she changed into a fresh T-shirt and track pants, set her glasses down on the bedside table and slid under the blankets.

"Thank You, God, for bringing Benjamin here to save me," she prayed as a sigh slipped through her lips. "Now help me protect my heart until he leaves."

Exhausted sleep swept over her before she'd barely finished her prayer.

A creak jolted her awake.

Piper opened her eyes and sat up.

Her alarm clock read four in the morning. The room was cold.

But it wasn't the temperature that sent chills down her spine. It was the figure was standing at the foot of her bed.

Chapter Four

Fear gripped Piper's body, pushing her back against the headboard. The intruder was nothing but an indistinct shape in the darkness. But she could see it. Standing there. Inches away from the bed. Not moving. Just breathing.

She reached toward her glasses.

"Don't move." A whisper hissed in the darkness.

Piper's hand froze on the nightstand.

"Don't scream, either. You just stay quiet, okay?" It wasn't the same voice as the man in the diamond ski mask. No, this one sounded uncertain. Agitated. Even nervous. Definitely higher-pitched, too. Female. "I don't want to hurt you. But I've got a gun, okay? I'll shoot you if I have to."

"Got it." Piper slid her body even farther back until she could feel her headboard press into her shoulder blades. She didn't know whether to believe the intruder, but didn't want to risk it, either. There were heavy wooden doors on the bedrooms below and thick carpets to muffle sound. If she screamed would anyone even hear her?

Help me, Lord. I'm terrified.

The intruder was jumpy, too, and even seemed to be pacing. Knowing she was frightened, panicking and apparently armed didn't make Piper feel any safer. How had anyone even broken in to her room? Piper's eyes adjusted to the darkness, just enough to make out shapes on her bedside table. A cold breeze swept up her arms. Wind howled in the darkness. The intruder must have climbed the fire escape and come through her window. Piper's fingers crept across the nightstand. "This house is full of people. Just leave. Now. Nobody needs to get hurt."

"I said don't move." The shadow moved closer. Her voice shook. "I have a gun, okay? I'm just here looking for something. I'm going to get it and leave."

Something or *someone*? Piper took a deep breath and fought the nerves from her voice. "What are you looking for?"

No answer.

"Who told you you'd find it here? Did he have a bear tattoo?"

Again, no answer. Just the wheezy, shallow gasps of someone battling for breath.

Piper gritted her teeth and beat down her fear even as it threatened to swallow the words from her lungs.

"Charlotte, is that you?"

The only response was a hysterical giggle, halfway between a laugh and a sob.

Piper's hand slid along the nightstand.

I'm sitting; she's standing. She's got a weapon. I don't.

Lord, I need a split-second distraction.

"I said, don't move!" The voice rose.

"And I said *leave*. Now. Whatever it is you think you're after here nobody needs to get hurt."

The shadow moved closer. She was slender. Long hair curled at her shoulders. The outline of a gun waved in front of Piper's eyes.

"I said I don't want to hurt you. I don't want to hurt anyone. But I will if I have to!" A face swam into view, featureless except for the eyes and mouth visible through the crude holes of a blue ski mask. The gun brushed Piper's forehead. "He'll make me kill you."

Whoever "he" was, he'd apparently sent a terrified coward to break into Piper's room and threaten her with a weapon she probably didn't even know how to use. Piper prayed her next question would hit its mark. "Who? Alpha? Did Alpha send you?"

The intruder leaned back with a gasp, as quickly and violently as if Piper had just slapped her. In one fluid motion Piper snatched the lamp off her bedside table and smashed it into the masked woman's head. The intruder screamed. Piper rolled off the bed and landed on her hands and knees. That's when she heard the barking below her. Harry was downstairs trying to get through her door.

A gloved hand grabbed a fistful of Piper's hair and yanked hard. Pain shot through Piper's skull. The woman bent down and hissed in Piper's ear. "Don't you dare say that name again. You don't understand who Alpha is. You don't have any clue what kind of man you're dealing with here!"

Maybe not.

But apparently Alpha didn't understand what kind of woman he was dealing with in Piper, either.

Piper's fingers grasped the hockey-goalie stick under her bed. She leaped up and with both hands she crosschecked her attacker hard in the chest. Her attacker stumbled and fell. Piper snatched up her glasses, pushed them onto her nose and then smacked the switch for the overhead light. Light filled the loft. The intruder was female, slightly shorter than Piper and thinner. Long blond curls poured out from under a navy blue ski mask. A small handgun shook in her gloved hands.

Blonde Bambi with bullets.

Just as she suspected, the bedroom window was open, and freezing rain poured through. From downstairs the barking grew louder.

Blondie was standing between her and the stairs. "Look, it's not too late for everybody to get out of this okay. Just go downstairs and make that dog shut up. Then tell everyone that everything's okay."

"Why would I do that?" Piper took a step back, holding the hockey stick firm in her grasp. There were four other people in the bed-and-breakfast below her right now and Benjamin was the only one she was sure could take care of himself.

"Because like I said, I don't want to hurt anyone! I just need to look around." She clutched the gun with both hands. "Just…just go shut the dog up. Then come back, lie still and stay quiet. I'll search your stuff and go."

I don't believe you.

Piper could hear the dog's paws scrambling as if Harry was now trying to dig his way through the door. Then she heard knocking at her door, and the knob rattled. Benjamin called her name.

"Benjamin! Call 911!" She shouted so loudly her throat ached. "There's an armed intruder in the bed-and-breakfast. Tell everyone to stay in their rooms and lock their doors!"

Green eyes narrowed inside the ski mask. "You should've have done that."

Maybe not, but I have more confidence in my ability to wield this hockey stick than I do in your ability to aim that gun.

Piper tightened her grasp. "Drop the gun, climb back out that window and run while you can."

"It's too late for that." The blonde's voice rose. "You don't understand him."

"You mean Alpha?"

The blonde closed her eyes and raised the gun.

Piper swung the hockey stick as a gunshot split the air.

Benjamin threw his shoulder into Piper's bedroom door, just as a bullet splintered the wood above his head. He leaped back against the wall, yanking Harry by the collar.

"Everyone, back!" He glanced behind him. Tobias was leaning out his suite door in a lush velvet bathrobe, like a posh rubbernecker on a highway accident. "Please."

When Harry had leaped onto his bed and started barking, Benjamin had presumed a raccoon had gotten into the garbage. But the dog hadn't been willing to shush. When Harry gripped his arm gently but firmly with his teeth Benjamin had realized something was terribly wrong.

Help me get to Piper, God. Help me save her.

Piper screamed. The sound seemed to shatter his heart in his rib cage.

"What in the blazes is going on here?" An irritated voice behind him spoke. "My wife is pregnant. We're trying to sleep!"

Benjamin wheeled around, coming face-to-face with a tall, angry young man with jet-black hair. He figured it was Gavin, staying here with his wife, Trisha. "Go call the police. Now! Lock your door and don't come out!"

Then he turned back to Piper's door without waiting for an answer. As much as he hated the idea of running into gunfire, he could hardly leave Piper alone up there. He lowered his head and charged the door. As his body hit the center of the wood the door cracked and flew open. Piper was crouched halfway up the stairs. Her hands were raised above her head, clutching two ends of a broken hockey stick.

"Benjamin?" She spoke his name without even turning.

"Yeah." He stretched one hand out into the empty space between them. "I'm here."

Harry pressed against Benjamin's leg, a deep growl rumbling in his throat. Benjamin grabbed the dog's collar and held it firm. His gaze rose to the masked, armed blonde at the top of the stairs. "Drop the gun and let her go. Nobody needs to get hurt."

"I can't!" She pointed the barrel of her gun directly at Piper's chest. The weapon shook, as if it had come to life and her hands were fighting to control it. "I don't want to shoot her but I will if you make me."

He heard a bedroom door open behind him. The blonde fired. Piper tumbled backward down the stairs. Benjamin let Harry go and caught her with both arms.

"My cell phone isn't working." Gavin's head peeked out a doorway.

Close your mouth and close the door! Benjamin fought the urge to yell. But the top of the stairs was empty now. The gun-wielding blonde was now nowhere to be seen. Neither was Harry.

"Fortunately, Trisha got the landline to work." Gavin was clutching a glass bottle of amber liquid. It sloshed. *Please, no! Don't let Gavin be getting drunk right now!* "The police said the roads are closed due to the ice storm, so it might take them a while to get here."

Piper slid out of Benjamin's arms. "Gavin, you and Trisha stay in your room, lock the door and don't come out until the police arrive."

Something inside Benjamin was fighting the urge to tell Piper to go hide, too, and let him handle this, even though he suspected she wasn't about to listen. Silence fell from above. He slapped his leg and whistled, but the dog didn't come back.

"Is that Charlotte?" he asked.

"I honestly don't know. She didn't give any reaction when I mentioned the guy with the bear tattoo. But I'm pretty sure she knows who Alpha is." Piper snatched up the pieces of broken hockey stick from the bottom of the stairs. "The Charlotte I knew wasn't quite that thin and her blond hair was straight, not curly. But those are all cosmetic changes and I don't know for sure without seeing her face. Whoever she is, she clearly doesn't know how to aim a weapon. She's terrified and out of control." Determination and fire flashed in the dark depths of Piper's eyes. "We need to find a way to hold her until the cops get here."

He reached out to hold her back but Piper had already pulled away and looked ready to charge back up the loft.

"My bedroom window was open and I'm guessing she'll try to run down the fire escape. It'll be really, really icy. There's no way she'll be able to shoot and keep her balance at the same time—"

"It's too risky." This time he grabbed her arm. "That woman just shot a hole through your door."

"And another in my bedroom wall, I know. But if there's even a chance she really is the woman who robbed my uncle and aunt six years ago, there's no way I'm going to let her just run away again without a fight. Either way, she's the only hope we have right now of finding out why Kodiak attacked me at the barn or why Charlotte's former boyfriend would send anyone here looking for her. Please, Benjamin, we have to stop her."

She was standing there, barefoot, in a T-shirt and

track pants, looking more like a college kid than the twenty-six-year-old woman he knew her to be.

He knew she was right. If he was alone, he'd chase after the intruder in a heartbeat. But he didn't want Piper to get hurt.

But it looked as if Piper was going after the masked blonde one way or the other. Short of physically picking her up and locking her in a closet he didn't expect he could stop her.

"How about this?" Piper said. "You head up into the attic and see if you can catch her before she makes it down the fire escape. I'll run outside through the garage and see if I can catch her coming the other way."

"Fine." He looked down at the thin gray T-shirt, track pants and slippers he wore. He wasn't exactly dressed to be chasing anyone around outside in freezing rain.

From above he heard the dog yip. At least Harry was okay. Then Harry yipped again. More insistent this time.

Piper squeezed his arm. "The dog—"

"What?" He looked up the stairs. "Oh."

Harry was holding a handgun in his mouth.

Chapter Five

Benjamin's jaw dropped. Had the intruder grown so desperate she'd thrown the gun at the dog? Or had the dog somehow disarmed her? Either way, the husky was now holding the weapon, gingerly but firmly upside down by the handle. If the situation wasn't so dangerous, he'd have laughed.

"I've got to go get that. You stay safe, okay? Just because she's lost her gun doesn't mean she's not dangerous."

"You, too." Piper squeezed his arm, then she took off running barefoot down the stairs.

Harry was sitting now, gun still in his jaws, and his tail was wagging. Benjamin started up the loft stairs slowly, his hands raised. "Good dog. Give that to me. Careful. Okay?"

The dog set the gun down right between his paws, then he stepped back and waited for Benjamin.

"You are the best dog ever, you know that?" His

eyes scanned the room. It was empty. He picked up the gun and slipped it into his pocket.

The sound of footsteps clattering on the fire escape drew his attention to the open window. He glanced out to see the blonde trying to break into a second-story window. "Hey! Stop!"

She glanced up, then pelted down the stairs.

He squeezed through the window and out into the storm. Freezing rain beat against his body. Cold metal stung his bare palms. His slippers pounded hard down the metal steps.

The blonde hit the ground and took off running through the ice-covered snow. Benjamin vaulted over the railing, catching her by the shoulder as they fell to the ground. The blonde kicked back frantically with both legs, and one lucky shot made contact with Benjamin's jaw, just hard enough to make his numb hands loosen their grasp.

She slipped from his hands and kept running.

His hand reached for the gun. No, surely he could catch her on foot without taking the risk of seriously hurting or even killing her.

Benjamin ran after her into the woods. Hail pelted his bare skin like rocks. His slippers were swallowed up in slush. The motion sensor lights flickered on in the forest ahead. She could run all she wanted, but the trees were lighting up around her like Christmas. Benjamin's legs ached. Thick branches heavy with snow pushed up against his body. His feet were bare now and numb.

A loud, guttural roar filled the air. He looked up just in time to see a bright light flying toward him. He leaped to the side. A neon yellow snowmobile swerved wildly through the trees, nearly knocking him over. Then it was gone.

He dropped to his knees as a groan filled his chest and left his lungs.

His fists hit the snow.

"Lord, was I wrong to show mercy?"

Yes, the woman had broken into Piper's room. But it seemed she was just a young, scared thing trapped in something she didn't understand. Under the circumstances he couldn't have guaranteed a nonlethal shot and even then he'd seen firsthand the damage bullets could do. He could no more ruthlessly shoot her—without at least trying to stop her in a more merciful way—than he could shoot a frightened animal.

Not that wild animals weren't lethal when spooked.

"Benjamin!" Piper was running toward him.

She had boots on her feet and a huge black cape enveloping her head. A new hockey stick was clutched in one hand. Harry trailed behind her, protective and alert.

She looked fierce. She looked vulnerable.

She was breathtaking.

There was something clunky slung around her neck. An unexpectedly hard heartbeat knocked his chest. His boots. She'd tied the laces together and tossed them around her before running out. She pulled his boots off over her head and handed them to him. There was a pair of oversize hockey socks stuffed inside one them. Not his, but they'd fit. His fingers brushed the back of her hand. "Thank you."

"No problem."

He paused for a moment, once again feeling the urge to hug her and not knowing how she'd take it. It was funny. Surely he was practically an expert on offering comforting hugs by now—between hugging his sister, his friends, people at church and even clients who needed that bit of extra encouragement to try some extreme sport they'd never done before. Yet whenever he was around Piper he was suddenly awkward about it.

He knelt down and put his boots on. "I'm sorry. She got away. I thought I had her for a moment but she had a snowmobile."

"Yellow with flame stickers? A neighbor reported it stolen this morning."

"That's the one." He tied up the laces. Something warm and heavy fell unexpected around his shoulders. He stood carefully.

Piper had thrown her large wool cape around him so that now it enveloped them both. Then she slipped both hands around his waist and gave him a firm, strong squeeze. "Don't beat yourself up, Benjamin. She had both a head start and a snowmobile. Now, come on, let's get somewhere warm."

She stepped back and slipped beside him again, holding her edge of the cloak with one hand. Conflicting thoughts flooded his mind, blocking his ability to think. She'd have been able to run so much faster if she hadn't stopped to grab his boots, let alone a pair of socks. And she'd have been so much more nimble if she'd just grabbed her ski jacket, instead of an oversize cloak that was large enough to cover them both.

She won't let me take care of her. Yet here she is taking care of me.

"Just don't freeze, okay?" Piper added. "You can't be in a wedding on Christmas Eve or on an airplane Christmas night if you've got hypothermia and frostbite."

"Thank you." His voice sounded as if it was coming from somewhere deep inside his chest. He turned to look at her. She was standing so close that if he tilted his head down just an inch or two he'd be kissing her on the nose. He had to stop that line of thinking. "Hopefully, the mechanic will have my truck back on the road before lunchtime."

She nodded slowly. "I just hope that when we get back to the house, the police will be waiting for us."

But before they could start back, the lights went out, plunging them and the forest into darkness.

In a heartbeat the forest was so dark she could no longer see Benjamin's face hovering just beside hers. The world fell silent, except for the beating of ice pellets on the trees.

"Did the motion-sensor lights go off?" he asked.

She could feel the cloak shake as he waved his hand around to reactivate them.

"They shouldn't, no. They're on a very long timer." She pulled away from him and from the protection of the cloak. Then she waved both hands above her head. The world stayed dark. She glanced through the trees but saw only darkness. "We should also be able to see the house lights from here, but I can't see them, either.

The bad weather must've caused a short in the electrical circuit somewhere."

"I'm sure it'll be okay." Benjamin's arm landed on her shoulders, warm, soft and strong. "Do you have a backup generator?"

"Yeah. It's in a shed by the garage. But it should have kicked in if the main power went out." She frowned. They started walking as she talked. "Hopefully it's just another quick power glitch. Fortunately, there's a fireplace for warmth, the stove is gas and I've got plenty of battery-operated flashlights and lanterns."

Benjamin kept pace beside her. She was in the crook of his shoulder now, with his arm holding the cape around her shoulder. His hand rested lightly on her forearm. A moment ago she'd hugged him without stopping to think. Now, in the darkness, the simple gesture of his hand on her arm somehow felt like more than she was ready for. But a part of her was grateful for the warmth he provided. Even through her gloves and cloak she could feel the cold and damp seeping through. Cold air and freezing rain stung her face. The dog slipped under the cloak between them. On this cold, wet night they all needed to stay warm. Even the dog knew that.

"I wish I knew if Blondie was Charlotte." Slowly her eyes adjusted to the dark winter night. "But she was wearing a mask and trying to disguise her voice. Not to mention it's been six years since Charlotte crashed through here like a tornado."

"I'm not sure I'm clear on what happened between you and her back then," Benjamin said.

Fair enough. For that matter neither was she.

"I did most of my college by correspondence, so I could be here to help my uncle and aunt. When I was twenty, I did one semester in Ottawa to finish up my degree. Charlotte had a two-bedroom apartment and had listed a room for rent online. I'd hoped we'd become friends, but we really weren't. She was the kind of person who kept to herself and never made eye contact. Her life revolved around her history degree and her boyfriend, Alpha. Sometimes I'd catch bruises on her arms and I wondered if he was hurting her. But she wouldn't talk to me. I was always planning on moving out at Christmas and coming home. So, I was really surprised when she asked if she could come here for the holidays."

She glanced at the dark sky above. A flurry of falling ice filled her eyes. "She was on her phone with Alpha the whole car ride here. Sounded like he was yelling at her. We arrived and went to a church party with my old youth group. I barely saw her over the next couple of days. She kept slipping out and going places. I'd wake up in the night and her bed would be empty. Uncle Des just told me that he caught her kissing someone in the woods and chased the guy off. Described him as young, tall and broad-shouldered. I assume it was Alpha. I guess Alpha's in his late twenties now. While there are a whole lot of things about this whole Charlotte-Alpha-Kodiak-Blondie situation that I don't know, I am convinced that Blondie knows Alpha. You should have seen her panicked reaction when I mentioned his name. She's terrified of him."

Which could mean Blondie was Charlotte and the man with the bear tattoo was Alpha. Except that Blondie didn't react at all when Piper had asked her about a man with a bear tattoo. She closed her eyes for a moment and listened to the storm pushing through the trees. Just when she thought the terrifying picture of what had happened these past few hours was swimming into some kind of focus, everything stopped making sense again.

Their footsteps crunched through the snow. Benjamin's arm tightened around her shoulder. "You said she robbed you?"

"She did, Christmas Eve." Piper opened her eyes. "While we were all down in the barn, singing carols and eating potluck, she snuck through the woods to The Downs and trashed the place."

"When you say trashed the place—"

"She went through every room and all the guests' things looking for stuff to steal. She ripped open presents. She knocked our Christmas tree through the front window and even smashed the nativity my aunt had on the fireplace mantel."

They stepped out from under the shelter of the tree canopy into the storm, which seemed to have intensified. Benjamin pulled the cloak over their heads as they jogged to a small shed behind the garage. The shed was windowless, smelled like gasoline and was every bit as cold as the outside air. Harry slipped in ahead of them and curled up by the wall. Piper slipped out from under the cloak and let its full weight fall on Benjamin.

"We never had a lot of money." She set down the

hockey stick and reached for a small battery-powered lamp hanging just inside the door. "So almost all the decorations she destroyed were homemade, mostly by me, including the nativity she broke into bits. A lot of the handmade garlands she ripped into pieces I'd made when I was five or six. The star on the top of the tree was something I'd made out of vintage newspaper when I was about eight, and I couldn't even find it in the wreckage. It was all too mean and petty for words."

She ran her hand over her face. *And I'm not even telling you the part about how she, or an accomplice, hit me over the head, knocked me out and locked me in the kindling box. Because even the memory of that makes me feel too pathetic and vulnerable for words.*

Holding out the lantern, she made her way over to the generator that sat in the corner, silent and cold. She bent down beside it, pushed the button and held it. It didn't start.

"I'm sorry. It must have been pretty hard to forgive her for all that." Benjamin's voice floated behind her in the darkness.

Was it even possible to forgive someone who'd never come back to ask for forgiveness?

She looked back up at Benjamin. "The generator's not working. Any suggestions?"

"If it's a motor problem I might be able to fix it. I've tinkered around with a lot of boat motors and vehicle engines." He moved passed her and knelt by her feet. He reached up, took her hand and moved the light over the generator. "Just hold that there, please, and don't move."

Thick snow dotted his hair and beard. His eyes were gray-blue in the lamplight. Oddly, she hadn't noticed the gray in them last summer. When he'd been standing outside waiting for her that last night on the dock by the pavilion, his eyes had seemed as dark and fathomless as the water spreading out behind him.

"Don't ever marry a sweetheart until you've both summered and wintered your romance..." Something Aunt Cass had said flickered in the back of her mind. It had been her aunt's way of trying to explain in the gentlest way possible why Piper's mother's whirlwind marriages never seemed to work.

But why was she remembering that now? She had no future with Benjamin. He wasn't her sweetheart and this wasn't a romance. He was just a friend and would be leaving as soon as his truck was repaired.

Benjamin muttered something under his breath. He stood.

"I'm sorry, Piper." His hands brushed her shoulders. "But it looks like someone sabotaged your generator."

Chapter Six

"Sabotage?" Piper's body was shaking. She couldn't tell if it was from cold, anger or shock.

In an instant, Benjamin had wrapped the cloak back around her shoulders.

"I'm sorry," he said. "Looks like somebody cut the fuel line. Probably why it smells like gas in here."

Her mouth opened but no words came out.

"And I think somebody stole your gasoline," he added. "It's hard to see in the dark, but the tank looks nearly empty. Thankfully, the police are already on their way and we can pick up a new generator tomorrow."

He was right. There was hardly anything she could do about the situation in the middle of the night. But right now, it just felt like one problem more than she was able to manage. She hung the lantern back on the hook by the door but she didn't switch it off. Light glowed in the tiny wooden room, sending shadows shifting back and forth across the floor and up the walls. Snow flew in the doorway toward them in a wild frenzy. She knew she should head back to the house, but her legs felt too tired to move.

"Piper?" Benjamin's voice dropped. "It's going to be okay. I promise. Before I leave tomorrow, I'm going to help you. My truck won't be fixed until lunchtime at least. Until then, I'm all yours, whatever you need."

I'm all yours. It was a common enough turn of phrase she'd heard dozens of times from people who'd offered to lend a spare pair of hands. *"You need a baker? You need furniture moved? You just tell me what you need. I'm all yours."* But somehow, hearing it from Benjamin's mouth right now turned her jaw tighter, like when the dentist used to tighten her childhood braces. Benjamin was there for her, for a brief, limited time, as the kind of friend who chased off intruders and helped with small engine repair. Nothing more.

His arms opened as he stepped toward her and she could practically feel the warmth of his chest, just inches away from hers. Did he think she didn't notice the support he was offering? Did he have any idea how hard she was fighting the urge to just fall into his arms? He was being a supportive friend and a friend was what she needed. But if she let herself hug him tonight, the simple touch of his hand could once again set her foolish heart up for failure.

"We might have a portable backup generator," she said. "I'll have to ask my uncle where he put it. We only got a permanent one installed a few years ago, after Charlotte—" Sudden tears rushed to her eyes—tears of frustration, exasperation, exhaustion. She blinked hard but still they flooded her voice. "After Charlotte robbed us. The lights on the path wouldn't light up that night. But Aunt Cass rallied. She called everyone and asked them to bring flashlights and lanterns, and we paraded through the trees to the barn in one long, glorious, beautiful line."

Piper should have stayed with them in the warm barn, drinking hot apple cider and singing songs about how God touched the earth on Christmas. But instead, when she'd realized Charlotte was missing, she'd grabbed a flashlight and slipped out. The lights had been off at the house. There'd been a swift, hard, painful blow to the head—and she'd woken up alone, terrified and locked in the kindling box beside the woodpile.

The shed door blew shut, cutting off the morbid memory. The lamp fell from the hook, casting shadows at their feet. Her lip quivered. It wasn't fair how the memories came back to disturb her every Christmas no matter how hard she worked to undo the damage she'd done in trusting Charlotte. Now Charlotte might be back and whatever she'd gotten herself into this time, she was bringing even more chaos, not to mention danger, to The Downs.

"Hey." Benjamin's hands touched her shoulders. "It's okay."

"No, it's not." She'd said the words under her breath, but still he'd managed to hear them.

"Yeah, it is." He looked into her eyes with that same soulful look he'd given her so many times back on the island. It was a look that said she could trust him. It

was a look she'd been so certain meant he was every
bit as drawn to her as she was to him. "Or at least, it's
going to be. You're strong, Piper, and you're going to
get through this. But even the strongest person alive is
allowed to fall apart sometimes. So, if you want a comforting hug, or a shoulder to cry on, or even a sparring
partner to box a couple of rounds with until the world
feels saner, I'm here for you, okay?"

He stepped closer, never breaking eye contact. His
hand brushed lightly along her hair, as if he was almost
afraid of touching her. Back on the island last summer,
they'd jostled and play-fought like pals. Now, though,
they both seemed uncertain about touching each other.
Slowly, tentatively, his hands slid down her back until
they reached her waist. Something pricked deep inside
her chest, like a lure slipping inside her rib cage and
pulling her toward him.

His breath brushed against her face. "If my flight
wasn't nonrefundable and if I didn't have that charity sailing voyage, I'd stay a bit longer, as long as you
needed me around to get things back on track."

How long would that have been, exactly? Until
Charlotte and whoever was after her were caught?
Until the renovations were done and her uncle and
aunt moved back in? All the while, he'd be pacing the
wooden floors like a mountain lion desperate to run.

The shed door flew open with a bang, a second before the cold wind rushed in. A light flashed across
their faces and they leaped apart.

"There you are!" Gavin stood in the doorway, knee-
deep in the snow and shivering in a shiny ski jacket

that was very stylish but way too thin. He clutched the industrial-sized flashlight she kept hanging beside the stairs for emergencies. "The power is out. The cell towers are out. That ramshackle bed-and-breakfast of yours is so cold my poor Trisha can't sleep. You do know she's pregnant?"

Yes, she'd barely seen the heavyset brunette since they'd moved in, but Gavin kept reminding her. Guilt filled her heart. Her guests had actually come tramping out in the snow looking for her—and found her in a shed, a breath away from falling into Benjamin's arms.

"Young lady, the police are here." Tobias appeared in the doorway behind Gavin, a long plaid scarf wound several times around his face. "They say they wish to speak to you regarding the incidents tonight. I trust that you're taking all this seriously."

"Yes, I'm taking it very seriously." She wrapped the cloak around herself picked up the hockey stick she'd brought for protection and started for the house, the two guests, Benjamin and the dog following behind her. She felt guilty for leaving Benjamin without the shelter of the cloak. But somehow she felt uncomfortable about the idea of sharing it with him now, too, and knew there was no way Benjamin would take it all for himself. Fortunately the house was only twenty feet away and Benjamin was able to run it in fifteen paces. She probably should have just grabbed two coats to begin with and not brought the hockey stick, but it was the quickest makeshift weapon she'd been able to find. But this wasn't a game. Charlotte's own unique brand of chaos was back. Only this time, Piper wasn't a frightened, trapped girl waiting to be rescued.

She stepped into The Downs's garage. Warmth filled her body and steam covered her glasses. She slid her glasses up onto the top of her head and stomped the snow off her boots. "I'm sorry, I didn't realize the police had arrived. I didn't see a car."

"They're in the living room with Trisha," Gavin said through chattering teeth. "They skied here, because the roads are bad and the salters aren't out yet. What kind of town is it where the cops can't keep their own roads open?"

A small town, she silently replied, *with only a few hundred people, in a place where the roads got really icy.*

"I'm sure they'll be open by morning." Piper grabbed a towel off a rack by the door, dried her glasses, then dropped to her knees and quickly ran it over Harry's snow-caked fur. "These things take time."

"The former mayor of Toronto experienced much derision for calling out the military to clear the snow one year." Tobias unwound his scarf. "But there is something to be said for military efficiency. Even the British troops were efficient enough during the eighteen hundreds to prime, load and fire at least three musket rounds in under a minute."

She would have laughed, if she hadn't suspected the tactics author wasn't actually trying to be funny. She stood up and started toward the kitchen door. "That's interesting."

A heavy hand landed on her shoulder. She turned.

Tobias leaned in toward her, his pale eyes focused intensely on her face. "I do want to assure you that if there's anything I can do, please don't hesitate to ask. I know how much the pressure of your college studies must be weighing on you, and I have studied extensively about how ordinary human beings react to extraordinary pressures in times of crisis."

"That's kind of you." She forced a smile. "But thankfully my college days are long behind me."

Though apparently the shadow they'd cast still lingered.

"There are cops in the living room." A young woman with short brown hair stood in the kitchen doorway. Trisha's narrow face was so pale it was almost white. A huge bulky sweatshirt swamped her form. Her arms cradled a very round stomach.

"Trisha!" Gavin ran over to her and threw his arm around her. "What are you doing out here? You should be in bed!"

Her red, puffy eyes glanced around the room. Trisha's voice was so soft and timid it was barely more than a whisper. "How long until the power comes back on?"

"Yeah." Gavin's voice rose. "How much longer will be the power be out? Because if it's much longer, we will be looking for a new hotel and expecting you to refund our stay."

Piper wouldn't blame them if they did. She closed her eyes, then drew in a deep breath and let it out again as she silently prayed. *Lord, it's the middle of the night. I'm exhausted. I'm overwhelmed. But as much as I need money to renovate The Downs, these people came here looking for a safe place to stay.*

"I'm afraid I'm going to have to close The Downs, at least for the next few days." She forced herself to say the words first. Then she opened her eyes.

Trisha's gaze dropped to the floor, Gavin gasped as if she'd just stolen his air and Tobias started to argue. She held up her hand and kept talking too quickly for them to get a word in. "I'll still be going ahead with the Christmas Eve event in the barn, and you'll all be welcome to come for that. But I have no choice but to close the bed-and-breakfast to guests. There've been two different armed trespassers on the property in the past few hours, the power is out and the weather is freezing. I will find you new rooms at good hotels in the morning, reimburse your stay and cover any financial difference. Again, I'm sorry."

"Sorry's not good enough." Gavin let go of Trisha and stormed toward her. He stepped in so close she could almost taste the stale smell of liquor on his breath. His finger jabbed toward her face. "Do you have any idea the inconvenience you've put us through?"

Did he have any idea what she was dealing with? All he had to do was change hotels.

Tobias took Trisha by the arm and steered her back into the kitchen.

Piper crossed her arms and faced Gavin's glare. "Again, I apologize. But there's only so much I can do."

"Oh, there's plenty you can and will do to make this right." Gavin snorted. "You think I didn't do my homework? You think I don't know there's not another decent hotel within half an hour's drive of here?"

"Hey, man, back off and give her some space, all right?" Benjamin calmly but firmly stepped between them. His hand brushed Gavin's arm. "She's doing the best she can."

And she was also capable of fighting her own battles and of hollering for the cops in the living room if she felt threatened. She wouldn't hide behind Benjamin now. Gavin was right about the lack of good hotels in the area, especially ones that offered full suites like The Downs. Depending on how long it took her to find her guests vacancies at this time of year, Benjamin might end up hitting the road before they did.

"Don't touch me." Gavin stepped back, his eyes darting from Benjamin to Piper. "I'll sue you. And I'll press charges for assault if he dares lay a hand on me again. Trisha and I own a successful law firm in Ottawa, and you can't afford the legal bill of making us unhappy. I saw that newspaper article last fall. I know you're saving up for some major renovation, with a ground-floor suite for some disabled relative. You can't afford the lawsuit we'll drop on you. You can't afford to make an enemy of me. Because we don't even need to win to ruin you."

A cold, threatening smirk crossed the young man's lips. But she didn't break his gaze.

"I'm sorry you feel that way. Now, I'm going to go talk to the police. Tomorrow morning I'll serve breakfast and then do my best to find you and your wife a suite somewhere suitable, especially as Trisha doesn't seem well. Then I'll expect you to pack up and kindly get out of The Downs."

The morning sun woke Benjamin. It was bright, glaring and shining down on him through the huge, towering windows of The Downs living room. He threw one arm over his eyes and stretched his legs, feeling for the large mass of heavy dog he'd gotten used to feeling curled up on his feet.

No dog. Then he remembered. After helping Piper replace her door with the one that had been on an upstairs linen closet, he'd insisted Harry bunk in Piper's room. After the police had taken statements and Blondie's gun, the rest of The Downs's residents had gone up to bed. But Benjamin had fallen asleep on the couch, fully clothed and with a full view of the entire second-floor landing, the front door and the front and back windows. All the bedroom doors were still closed. He reached for the lamp on the end table behind him and barely managing to stop himself from slipping off the narrow couch and landing on the floor.

He flicked the switch. Nothing happened.

The Downs was still without power.

The old grandfather clock in the corner of the living room said it was a quarter to nine. So, he'd had five hours of sleep, then. Well, he'd survived before on less. Soon enough, he'd be living full-time on a sailboat and would have to get used to grabbing sleep when he could.

A smile crossed his lips. Tomorrow was Christmas

Eve. Only two days left until he got on that plane and left the bitter cold of Canada behind for the glorious heat of an Australian summer. Of course, he should really trim his beard before his sister's wedding rehearsal tonight, not to mention get a haircut, too. Before that, he'd need to collect his truck. And say goodbye to Piper.

Through the window he could see a thin layer of ice coating the world outside. Dazzling blue sky peeked through the glistening branches. *Lord, there's so much more I wish I could do to help Piper before I go. Help me do the best I can, in the short time I have left.* That was a good prayer and one that made him feel better. He'd never be able to solve everything and it never hurt to remind himself of that. But there was always something he could fix.

Starting with coffee.

He threw a couple of extra logs into the fireplace then walked into the kitchen. No power meant no coffeemaker. But the burner on the gas stove turned on without a hitch and a quick rummage in the cupboard beside the sink turned up a couple of solid pots plus a large skillet. There was a loaf of fresh thick bread in the bread box, real maple syrup in the walk-in pantry, and butter and a carton of eggs in the fridge, which was still fairly cold. He piled his finds on the counter and started a pot of water boiling for coffee. Wouldn't be much of an outdoorsman if he didn't know how to brew a decent cup over an open flame and this morning, campfire coffee would have to do. He ground some coffee with a mortar and pestle, and then added it to the boiling water. A blob of butter went into the hot skillet on the stove. He'd just started whistling when he heard noise behind him.

"Where's Piper?" Gavin stood behind him, scowling.

Benjamin wondered what had brought him and Trisha to book their holidays at The Downs, anyway? As much as Gavin had protested about moving out, neither of them seemed happy staying here, either.

A warm smile crossed Benjamin's face, learned by years of customer service. "Good morning. I'm not quite sure where she is. But there's some fresh coffee brewing if you'd like a mug. Did you sleep well?"

The young man snorted. "The power's still out."

"Well, then it's a good thing you and Trisha will be moving to a new hotel."

Gavin's forehead furrowed. Benjamin had seen that same overly worried look before. Usually on the face of someone who was thinking twice about his decision to book a tandem leap after the plane had reached altitude and a parachute was already strapped to his back. Not from someone about to be asked whether they'd prefer milk or sugar. Benjamin's gaze ran from the man's overly styled hair down to his designer boots. If he had to guess, he'd peg Gavin as someone who'd come from the expectation of money, but actually lacked a decent jingle in his pocket.

Gavin's eyes narrowed in return as if he didn't appreciate the appraisal. "Tobias said your last name was Duff. Are you the same Benji Duff who nearly killed himself because he didn't know how to drive a motorbike? We had to watch some stupid documentary about you every single winter in school assembly, from like grade seven onward."

Benjamin remembered when one of the national television current-affairs shows had done a sensational hatchet job, heavy on the scare tactics. Schools loved it.

"That's me," he said, "but it was a snowmobile accident actually. And the friend I was riding with died. His name was Chris." He turned his back on Gavin, cracked eight eggs in a bowl and whisked them until they were frothy.

"Gavin, my good man! Good morning! How did your wife sleep?" Tobias's voice boomed through the doorway. "I do hope the fact breakfast is late isn't a sign some tragedy has befallen poor Piper."

Did he mean some new tragedy besides everything that happened yesterday? Benjamin gritted his teeth. He didn't know how Piper did it. Sure, as a sports instructor he'd dealt with his share of difficult people. But not the self-centered kinds like these.

"Trisha isn't feeling well this morning," Gavin said. "Headache."

Which considering whom she was married to wasn't a surprise.

Tobias clicked his teeth. "Well, it's no wonder. Studying for a university degree can be very stressful on a young woman, not to mention quite expensive."

Pregnant, a lawyer, studying for a university degree and married to Gavin? Yeah, that would be more than enough for anyone. Benjamin tuned the conversation out, slid a large knife from the cutting board and sliced the bread in quick, even strokes.

"What university do you attend, young man?" Tobias hovered over Benjamin's shoulder. He couldn't help but notice the older man had shown up for breakfast in a tweed jacket, bow tie and fedora.

"I never went to university." Benjamin dipped the slices of bread in the eggs and laid them in the skillet. "I was a lifeguard and camp counselor as a teenager, then went straight into working for a sports store after high school, while taking some business courses by correspondence." He flipped the bread. It was golden brown. "Opened my own business when I was twenty-three."

Tobias sighed pityingly. He laid one hand on Benjamin's shoulder and leaned in as if delivering terminally bad news. "Well, not everyone has what it takes to handle academia."

"Guess not," Benjamin said. He dropped the piece of French toast onto a plate, just barely managing to keep from swatting the pompous older man with the spatula. "I mean, getting offered a full scholarship to both McGill and the University of British Columbia because of my straight A average was sweet. But my sister was dealing with some personal stuff and I didn't want to leave her. Now, if you want to have a seat at the dining-room table, I'll be out with a pot of coffee in a second." Benjamin pushed the jug of maple syrup into older man's hands and handed the younger one a fistful of cutlery. Then he turned back to the stove.

"Benji's unflappable!" his big sister, Meg, liked to

say, as if being steady was some magical power he possessed, instead of a side effect of growing up with an anxious sister, a distant father with a heart condition and a hysterical mother. Someone had needed to bring some calm into that house. Besides, why get all flapped up about something as minor as somebody else's bad attitude? There were already too many things in life you couldn't control and only a few that actually mattered.

Once breakfast was made and served, Gavin took some up to Trisha in her room, and then sat with Tobias who cheerfully showed off what looked like a replica World War I hand grenade that the author wore on a loop on his belt. It was almost ten by the time Benjamin was alone again. He hadn't seen Piper yet. But last summer it had been pretty clear she wasn't really much of a morning person.

His cell phone rang. It was his sister, Meg. Also, he'd apparently missed a call from the mechanic. "Hello?"

"Benji! How are you? I got your message about last night. Where are you?" His sister spoke so quickly her voice was almost breathless.

The familiar gnawing of guilt filled his gut immediately. Meg might be four years older than him. But she was also a tiny slip of a thing who'd been fighting an anxiety disorder for years. She was on the verge of getting married and he was still a seven-hour's drive away.

"I'm so sorry, sis. I'm still at The Downs." He ran his hands down his jeans. "Just finished making the guests French toast and coffee. You'd be impressed. I used a mortar and pestle and everything. Even added some cinnamon. Or nutmeg. Not sure which. Piper doesn't exactly label her spices."

There was a slight pause on the other end of the phone. "Where's Piper?"

"I don't know. Thought I'd let her sleep in. Haven't seen Harry yet and the two of them are sharing a room." He ran his hand over the back of his neck. "But I promise, I'll do everything in my power to be at the rehearsal tonight."

"Whatever you do, don't leave too late. There's a wickedly heavy snowstorm scheduled to come in later tonight that could cause all types of chaos on the roads. They're already pretty terrible as it is. Black ice, strong winds, accidents everywhere. If anything goes wrong, call me. There's still something major we need to talk about. It's kind of important, but I'd rather do it in person and it can wait for tonight."

"Don't worry. My truck has four-wheel drive and really great snow tires. There's nothing better I could be driving. I'll take it really slow and drive safely, I promise."

After another long pause on the other end of the line he was sure something was wrong. He and his sister had shared a house and each other's lives ever since their parents had moved to Florida years ago. He could read trouble in her silences at a dozen paces. *Please, Lord, protect her from having another panic attack. Not over this. Not because of me.* "Look, sis. I know you're worried, but it's going to be okay. You've got a great man by your side and people who love you—"

A laugh echoed down the line. Gentle. Genuine.

"No, no, bro, I'm fine! I'm better than fine. I'm really excited about getting married tomorrow. *You* are the one I'm worried for right now."

"Me?" Benjamin blinked. "What? Why? I'm just fine…"

"Are you sure? You're standing in Piper's kitchen, making breakfast—"

"Because this is a bed-and-breakfast. I'm just being a good friend."

Last summer his sister had totally misread his friendship with Piper. He could still picture the way Meg had looked up at him over her coffee mug and said, "You really like Piper. I do, too. Just be careful there, okay? Don't hand your heart away to someone here if you're planning on heading overseas. I'd hate to see either of you get hurt." He'd already caused more than enough hurt to the people he loved, enough to last a lifetime. That very night when he and Piper had gone out to dinner he'd explained to her, in no uncertain terms, that he'd decided he'd never have the kind of close relationship with anyone where they'd be relying on him for their security or happiness, including a wife or family of his own.

Still, when he'd first told Meg that he'd asked Piper to give his dog a good home, he'd gotten a whole new warning for his troubles.

Looked as if he was in for round three.

"You got a call this morning from your friend in Brighton," Meg added. "He's flying out from England to Australia on the twenty-sixth to join your sailing team. Also, the final payment went through on the boat—"

"Wonderful. Honestly, Meg, I can't wait to hop on that plane Christmas night. Stop worrying, okay? I've been waiting and saving all my life for this. I'm not about to let the dream go now. Not for anything—"

"But, Benjamin, are you sure?"

He opened his mouth to argue. Then shut it again. His sister was so concerned she'd actually called him Benjamin—not Benji, bro, or any number of the other things she called him from time to time. He gripped the counter with both hands. "I don't get it, sis. Why are you being like this? You've never once given me grief about a woman before."

"I've never seen you look at anyone or talk about anyone the way you do with Piper. This boat, this adventure, is all you've ever wanted. You put your dream on hold for me for years, didn't you? And now, I don't know what to think. I'd hate to see you give up your boat. But at the same time, I know someone like Piper doesn't come along that often in a lifetime, and if being with her at that bed-and-breakfast had even a chance of making you happy—"

"Meg, listen to me." He was so frustrated with her for inventing a concern like this, especially when she already had more than enough to worry about. Sure, he was attracted to Piper as a person, as a friend. And sure, she was more than a little easy on the eyes. But just because he recognized and admired who she was didn't mean it was a romantic attraction. Certainly nothing so deep that it would threaten the course of either of their lives. "I promise you, there is no way I see this bed-and-breakfast playing any kind of role in my future. Yes, I spent years living on the island, because I loved you and you needed me. But you're my *sister*. Plus, living there allowed me to build an amazing, successful sports business on the biggest freshwater island in the world. I know where I'm going. No pair of pretty dark eyes is ever going to make me give up a dream I really care about to hang out in a stodgy, boring old bed-and-breakfast in a tiny little town, making miserable people eggs and coffee. Being trapped here does not and will not make me happy. I'd rather move back into your basement."

There was a crash behind him. He turned.

Piper stood in the doorway.

Bright sun cascaded down her wet hair and illuminated her cheekbones. Deep eyes fringed with long dark lashes met his. Shivers ran down his arms, so powerfully that his heart leaped a beat. *Okay, so maybe there is a little bit of an attraction.*

And judging by the hurt in her eyes and the broken dishes scattered by her feet, she'd heard every thoughtless word he'd just said.

Chapter Seven

$\sim$

Benjamin spun toward her. One hand clutched a phone to his ear and the other hand waved through the air as if trying to erase the words that had just flown out of his mouth. But it was too late. She'd heard them. What's more, she believed them.

There was no way a man like Benjamin was ever going to be happy in a place like The Downs. It would be completely contrary to the adventurous, daring man that she knew. *Don't worry. I was never going to ask you to trade in your dream for me.* But she could've done without hearing him call her home a stodgy, boring old place for miserable people.

His eyes met hers for a second with a look so pained it almost bordered on panic. Then he turned back to his phone. "Meg, I've got to go. I'll give you a call once I get my truck. You, too. Bye."

She bent down and started picking up pieces of the broken dishes.

He bent down, too. "I'm sorry about that. I don't

know how much you just heard. But I think I phrased something really badly. I definitely didn't mean to imply—"

"Don't worry about it." She stood quickly and dropped the pieces into the garbage. "I'm sorry. I didn't mean to eavesdrop."

Benjamin stood slowly and walked over to the stove. She grabbed some paper towels and wiped the floor where the dishes had landed.

"That was just my sister. She wanted to make sure I was still planning on being there for the rehearsal tonight. And apparently I missed a call from the garage."

"You should probably call them." She walked past him to the sink. "Thank you for making breakfast. That was very thoughtful of you."

"Well, yeah. Anything I can do to make things easier for you while I'm here."

"I know you're in a hurry to go." She ran both hands through her hair. It was still damp from the shower. "Just give me a few moments to make some phone calls. Then I'm going to walk into town to visit my uncle and aunt. If you don't mind waiting, I'll show you how to get to the garage."

"Great. I should really go get changed and pack." He started toward the living room, then paused. "Oh, and if you're going to have coffee from the saucepan skim it off the top. The grounds will have settled at the bottom. And I left a couple of slices of French toast in the oven."

"Thanks." She grabbed a bag of dog food from the pantry, then slipped past him to pour some in the bowl by the back door. It was amazing how much two people could move around such a tiny space without touching or even making eye contact.

She turned back. Benjamin was leaning in the kitchen doorway, one arm up against the lintel. His gaze seemed to sweep over her like an X-ray. "Is everything okay, Piper?"

Please, don't make me have this conversation.

She forced a smile across her lips and nodded. "Just give me a few minutes, and then we'll go get your truck."

While he went to pack his bag she pulled The Downs credit card out of her wallet and picked up the phone to book luxury hotel suites for her guests.

Forty minutes later, Piper sat on the front steps of The Downs. She looked down the road where Benjamin had gone to give Harry one final walk. Ice seemed to coat the whole world. A thin layer enveloped every twig, pine needle and stone like glass. Fresh snow danced from the sky. The great irony of winter was that the world kept getting more beautiful the more dangerous it became.

She twisted her hair behind her head and tied it into a knot. Finding new accommodations for her guests had been easier than expected. A high-priced spa near Niagara, with an indoor pool and gourmet buffet, had a couple of one-bedroom suites available on short notice at a steep markup. But considering the amount of eye rolling, complaining and protest it took to get the irritating lawyer, his withdrawn wife and the middle-aged author to take the very generous trade and leave, it almost made the money she'd be losing worth it just to have some peace.

Almost.

Between paying out refunds and booking the last-minute rooms at a higher cost, The Downs restoration fund had just lost over a thousand dollars.

Harry's wet, furry body bounded around the corner, followed by Benjamin at less than half the speed. "Careful. It's insanely slippery. I've already fallen down twice. They're all gone?"

"Yeah." She stood. "Wasn't easy. Gavin was still threatening to throw the full weight of their law firm behind suing us as they drove away. If he makes good on his threat there's no telling the damage he could do."

"I don't think you have to worry about that." Benjamin shook his head. "I'm pretty sure Gavin won't sue. In fact, I'm pretty sure I caught him out on a lie this morning. I didn't really put two and two together at first. But you know how he said that he and Trisha own a law firm? Well, he also told me that he had to sit through that horrid documentary about my accident, every winter in school, starting since grade seven. Well, I can tell you for a fact that documentary came out when I was eighteen. Which means he's only about twenty-five. He may very well have already passed the bar, but that's a bit young to have already built your own successful law firm."

But not too young to be Alpha though, she realized. But was Alpha brazen enough to book a room in the very hotel he was getting Blondie to break into?

"In fact, the more I think about it the less I think his

bluster is anything you need to worry about," Benjamin added. "The lawsuit would be terrible publicity for a small firm. Also, for what it's worth, Tobias seemed to think that Trisha was still in university. But he thought both you and I were university students, too."

"Although, I'm not sure Tobias listens very well." She walked over to Harry and ran her hand through his fur. "It's like he's not all there. I could never tell if he was eccentric, self-absorbed or slightly off his rocker. At least it's one less thing I'll have to worry about now."

"Are you sure?" The tone of Benjamin's voice was so serious that her feet paused on the ice.

"Of course." Of all the heavy things weighing on her mind right now, the ramblings of an overweight, middle-aged author didn't even budge the needle. "Tobias should be settling into a beautiful suite in a rather expensive spa right now surrounded by all sorts of people happy to hear his rambling stories."

"Not him—Gavin." Concern filled the depths of his eyes. "As far as lies go, it's an odd one for Gavin to tell. I don't like coincidences and here you have a young man telling stories and throwing his weight around at the exact same time you've got people breaking in and threatening you. We still don't know what Kodiak and Blondie were even after. And might I add Gavin isn't too young to either be Alpha or to be mixed up in this some other way."

"You're right." What else could she say, exactly? "But Gavin doesn't have the right build to be either Kodiak or Blondie."

"Well, I don't like uncertainty." Benjamin's voice

sounded so deep in this throat it was nearly a growl. "There's something seriously wrong going on here. We don't know exactly what, let alone why and you're altogether too casual about it. There has to be something we can do."

She shook her head and crossed her arms. Did he miss the fact she'd just shut down the bed-and-breakfast, kicked out her guests and lost a huge chunk of money? What did he expect her to do? Start crying, fall into his arms and stay curled up there until the danger disappeared? "There are things that I can do, and I am doing them. You have a truck to pick up and a wedding rehearsal to get to."

But now he'd picked up such a verbal steam it was as if he hadn't heard her. "You told me that your uncle saw Charlotte kissing someone in the woods the night before she robbed you. What did he say he looked like again?"

Why was he pushing this? She appreciated the effort, but this wasn't the kind of problem that could be solved in five minutes before he took off.

"Tall, broad shoulders, young." She opened the door and whistled for Harry to come inside. The dog raced in. "But while Gavin is definitely young and tall, I wouldn't consider him to have broad shoulders."

"Clothes can do a lot to disguise someone's build—"

A horn honked, cutting off his words. She looked up to see a small red hatchback inch off the road and down into her driveway. A dark-haired man with a dazzling smile waved one hand out the window. She recognized him immediately. The back of the car was so overflowing with boxes and bags it looked as if it was starting its own garage sale.

"Dominic!" She skidded down the driveway toward him. "What are you doing here? And what's going on in the back of your car?"

"Hey, Pips!" Dominic unfolded his six-foot frame from the driver's seat. "My mom packed up my stuff when I was working out west. These are the remains of my misspent youth. It was taking up too much space at my sister's, so I moved it out to the car." He paused only for a second before he went on. "Just saw your aunt when I was visiting my grandma. She told me about the problems you were having. Suggested I swing by and see if you needed a hand."

"Oh, she did, did she?" Why was she not surprised?

"Please, don't send me away, Pips." He slapped a gloved hand over his heart. "It's a nonstop noise machine over at my sister's. She has five little kids under the age of seven. Five! I love them more than life itself, but I'm not cut out for that much noise and chaos. I haven't had five minutes of quiet to myself to study, and the police exam is in three weeks."

She glanced back at the empty house. Yeah, having a big, strong man sitting in her living room deterring trespassers while she was visiting her uncle and aunt probably wasn't the worst idea. She reached into her pockets and handed him the keys. "Go ahead. There's a dog in there somewhere, too. His name is Harry."

Benjamin frowned slightly.

She took a step back. "Oh, I'm sorry, I should do introductions. Dominic Bravo meet Benjamin Duff."

Benjamin reached for Dominic's hand and shook it firmly. His eyes darted down to their hands for barely a second. "Nice to meet you."

"No way!" Dominic's smile grew wider. "Piper, you're friends with Benji Duff? *The* Benji Duff, the extreme sports guy from Manitoulin Island?"

"The one and only."

"Dude!" Dominic clasped Benjamin's arm firmly and slapped him on the back. "I heard you speak last year. Went and downloaded one of your talks after that. Even gave Pip's Uncle Des a copy. You were incredible!" Dominic crossed his arms and looked at Piper. "This guy is the absolute best. Made me realize I had to quit mucking about and get serious about my life. Please tell me you're getting him to stick around and give a talk tomorrow night at your Christmas Eve shindig. I'll call around to all the neighboring youth groups. You will totally pack the place."

Pack the place? She was just barely hanging on to the hope she'd still be able to pull off a halfway decent carol night without worrying about pulling in extra mouths to feed.

"No, thank you." Benjamin held up a hand. "That's really kind, but I'm actually about to hit the road."

"Merry Christmas, then." Dominic gave him one more thump on the shoulder. "Give me a shout next time you're down this way."

"Won't be for a while, I'm afraid. I sold my business. Bought myself a boat. Real beauty. I'm picking it up in Australia the day after Christmas. Going to sail around the world for charity and then start up a charter business."

"Of course you are." Dominic chuckled. "Wow. Stuff like that is why *you* are the man."

The image of Benjamin's sundrenched boat floated in the back of Piper's mind as they slid down the sidewalk into town. Had there been that much joy in his eyes this summer when he'd first told her of his dreams to buy a boat? Or had she been too caught up in her own foolish fantasy of somehow shoehorning this big, strong, adventurous man into her tiny little life?

"How well do you know Dominic?" Benjamin asked. "I mean, you're sure he's a good guy? You can vouch for him?"

Was that why Benjamin was looking down during their handshake? He was trying to check Dominic's wrists for a bear tattoo?

"Yes, I'm sure Dominic is a good guy!" Her eyes rolled to the thick clouds now filling the sky above. "He's the guy who found me when—"

Her words froze in her·mouth as Benjamin's eyebrow rose. "He found you when?"

When I was hit over the head and locked in the kindling box. Only I never told you about that.

"Listen to me," she said. "I've known Dominic since we were kids. We went to the same church. He was a year behind me in school. Yeah, he was always a bit awkward and got into a few scrapes as a kid. But he has a good heart. He'd do anything for his family. Anything."

"All right, then."

Did that mean he believed her? Or just that he was done arguing about it?

Well, there was nothing to stop Benjamin from contacting the police and telling them all his suspicions about Dominic, Gavin or anybody. In fact, she wouldn't be surprised if he did.

"Dominic treated you like some kind of celebrity," she said. "Do you get that a lot?"

He shrugged. "Sometimes. People tend to think they know me. Either because of the talks I've done or that awful documentary on winter safety that schools keep showing. Most people are curious more than anything. But there've been plenty, like Gavin this morning, who've been downright rude and practically mocked me about it."

They walked slowly. The sidewalk was unevenly shoveled and only a few of the stores had sanded. Her eyes ran over the old familiar buildings of her childhood. The small independent grocery store had been bought out by a chain franchise a few years ago. The gift-and-flower shop seemed to change ownership once a year or so. But most of the street was the same as it had been since she was younger. She'd been desperate to escape The Downs as a teenager thinking adventures and excitement lay somewhere else.

Was that why she was so bothered by Benjamin's dreams to travel the world and live a carefree life?

A man with shaggy blond hair was slouched in front of the town's one bar puffing on a cigarette. A dirty red tuque was pulled down low on his scarred face. She nodded at him as they passed. He didn't look up so they kept walking. This dingy bar was the closest thing the town had to danger or excitement. When she'd realized Charlotte had been sneaking out, it's where Piper thought she'd been going.

Benjamin waited until they'd passed the bar then started talking again.

"Three years ago, a friend of mine was starting this white-water rafting business. I wanted to come in as an investor. I was really excited about it." He ran one hand across his head and adjusted his tuque. "But the rest of the team took a vote and decided they didn't want me. They were afraid it might lead to bad publicity and unwanted attention. Thought it might tarnish what they were trying to do."

"You can't be serious!" An icy breath caught in her throat. "You're such an incredible person! You're so good at what you do!"

He stopped walking and looked at her square on. The smile faded from his face. "Thank you. But think of it from their perspective. Imagine you're running a small, financially strapped business, and there's someone on your staff who's capable of bringing all sorts of unwanted drama and chaos through your door at any moment. Stupid teenagers are going to crank call you every single winter because that old documentary's running again. People are going to walk in and demand a selfie with the guy, or tell you to fire him because he's an example of everything that's wrong with the world. Every time helmet laws, snowmobile licenses, or tragic winter accidents are in the news—or the calendar rolls around to the middle of February—you might wake up to see a news camera outside."

Was he still talking about his friend's business? Or hers?

No. As much as part of her would be willing to take all that on if it meant being near Benjamin, she also couldn't imagine bringing that much chaos into The Downs. Her uncle and aunt deserved far better than that.

His blue eyes focused on hers. "See, I chose to see my accident as a mantle. I accepted it and did my best to turn it into something awesome. But that doesn't mean it's easy or that I'd wish it on anyone. With my sister getting married tomorrow, it's time to start a new chapter in my life. I'm almost thirty-one, and I can't remember the last time I went two weeks without having to talk to someone somewhere about that day. I'm really looking forward to being where I can be anonymous, far enough away from Ontario that people don't know that story." He emitted a wry chuckle. "Also, I really, really don't like snow."

She looked past him. They were steps away from the mechanic's garage.

Guess this was where they said goodbye.

"Travel safe, Benjamin." She reached out to hug him. But he took her shoulders and gently held her out at arm's length.

"Wait. There's something else I need to say." His eyes were still fixed on her face, with such a raw unrelenting gaze that it made her heart tighten in her chest. "I want you to be happy, Piper."

"I am happy."

"No, I don't think you are. I respect that you want to renovate The Downs for your uncle and aunt—although you still haven't told me the details of their health problems, so I don't quite understand why you're as stressed-out about that as you are. But I know a thing or two about existing versus living. The Piper I met this summer on the island was so very *alive*. You were so excited you practically sparkled. Now that light is gone."

"You're right. You don't know the whole situation with my uncle and aunt." She dug her heels into the slippery snow. "But anybody can be happy swimming and hiking or floating off into the sunset. Now I'm at work."

"But your whole life is your work. Christmas Eve is work. Your home is your work—"

"Because I'm helping my uncle and aunt keep their home and only source of income!" She heard her voice rise, despite the cold air rushing into her lungs. "What else am I supposed to do? Let them lose their only source of income while I travel the world? They have no retirement savings. Their only asset is The Downs and it's mortgaged. They took me in when my dad left and my mom had one foot out the door. I'm not going to abandon them now."

Benjamin ran his hand through his hair. "Look, I'm sorry, I'm saying this all wrong and I didn't want to say goodbye this way. I just think you should try to find a compromise between the life you want and the one you're currently trapped in."

Trapped. There that word was again. Life here, with her at The Downs, was just some trap to escape. Benjamin's words to his sister flickered in the back of her mind. *"Being trapped here does not and will not make me happy."*

The blond smoker pushed off the wall and started sauntering their way. She didn't recognize him, but she couldn't know everyone, even in a town this size. She looked back at Benjamin. This wasn't the kind of conversation she wanted to have on a public street in front of an audience.

Better this conversation ended right now, before either of them said anything they regretted.

"Thanks for caring so much about my happiness. Thank you for everything." She gave Benjamin a quick hug and her lips brushed his cheek. "Safe voyage and merry Christmas."

Then she slipped into the alleyway beside the mechanic shop and hurried along the back route to Silver Halls before Benjamin could follow.

Piper disappeared around the corner leaving the scent of maple and cinnamon in her wake.

Was that goodbye?

He stared at the empty patch of snowy air where the tenacious brunette had been standing just moments ago. All the while he'd been packing his bag and walking Harry, he'd been practicing this great goodbye speech in his head. Probably for the best he never got to give it. If he was honest, he'd have probably just rambled on far too much about what a wonderful person he thought she was.

He pushed open the door to the mechanic's shop.

A tall, smiling young man in grease-stained overalls looked up at him from behind the counter.

The smoking blond man brushed past him, so close their shoulders almost bumped. He glanced back to see the man disappear into the alley behind Piper.

Benjamin froze in the doorway, with one foot on either side of the threshold and his hand still on the knob. Every warning signal in the back of his skull was clanging.

Was that man following Piper?

"Mr. Duff." The mechanic wiped his hands on a cloth. "Your truck is all ready to go."

"Thank you. That's awesome. I'll be with you in just one moment." He stepped back outside onto the street and let the door close behind him. He hiked his hockey bag up onto his shoulder and started toward the alley.

Maybe he was overreacting. After all, lots of people probably used this alley as a shortcut. But if there was even a chance that man was trailing Piper...

I can't risk it.

He stepped into the narrow alley.

It was deserted.

Now what? Benjamin started down the empty alley feeling increasingly foolish with every step. He passed a closed metal door that he presumed led to the back of the mechanic's shop. A towering pile of garbage bags loomed out of a Dumpster ahead on his right. The air smelled like grease. Slush and motor oil mingled together under his boots. Up ahead he noticed boxy letters spelled out what looked like Silver Halls on a building in the distance—Piper's destination. He'd just walk to the end of the alley, take a quick look around to make sure everything was okay, and then he'd go back and get his truck.

He reached the Dumpster. A sucker punch hit his jaw without warning. Then the man he'd been following leaped out from behind the trash, hands cocked to fight.

Benjamin stumbled and for an unsettling moment thought he was about to fall backward. But then he braced his feet and his grip held sure.

"Hey, man." Benjamin held his hands up and started into the man's ugly, scarred face. "I don't know what your problem is, but I don't want to fight."

Not because he didn't think he'd win. But because he really didn't like hurting people. Even sneering and snarling brutes who looked ready to pound him into the pavement.

"Nice try, but I ain't playing." The blond man pushed his sleeves up over his elbows, exposing muscular, tattoo-covered arms.

Including the tattoo of a brown bear and the word *Kodiak*.

Benjamin raised his fists to fight. He wasn't playing either. Not anymore.

A knife flashed in Kodiak's hand. Benjamin swung his bag out in front of him, catching the blow in the canvas. The bag ripped. Clothes and papers spilled out onto the ground.

Kodiak lunged at Benjamin.

Benjamin leaped sideways, but the knife tip came within an inch of piercing his stomach. His attacker stabbed again. This time Benjamin knocked the knife from Kodiak's hand and shoved him into the wall. His forearm pressed into the man's neck, pinning him firmly. "What do you want? Why are you following Piper?"

"Hey, dude!" A voice floated down from the end of the alleyway. "I think that guy's beating up that other guy!"

Benjamin's head turned. Two teenagers stood at the end of the alley, their forms almost indistinguishable in puffy jackets and floppy tuques. Both clutched cell phones.

"Call the police," Benjamin shouted. "Now."

"Yeah!" Kodiak shouted. "He's got a knife. He's threatening to murder me. You got that? You tell the police. I was minding my own business and he attacked me."

Benjamin gritted his teeth and fought the urge to knock the lying thug's head against the wall. Neither boy was dialing. If anything, it looked as if they were either recording video or taking pictures. He winced to think of how this all must look from their perspective. They wouldn't see the man who cared for Piper battling the man who'd terrorized her. All they'd see were two large men, equally matched in size and strength, fighting in an alley—with one of them pinning the other up against the wall.

He could almost see the cover of the newspaper

tabloid now: Notorious Snowmobile Accident Survivor Benji Duff Arrested in Niagara Region for Violent Street Fight. Pictures on Page Three.

Hardly the headline he wanted Meg waking up to on her wedding day.

Benjamin loosened his grip on his throat. "Look, I don't want to hurt you. But I'm not going to let you get away with stalking and threatening Piper."

"I surrender. Okay?" Kodiak's hands inched up the wall. His fists were clenched. "Let's go to the police station together and let them sort it out. I'll tell them you followed me into this alley and I was only acting in self-defense."

They'd see how well that held up once Piper identified him as the man who tried to strangle her outside the barn.

"Okay." If Kodiak was willing to take this to the police station, even under duress, Benjamin didn't need to stand there insisting they fistfight. He stepped back, his foot nearly landing on the remains of his sliced hockey bag now lying on the grease-soaked ground. "We're going to walk nice and slow to the police station, and let them sort it out, all right?"

"Sure thing." Kodiak smirked. His fingers uncurled and the bright blue flame of a cigarette lighter flickered to life in his palm.

Benjamin lunged for the man's hand but it was too late.

Kodiak tossed the lighter down into the remains of Benjamin's oil-soaked belongings.

His bag caught fire.

Chapter Eight

Benjamin threw himself onto his belongings, pounding out the flames with his gloved hands before they could spread.

"Tell Piper I'll be seeing her." Kodiak spat a curse and sprinted back down the alley, knocking the two teenage gawkers aside like bowling pins.

Benjamin leaped to his feet and ran down the end of the alley, but Kodiak was already gone. So was the teenaged audience. Guess they'd seen no point in sticking around once the show was over. A large, rusty truck peeled out of the bar parking lot so quickly it fishtailed. A growl of frustration rumbled in the back of Benjamin's throat. At least Kodiak seemed to have gone in the opposite way from Piper this time.

Benjamin walked back down the alley, sat back on his heels in the slush and shoveled his belongings back into his bag as quickly as he could. A couple of his shirts were now nothing but rags and ashes. His favorite sweatshirt had a burn hole in it the size of his fist. But, thankfully his passport, traveling money and airline ticket had been spared.

He could buy a new bag on his way back to the island. He could grab a few new T-shirts and a sweatshirt anywhere. But replacing the passport would have taken days. Maybe even weeks. His flight was not only nonrefundable, but he'd saved a bundle on airfare by flying on December 25. He'd have missed the start of the charity sailing race. Not to mention, every penny he'd made from selling his business was wrapped up in his boat or already converted into the starter money he was counting on to start his new charter-boat business.

Well, maybe it was a good thing he was leaving the country. That way God would find someone better to help protect Piper.

An ugly gash now ran along the length of his bag. He pulled a roll of duct tape from his bag, yanked off a strip and taped it shut.

His cell phone started ringing. It was Meg.

"Hello?"

"Hey, bro!" Her voice was so cheerful and hopeful he almost groaned. "Got your message about picking up the truck. How does it look?"

He glanced back at the brick wall behind him.

"I've reached the garage, but I haven't picked up the truck yet. Hang on." He yanked off two more strips of duct tape and made sure the hole was well patched. Then he grabbed the handles and stood up again. Slush and oil froze to his soaked jeans. "It's going to be a few more minutes before I can leave town. But I'll send you my GPS coordinates and route as soon as I hit the road."

There was a long pause. Then Meg said, "What happened?"

He trudged back down the alley toward the mechanic. "Don't worry about it. Please, I'll be on my way soon."

"Benji. Don't do this."

He sighed and leaned against the wall. "I saw the man who attacked Piper following her down an alley." He explained what happened. "I eased up because I'm a fool, and he got away."

Meg sighed. "You eased up on him because you're a good guy."

Yeah, but that still left Piper in serious danger.

And he didn't feel like much more than a waste of space right this second.

"Are you hurt?" she asked. "How's Piper?"

"Piper wasn't here. She doesn't know what happened. I'm fine. But my bag's seen better days." He glanced at the clock on his phone. It was almost twelve. "Obviously I have to talk to the police before I leave. The one piece of good news is that I saw his face, so I can give the cops a pretty solid description and hopefully they can catch the guy."

Although the fact the Kodiak was daring enough to attack him in broad daylight wasn't too comforting.

Another pause on the other end of the phone. "Are you going to go talk to Piper?"

"And tell her what, Meg? That I had the guy who attacked her in the palm of my hands and I let him go?"

"You need to tell her."

"I know." He ran his hand over the back of his neck, barely managing to stop himself when he remembered the muck he'd been kneeling in just moments before. "And yes, I know it's better to tell her in person than just call her. But I left things a bit…off with Piper when I said goodbye. I think I said something that hurt her feelings, and she kind of took off before I could really apologize properly. It's probably nothing. It just felt like a stormy goodbye."

And the news that he'd now let Kodiak escape wasn't going to help.

"What did you say to her?"

"I told her I wanted her to be happy, but it came out like I was insulting her decision to take care of her uncle and aunt." He blew out a hard breath and kept walking toward the police station. Picking up his truck would have to wait. "She's just so unhappy, Meg. Reminds me of how you used to be before Jack. She processes it very differently from you and tries to hide it. I don't think she'd admit it, even to herself."

"Well, there have been a couple of break-ins. Last night she was attacked."

"I know. But it's more than that. Last summer she was so happy, like there was all this light inside her. Now it's like she's killing herself to make other people happy. I was only trying to encourage her not to give up on her dreams, but somehow I messed the whole thing up."

Probably because she thought he wasn't listening and was just telling her she was wrong.

"So, go fix it."

He nearly laughed. Meg's advice sounded exactly like the kind of thing he'd said more times than he could count. *So, you messed up? Go fix it.*

Turned out the words felt a whole lot different on the receiving end.

Especially when he still had to file a police report, pick up his truck, talk things out with Piper and make it to his sister's wedding rehearsal. "I can't fix things with Piper now. The rehearsal's tonight and I'm seven hours away."

"Sure you can." Despite the rush and stress the bride must be feeling, he could still hear a smile in his sister's voice. "I'll move the rehearsal to nine or ten if we need to. Not like I'm going to be able to sleep tonight, anyway. Everything today got pushed back, anyway. Jack's best man, Luke, was delayed getting here from Muskoka because of the bad weather. So, that gives you a little more time. Not much. But enough that after you file a police report you can go find Piper, fill her in on what happened with Kodiak, say you're sorry for the misunderstanding earlier and try your hand at a better goodbye."

"I'm not sure I know how."

"You'll think of something." Warmth filled his sister's voice. "I have faith in you. Just make sure you make it back to the island tonight. There's still something very important I need to talk with you about at the wedding rehearsal."

His footsteps reached the police station. He glanced back at the clock. As long as he was on the road by two o'clock, he'd be okay. That gave him just two more hours. He set the alarm on his phone for a quarter to two, just to give him a small window to grab coffee before getting on the road. "Okay. Thanks. I'll be there, I promise. Love you."

"You, too. Now go file your report and say whatever needs saying to Piper."

Whatever needed saying. Okay, but what was that? He still meant every word he'd said to Piper, despite the fact he'd somehow mangled them and said them in a way that upset her.

Now he was skating in overtime, had just let the opponent deke a shot past him and still didn't know how to make things right.

The retirement home was a large beige rectangular building with featureless square windows. Ornate letters on the door read Silver Halls but didn't do anything to change the fact that the structure looked like a cardboard box. He walked through the front door and crossed through a lobby with blue-tiled floors. Bits of silver tinsel draped limply over fake plants. A few velvet bows were clipped haphazardly onto the plastic leaves.

A young woman who didn't look much more than eighteen sat at the front desk. She didn't move, and barely even glanced his way when he walked in.

He raised a hand. "Hi. I'm looking for my friend Piper Lawrence. She's here visiting her uncle and aunt?"

The receptionist shrugged toward the doorway on

the other side of the room and then looked back down at her cell phone, which he took as an invitation to walk in. A pair of open, shuttered doors led to a long, multipurpose room. The carpet was industrial green; the air smelled like disinfectant mixed with peppermint air freshener. He glanced out the nearest window and saw the wall of the apartment building next door.

While The Downs wasn't exactly his cup of tea, either, he knew which place he'd choose to live out his last days.

Then he saw the couple. They were sitting together with their backs to him, on a settee on the far side of the room. The man was tall and bald, with a soft green holiday sweater and one arm around the woman curled up next to him. Her long salt-and-pepper hair fell lush against his shoulder. A plain gold wedding band shone on his hand. She leaned toward him and said something Benjamin couldn't hear. He turned toward her, with a look both so tender and caring, it suddenly reminded Benjamin of the couple, half their age, whose wedding he was going to witness tomorrow. The woman's eyes twinkled. Her husband brushed a quick kiss across her lips.

Benjamin turned away, feeling like an intruder on their private moment. An unexpected ache clenched his heart. The couple must be older than his own parents, by a few years, at least. Yet, he'd never seen his father look at his mother with that kind of tender, loving respect. Nor his mother look at his father with such trust. True, they'd kept their marriage going all these years, which was something, and he'd barely seen them since they'd retired and moved to Florida.

He thought of Meg and Jack. There was something so raw, vibrant and real about the love he'd watched grow between them in the past year and a half. He hoped they'd never lose that.

"Benjamin!" Piper's voice broke into his thoughts. "Come meet my aunt and uncle." A smile of surprise lit her eyes as she hurried across the floor.

"Hi!" Her hand brushed along his side in a gesture that was half like a hug and half like pulling him toward her.

"Hi." His cheeks felt warm.

"What are you doing here?" Her fingers curled lightly into the fabric of his coat. "What happened with your truck? Is everything okay?"

How did he put this?

"Well, the good news is that the police think they might have a lead on Kodiak. I'll fill you in on the rest after I meet your uncle and aunt. I've got almost an hour and a half before I need to leave."

The happiness glittered in her eyes. "Well, whatever it is, I'm glad you came to talk it out with me in person. I'll do my best to keep this brief." Her hand brushed over his. She steered him toward the couple on the settee. "Uncle Des, Aunt Cass, I'd like you to meet my friend Benjamin Duff. Benjamin, meet my uncle and aunt, Desmond and Cassandra Lawrence."

It seemed fitting that Piper had their last name, as opposed to the surname of the father who had abandoned her.

Benjamin smiled. "It's very nice to meet you."

Des didn't stand. But his grip was firm and his eyes were clear. "Nice to meet you."

It was then that Benjamin noticed the walker tucked against the wall. Just how bad were Piper's aunt's health problems?

"Please, sit." Cass took his outstretched hand in both of hers. Her hands were delicate, soft. Like her husband, Piper's aunt still had a strong British accent. "Piper and I were just talking decorations."

Benjamin found himself pulled down onto the settee. Cass slid a large photo album onto his lap. Piper held up her fingers and mouthed, *Ten minutes. Okay?*

He nodded. He looked down at the pages. They were photos of a small English village. A beautiful ridge of mountains lay on one side, the rocky shore and gray expanse of the waters of the English Channel lay on the other. Beautiful shops and town houses wound through the narrow streets, wreathed in pine branches, large wide bows and sprigs of real holly. There was just the faintest dusting of snow on the ground.

"Have you ever been to the south of England, son?" Des asked.

Benjamin nodded. "Yes, sir. I've taken part in a couple of sailing tournaments out of a wonderful extreme sports resort and marina run by a friend just outside Brighton and traveled the coast in both directions. It's a wonderful place."

"It is." Cass's eyes shone as he turned the page.

Benjamin sat for a moment and just listened, turning the pages as instructed, and listening as the older woman pointed out the buildings and streets of her childhood. Piper sat on the footstool beside him and leaned back against his legs. "My aunt and I often look to her Christmases back home as inspiration for Christmas Eve at The Downs."

"Oh, we had beautiful Christmases there." Cass smiled softly. "We didn't get the piles of snow you do here. Just enough to make the world feel special. Our church would do a special dinner for the community. We used to roast chestnuts."

Her eyes misted softly.

Her husband slid his hands over hers. "Cassy didn't know what she was getting into when she married a man who was headed to Canada forty-two years ago."

She smiled softly, and poked her husband in the ribs. "Of course I did."

Des looked down at his wife. "Yes, but the plan always was that we were going to go back."

Her eyes met his. "Plans change."

Benjamin nodded slowly. Yeah, sometimes they did. Remodeling the beloved bed-and-breakfast to make it accessible might be hard, but it still had to be a lot easier than packing up their lives and moving back overseas at their age and stage of life.

"Have you managed to chop down a tree yet?" Cass asked Piper.

"No, not yet. Time sort of got away from me today."

Benjamin glanced at the clock. "How about I go help you chop down a tree? I've still got some time before I need to leave. My sister's delayed the wedding rehearsal until nine tonight."

Besides, maybe both conversations they needed to have would be easier if he knew he'd managed to do something productive.

She nodded. "Thank you."

They didn't talk much on the drive to the Christmas-tree farm. Benjamin focused his attention on steering down the unpaved back roads through the woods, while Piper gave directions. It was only when the truck came to a stop and he turned off the engine that she turned to him on the seat.

She looked down. "I'm really glad you got a chance to meet Uncle Des and Aunt Cass. They are the most solid people and I've always been able to count on them. I owe them my life."

Then her eyes met his, and for a moment there was something in their depths that reminded him of the rush he got the first time he set eyes on a new path of wilderness. Boundless. Fathomless. Filled with awaiting adventures.

His rational mind kicked him to say what he needed to say. But something deep in his chest rebelled. He needed to tell her he'd had a run-in with Kodiak and let him escape. But first, maybe they should just relax and enjoy this moment. It might be their last chance to ever be alone.

They got out of the truck and walked through the woods without talking, enjoying the easy, comfortable silence they'd fallen into back on the island. Her dark hair was tucked behind her ear, under her bright blue tuque, falling in dark waves around her shoulders in between the folds of her scarf. Snowflakes fell from the sky and swirled around them on the breeze. A glimmer of a smile curled at the corner of her lips.

This was the Piper he remembered from the summer. This was the Piper who'd made him excited to get up out of bed every morning. This was the Piper he'd—

The train of thought caught him up short and made a freezing cold breath catch in his lungs.

He'd what exactly? Been attracted to? Been drawn to?

Had felt himself falling for until his sister reminded him how foolhardy that would be?

"This'll do. Don't you think?" Piper stopped in front of a fir tree, at least fifteen feet tall, he'd guess, with thick, lush branches.

"It's a beauty all right." He let her pull the ax from his hands. "How were you ever going to cart a tree like this back to the barn by yourself?"

"Oh, I'd have figured something out." She gripped the ax with both hands and swung. The loud, satisfying sound of the ax hitting the wood echoed through the forest. Her grin grew wider.

His eyes rose to the heavens.

Lord, my flight's in two days' time. How can I get on that plane without knowing that Piper is perfectly, totally and utterly safe?

The sound of Piper's ax swings filled the air around them. He closed his eyes as his prayer deepened.

But I want so much more for her than just safety. I want her to be happy. I want her to have everything she's hoping for, everything she's dreamed of, every adventure she's capable of having.

His heart ached knowing he'd never be the one to give all that to her.

He opened his eyes again, and stared at the ice-covered tree branches above him.

"Timber." Piper stood back as the tree fell into the snow. "I've always loved *this* part. I might not be as big a fan as Aunt Cass of decorating or planning meals, but I could be out here chopping trees for hours."

"Well, it suits you."

Piper swirled the ax around in slow motion. "You think I should give up the bed-and-breakfast business to become a lumberjack?"

"No, I think you should come sail the world with my friends and me."

Chapter Nine

Piper's jaw dropped. The ax slipped from her hands and sank into the snow at her feet.

"There are several boats on this sailing trip, not just mine." Benjamin said it so casually, as if he was just inviting her to join him and some buddies for pizza. "One's an all-women crew and I'm sure they'd have an extra bunk if you wanted to join us for even part of the journey. A few months or a few weeks. Whatever. It wouldn't have to be a big thing."

Right, because spending thousands of dollars to fly overseas and go sailing for a while wasn't a "big thing" at all. Not to mention her responsibilities here.

He ran his hand over the back of his neck. "Bring a friend if you'd like and we'll find a space for them, too. I don't even know half of the people I'll be sailing with. It's no biggie."

So now he'd pointed out twice how little the invitation meant to him.

She held his gaze for a long moment. Then she bent

down and picked up the ax. "Thank you for the suggestion, but that's not really something I'd be able to do."

Even if she did have the time and the money—which she didn't—how could she possibly consider flying halfway around the world to spend time with someone who'd take something like that so casually? It had been hard enough to forgive her father for bailing on them when she was little and forgive her mom for chasing after a whole string of temporary relationships with men just as unwilling to stay. When Benjamin had walked into the retirement home like that for a split second she'd almost let herself believe that it meant something.

He reached into his pocket, pulled out a thick ball of twine and carefully helped her bind the branches. "I mean, obviously, you're not going anywhere until those renovations are saved up for and sorted, and your uncle and aunt are able to move back in. But the initial trip will be about a year, and there will hopefully be more group trips after that."

"Thanks. But I won't be going anywhere, even after the renovations are done."

"Oh. All right, then." His shoulders dropped as if she'd just let the air out of his chest.

They dragged the tree back to the truck in silence and drove back to The Downs.

Piper's eyes stayed locked on the window.

"I hope I didn't say the wrong thing or offend you when I suggested you take a holiday from The Downs," Benjamin said when he'd pulled his truck past the bed-and-breakfast driveway, down the hill and up to the barn. "Your uncle and aunt are obviously amazing people. I know how much they mean to you and I really respect your dedication to running The Downs."

She pressed her lips together but didn't trust herself to speak. Was she being oversensitive? After all, it was hardly Benjamin's fault that he didn't realize how serious her aunt's health problems were. She hadn't told him. But she didn't know where to start.

The whole thing felt so huge and unwieldy in her head. It was the kind of conversation that took time. Time they didn't have.

She turned away from him and looked out her window. All around the property the trees were bent low and some had split from the weight of the ice. A fleeting shadow on the barn roof caught her eye. *Please, not raccoons on top of everything else.* There had to be at least six feet of snow on the barn roof and by the looks of things the branches of a huge tree were practically smacking the roof in the wind. She should really cut some before one cracked off and fell through the roof.

Benjamin's eyes glanced at the cell phone mounted in the cradle on the dash. Her eyes followed. Twenty minutes, then he had to go.

Piper undid her seat belt and opened her door. Then she stopped, sat back against her seat and wrapped her arms around herself.

Lord, I need something solid right now. Everything seems to be crumbling around me right now. And my aunt, the strongest, most solid woman I know, is withering away in front of me.

"Hey," he said softly. "Everything okay?"

"Aunt Cass couldn't brush her hair this morning. My uncle brushed it for her, even though it probably hurt him a ton because of his arthritis. Not that he'd ever complain." She ran both hands over her eyes. "Doctors don't know what's wrong with her yet. Her limbs are just kind of numb sometimes and don't work like they should. We're still in that phase where it's all tests and waiting."

"I'm sorry." His voice was so soft it was barely more than a whisper.

"It's okay. That's the way life is sometimes, I guess. But you asked me what's wrong with her. I don't know what to say, because we really don't know. I mean, when you hear words like amyotrophic lateral sclerosis or multiple sclerosis they sound like they should be kind of the same thing, but in reality they're different and would mean totally different things for her life expectancy or the kind of help she's going to need in the future. And those are just two of the many things doctors haven't actually ruled out yet."

His hand was lying right there on the front seat between them. She reached for it. He wrapped her hand in his and held it tightly.

"Maybe she only has a couple of years left to live, in which case I'm not about to head off on some fantastic trip overseas. I'm going to be here for whatever time she has left. Or maybe she's going to outlive Uncle Des by a decade or more, in which case she's going to need someone to live with and make her tea, brush her hair, fix her meals, run The Downs…"

Tears choked the words from her throat. Did he

have any idea how helpless this whole situation made her feel? Yeah, more than anyone, Benjamin probably would.

"And you're going to be there for them." Benjamin slid across the seat and wrapped his arms around her. "No matter what they need. You're going to be there."

She let her head fall against his shoulder. "Yes. I really will."

Because they took me in where my father abandoned us. Because they raised me when my mom kept wanting to run off chasing whichever man turned her head. Because I love them. Because they're my family.

A tear slipped down her cheek. He held her tighter.

"I want to apologize." His lips brushed the top of her head. "I'm really sorry if I ever made it sound like I don't respect the sacrifices you're making or how hard you're working. I think you're doing an amazing job. I respect you so much—you have no idea."

For a long moment she didn't say anything. She just let her body lay in his strength and watched the minutes count down until Benjamin had to leave. Tears filled her eyes and fought to escape her eyelashes. She didn't pull away. He didn't her let go.

"Remember that feeling of helplessness?" she asked, "Like everything's falling apart and you can't do anything to stop it?"

"I really do. In fact, I feel pretty helpless right now." Benjamin's voice dropped. She turned around until they were facing each other. His left hand spread across the small of her back, as his right slid up her cheek. His fingers brushed a tear from the corner of her eye.

"I haven't actually felt this helpless since I was lying flat on my back in a hospital bed with all four limbs in a cast. Only that time was almost easier because the pain was mine to fight. This time it's not. The pain is yours and I can't figure out how fix it, even though I'd do anything in my power to make things right for you."

"I know." She leaned her forehead against his. "And you can't. But thank you for wanting to."

She closed her eyes. She could feel him there, breathing the same inch of frosty air, her tears brushing the soft scruff of his jaw.

Then slowly, as naturally as breathing, his lips found hers. They'd barely met when a loud, incessant ringing filled the cab.

"Your phone!" She pulled back from the kiss.

Benjamin leaped back so quickly his head bumped against the roof. "That's not my phone. Mine's not ringing."

"Well, I don't have a cell phone. Mine was destroyed yesterday."

The ringing grew louder and seemed to be coming from the backseat. Benjamin reached around behind him and yanked his bag into his lap. Her jaw dropped. What had he done to his bag? It was filthy and patched with duct tape.

He ripped back the zipper, rummaged around inside and pulled out a phone. "This isn't mine. I must have accidentally picked it up from the alley."

"The alley? What alley?"

He glanced at the screen. His face paled.

"Benjamin, what's going on?"

He held up the phone toward her.
And she saw who the incoming call was from.
Alpha.

Chapter Ten

Benjamin stared in disbelief at the ringing phone in his hands. Kodiak must have dropped his phone in the alleyway during the fight and, somehow in all the confusion, Benjamin had scooped it into his bag with his things.

And now Alpha was calling it.

Piper was staring at him now. Her hands rose to her lips. "Why is Alpha calling you?"

"He's not calling me. This is obviously Kodiak's phone and I picked it up by mistake when we fought in the alley." But now what? The only question that really mattered now was whether or not he should risk answering it. His gut was dying to, but if Alpha realized someone else had Kodiak's phone, it could rob the police of a valuable lead. *Lord, I don't know what to do—*

"I don't understand what's happening here." Piper's voice rose. "What fight in what alley?"

The phone stopped ringing.

Benjamin sighed. Probably just as well he hadn't answered it.

He looked at her. "After you dropped me off at the garage, I saw a man walk into the alley after you. It was same man we saw smoking outside the bar and I thought he might be following you, so I followed him. He jumped me and we fought. Turned out to be Kodiak."

Her eyes grew wide.

He glanced down at the phone. The screen read: *Missed Call.*

"And then?" Piper was still looking at him. Not at the phone in his hand. At him.

"Then he got away, I went to report it to the police and then came to find you and tell you about it." *Only I didn't tell you. I held off because you seemed to be happy and that made me happy, and I didn't want to ruin the moment.* In fact, he basically tried to leave it to the last possible second. And then, he'd gotten swept up in the feeling of her in his arms, and he'd kissed her. He couldn't begin to guess what she might think of him now. He didn't even know what to think of himself. "But that's the reason my sister agreed to delay the rehearsal."

"Oh." Piper sat back on the passenger seat. "So, that's why you hadn't left town yet."

"Well, yeah. Why else did you think I'd still be sticking around here?"

Piper's eyes dropped to her knees.

Oh. Guilt stabbed Benjamin's heart. She'd thought he'd come back for her.

The phone started to buzz as texts appeared rapid-fire on the screen.

When I call your phone I expect you to answer!

Did you find Charlotte?

Answer me!

Did you find her?

She told me she was going to the Downs for Christmas!

The messages stopped. Piper leaned in and read over Benjamin's shoulder.

"He still thinks Kodiak has his phone," she said. "And apparently Charlotte told him she was coming here. Although there's no reason why she couldn't have been lying about that."

He nodded. "Looks that way." Now he was grateful he hadn't answered the phone call. These texts might actually lead to something useful.

The messages faded from the screen. He pressed the unlock button to read them again, but the phone demanded a password. He set it down on the dashboard. "I'm going to drop it off to the police on my way out of town. I was already able to give them a good description of Kodiak without a mask on. Might take them a few days, but hopefully between the phone and that description they'll have enough to be able to catch the guy."

She shook her head, then looked straight ahead to the snow falling thick and fresh on the windshield. "You should have told me. Right away. Kodiak tried to kill me. You had no right to hide something like that from me."

"You were already dealing with a lot." Heat rose to the back of his neck. "I was trying to protect you."

She spun back. Her eyes flashed at him. "I never asked you to protect me."

The phone began to buzz again, rattling across the dashboard toward Piper. She caught it and held the screen up where they could both see it.

Hello? Hello?

Where are you?

She said something about a Christmas thing. Did you check all the Christmas things?

Did you check the brick? I think I heard her say something about bricks to that guy.

You know, that guy she's cheating on me with!

If you find and hurt the guy she's cheating on me with I'll pay you double.

Fifty thou for bringing me her. Fifty thou for killing him. Got it?

Got it?

You're starting to make me mad.

Get to the usual place now and wait for me.

I'm not texting you again! So you'd better get there. Now. Or you'll be sorry.

After the wild flurry of texts, Kodiak's phone fell silent again. A shiver ran down Benjamin's neck. Whoever this Alpha was he sounded both psychotic and dangerous.

And there was only one other young man he'd met recently who had that bad impulse control. *Gavin.* "I don't like this."

Piper sucked in a deep breath as she wrapped her arms around her body. "Neither do I. It's all too fresh. It's like six years ago all over again. Exactly like six years ago. Like I'm twenty again and Charlotte is coming here for Christmas. I feel like I'm stuck in a time loop where history's repeating itself."

"Do you have any idea why she'd come here for Christmas this year? Or what he could possibly mean about Christmas things or bricks?"

She looked so lost that for a moment it took every impulse in his body not to reach out and hold her. "No. I wish I did. But I don't."

The cell phone began to chime. But this time it wasn't Kodiak's with a new text message. It was his phone alarm. He groaned.

"Piper, I'm sorry. I'm so very sorry. But I have to go. I promised my sister I'd hit the road by two... And I... I didn't expect to take this long."

"Okay. Let's get the tree off your truck and into the barn. Then you can drop me and Kodiak's phone off at the police station. I'll call Dominic to come pick me up from there."

Piper jumped out into the snow. It was falling thicker and faster now than the forecast had called for. The door slammed behind her. Seconds later she was hauling the tree off the back of the truck without even waiting for him. He slipped the phone into one of the oversize pockets of his winter jacket, along with his army knife and windup flashlight. Then he hopped out. "Here, let me help with that. You take the top, I'll take the bottom."

"Makes sense." She stopped. "But then I've got another favor to ask you, okay?"

"All right. Anything."

She stood there a moment, under a dark gray sky, her eyes on his face, and his eyes on hers, as if they were tied there by some invisible string.

"After we take the tree into the barn and you drop me off at the police station, you're just going to go. Okay? No speeches. No big affectionate gestures. Don't even say goodbye. Give me a quick hug, like a friend would do, and go. Head to your sister's wedding. Head off to the other side of the world and enjoy your life."

Piper crossed her arms. "Stop worrying about me.
Please. Don't worry, not about me, or The Downs, or
my aunt's health, or whether I'll be taking smart pre-
cautions to protect myself from Alpha. I know you're a
good guy. I know you want to help me and rescue me.
But I'm fine. I promise you. This isn't some trap I'm
stuck in. This is my life. I've chosen it and I'm going
to manage it. I don't need saving."

He nodded slowly. "Got it."

He grabbed the other end of the tree and helped
her carry it through the snow and up the stairs. They
stepped inside the cold, dark barn and set down the
tree. The power was still off so he pulled a windup
flashlight from his pocket and shone the beam back and
forth over the room. As he did, a cry slipped through
Piper's lips.

The barn had been trashed. Tables were knocked
over. Boxes of decorations were scattered across the
floor. Stacks of chairs had been tossed. The cement in
the fireplace looked as if someone had taken a couple
of whacks at it with a sledgehammer. Even the hay
under the wooden loft overhang had been torn into
shreds and tossed.

"I don't understand!" Piper's hands rose in exasperation. "I don't know what I ever did to Charlotte that she
decided to trash our Christmas decorations six years
ago. I don't know why she'd ever come back here now!
Let alone why she'd drag her abusive former boyfriend
into this and some other guy he thinks she's cheating
on him with." Her arms spun toward the wreckage.
"Is this what Alpha meant by checking the 'Christmas

things'? Did Charlotte do this? Did Kodiak or Blondie or someone else Alpha sent after her?"

Benjamin ached to go to her, to hold her, to make it right. Yet she'd demanded a promise from him and he'd given it. But, how could he just leave Piper and not try to help her now?

The barn door slammed shut, plunging the air around them into a deep murky gloom. Piper strode over to the door and pulled. The door didn't move. She tossed down her gloves, gripped it with her bare hands and pulled harder.

"Everything okay?"

She shook her head hard, tossing her hair. "No. I can't even budge it."

A loud crack boomed through the air above them. Then came a creak from above, as if something was trying to split the roof like a giant nutcracker.

Benjamin grabbed Piper's arm and pulled her into the soft hay pile under the loft.

"Get down!"

An avalanche of wood and snow caved in on top of them.

Chapter Eleven

Piper was so cold. That was the only thought that went through her head as she opened her eyes to survey her surroundings. But she saw only dark blurs. Her glasses were gone. She tried to move, but her frozen legs would not budge. She was wedged in, snow pressing in to the right and left of her legs. Able to move her arms, she felt around in the darkness. Snow formed a wall all around her, and thick wooden planks crossed just inches above her head.

Fighting panic, her mind scrambled to focus. Memories assailed her, one at a time.

There had been a loud cracking noise. Benjamin threw her into the hay. The roof caved in on top of them.

Then the barn had collapsed, burying them alive.

She closed her eyes again as tears ran down her cheeks. *Lord, I'm scared. I'm trapped. I don't know what to do.*

There was a groan to her right.

"Benjamin?" She turned toward the sound. Her bare fingers dug in the densely packed snow. "I'm here. Can you hear me? I'm coming to you."

The groaning grew louder. She dug furiously, until her fist punched through the snow wall and into another larger air pocket. She scrabbled away at the hole until she could slide her body through. She turned onto her hands and knees and crawled forward in the darkness. Her hand brushed against something soft. Her fingers trailed up the lines of Benjamin's coat, to his shoulder, then finally onto his soft beard. Then she felt a hand brush hers.

"Piper." Benjamin's fingers looped through hers. "Are you okay?"

"My body seems to still be in one piece and everything's moving all right." She tried to get up, but the ceiling of the pocket was barely a foot above her head. "How about you?"

"Yeah. I'm okay. Just sore. I think I bumped my head, but I've felt worse."

She curled into the snow beside him. "I'm sorry you're going to be late for your sister's wedding rehearsal."

A chuckle slipped through his lips. "Yup. Well, one problem at a time. Right now I'm going to worry about getting us out of here. I'm guessing there are several feet of snow on top of us now, along with a bunch of broken boards and pieces of the barn roof. Hang on, I think I'm sitting on the flashlight." He dropped her hand. She heard a whirring sound, then a bright light flashed across her eyes, replacing the gray spots with yellow spots. She blinked and saw nothing but splotches.

"Hey," his voice dropped. One hand reached up the side of her face, brushing along her skin. "You don't have your glasses."

She shook her head. "They're gone. Somewhere. I can't see a thing. Just shadows of light and darkness."

"Don't worry about that. We'll figure something out." He wrapped one arm around her and squeezed her tight. The warm, rough wool of his coat pressed against her cheek. He kissed the top of her head. "Just give me a moment to look around and think, then we'll come up with a plan. Don't worry."

How could she not worry? She was terrified. As silly as it would probably sound if she admitted it, not being able to see was scaring her more than being crushed by snow and a falling roof.

She clenched her jaw and told herself to be strong. But still she could feel the tears there, pooling in her eyes. She blinked hard and for a fraction of a moment thought she'd regained control. Then she felt a treacherous tear slip down her cheek.

No. I won't cry again. Not in front of Benjamin.

He shifted sideways, as if changing his angle, and pushed her back into the snow. "Oh, I'm sorry. I should have warned you before moving."

"Just focus on finding us a way out."

"I remember from spelunking over the summer how being in tight spaces kind of bothers you."

Bothered her? She could feel a sob building in the back of her throat and hoped he hadn't been able to hear it in her voice. She felt far more than bothered. She felt helpless. What's more she hated that this was probably how Benjamin would remember her now: blind, trapped, scared—and kissing him back in the truck when she should have been strong enough to push him away.

"Charlotte locked me in the kindling box." The words were out before she could rethink them. "At least, I think it was her."

"What?" Benjamin's body froze. "That's terrible."

"Yeah, it really was." She couldn't make out the features of his face without her glasses. But she could feel him there, his breath on her face and his chest rising and falling softly. "I'd been in this barn, with Uncle Des, Aunt Cass and everyone celebrating Christmas Eve. I should've stayed. But I saw Charlotte slip out and tried to follow her. I didn't even make it back to the house before someone—and I've always been pretty sure it was Charlotte—hit me on the head, shoved me into the box and locked me in. It was half an hour probably before Dominic found me. I'm just thankful he noticed I'd left and went looking for me. I don't know if I was more scared or angry. But ever since then I panic in closed spaces."

Benjamin pulled her tighter. "I was terrified in traction after the snowmobile accident because doctors didn't know at first how I'd recover. But I was livid with myself, too. I was so angry with myself for putting the people I loved through that. I promised myself that I would never put myself in a situation where I could break someone's heart like that, and that once

I was able to run I'd never let myself get trapped ever again." His hand brushed her back. "But as much as I hate being trapped right now, at least I'm trapped with you."

She let out a long breath. Funny, as much as she liked Benjamin, right now, if she had a choice of whom to be trapped with it wouldn't be someone who'd be sprinting to their truck the moment they broke through the snow.

"How big is the hole we're trapped in?" she asked.

The flashlight started to whirr again. "I'd say four feet high, eight feet long and about six feet wide."

That meant they probably had thirty minutes of air, maybe more, depending on whether they could find a ventilation hole. It was now a question of whether accidentally causing a cave-in by rushing to dig a way out was more or less dangerous than taking their time and maybe running out of air.

She wondered how it all happened. "Did a tree fall through the roof?"

"Maybe," he said. "We're under a pile of broken wood right now. There's a solid wall of wood to our right, which has kind of splintered in. On the other side there's a lot of snow, with a hole."

"Yeah, that's where I was buried."

He shifted away from her. "I've got to be careful, otherwise this whole thing could come toppling in on us."

Light and dark shapes and shadows swam in front of her eyes. She had backup glasses back at The Downs, but for now she might as well be blind. Frustration screamed inside her, but she swallowed it back. She might not be able to help Benjamin, but at the very least, she didn't need to make things harder for him.

"Hang on," he said. "There's what looks like a branch just above us to the left. I'm going to try to move it an inch or two and see what happens. We might be able to create a small ventilation pocket. Also, it might give us an idea of just how deep this mess is. We might even be able to just dig a hole and climb straight up. Just stay back and out of the way."

She couldn't see well enough to even know what constituted "out of the way." Still, she curled into a ball and slid back until she felt snow against her back.

"Okay…it's moving. Which is good. I'm just going to try to— Oh, Lord, please help us!"

His sudden, shouted prayer was swallowed by the rush of falling wood and snow. Piper tucked her head into her knees and cradled her arms above it. Benjamin's arms flew around her, sheltering her body with his. Silent prayers flew from her lips, mingled with the pleas for safety coming from Benjamin's.

Finally the rushing of snow stopped. When silence fell, Benjamin sat back and loosened his arms. "I'm really, really sorry about that. You okay?"

"It's not your fault. You had no way of knowing." But now she was buried in snow up to her waist. "I'm fine. Cold, though. Feels like my legs are frozen."

"The bad news is we're now in a lot smaller space," he said. "The good news is we still have the flashlight. I'd suggest we climb straight up, but there are broken boards and nails everywhere. Not to mention there's

probably a big heavy tree somewhere over our heads."
He sighed loudly. "It's like being trapped inside one
of those wooden puzzles where if you pull the wrong
thing it all crashes down, with us inside, and I pulled
the wrong piece. In the meantime, let's focus on keeping warm while I figure this out."

He unzipped his coat and pulled her into his chest.
Warmth radiated from his body into hers. The flashlight started up again. She waited, curled against his
chest, tucked in the strength of his arms and battling
the urge to cry. Her mind yelled at her to be stronger
than this. She should be figuring a way out of this, not
lying buried in the snow, in the arms of the man she'd
fought so hard not to let herself fall in love with.

*But what good am I right now if all I can see are
blobs of light and shadows?*

She took a deep breath. "Turn off the flashlight,
please. I want to give my eyes a moment to adjust to
the darkness and look for something."

The whirring stopped. "But I thought you couldn't
see anything."

"Yeah," she said. "But when you've spent your entire life figuring out one set of blobs from another
every time you're in the dark and need to find your
glasses, you also get surprisingly good at telling shadows apart."

The light slowly dimmed to black. Slowly she turned
her head, scanning every inch of the infuriatingly indistinct shades of light and dark gray that swam past
her eyes.

Lord, help me now. If there's something I'm supposed to see, help me see it.

"There!" She pointed. "There's a light source over there. It's like the change you see behind your eyelids when you turn toward a light with your eyes closed. We need to dig in that direction."

There was a long pause. Then he said, "Okay. We dig in that direction. We tried it my way earlier. Now we'll try yours."

He started to dig. She closed her eyes and prayed not to feel another rush of snow caving in on top of them.

"Okay," he said after a long moment. 'I've got a bit of a tunnel dug now. I'm going to crawl in and keep digging. Just feel for my foot, and you can follow me out."

She didn't miss the irony. She'd distanced herself from Benjamin after the summer because she didn't want to foolishly chase after a man who'd just end up breaking her heart. Now she was literally following him blindly.

"Quiet." His hand brushed her arm to still her. "Listen."

She focused her ears on the silence. Then she heard it—barking and then Dominic shouting her name.

"Hey! Hey! We're in here!" they shouted back.

As Benjamin dug faster, hope leaped in her chest. After a few moments light burst through her vision, then a large bundle of fur landed on her chest. *Thank You, God!*

"Hey, you okay?" Dominic's voice came from above her.

"Yeah," was all she could manage to say.

Benjamin stood up. "We were in the barn and the roof caved in. Piper, it looks like a pretty major tree fell."

"That's some dog you've got," Dominic said to her. "Practically dragged me out of the house and then wouldn't let me rest until I found you two."

She felt his hand on her arm ready to help her up. Instead, she stayed on her knees for a moment and wrapped her arms around Harry. The dog licked her face.

She was out. She was alive. She was safe.

Benjamin might even make it back to the island before the wedding rehearsal was over.

"Hey." Benjamin's voice floated over the air. "What happened to my truck?"

Chapter Twelve

Benjamin looked down onto the living room from the second-story balcony as he dialed his sister's cell phone number. Below him, Piper was curled up on the sofa in front of the fire, blue backup glasses on her nose and a blue-and-white Maple Leafs hockey jersey draped over her frame. A police officer and Dominic flanked her on either side and the dog was curled in a ball at her feet. The grandfather clock read four thirty.

Meg answered on the first ring. "Benji?"

He turned his back on the scene below. There was no easy way to say this. "My truck's been stolen. I'm not going to make it to the rehearsal."

His sister sighed. "But are you okay?"

"Yeah." He slid all the way down until he was sitting on the floor. "But I had everything in that truck—my bag, my passport, my airline ticket, emergency credit card, traveling money. It's all gone. Literally all I have now is my driver's license and twenty bucks."

She gasped. "Oh, Benji, I'm so sorry."

"Yeah, sis. Me, too." He stared up at the wooden beams crossing above as wind howled outside. The predicted storm had arrived full force, bringing heavy snow once again. The town was still without power, but Dominic had brought over a portable generator and hooked it up to a few essential circuits, including a couple of standing lamps. "A friend of Piper's has offered to lend me his car, as long as somebody's able to drive it back down to him after the wedding."

"Of course, we have several guests heading back that way. But what about your flight?"

Benjamin blew out a long breath. "Doesn't look good. It's unlikely I'll be able to get a new passport issued in time, not with everything being shut down for Christmas. And the airline won't refund my flight. I'm just hoping that once I get home to the island and visit a government office there, they'll be able to do something. I'm about to hit the road now and I'll grab food on the way. I should be there around midnight."

"The bridge to the island is closing tonight until tomorrow morning," Meg said gently. "It's iced up and they're saying a whole lot of snow is going to keep falling overnight. Stay there, get some sleep and get here as soon as you can in the morning."

"But tomorrow's your wedding!"

"Yup. Ironic, I know. I'm a wedding planner who spent years panicking about the safety of her baby brother, and now circumstances are conspiring to keep you from making it to my wedding. The old Meg would be hanging from the ceiling by her fingernails." She chuckled. "Maybe God's showing me just how far I've come in the past year and a half, and just how ready I am to marry Jack tomorrow. Fortunately, all the other guests have now made it here safe and sound. We'll all pray that you make it here on time."

He closed his eyes and dropped his head into his hands. "But what if something happens and I don't make it?"

"You will. I'll dance with you at the reception, open presents with you Christmas morning and have Christmas brunch with you and the family before you leave for Australia and we leave for our honeymoon."

"Okay." He closed his eyes. He was exhausted and couldn't help feeling he was letting his sister down on the most important day of her life. The fact she was being so awesome about it didn't make him feel any better.

The gentle murmur of Piper's voice floated up through the air behind him. Even though he couldn't make out her words the mere tone of her voice seemed to brush the back of his neck like gentle fingertips, calming him a bit. He was so frustrated right now he was ready to grab Piper's boxing gloves and start punching at the snow. Meg had tried to warn him about showing up in person to drop off the dog. But he hadn't listened. Now he was messing up his sister's wedding plans. And all he'd succeeded in doing with Piper was letting the man who'd attacked her escape, fumbling another goodbye and kissing her.

If he hadn't decided to drop Harry off in person, Piper might never have been at the barn so late that Kodiak was able to attack her like that. Yes, Benjamin had stepped in to protect her, twice. But if he hadn't been here, wouldn't God have provided someone else? A better guardian? Somebody smarter and wiser than he had been? His sister had been right. He never should have insisted on driving down and dropping the dog off himself. He'd selfishly given in to his own desire to take one last look at Piper. Hadn't he learned anything from hearing Piper's stories? Her life had been damaged enough by selfish people—her father, her mother, Charlotte and the evil, cruel brutes who were threatening her now. It didn't matter that his heart was in the right place. Piper needed stable people to stand by her. Not the kind of man who was going to give her a quick hug—let alone a reckless kiss—before dashing off to chase his own dreams.

Well, Lord, I'm just going to have to trust that You have Piper's back and will help surround her with the kind of people she needs.

"Don't worry." His sister's voice drifted down the line. "Everything's going to be okay."

He should be the one standing there, in person, telling her that. "There was something you wanted to talk to me about at the rehearsal—"

"Don't worry about that right now."

"You told me it was important."

"Yes, but not as important as you just getting here safe." She was using her "I'm trying to protect you" tone of voice. It bothered him just as much as it probably bothered Piper when he did it.

"Sis? Just tell me."

She sighed. "I was going to ask you to walk me down the aisle tomorrow."

He felt his breath leave him, as if someone had just sucker punched him in the gut. Certainly he'd known she wasn't going to ask their father to do it; he'd never been emotionally there for her. But Benjamin had never imagined... "I thought you'd decided to walk in alone."

"I wanted to tell you in person." Sounded as if there were tears in Meg's voice, too. "Jack and I are having all four of our parents come in together. Then he's coming in with his best man, Luke. Then you and I walk in. You're my best friend, bro. After everything we've gone through together, it just felt right to have you beside me."

"I'll be there." Benjamin stood up and looked down over the balcony. Piper was walking the police officer out. He couldn't see where Dominic had gone. "I promise. Whatever it takes."

Otherwise he'd never be able to forgive himself.

Piper looked up. Benjamin was standing alone on the balcony above her. He slipped a cell phone into his pocket and then started down the stairs toward her.

"Where did everybody go?" he asked.

"The police finished up their report," she said. "They already have someone trying to match the description you gave them of Kodiak and they'll apply for a search warrant to go through his phone. They're on the lookout for your truck and will also try to have someone drive by The Downs a couple of times in the night, just to make sure everything's okay and to show anyone who might be prowling around that they're watching. Dominic's gone home to grab a few things. Now that the guests have moved out he's taking a second-floor suite for tonight, so that you and I have another person here for backup."

Benjamin dropped down on the couch beside her. "So you guessed that I'm going nowhere tonight."

"I had a hunch." The back of her hand brushed the back of his. Then she folded her hands in her lap. "Are you okay?"

"Depends how you define *okay*." He looked so tired she was amazed he was still standing upright. "I have no passport, no truck, no clothes, there's another snowstorm outside, the bridge to Manitoulin Island is closing tonight due to ice and my sister is getting married tomorrow." He shook his head in what she assumed was exasperation. "But you and I are both safe, and it could be a whole lot worse. So, sure, all things considered, I'm okay."

"Yeah, I'm pretty much the same," she said. "The barn has collapsed, taking the tree we chopped down and the Christmas decorations with it. I have no idea what I'm going to do about Christmas Eve at The Downs, since we obviously can't hold it in the barn now. Kodiak, Alpha and the blonde who broke into my room are all still on the loose. According to police, it sounds like no one's heard from Charlotte since the night she trashed The Downs. It's like she evaporated into thin air. As far as the police can tell she did a complete disappearing act."

Which did not bode well for either finding her or stopping those now after her.

"Maybe she changed her identity," Benjamin said. "Especially if she was trying to escape Alpha. Do they have any idea why the barn collapsed?"

"Yup, but you won't believe it, because I barely believe it myself. Someone walked around on the barn roof and tried to break into the top of the chimney."

He blinked. "You're joking."

"No word of a lie." She ran both hands through her hair and let it fall. "The stupid thing is I thought I saw something up there when we were driving in to drop off the tree. I just never realized it could be a person. But that's the theory based on the footprints, broken branches and what they could piece together. They actually found a sledgehammer in the rubble. Looks like someone climbed up, took a few swings at the brick. They tried to climb back down, but the branch broke and everything caved in. They fell through but obviously managed to crawl out while we were still buried, and then stole your truck, I'm guessing."

"Did you check the brick? I think I heard her say something about bricks to that guy."

One of Alpha's angry texts floated through her mind. But that couldn't be the "brick" Alpha was talking about. Could it? After all, whoever trashed the barn also took a couple of swipes at the fireplace and stopped when they hit the heavy wall of concrete Uncle Des had poured in.

Benjamin's mouth gaped. "You're telling me that someone was actually climbing around on your barn roof, trying to break into the chimney with a sledge-hammer?"

"Yup." She nodded. "The police said they'd check The Downs's roof for footprints, too, but they figure it's too steep to climb on."

"Do you realize how ridiculous that sounds? They could have been killed. We could have been killed. I shouldn't be finding this funny."

Benjamin looked on the cusp of bursting into laughter. But Piper was almost ready to cry.

"It's ridiculous. I know!" She threw her hands up in the air. "It's too absurd for words. Six years ago I try to do the nice thing and let some girl I'm sharing an apartment with come visit The Downs because she's curious about the rumors of its Prohibition history. Instead, she sneaks out to kiss some handsome young man in the woods, robs my family and our guests, and destroys pretty much every special handmade Christmas ornament we have. And why? I don't know! Now my aunt is ill, I'm saving every cent I can for renovating this place and suddenly she's back to wreck my life even more spectacularly than before. Only I haven't *seen* her. Not specifically. All I've seen is a masked blonde girl, who could be Charlotte. Thanks to the phone you inadvertently picked up after fighting Kodiak, we now have pretty strong confirmation he was sent here by Charlotte's former boyfriend. But why Alpha is looking for Charlotte here after all this time is still a giant mystery, because as far as I can tell, *she's not here!* And there's nothing I can do!"

That was probably more of an outburst than Benjamin had ever heard from her before. But, while she might have been born in England and raised by a couple who were strong believers in staying calm and carrying on, with everything that had been mounting the past couple of days it was getting harder and harder not to throw her metaphorical hockey gloves down on the ice and pound something.

She took a deep breath, afraid she already knew the answer before she asked the question. "What happens to your flight to Australia?"

He sighed. "I don't know. Whoever stole my truck now has my passport. I don't know how fast I'll be able to get a new one, but it doesn't look good. Worst-case scenario, I wait days or weeks for the passport to arrive, book a new flight, get over there as soon I can and figure out how I'm going to join the charity sail after it starts."

He was sitting so close to her on the couch now she caught his scent—like the forest after a rain, like spices, like comfort. If she moved her body just an inch they would be touching. Shadows from the flickering flames danced along the lines of his jaw. Piper ached to reach up and feel the softness of his beard under her fingertips, to brush her lips along the soft skin where it met his cheek.

No. She'd kissed him once and that had been a mistake. They couldn't let it happen again. She leaped up. "I have some mulled cider in the pantry. I'm going to go heat it up over the stove."

A question flickered in his eyes, but he didn't follow her.

The kitchen was dark. She walked through the narrow room and headed for the pantry.

Lord, please help Benjamin catch his flight. I never thought I'd say this, but I need him to leave. The next goodbye has to be the final one, no matter what. I can't keep having my heart yanked up and down like a yo-yo anymore.

She opened the pantry door and pulled the cord for the light out of habit before remembering the power was still out and they were reliant on a generator. She stepped in and ran her hands along the jars and cans, feeling for the cloth-wrapped cider lid.

Something moved in the darkness. Then before she could barely make a sound, a gloved hand clamped tightly over her lips and the tip of a knife brushed against her neck.

"Don't move!" the man whispered. "Or I'll have to kill you."

Chapter Thirteen

A crash came from the kitchen.

"Hey, everything okay in there? You need a hand?" Benjamin glanced over his shoulder. He thought he heard a muffled sound but couldn't make out any words. He stood up. "Hang on, I'll come hold a flashlight—"

The words froze in his throat as Piper walked, slowly and awkwardly into the living room. A black-gloved hand was clamped over her mouth and the tip of a jagged kitchen knife was pressed into the soft flesh at the base of her throat.

Oh Lord, help me save her.

She took another step toward him and it was only then he saw her attacker. The man was about Piper's height but had an athletic build. He wore a shiny red ski jacket and a striped balaclava that hid his face, but not enough to hide the bruised eye and bloody lip.

Not Kodiak. Not Blondie.

Was he face-to-face with Alpha?

Benjamin focused his gaze directly on Piper. "Don't worry. It's going to be okay."

"Don't talk to her!" the man snapped. "Just tell me where I can find what I'm looking for or someone's going to get hurt!

Piper's hands rose in front of her. "Okay. We hear you."

But her eyes met Benjamin's, determined, fearless.

He took a step forward, praying for an opportunity, his limbs tense and ready to strike. "We have no idea where Charlotte is."

"What?" The masked man's head snapped toward Benjamin. "Who's Charlotte?"

But the final syllable froze in the masked man's throat.

Piper swiftly grabbed his wrist with both hands and pulled it out in front of her face. For a second the blade reflected in her eyes before she twisted his wrist, wrenching the knife from his grasp.

He screamed in pain, dropping the knife to the floor.

She tossed him over her shoulder.

The masked man landed on his back on the floor and lay there, staring up at her with bulging eyes. She still hadn't let go of his wrist.

Then Piper tossed her hair and looked at Benjamin, fire flashing in her eyes.

Benjamin's mouth went dry.

He couldn't remember ever seeing anything stronger, braver or more beautiful in his entire life.

"Got the knife?" she asked.

"Yeah." Benjamin picked it up and held it out firmly,

just enough to show the intruder that even though Piper had the situation covered he was more than happy to step in as needed.

Only then did Piper release her grip just enough to let the man rise to his knees.

He spat on the floor. "You broke my arm."

"Probably just sprained. We'll call an ambulance when we call the police." Benjamin reached down and yanked off the ski mask.

It was Gavin.

Benjamin almost laughed. The same arrogant jerk who'd stood in this kitchen just this morning insulting him had just threatened Piper at knifepoint, and was now down on his knees, his bruised and bloody face glaring defiantly at them.

Benjamin hoped the disgust he was feeling showed clearly in his eyes.

"Who sent you here?" Piper turned on Gavin. "Was it Alpha? Why do they think Charlotte is at The Downs?"

A snarl passed Gavin's lips. "I told you, I don't know anyone named Charlotte and I've never heard of Alpha. I don't know what's going on here any more than you do!"

Benjamin snorted. Even though Gavin had spit the words out with so much anger and frustration it was likely he'd convinced himself they were true. But Benjamin wasn't about to listen to the hotheaded liar and sneak who'd assaulted Piper claim that he was the victim.

"Well, I hope whatever you're after is worth losing

your legal career for. If you even are a lawyer." Piper turned to Benjamin. "There's a phone behind you on the counter. If you call 911, they should hopefully be able to get us through to the right officer for our case."

"Agreed." Benjamin reached for the phone.

"Wait! Please!" Sweat was pouring down Gavin's face. "Don't call the police. Just get someone to take me to the hospital. Or call a taxi and I'll make my own way there. Okay, okay, so I don't have my own law firm yet. But I did just pass the bar exam and I'll agree not to sue you, or press charges for assaulting me or…or for the fact I fell through the roof of your obviously unstable barn. We can all just chalk this up to one big misunderstanding and go on with our lives."

Fury built at the back of Benjamin's neck, tightening his shoulders and pushing through his voice with so much force. "You *attacked* Piper! You broke into her home. You put a knife to her throat. Not to mention vandalizing the power generator, taking a sledgehammer to the chimney of her barn, and conspiring with some creep with a bear tattoo who choked her at the barn last night—"

Gavin's hands rose higher. "I don't know anything about any of that!"

Benjamin's eyebrow rose.

"Okay, yeah," Gavin conceded. "I did threaten Piper with a knife right now and I did sort of trespass on the roof of her barn, and hit the chimney with a sledgehammer. But in my defense, I didn't know her barn roof was so weak. And I didn't touch her generator, or do any of those other things. And I only threatened her right now because I was getting so desperate and frustrated. I was hired by somebody to find something, okay?"

"Hired to find what?" Benjamin demanded.

"I don't really know."

"Who hired you? Was it Alpha?"

"I don't know! Look, I'm kind of a subcontractor. Trisha hired me." His whole body seemed to deflate and sink into the floor. "Trisha's not really my wife. She's definitely not a lawyer and she's only twenty-two. She came into the legal clinic where I was working and offered me five hundred dollars to go away with her over Christmas."

Benjamin snorted. Gavin was claiming Trisha had paid him to come to The Downs with her and pretend to be her husband? "Really? That's the story you're going with now?"

Benjamin reached for the phone again.

"Wait! Look, I'm telling the truth!" Gavin yelled. "I met her a few months ago. She seemed to be in some kind of trouble with a really bad boyfriend and I'm a nice guy, so I found out her contact details and tried to keep in touch with her afterward. I kept texting and asking her out every now and then over the next few months, trying to build a rapport. She kept saying no and telling me to leave her alone. Then all of a sudden she offers me money to go away with her over Christmas and pretend to be her husband. Should've known it was too good to be true. I hadn't even realized she was pregnant and she wouldn't let me get anywhere near her. But I needed the money and thought she might've started liking me. But when we got here she basically just hid in the room and got me to do all kinds of stupid stuff for her."

Okay, that much Benjamin could believe. If Trisha had been looking to use someone—for whatever reason—Gavin might have seemed both arrogant and foolish enough to be a dupe.

"Did Trisha have anyone else working for her?" Piper loosened her grip on Gavin. "Or was she working for anyone?"

"I don't know." Gavin frowned and cradled his sore arm. "Her story kept changing. At first she told me she was here looking for a person. But then the person wasn't here and suddenly she says we need to go through the Christmas decorations in the barn and take a look inside the barn chimney. And why the chimney? I don't know. It was as if her connection with reality was totally slipping. Or maybe someone was just giving her really weird directions. She was texting someone a lot. All I know is I got tired of being her lackey and began to worry I was never going to see my money. Especially after you kicked us out. Falling through the barn was the last straw. So I decided to take matters into my own hands. Figured Piper might know what was going on."

As ridiculous as this sounded, it was also consistent with what he'd seen on Kodiak's phone. So that made multiple people under Alpha's command. Benjamin met Piper's eyes.

"I'm pretty sure Trisha was getting instructions from Alpha, too," she said, "and that she's scared witless of him."

Yeah, he could see that, too. But Uncle Des had seen Charlotte kissing a strong, young man. If neither Kodiak nor Gavin were Alpha, they were running out of suspects. The only other person he'd met in town who met that description was the mechanic.

"Where is Trisha now?" Benjamin asked.

"Where's Benjamin's truck and stuff?" Piper spoke almost at the same time.

"I have no idea." Gavin's shoulders rose and fell. "After I climbed out of the barn, I told Trisha I was done. So she stole your truck and split, because it was my vehicle we'd come up in. No girl, no matter how cute, is worth that much trouble, am I right?" Gavin grinned, foolishly. "But I have her cell phone number and I really can't afford any legal problems at this stage of my career. So, how about you help me figure out what she was looking for, and then help me find it, and I'll cut you in for a share of the money to help you renovate this old dump. What do you say?"

Piper's eyes rolled. Benjamin just looked down at the phone and dialed.

"911. What's your emergency?"

"Hi, this is Benjamin Duff calling from The Downs—"

Gavin shouted. Benjamin turned, just in time to see the man lunge for Piper's legs in an apparent last-minute attempt to escape justice. Piper swung, her elbow catching Gavin square in the jaw. He crumpled to the floor. Benjamin shook his head. The whole thing had taken less than a couple of seconds.

"Hello?" The 911 operator was back in his ear.

"There's been a break-in. We need police and an ambulance. The intruder threatened the proprietor with a knife and clearly underestimated who he was dealing with."

Gavin was taken away in an ambulance, all the while demanding loudly that the police go find and arrest Trisha instead, because everything was entirely her fault. The same flurry of police cars and people in uniform that had become all too common a sight at The Downs in the past two days came and left as quickly as a winter snow squall. By ten thirty, Piper and the dog had gone upstairs to her room, Dominic had settled into the large suite Tobias had vacated, and despite having a more than adequate four-poster bed on the second floor to himself, Benjamin once again found himself tossing and turning on the living-room couch.

He couldn't sleep.

Snow buffeted gently against the towering windows. A thirty-five-foot ceiling vaulted high above his head.

The expansive room twisted and turned at the edges into nooks, crannies and alcoves. He lost track trying to count the number of walls the room even had. No wonder people suspected The Downs had been used as a hidden speakeasy or some other criminal enterprise with illegal alcohol and dirty money. Everything about this house projected mystery, suspense and intrigue.

He could also see why Piper's uncle and aunt loved the place so much and hoped to live out their last days here.

The fire was burning down to embers and the box

of wood beside the fireplace was running low. He grabbed his coat and started for the woodpile out back. The grandfather clock chimed midnight. His footstep paused. He was down to eighteen hours to his sister's wedding.

Christmas Eve had arrived.

Not that it showed in the space around him. The lights Piper had strung outside hadn't come back to life since the power had gone out yesterday, and there wasn't so much as a string of tinsel or a sprig of holly inside The Downs.

He held out the battery-powered lantern in front of him as he walked. The track pants and T-shirt he'd borrowed from Dominic were a size too big, but the clothes were warm enough against the cold. Thick white snow fell down from the sky, brushing his skin and sticking to his beard.

Lantern light ran over the large kindling box. It was about three feet tall and five feet long. The idea of anyone being cruel enough to lock Piper inside it burned through his veins like fire. No, he didn't judge Piper for relegating Christmas Eve at The Downs to the now-damaged barn. If anything, he admired her all the more for taking on the community event in her aunt's place. He couldn't blame her for not filling her living room with memories of Christmas, either. It was as if someone else's cruelty and malice had taken even the happy symbols of the holiday and smashed them to bits.

He filled his arms with small branches and kindling. The remnants of the broken hockey stick from when Piper had fought off Blondie last night had been tossed on top of the woodpile. In fact, there was more than one broken hockey stick, a broken paddle and half a cross-country ski scattered among the logs and branches. He chuckled. Yeah, the Piper he'd gone running, kayaking and sailing with that summer had been strong, daring and utterly fearless. But not always easy on either herself or her sports equipment.

The dull ache he'd felt in his chest at the memory of Piper's smile strengthened to pain. It was like hunger pangs for something that he couldn't quite put a name to. He'd thought the pain was bad that hot summer night when Piper had said goodbye and walked out of the restaurant, and that swinging by to drop off Harry would somehow put it to rest. Instead, it had just kept growing stronger every moment they'd spent together.

He turned his face to the sky and prayed aloud.

"Lord, You've got to know how awesome Piper is. I trust that You want an amazing life for her, just as much as I do. It was incredible the way she took Gavin down. Right now everything inside my heart is aching to help her, save her…or even just to give her a reason to smile this Christmas. But I've never felt so helpless and I don't know where to start."

His eyes slid over the tree line as a memory filled his mind. A year and a half ago, he'd picked up his reporter friend Jack from the police station on the island. This was long before Jack was his sister's fiancé or had even admitted to himself how perfect he and Meg were together. Benjamin had been driving and drinking coffee. Jack had been ranting about how impossible his situation was, almost on the verge of falling apart. A serial killer was stalking Meg. Jack was in trouble with the police and about to lose his job. And Benjamin had turned to the reporter, told him some camping story about a nonexistent bear, and then said something like, "I didn't ask what you can't do. I asked what you're gonna do."

Now here he was standing in a snowstorm, freezing his feet off, worrying about everything he couldn't fix. To be fair there was whole lot he couldn't do right now. But figuring out what he could still do wasn't a bad place to start.

He grabbed the broken hockey stick.

Piper woke with a start and stared into the darkness, unable to tell if she really had just heard a noise downstairs or if it had just been an echo of the nightmare she could barely remember. Silence filled her ears, interrupted only by the sound of Harry snoring at her feet. The clock read six thirty in the morning. It was Christmas Eve. The world was still pitch-black outside her window, but she might as well get up.

Her mind urged her to start making plans about how she was going to salvage the Christmas Eve potluck now that she'd lost the barn. But that would have to wait until after some coffee. She threw on jeans and pulled on a hockey jersey. Her feet dragged across the floor. Harry didn't even follow, just stretched out on the full length of her bed. Guess that meant that he wasn't bothered by whatever she might have heard. She felt her way down the stairs in the darkness, pushed the door open and stepped out onto the second-floor landing,

"Hang on! Don't move." Benjamin's voice floated up to her through the darkness. "Just wait one second."

"Okay…" What was going on? She couldn't see a thing.

"All right," he said. "This isn't much, I know. But my goal was to come up with something totally different and unique, that you probably hadn't ever seen in The Downs before. And seeing as I didn't manage to get you a Christmas present, I wanted to leave you with something."

She heard the whirring of the windup flashlight. The outline of a tall Christmas tree slowly came to life in the gentle glow of white fairy lights. She walked down the stairs watching as the lights grew brighter. A tall, handmade wooden Christmas tree stood beside the fireplace. A long, worn board formed the trunk. Bits of wood, hockey sticks and pieces of a canoe paddle formed the branches. Intricate crisscrossing twigs formed the star on the top. Christmas lights weaved through and around makeshift branches, plugged into the power outlet of Benjamin's windup flashlight.

His eyes met hers, hopeful, questioning. "So, what do you think?"

"It's incredible." She felt a smile tug at the corner of her lips. "I don't know what to say."

"I'm glad you like it." His eyes drew her in deeper. "I found a toolbox in the garage and pulled the wood from the woodpile. I know it's not much and I figured if you didn't like it, it would be easy enough to dismantle—"

"Stop it." She ran across the floor toward him.

"You're being hard on yourself and you don't need to." She slipped her arms around his waist and hugged him. "I love it. Thank you. It's too beautiful for words."

"Well, you're beautiful. After everything you've been through I wouldn't blame you if you hated Christmas. I just wanted to leave you with something to hopefully help build a happy memory." His arms encircled her shoulders, his fingers locking behind her back. The tree lights began to slowly dim again. "You're the kindest, most caring, pluckiest person I've ever met. Someone came along and stepped all over your Christmas memories and you just rolled your shoulders back and carried on making sure the holiday was still special for other people. I just hope you know that I'd do whatever I could to make sure you had a really amazing Christmas."

Then don't leave. Don't go to Australia. Her cheek pressed against his chest as the words she didn't dare let herself say filled her heart. *Forget about your boat. Forget about sailing the world. Just stay here with me and help me run this old, boring bed-and-breakfast in the middle of nowhere. I know it's selfish to even think of asking you to give up your dreams. Because you're right about this not making me happy. I wish my aunt Cass wasn't sick, that The Downs wasn't broke and that I could just pack up and leave here, too. But I can't. I'm needed here.*

So, I wish what made you happy was being here, in The Downs, with me.

Because right now the only thing that makes me truly happy here is you.

No, she wouldn't say that. She'd never say anything even close to that. Because the only thing that hurt worse than the thought of Benjamin leaving was knowing she sent him off with a heavy heart. Whenever he managed to catch that plane, the last thing she wanted him carrying with him was the weight of knowing just how sad she'd be.

She took in a deep breath and breathed him in. She memorized the feel of his arms around her shoulders and the scent of him filling her lungs. Her eyes closed. Then she felt his lips brush her forehead. His fingertips lifted up her chin right before she felt the sweetness and scruff of his lips finding hers.

The kiss lingered, as naturally and tenderly as breath filling their lungs.

Then Piper stepped back. Benjamin did, too.

"How soon do you leave?" she asked.

"Soon." Benjamin ran his hand over his face. "Very soon."

She didn't know which one of them had initiated the kiss or which one of them had stopped it. But maybe it didn't matter. They were like two of the little magnet dogs she had as a child. They kept pulling together and pushing apart, the two of them trapped in an invisible orbit.

The pale gray light of winter morning began to fill the windows above their head.

"I want to make sure the bridge has been reopened and that you're ready for your party tonight," Benjamin said. "But I hope to leave by ten at the latest. Do you know what you're going to do about tonight yet?"

"No, not yet." She dropped into a chair by the window and pulled a blanket over her knees. For a moment she just sat and let her eyes run over the intricate work he'd done on the makeshift Christmas tree. Benjamin crossed the floor, sat down on the carpet and leaned his broad shoulder against her legs.

"Aunt Cass used to host Christmas Eve in this room when I was little. They'd push all the furniture back, set up a string of potluck dishes down the kitchen counter and let everyone come through and feed themselves. It was a big, happy, chaotic mess." She glanced up. "People used to sit on the second-floor balcony with their feet dangling down. Sixteen-year-olds. Sixty-year-olds. It was a madhouse."

He looked up at her face. "Sounds amazing."

"Oh, it was. But it was hard, too, because I was an only child, and this was my home and I never liked having all these people galloping through my space. I'm hardly an extrovert like Aunt Cass. Sometimes I wonder if she moved the whole thing out to the barn because she suspected it would be easier on me that way." She sighed. "I love knowing that I'm helping my uncle and aunt keep their home. I love knowing I'm part of something that's done so much for this community. But I don't love the chaos of it all."

"All tacking, no sailing?" Benjamin asked.

"Lots of loudly heralding angels and banging drummer boys. No 'Silent Night'."

Feet padded above them and she looked up to see Harry making his way down the staircase. Benjamin got up and disappeared into the kitchen. She heard him pouring kibble into the dog bowl, then he reemerged, a cup of coffee in each hand.

"You know how we did all that wilderness stuff together this summer?" He handed her a cup. "Well, I don't do all that with just anyone. Not for fun. Most people are either too shy or too loud. But you've got a really good combination of getting things done and knowing how to just exist in the moment and let a guy think." He sat down beside her. "You're the most comfortable person I've ever been around. I think you'd be awesome to go on a sailing voyage with. I'm going to miss you so much, Piper, you have no idea."

Her fingers slid through his. "I'm going to miss you, too."

"Hey! Good morning!" A loud, cheerful voice floated from above them. Dominic was standing on the second-story balcony. The wannabe cop strode down the stairs. "Do I smell coffee?"

"Yes." Piper stood quickly. "Benjamin was kind enough to make some."

"Awesome." Dominic smiled broadly. "Whoa, that hockey tree is something else! Did Benjamin make that?"

Piper ran her hands up and down her arms, trying to brush away the shivers Benjamin's words had left on her skin. "Yes, he's quite the craftsman."

Dominic clasped his hands together like a fighter ready to enter the ring. "Now, Pips, tell me what I can do to help you pull off Christmas Eve at The Downs. You want me to start calling around to church and school halls? You want me to round up volunteers and see who's still able to get here? I can get my whole extended family worth of cousins, plus the youth group of my church here in minutes."

"Thank you. Get some coffee into you and then we'll make a game plan." Piper's gaze ran over Benjamin's tree. "I think we're going to hold Christmas Eve here, in this room. It will be crowded and mean some last-minute adjustments. Especially if the power doesn't come back on. But people can bring backup generators and hot plates, and we can light candles. We can make it work." She felt Dominic nod his assent, but she only had eyes for Benjamin. "It's been a long time since we've held Christmas here. I think it's time to bring it home."

By the time the clock chimed nine thirty, The Downs was standing room only. Good to his word, Dominic had not only rounded up his entire extended family, but teenagers from three different youth groups, many of whom had brought friends and family members of their own. Boxes of donated Christmas decorations filled the garage. Uncle Des had organized a minibus of seniors from Silver Halls, many of whom were now seated around the dining room table teaching the youngsters how to make decorations. Aunt Cass had hit the phones and was getting a faithful crew of volunteer cooks to amend their menus. The driveway was being plowed to make more space for cars. A bonfire was coming together on the wide expanse of snow between the house and hill. Garlands of freshly cut pine branches and bows were being strung from the balcony railing above her. Even Tobias had turned up after hearing the news from someone at the local bookshop. The plump professor was now directing a makeshift Christmas choir on the staircase. And every few moments the front doorbell rang with loans of plates and cutlery, candles, battery lamps and backup generators.

Piper stood in the living room and watched the hustle of energy and life flow around her.

Lord, I had no idea this was possible. Just... Thank You.

"You doing okay?" A comforting hand brushed her shoulder, as Benjamin's voice rumbled softly in her ear.

"Yeah. I'm good." She stepped backward into his chest and pulled his arm around her shoulders. "You're going now, right?"

He'd changed back into the clothes he'd been wearing the day before. He'd hand-washed them and gotten out the dirt, but there was no helping the gaping holes and grease stains in his jeans.

"Yeah, I'm sorry. I have to. My sister's getting married in a little over eight hours, and I've got a seven-hour drive ahead of me. But call me if you need anything. Or if you can't reach me because I'm out of cell phone range, call my sister and leave a message there. I left her number on the pad beside your phone."

"It's okay." She turned around inside his arms and his strong hands brushed the small of her back. "You go be where you need to be. I'm going to be just fine. Promise."

They were standing in the middle of the living room, while people rushed around and chaos reigned around them. But, in that moment, it was as if nothing else existed but his eyes on her face and his arms hugging her goodbye.

"I wish you could come with me," he said softly. "And I wish I could stay to help with Christmas Eve."

"Well, I don't wish you could stay." *Not at The Downs. Not forever. Because it's not who you are. It's not where you belong or what would make you happy.* "You've waited all your life for this trip. So you go. Just say goodbye, hug me tight and then go."

"It might take a few days before I leave. I still have to sort my passport and rebook my flight. If I have a bit more time—"

"Just go. Don't look back. I don't want to have to keep saying goodbye to you over and over again."

She closed her eyes and felt the scruff of his beard on her cheek. Then his lips hovered over hers.

"Hey! Isn't that Benji Duff?" a young voice shouted from somewhere behind her. "Hey, dude, look! I think that's the snowmobile crash guy! Yo! Benji! What did it feel like to almost die?"

Benjamin kissed her on the top of her head. Then he stepped back. "Goodbye, Piper."

She took in a deep breath and let it out slowly. When she opened her eyes, he was gone. She blinked hard. No, she wasn't going to cry.

"Piper, honey? Can you come here a second?" Aunt Cass's voice cut through the noise inside the house. "I was just telling people about the wonderful paper decorations you made for us years ago. I was wondering if you wanted to show us."

Piper nodded. "Sure thing."

She suspected her aunt was trying to give her a distraction, something to keep her hands busy while she calmed the raging battle of emotions inside her heart. For that, she was grateful.

She walked over to the dining-room table and sat down. Her hands reached, unseeing, for a scrap of newspaper and tore it into triangular strips. Tear, fold, weave. Set aside. Grab a new sheet. Tear, fold, weave. If she just keep her hands moving, let the pain move through her like a river, she'd be fine.

"Hey, who taught you to make paper stars?"

She looked up. Dominic was standing above her on the stairs. His eyebrow rose. Oddly, he looked more than a little troubled. It was worrying.

"Nobody taught me to do this. It's just some craft I invented as a kid."

Aunt Cass patted her arm. "She made a huge, beautiful newspaper star for me this way when she was about eight or nine. Used to sit on top of my tree." Her aunt's eyes darkened. "It was one of the things that we lost that Christmas Eve six years ago."

Dominic's face paled. As Piper watched, his hand rose to his mouth. Then he turned and darted up the stairs.

What on earth?

Piper jumped up and followed after him. She caught up to him part way up the stairs. "What's up with you?"

"I'm so sorry, Pips! I think I did a really stupid thing. But believe me, I didn't know!"

Chapter Fourteen

Dominic clenched his hands. Whatever he'd done had left him so agitated it almost frightened her. She glanced through the large front windows. Benjamin was standing in the driveway, saying goodbye to Uncle Des. By the look of things, two teenaged boys had followed them out. One of them was now trying to get Benjamin to autograph his hat.

Dominic edged his way up the staircase, weaving his way around the staircase choir. He disappeared into his guest room.

She rapped on the door. "Look, Dominic. I'm your friend. Whatever you did, whatever you're upset about, you can tell me."

There was a long pause. Then the cop-in-training opened the suite door. His shoulders hunched. "I kissed someone I shouldn't have kissed."

That's it? Piper's gaze ran down to the mass of people teeming below. Her friend was having a crisis, on

Christmas Eve, over an ill-advised romantic interlude?
"Who did you kiss?"

Dominic's gaze dropped to his feet. "Charlotte."

"You kissed Charlotte?" Piper's voice rose to a shriek.

Dominic nodded miserably. "I'm sorry. I didn't know what kind of person she was."

How could he have possibly kept a secret like this from her?

She ushered him into the room. "When was this? Recently? Is she nearby? When are you seeing her again?"

"No, of course not! It was six years ago!"

Piper's shoulders sank.

Dominic's gaze dropped to his feet. "We hit it off the night you brought her here. But she told me we could only be friends in secret and you could never know. We used to meet in the trees. She had this terrible former boyfriend she was really scared of. She was afraid he was going to come to The Downs and cause trouble. One night I was comforting her. Then the next thing I knew, she was kissing me."

She probably shouldn't be surprised, after all this lined up with everything she already knew.

"I didn't know she was going to rob you," Dominic said, his voice rising. "She said she was going away for a while and that I shouldn't try to find her, but that she'd come back as soon as she could. She gave me this beautiful newspaper star on Christmas Eve and told me she'd made it for me because I was such a nice guy. I had no idea she'd stolen it from you. Honest, Piper! If

I had, I'd have made sure you got it back. She made me promise I'd keep it forever. But I was so embarrassed after everything that happened I just hid it in a box in the cupboard because I thought it was just some random Christmas thing."

Piper ran her hand through her hair. He'd been only about nineteen at the time. She couldn't begin to imagine the turmoil his emotions must have been in. "Where's the star now?"

He looked around the room. "In one of the boxes of stuff in my car. That's why I ran to my room right now. I thought I might've brought it in. But it must still be in the trunk of the car."

In Dominic's car? The car that he'd lent to Benjamin to drive to Manitoulin Island? She ran to the window and looked out just in time to see Benjamin shut the driver's-side door. She squeezed Dominic's shoulder. "It's okay. Please don't worry about it. Charlotte made a fool out of a lot of us. I'm going to run and try to grab Benjamin before he leaves."

A handmade newspaper star from her childhood might be a small thing. But it would still be one special thing she could do for Aunt Cass. She dashed down the stairs, grabbing her coat as she sprinted out the front door.

"Benjamin!" The car was pulling away. She chased it down the driveway, waving both hands over her head. "Hey, wait!"

But the small red car pulled onto the road and disappeared.

She went back to the house and shrugged off her

coat, feeling like a balloon whose air was slowly seeping out. One of his sister's friends would be driving the car back for Dominic a few days after the wedding. She could get the star back then.

But, watching Benjamin drive away while she'd run after him waving frantically caused a pain that stung her chest.

True, he hadn't noticed she was there. Yet, she'd really wanted to remember the other goodbye, the final one of this Christmas. The one where she was strong, composed and encouraged him to go. Not one where she chased after him frantically, even if she was only after a sentimental newspaper Christmas craft.

"Hey, did anyone bring some string? I'm running low and wanted to weave some bows through the banister." The request came from the teenaged boy standing above on the balcony.

"Absolutely," Piper called up. "Pretty sure I've got both fishing wire and a roll of twine downstairs."

Her feet echoed down the stairs into the empty basement. A cold breeze brushed her body as the door swung shut behind her. She paused a moment and let her eyes to adjust to the darkness. A few moments alone to compose herself probably wasn't a bad idea. Besides she'd always liked the cellar. It was crowded, cluttered and comforting, far too small for a house the size of The Downs, and full of hidden nooks and crannies. Mysterious and peaceful all at once.

She heard something crash in the darkness. She glanced up, just in time to see a flash of blond hair peeking out from under a navy ski mask. Blondie!

"Hey! Stop!" Piper dashed after her.

Blondie climbed onto a low shelf and then leaped through the open basement window.

If the woman thought after all this Piper would let her just run, she had another thought coming. Piper sprinted across the basement floor, dove through the window and crawled out into the snow. Ahead of her she could see a slim figure running for the trees.

Nice try, Blondie, but nobody outruns an athlete on her home turf.

Piper dashed after her through the snow. When Blondie hesitated, Piper lunged, catching the slender woman around the knees and throwing her into the snow.

Blondie struggled wildly, but Piper flipped her over and pinned her down hard.

She yanked the ski mask off, taking the fake blond wig along with it.

She stared down at the thin, short-haired brunette lying in the snow.

Trisha.

So, the blond hair had been fake. Did that mean... She glanced at the woman's slender waist. Trisha's pregnant belly had been fake, too. Piper shook her head. Benjamin had been right when he said the right clothes could do a lot to disguise the shape of someone's body.

"Where is Alpha?" Piper said. "What on earth has he gotten you into?"

The windshield wipers cut back and forth past Benjamin's eyes. Less than an hour after leaving Piper's he was caught inside an unexpected snow squall. He'd taken Des's advice and stuck to empty back roads instead of the main highway and, according to the snippets of traffic and weather he was able to catch on the intermittent radio, he'd made the right choice. But still the car was crawling forward and the snow was so thick it was practically a whiteout.

Dominic's car was tiny. Way lighter on the road than the comforting bulk of Benjamin's four-wheel drive truck. Even with the front seat slid all the way back Benjamin could barely make room for his cramped legs. The boxes Dominic had left in the back made visibility even harder. He'd driven his sister's hatchback from time to time, when circumstances demanded it, but why any grown man would voluntarily drive such a small car was beyond him.

A sudden pang of sadness nicked his heart.

He really missed his truck.

Along with his torn bag, his clothes, his passport—and the sense of certainty he'd had in his heart just two days earlier.

He glanced in the rearview mirror. Was that another set of headlights behind him? He couldn't even remember the last time he'd been passed by another vehicle. There was no music on the radio, nothing in the tape deck and nothing to see out the window but an endless stream of white in all directions.

Nothing to distract him from thoughts of Piper.

Nothing to keep the smell of her hair, the touch of her hand, or the curve of her smile from taking over the corners of his mind and driving him crazy. How was he ever going to manage missing her this much? How soon would it be until thoughts of her faded away?

His cell phone started to ring from its mount on the dashboard. He pushed the button. "Hello?"

"Benji?" Meg's voice echoed through the tiny car.

"Hey, sis! All is well. I'm still on my way. At this rate I'll be there by five thirty."

He heard Meg breathe a prayer of relief under her breath.

His eyes rose to the rearview mirror again. Those headlights were growing closer.

Was someone actually going to try to pass him in weather like this?

"You've got to speak louder," he said. "I'm using the phone hands-free. In fact, I should hang up soon. It's like driving through a milk shake."

"Okay. Can you send your GPS location to my phone, so I have a sense where you're at?"

"Sorry, I forgot." Fortunately he had a map function installed on his phone that not only kept track of where in the world he was, but emailed it to others. Meg was already preprogrammed in. All it took was the push of a button. "Done. You should be able to see my whole route. But my exact location may not be that accurate, though, as I keep blipping in and out of cell-tower range." The headlights behind him now filled his rearview mirror. "I've gotta go. See you soon."

"Drive safe."

"Will do." He hung up and gripped the steering wheel with both hands.

The vehicle behind was far too close for his liking

now. It was big, too. A large, old pickup truck apparently being driven by the kind of person who thought they owned the road. The truck inched closer.

Hey, buddy, back it up, okay. There's no reason we can't share. Benjamin slowed even more and nudged the car over to the side of the road, giving as much room as possible for the other vehicle to pass. The truck pulled alongside him. Benjamin glanced toward the other vehicle and gave what he hoped looked like a friendly wave toward the tinted window. *Just go ahead and pass. This doesn't have to be a race. We've all got places to be this Christmas.*

The truck didn't pass. The truck's passenger window rolled down. Benjamin's blood froze as he looked over into the cold dead eyes of the man who'd threatened Piper and come hunting for Charlotte.

Kodiak raised his gun and fired.

Benjamin's window exploded inward. The bullet barely missed him before coming to rest in the passenger-side door. Glass filled the front seat.

Benjamin gripped the wheel tightly. He forced his gaze on the road ahead and his heart to the God above.

Help me, Lord. Help me. I can't outrun Kodiak in this car. I can't escape him. I—

Another gunshot.

This one clanged somewhere on the body of the car.

The prayer choked in Benjamin's throat. His mind froze. He was trapped.

Just like that moment, almost sixteen years ago, when he'd seen the headlights of that transport truck barreling through the snow toward him and had been convinced he was going to die.

Another shot exploded his front tire and the car spun off the road. It crashed through the barrier and careened down the hill.

He rolled, side over side, through the trees. Then slammed to a stop upside down as an air bag exploded in his face.

The seat belt snapped him back against the seat holding him upside down in the overturned car.

The sound of the horn filled his ears.

He started to pray. *Lord, please don't let me die this way. Not on Meg's wedding day. Not on Christmas Eve. Piper needs...*

Darkness swam before his eyes. He could feel the deep pull of unconsciousness at the corner of his mind now, like an old enemy waiting to strike. He gritted his teeth and tried to resume his prayer but he couldn't shake the feeling that he was about to pass out. His eyes wouldn't open. His limbs wouldn't move. Time seemed to ebb and flow around him, as he fought to stay in control.

From outside the vehicle he thought he heard footsteps crunching in the snow. Or was he hallucinating?

"Move a muscle and I'll shoot you." It was Kodiak's voice, right in his ear. Cold fingers grabbed his face and held them in their viselike grip. "I will find Charlotte. You can't stop me."

A hard, sudden blow snapped Benjamin's head back against the seat.

Unconsciousness took hold.

Chapter Fifteen

A light flashed somewhere in the distance. Benjamin could hear a voice shouting, but far away, like someone trapped in the distant fog. His entire body ached and he could barely move. He forced his eyes open. He was in the upside-down, crushed hatchback—suspended by a seat belt with a face full of air bag. The beam of light scanned back and forth on the hill above him. A voice echoed, disjointed on the wind. "Hello? Hello? Is anyone there?"

"Over here!" He tried to shout but the words left his throat as barely more than a groan. He fumbled in the front pocket of his jeans for his pocketknife, yanked out the blade and hacked away at the seat belt. He fell free and crumbled into a ball on the ceiling of the car. The door was bent in and the handle wouldn't move, but he kicked the door hard with both feet, pounding into the metal until it flew open. He crawled out.

He was at the bottom of a steep hill. A wall of snow

and trees rose above him. It was a wonder anyone had been able to find him down here.

"Benjamin!"

He blinked, unable to let his heart believe what his eyes were seeing.

Piper was running down the hill toward him.

Strength surged in his chest. He pulled himself to his feet. She flew into his arms and her lips brushed his cheek. "Benjamin! Are you okay? What happened? Where are you hurt?"

"Kodiak ran me off the road." And that was it. He suddenly lost the ability to find words to speak. One moment he'd thought he was about to die. The next, Piper was running down the snow toward him. He held her close. "Piper…" His hands cupped her face. "Is it really you?"

"Yeah." A laugh of relief slipped through her lips. "It's really me, I'm really here. But more importantly, how are you? What happened? Can you walk?"

His arms slid around her waist and pulled her tightly against him. Was she kidding? Just knowing he was still alive and she was here, he felt as if he could fly. "Yeah, I can walk. Everything aches, but I've been worse. Between the air bag, the seat belt, the deep snow and the layers of winter clothes I have on, I seemed to be pretty well cushioned." His lips brushed her cheeks and he tasted tears. So many questions were tumbling through his mind that he didn't know where to start. There were probably just as many tumbling through hers. "How did you find me?"

"When you didn't answer your phone, I called your

sister." Piper had called Meg? But why? His head was still spinning and Piper was talking so fast she was barely pausing for breath. "She told me the route you were taking and told me where she'd lost your signal. When I spotted the smashed railing I followed the footprints down and trail of debris and Dominic's things—"

"Dominic's things?" He pulled back and followed a few steps around the back of the car in the direction she was pointing. The back of the hatchback was smashed open. The contents of Dominic's boxes were strewn in the snow. "Kodiak must've come down the hill through the snow to steal something by the look of it. But what could he possibly be after in Dominic's stuff?"

"My guess? The newspaper star I made my aunt. Dominic's the guy Charlotte was sneaking out to see. Probably even the person Uncle Des saw her kissing. She apparently stole my newspaper star and gave it to him. Maybe that's even what Trisha had Gavin looking for when he trashed all the Christmas decorations in the barn. Alpha did text something about checking in 'Christmas things.'"

There were so many questions cascading through his mind he didn't even know where to start. "How would he find Charlotte from a newspaper star you made your aunt as a child?"

"No idea. Maybe Charlotte wrote something on it before she gave it to Dominic. Some sort of address, phone number or clue to where she is now. Then again, I made it out of very old newspapers I found in the basement and Charlotte was studying history. Maybe she thought it was worth something. Because Alpha was tracking her down, maybe she gave it to Dominic for safekeeping. We might never know." Her hand slid over his arm. "There's a whole lot we still need to talk about, but all that really matters right now is that it's cold, you just survived a car accident and we still have to get you to your sister's wedding. Come on. There's hot coffee and cookies in the truck. I called 911 before I walked down the hill, so police and ambulance are already on their way."

They climbed up the steep hill, walking slowly as Benjamin gingerly tested his limbs for injuries. The remnants of Dominic's boxes lay around them, slowly disappearing under a dusting of snow. The star was nowhere to be seen. They trudged upward. Something was niggling at the back of his mind, something very important about Christmas and Piper being here. But his head still ached and his mind was swimming in so many circles it was hard to focus.

His eyes rose to the highway above and he was so shocked by what he saw that he could barely believe he wasn't hallucinating. "Is that my truck?"

"Yes!" Happiness shone in Piper's eyes. "That's why I called your sister to begin with and then came after you. I managed to get it back for you, along with your bag, your passport, your ticket—everything. All of it. It's all right there. Now, you can catch your flight tomorrow."

For a moment he couldn't tell if she was laughing or crying. He grabbed her around the waist and hugged her so tightly her feet left the ground. Then they climbed into the truck. She pulled out a Thermos from behind the passenger seat.

"Like I said, we have a whole lot to talk about. Blondie in the navy ski mask was Trisha. She wore a wig and mask when she was stalking me and a fake belly when she wasn't. You were right when you said we should think about how clothes disguise people." She poured him a cup of coffee. The steam rose. "I caught her poking around the basement, chased her down and tackled her."

"Nice!" Again that unsettling feeling that he was forgetting to ask her about something important kicked at the back of his brain. He glanced at the clock. Quarter to twelve. He'd been out for over an hour.

"Thanks." Piper smiled. "I convinced her to tell me where she'd hidden your truck. She also backed up everything that Gavin said and most of what we suspected."

He raised the cup to his lips and drank. He'd never tasted better coffee. "She was working for Alpha?"

"Worse. She was dating Alpha. Exact same story, just six years later. They met online. He got scary. She wanted to get away from him. Only she says he started slipping sometimes and calling her 'Charlotte' when he was upset and demanding she wear a blond wig so she looked like her, too. Creepy stuff. She thought finding Charlotte for him would be her way out. When he told her that Charlotte said she'd be here this Christmas, she offered to come to The Downs and convince Charlotte to take him back. Took Gavin with her as backup, pretended to be sick and pregnant so Gavin would keep his distance, and created a cover story for them in case Charlotte needed convincing." She leveled her eyes at him over the mug. "I get the impression she was more than ready to kidnap Charlotte if that's what it took to get Alpha off her back. Only when she got here, she couldn't find Charlotte."

"Did she give you Alpha's name?"

"No, that's one thing she wouldn't spill. I get the impression she's really scared of him. It was like part of her was kind of relieved to be arrested. But she didn't deny it when I accused her of breaking into my room at night. Alpha apparently texted her that he'd actually seen Charlotte go into my room, so she was really surprised when she broke in and it was just me. The weirdest part of the whole thing for me is, just like Gavin said, Alpha's texts started getting bizarre until she had no idea what she was looking for or where."

Like "check the Christmas things" and "check the brick."

Flashing red-and-blue lights were coming toward them. "How did Kodiak know that I had the newspaper star? And even if Charlotte had written her address and phone number on the thing, why would Alpha think he could still use it to trace her six years later?"

A police car pulled in front of them. Another stopped behind.

"No idea," Piper said. She ran both hands through her hair. "Aunt Cass and Uncle Des are working out an arrangement with Dominic where he takes a suite whenever we have guests so I'm never staying there alone with strangers. And if I ever do manage a night without guests, I'll stay over at Silver Halls with Aunt Cass and Uncle Des. Now that Trisha and Gavin have been arrested, police are hopeful the harassment will stop. But they'll also be doing a media blitz about everything that's happened, which will hopefully get word back to Alpha that there's no point looking for Charlotte at The Downs. Oh, and they have a pretty good suspect on Kodiak, too. They think he might be a career criminal called Cody Aliston, so they're issuing a warrant. Hopefully, this will all be the end of it."

The end of it. So that was it? It was over? Benjamin ran both hands over his face feeling as if he'd been knocked out for months instead of minutes. It was like waking up from a coma to catch up on the story that had been his life. Only instead of having people urgently trying to tell him everything that had gone wrong in his absence, this time everything had been wrapped up. He'd missed the finale, and other people had stepped up to do what he hadn't been able to.

Piper didn't need him as her hero.

There was nothing to stop him from catching his Christmas flight.

"Christmas Eve at The Downs!" He grabbed her hand, as he suddenly realized what had been kicking the back of his brain. What was Piper doing here, sitting beside him in his truck, when she had a huge event to run? "You've got to get back to The Downs!"

"It's fine." She pulled her hand away from his. Cops were walking to her door. "Aunt Cass and Uncle Des have it covered. They're scaling things down to what they can manage and relying on a lot of volunteers. Someone needed to bring you your stuff and it made the most sense for it to be me. Not to mention your truck is so much better for this weather than the hatchback you were driving. I was going to try to meet up with you, switch vehicles and drive Dominic's car back."

He glanced toward the cliff where the hatchback lay crushed at the base.

"Don't worry," Piper said, following his gaze. "My aunt's friend on the island has a spare car she'll lend me to get home."

He felt as if he should be arguing, but wasn't sure quite what to say. She couldn't just show up, say she was skipping the event she'd been single-mindedly focused on and not give him a real explanation.

What happened when I was unconscious? What am I missing?

And why won't Piper meet my eye?

An officer knocked on the truck door.

"Christmas Eve happens every year. Your sister and her fiancé only get married once." She squeezed Benjamin's arm, but her gaze wouldn't quite meet his. "There isn't enough time to get me back to The Downs and you to the island both, and we can hardly expect the cops to ferry us around the province. Let's just hope we can file a report and get you checked out quickly, so you can still make it home for the wedding."

They drove to the island in uncomfortable silence, both of them staring straight ahead through the windshield at the lightly falling snow.

Piper glanced over at Benjamin as he slowed the truck to cross the swing bridge to Manitoulin Island. Thankfully, despite the fact Benjamin's jacket hid some impressively large bruises on his arms and chest, the paramedics had been convinced to let him continue on to Meg's wedding. The police had even given them an escort for a while, until the cruiser turned off to head back to the closest provincial division.

But the joy-filled thankfulness and relief that seemed to fill Benjamin when she'd first found him had descended into awkwardness. He wanted her to go back to The Downs. That much was clear. But there wasn't any time. Benjamin's large, sturdy four-wheel truck had the best possible chance of cutting it through the storm and getting him to the island on time. Dropping her off at a car-rental place at night on Christmas Eve was silly when there was a vehicle waiting on the island she could borrow.

But still they'd argued and when she hadn't given in, he'd lapsed into stony silence.

She'd made peace with her decision to miss Christmas Eve. Why couldn't he? As the truck mounted the bridge she looked down at the frozen lake spread out on either side, icy gray with dark waters showing here and there through the surface.

He didn't understand what had happened in those minutes between when he left and when she found him, and she'd never explain it to him.

Her uncle and aunt had taken her aside. Aunt Cass had held her hands when she had told her, *"Get in the truck, go after Benjamin. Make sure he gets his stuff*

*on time and that he walks into his sister's wedding with
none of that stress on his shoulders."*

"I'll miss Christmas Eve."

A soft light had twinkled in her aunt's eyes. *"But,
you'll be giving someone you love both peace of mind
and joy—which this Christmas might just be the best
gift you can give him."*

Someone she loved? What did her aunt think she'd
seen when she'd watched the two of them say goodbye?

"Trust me." Uncle Des's hand had fallen on her
shoulder. "Your aunt and I have been managing bigger crises than this together long before you were born.
We're built of stronger stuff than you seem to think
sometimes. Benjamin's a good man and that's some
talk he gives on chasing dreams and taking chances.
So go. Wish him a merry Christmas from us and then
come home in time for Christmas morning. We'll be
okay."

So she'd followed Benjamin. She'd followed the
route he'd sent his sister, down snowy, twisting back
roads in a storm. She'd done that one thing she promised herself she'd never do—left what mattered most
to her and followed a man, because she realized she'd
loved him.

Even though everything about him now seemed to
indicate he wished she wasn't there.

Benjamin looked at the clock on the dashboard. It
was five thirty. He frowned. "The church is still half
an hour from here. We're not going to make it for the
start of the service. I'm just going to skip it, go home,
get changed and show up at the reception."

"You'll make it. It'll be tight but—"

"I'm wearing grease-stained jeans with giant holes in the knees. I'm a mess from the car crash. I have to get cleaned up and change into my tux. I need to shave and—"

"Your sister won't care about any of that!" Why was he even arguing about this? Her eyes scanned the torn jeans and plaid shirt that fit him as comfortably as a second skin. "Your sister loves *you*, more than anything! You can show up dressed just as you are and she won't care."

No response. Just a deeper frown. It was as if he wasn't even hearing her and instead just listening to a voice in his head that only he could hear—one that seemed to be berating him.

"It doesn't matter," he said. "It's too late, anyway. While you were talking to the police, I borrowed an officer's phone, called her and told her she'd have to go ahead and get married without me."

"But we're so close now!" Piper argued. "We can call her on my phone, tell her we're only thirty minutes out, and ask her to postpone the wedding for an hour. You know she will."

"But she shouldn't have to!" Benjamin smacked the steering wheel. His voice echoed through the cab. When he glanced at Piper her heart leaped in her chest. Behind the frustration burning like flames in the blue of his eyes echoed a deeper pain than she'd ever seen there before. "You don't get it, Piper. I've let my sister down. Again! And I made you miss your big important Christmas Eve thing."

But you don't understand! I chose to miss it. I chose you.

And I don't know how to tell you that.

She opened her mouth to speak, but he waved her down.

"Please, don't try to tell me it's not my fault, that it's because of Charlotte, or Gavin, or Trisha, or Kodiak, or Alpha. I made choices. Me. I chose not to lock my truck outside the barn when Trisha stole it. I chose not to shoot Trisha when she escaped through the snow and not to choke Kodiak until he was unconscious when I caught him in the alleyway. I chose to take an empty back highway to get to the island instead of inching along the main road. I..." He took a deep breath. Then his chest fell. "I chose to come see you and drop the dog off in person, because I wanted to see you one more time before I went. If I hadn't done that you might not have even been down by the barn for Kodiak to attack you."

But you saved me!

She waited a moment while he crossed the bridge. Then they hit shore.

"Everyone makes mistakes," she said softly.

"Yeah, but my mistakes hurt people, Piper. Don't you get that?" The truck wound through the narrow, island highway. "My mistakes hurt people. I made the mistake of not wearing a helmet snowmobiling when I was fifteen years old, and my sister spent years paying for that. You know the accident happened just two weeks before her birthday? So instead of having a party and opening gifts, she spent the day huddled around my hospital bed, wondering if I was ever going to wake up from the coma."

She slid her hand across the seat toward him. He didn't take it.

"I made my sister miss her high school graduation, too," he added, "and her plans to go away for university, and my folks' plans to go to Florida for their thirty-fifth wedding anniversary. My sister couldn't go anywhere on the island, for the whole rest of her life, without people trying to talk to her about the most traumatic thing she'd ever lived through. No wonder she had anxiety. She lost so much all because I was the dummy who went snowmobiling without a helmet."

He ran his hands over his head. "So, I don't do that anymore. Got it? I'm not the guy who causes problems anymore. I'm the guy who fixes them. I'm the one who finds solutions and makes them happen. I'm not the problem that other people have to worry about. Not anymore. Not for Meg. Not..." His eyes glanced at her face for a moment before snapping back to the road. "Not...for anyone."

What was he saying? That he thought *he* was a problem for *her*?

He looked so pained and frustrated with himself.

She pulled her hand back and crossed her arms. "You're right. You went snowmobiling without a helmet, underage, on a highway, without a license, and got hit by a transport truck. You were badly hurt. You hurt people who loved you. Those were some colossally dumb decisions you made right there."

His eyebrow rose. "I can't believe you just said that."

"I'm not going to sugarcoat it," she said. "I don't think you'd want me to. But it's the decisions you made after that which matter. You decided to own up to what you'd done, and create an incredible sports business. You encouraged other people to take risks, be brave and live their life to the fullest while teaching them to also be smart and safe at the same time. That's pretty amazing. Now you're about to fly overseas and sail the world. You take more risks than anyone else I know."

Benjamin didn't meet her eye. "No, I don't," he said quietly. "Not where other people's hearts are concerned." He slowed at a traffic sign. "Oh, sure, I bungee jump and kayak and rappel. But that's just the science of levers and pulleys and helmets. Controllable, predictable elements. But other people's feelings…" His voice trailed off.

Shivers ran down Piper's arms and down her spine. She knew what he didn't say. Other people's feelings weren't always controllable or predictable.

He pulled through the intersection and kept driving. "Your uncle Des came out to say goodbye when I left. Thanked me for a talk of mine he'd heard. Said it really encouraged him to think through what risks he was willing to take in his future. Called me brave." He shrugged. "All I could think was that he was the brave one. Your uncle has been with the same woman for over forty years! They survived moving from one country to another, the bottom falling out of his work and not being able to move back. They went through not being able to have kids of their own. They took you in and raised you. Now they're facing years of health problems."

The truck left the small town and pulled onto another rural road.

"Your uncle is a braver man than I will ever be. I've been responsible for only one person my whole life, my sister. But I always had total faith that was temporary, and one day she'd be standing on her own two feet. That was it. That was my one shot being somebody else's guardian. I can't ever be anyone's full-time, solid rock and anchor person. Not like your uncle and aunt are for each other. Because if I did and I let that person down, I'd never forgive myself. That's what I was trying to tell you back in the restaurant on the island last summer, when you suddenly had to get up and go. I just can't ever let myself—"

A car whipped around them and Benjamin hit the brakes in a controlled skid.

His hand landed hard on the horn.

Finish the sentence, she wanted to yell at him. *You can't let yourself what?*

But he obviously wasn't ready to finish his thought and she wasn't about to push. She pressed her lips together and forced herself to wait. The sign for his town loomed ahead of them.

"Meg asked me to walk her down the aisle," he said after a few long minutes. "Now, she's the kind of independent woman who'd be quite happy walking herself down the aisle. But she asked me. And…and everybody in that church is going to look at me and still think of me as that irresponsible younger brother who wrecked the family's life, no matter how hard I worked to fix what I'd done. They're all going to see me run in late, making her wait, in torn, stained jeans, and roll their eyes at how foolish, irresponsible Benji Duff is same as he ever was.

"I'm going to ruin her special moment!" His voice rose. "It was always going to be like that. Even if there was some way I could rush home, shave, cut my hair, put on a tux and show up looking like a million bucks, what difference would it make, really? They're all going to know that I'm not good enough for that honor! I'll know that I'm not good enough."

And there it was.

"So, don't be good enough." Her hand slipped onto his arm. "Whatever being 'good enough' is even supposed to mean. She didn't ask you to be good enough. She asked you to be there. So, go. Go be your sister's guardian and best friend one last time. She's strong enough to tell you to go home and change, and delay things while you do. Just show up, right now, in your old jeans and red plaid shirt, and be her brother. Not because you're perfect, worthy, or what somebody else might say is 'good enough.' But because you're the only sibling each other has got and you love each other, and that's all that actually matters."

He blew out a long breath. She closed her eyes, leaned her head back against the seat and let her heart pray with feelings she didn't even know how to put into words.

The truck stopped and she opened her eyes. A small

country church sat ahead of them. The clock read six fourteen.

Benjamin unbuckled his seat belt. "Come on. If I'm doing this thing you're coming in with me."

He leaped from the truck and ran through the snow toward the small church. Piper followed. His footsteps pounded up the church steps and he opened the door. There stood Meg, beautiful and breathtaking in a dazzling white beaded dress, trimmed with a white cloak lined with deep red velvet.

Tears slipped from the bride's eyes. "You made it!"

Benjamin swallowed hard. "Of course."

Piper stepped back. But Meg's joy-filled eyes swept over her, her gaze pulling her in. "Thank you so much for bringing my brother to me. Please stay. I'd be so happy to have you. You're welcome just the way you are, but if you want something fancier for the reception, one of my friends runs a consignment formal-wear shop. I'm sure she will be more than happy to help you pop out and find something to wear right after the service." Then Meg squeezed her brother's arm, pulling him to her. "Come on, baby bro. Let's go do this."

Piper waited until the bride and her brother started down the aisle toward her groom. Then she slipped in the back of the church and found space at the end of a pew.

The service was beautiful. She'd never seen two people more excited to start a life together. Carols were sung, candles lit, vows exchanged. Jack's best man, Luke, and his fiancée, Nicky, stood up to read the beautiful familiar Old Testament reading. "Many waters cannot quench love. Rivers cannot sweep it away."

Yet somehow, through it all, she only had eyes for the scruffy, beaming, jean-clad Benjamin. Her heart sobbed.

Her uncle and aunt were right, as much as she didn't want to admit it to herself and would never admit it to Benjamin. She loved him. She'd cared for him since the first moment she'd laid eyes on him last summer, and the feeling had grown inside her until she ached just to be near him. She loved him so much she wanted him to get on that plane tomorrow, fly to Australia, sail the world and make every one of his dreams come true.

She loved him so much she wanted him to leave.

Lord, why is it the only man I could ever imagine going through this life with is the one so determined to never share his life with anyone?

Was she so much like her mother that she was only attracted to men who were destined to leave? At least Benjamin had always been honest with her.

The congregation stood to sing "Joy to The World" as the wedding party started back down the aisle. Piper got up from her seat and slipped out the door.

She couldn't do this. She couldn't stay. She couldn't get dressed up and go to the reception and hang on to Benjamin's arm as if she belonged there, only to watch him leave again.

Lord, give me the strength to say goodbye to this dream.

She walked through town, her boots crunching through the snow as the dark night settled in around her. She reached her aunt's friend who'd offered her a car. After a quick hug and thank-you, Piper was back on the road, driving back over the bridge, toward home. Her phone started ringing. She glanced down. It was Benjamin. She ignored it, even when it rang again. She didn't pick up but instead texted back a quick line to tell him to thank Meg for the invite but that she was heading home.

Then she turned her phone off.

Benjamin frowned at his phone and then set it down on the table. Piper wasn't answering. The flurry of well-wishers who'd come by the head table to ask about his sailing trip had finally trickled off. He'd heard every conceivable joke about showing up at his sister's wedding dressed as a lumberjack. But Meg was happy. The moment he'd seen that joy light up in her eyes he'd known he'd made the right decision.

He looked down at the wedding cake in front of him. Considering how many years Meg had run the top wedding planning business on the island, it was no wonder the food was impeccable. But somehow, every bite had seemed to land in his stomach like sawdust.

Meg swirled off her happy husband's arm and spun across the floor toward Benjamin. She dropped into a chair beside him and squeezed his arm, her face flushed with both excitement and fatigue. "Did you ever manage to get through to Piper?"

"No." Somehow he'd lost sight of her in the hustle of the wedding, but had tried calling to give her the location of the reception. She'd have known the restaurant, since it was where they'd had their last meal together before she'd left the island last summer. In fact, the door she walked out of was right over there. "She isn't answering her phone, but she did send a text message saying she'd decided to go back home."

"Oh?" Meg said. It was amazing how much inflection his sister was able to put in one syllable.

Suddenly, he felt himself blushing. "Yeah, well, the drive here was a bit tense. I told her to head back to The Downs. Maybe she thought I didn't want her here."

Meg's eyebrow rose.

"But it wasn't that," he said quickly. "It was more that I didn't want her to go to any trouble for me or give up on anything that mattered. I tried to explain that I never wanted to be responsible for anyone else's happiness, because I can't trust that I'd never let them down or hurt them."

He slid his head into his hands. It had almost felt as if they were arguing. But he wasn't quite sure what about. Being run off the road like that had reminded him of just how determined he was to never make a commitment to someone else that he might not be able to keep. She hadn't even disagreed with him on any of that.

Meg pulled her chair back against the wall and gestured to him to follow. He did so.

"Two of the people who were stalking The Downs have been arrested," he added. "She's going to have a friend stay there whenever she has guests so she won't be alone with strangers. She tried to make it sound like all the problems of the last few days are sorted and there's nothing else I can do. And she's right, there's not really anything much I can do. So, I don't understand why I'm beating myself up for letting her leave and why my insides feel like they're being mangled in a car crusher."

"You are unbelievable." Meg crossed her arms. Her smile was somewhere between frustrated and amused. "For a long time I thought you were the smartest guy I knew, and now I've never heard you sound so clueless. You're in love with this woman, Benjamin. I saw it in your eyes the first time you mentioned her name, and here she loves you well enough to skip the biggest night of her year and drive fourteen hours round-trip just to make sure you had your passport."

Benjamin could feel a flush rising to his cheeks. "You don't get it, Meg. Even if I did have feelings for Piper, there's nothing I can do about it. I'm sitting at my sister's wedding. I'm flying to Australia tomorrow night. I have a boat, a sailing trip and a new life waiting for me on the other side of the world. She's committed to spending the rest of her life taking care of her uncle and aunt, running a bed-and-breakfast in a town even smaller than this one. She's not happy there and I for sure wouldn't be. Look, it doesn't matter how I *feel*. There's absolutely nothing I can *do*."

His words spluttered to a stop like an engine that had just run out of steam.

Meg nodded. She leaned forward, gathering her billowing dress around her just like she used to do when she was playing dress-up as a child. "Remember that game we used to play as kids where one of us asks a question and the other has to answer it as fast as they can with the first thing that pops into their mind?"

"Yeah?"

"Where do you want to spend Christmas?"

"With Piper." The answer flew from his heart to his lips without a second's hesitation.

"Then what are you doing here? Get yourself back in your truck and go spend Christmas with her."

"But that's a seven-hour drive!"

"I know."

"And I'm flying to Australia tomorrow night."

"Yup. Good thing your bag is all packed and The Downs is only a couple of hours from the Toronto airport." She was smiling now. It was infuriating.

"Meg! I'm at *your* wedding reception!"

"Yes, and you've walked with me down the aisle, I've gotten married, the pictures have been taken and the cake's been cut." She grabbed his arm and yanked him out of the chair. "We can open presents without you."

He was already climbing to his feet. "But I don't know what I'm going to say to Piper. I don't know how to explain why I'm back. I don't even know what I want to do. She still can't come to Australia and I still don't want to stay at The Downs."

"It's okay." She stood, too, and slipped her arms around her brother. "You've always been good at figuring out what to do on the fly. Just pretend you're skydiving, or bungee jumping, or some other crazy, risky thing you went and did that scared the life out of you right before you leaped. Now go, before anyone tries to stop you and talk. I'll say goodbye for you." When he hesitated, she pushed him hard with both hands. "Go!"

He got in the truck and drove through the night. Crisscrossing the province on Christmas Eve probably wasn't the wisest, most well-thought-out decision he'd ever made. But for the first time since Piper had walked out of that restaurant back on the island, he felt as if he was doing exactly what his heart wanted to, and as if every part of his body, heart and mind were finally playing on the same team.

No matter what happened next, it was a wonderful feeling.

It was almost four thirty when he pulled into The Downs parking lot. The lights were still out. Not even a twinkle of Christmas lights in the window or the gentle glow from an upstairs room. He got out of the truck and walked across the snow. Three sets of footprints lay in the snow in front of him. Piper, Dominic and…somebody else? He pulled the hidden key from under a rock by the door, but when he tried it, the front door wouldn't open. The garage door wouldn't open, either. He rounded the back of the house. The back door wouldn't even budge. His eyes scanned the darkened house.

Okay, now what?

He hadn't thought through how he was going to get in the house and didn't want to bang so hard he woke Piper up. But a window on the second floor was open. Well, looked as if his options now were climbing the fire escape and shimmying through a window or sleeping in his truck.

Then he heard the sound of crying. The sad, high-pitched sound floated on the winter air. He followed the sound. It was coming from the wooden kindling box beside the woodpile.

He ran toward the sound. "It's okay. I'm coming."

The whimpering grew louder. He pulled back the latch and threw the lid open. A ball of black-and-white fur launched himself into Benjamin's arms.

"Hey!" Benjamin cradled the dog in his arms and set him gently in the snow. "Are you okay? Did someone hurt you?"

Harry galloped out into the snow a few feet and then back again. Benjamin crouched and ran his hands through the dog's fur checking for injuries. It smelled sickly sweet.

Like chloroform.

A loud boom sounded below him, as if someone was shaking the very foundations of The Downs. A dim light flickered in the basement window. He crouched and looked in.

A figure was standing in the basement, swinging a sledgehammer, knocking blow after blow hard into The Downs's foundation. Benjamin couldn't see his face.

The man disappeared from view and what he saw next made Benjamin gasp.

Piper was sitting in front of a small folding table. Her head drooped against her chest. Her hands were tied behind her to opposite legs of her chair.

The newspaper star was spread out in pieces on the table in front of her.

Chapter Sixteen

Piper's mind swam slowly up into consciousness, as disjointed thoughts and feelings filled her senses. She felt rope dig sharply into her wrists, saw scraps of newspaper float on the table in front of her like scattered islands of letters and shapes. A flashlight lay nearby sending a triangle of yellow light across the table and over the floor. A loud, constant thumping split the air, shattering the concrete walls, exposing the bare brick beneath. The sound seemed to rattle her eardrums and shatter the inside of her skull.

It was as if someone was trying to bring The Downs crashing down with her inside it.

Her eyes fluttered shut again, as memories assailed her.

It had been quarter after three when she'd gotten home. The Downs had seemed eerily empty. No Dominic. No dog. Yet candles had flickered in the living room, covering every possible surface of the room like someone's creepy idea of a romance.

Then a hand had grabbed her neck, and a gun barrel had pressed against her temple. A cloth had been clamped over her face filling her nose with the smell of something sickly sweet.

Now she gasped in a deep breath, filled her lungs and screamed.

"Piper!" The thumping stopped and a man ran out of the darkness toward her. "Don't scream. It's all going to be okay. Just do what I say, and then I can let you go."

Slowly her eyes rose toward him. His hand clenched a sledgehammer. Brick dust covered his body. His face was half-hidden in shadows, but she saw enough to gasp in horror.

"Dominic?"

No. It couldn't be. The young man she'd known since they were kids, who loved his huge family of nieces and nephews and was training to be a cop—*he* was the man now standing over her as she was tied, helpless, to this chair?

"Let me go. Please, Dominic. I don't know what's going on here or what you think you're doing but you have to let me go."

He broke her gaze and gestured toward the scraps of paper on the table in front of her. "Figure out what that means, then this'll all be over."

He raised the sledgehammer high, turned back to the wall and swung. She didn't even glance down at the paper he pointed to.

"I don't care about some paper star or where Charlotte is now!" Her voice was swallowed up by the deafening blows landing against the brick in the darkness.

"I care about the fact my friend attacked me and tied me to a chair. What happened to you? What happened to the Dominic I know? Remember when we were seven and I climbed that tree in the park to get your kite back? Or when we were ten and your family went on holiday so you asked me to come over every day to feed your turtle? Please! Dominic, you're scaring me!"

The thumping stopped. Dominic turned. His face was so pale in the lamplight it was almost white. His eyes darted past her into the darkness.

"It's okay, Piper. I don't want to hurt you. Just focus on solving the puzzle, and it'll be all over soon enough. Please."

The puzzle? She stared down at the table. Someone had taken apart the Christmas star she'd made as a child and spread the pieces over the table, pushing the pieces together at the corners and lining up the lines as best they could. It was a page of newsprint, with headlines about Christmas holidays and fairs, just like a regular community paper.

The date at the top read *December 25, 1924.*

It was issued during American Prohibition, and when Canada's alcohol was under tight government control.

Right around the time of The Downs's rumored speakeasy and smuggling past.

"What are you doing?" she asked him. "What do you think is behind those walls?"

He didn't respond.

Years ago Charlotte had come here looking for a speakeasy. She'd always told Piper so.

And I hadn't believed her, because I'd stopped believing it was real.

But Charlotte had believed. She'd fallen hook, line and sinker for the tales of walls stacked with old, frosted glass bottles of bootleg rum, hidden envelopes of money, bags of jewelry and loot from ill-gotten gains. Charlotte hadn't just robbed The Downs. She'd searched it for some hidden treasure she could use to get away from Alpha.

What if she'd found it?

Piper stared back at the paper. Some lines were darker than others, just slightly, as if the printing plates had been uneven with ink. Subtly, in ways she'd never noticed as a child. Now her adult eyes traced and connected the darker letters like a grid. It looked like there were *blueprints* hidden within the words on the page. If she joined up the vertical and horizontal lines the pattern they formed created walls, entrances, and hallways. But pieces of the page were missing. Strips here. Jagged pieces there. Holes from where she'd torn the paper in her youthful enthusiasm.

"This isn't the whole page," she said. "There are pieces missing."

"Just focus on remembering." Dominic shifted his weight and started on another wall. "Keep reading and fill in the blanks."

So he didn't know about the blueprints and thought it was nothing more than newspaper articles. He might have no clue why Charlotte had stolen this star or what it had to do with finding her. Dominic's swings grew faster, harder. At this rate he'd bring the entire house down.

"But I was a child when made this. I have no way of knowing what was here."

"Piper, please!" Dominic's voice rose, filling the basement. "All we have to do is find Charlotte and then this will all be over."

Find Charlotte? Charlotte was a person. Not a hundred-year-old rumor from history, an object hidden in a box of Christmas decorations or something to find by bashing holes in a wall. Had Dominic lost his mind?

The longer she stared at the paper the clearer the hidden blueprints were appearing. Tunnels were appearing on the page now, a passageway, and what looked like a hidden room.

"Untie my hands. Please." She kept her voice level and firm, pushing through the fear even as it threatened to take her over.

"I'm sorry. I'm so sorry, Pips. I would if I could, but I can't."

Again, Dominic's eyes flitted to the shadows and then around the room, like a mosquito trapped in a jar. Her head turned. But all she could see was the darkness looming in from the corners of the room and filling the cluttered basement.

"Why? Why can't you, Dominic?"

No answer. Sweat ran down Dominic's face. Was he frightened, paranoid, on drugs?

"Dominic! Talk to me! This is crazy. Whatever's going on, I can help you!"

"Just find Charlotte, Pips. Please."

He stepped out of the light and into the darkness. She watched his shadow on the floor as he swung a sledgehammer high over his head. The banging started up again.

Oh, Lord, help me please.

She lowered her head as fear and frustration battled in her mind, laced with a toxic confusion that threatened her ability to even think straight. Her vision swam before her, the pieces fading in and out of focus. They were definitely blueprints, a map. But not for the basement Dominic was desperately chipping away at piece by piece. Nor the barn that Gavin had demolished.

These were blueprints for the main floor of The Downs.

There was the staircase. Here was the entrance to the basement. There was the fireplace—

Something about Christmas things...

Something about brick...

Then suddenly, her gut told her all too well what Charlotte had discovered and why she'd demolished the Christmas tree and decorations to find it. Even why someone would come back here looking for her now—the final winter before they were due to break ground for The Downs renovations.

"I think I know where Charlotte went!"

Dominic froze. Something rustled behind her in the darkness.

"But I won't know for sure without my hands. Some of these pieces aren't in the right place."

Dominic nodded. "Okay. But just one hand."

One hand would have to do.

"Okay. Just one. That's all I need."

Dominic stepped closer. Then he bent down and touched her left hand. His voice dropped until it was barely a whisper. "You know I care about you, Pip, right?"

She nodded to show she'd heard him. But she didn't trust herself to respond.

"Forgive me, Pip." He untied the rope. Her left hand fell free.

"I forgive you, Dominic."

She gripped the chair with her right hand and leaped up, swinging the chair around above her head. It hit Dominic hard on the side of the head, knocking him to the ground.

She scrambled across the floor, yanked her other hand free and grabbed the sledgehammer from the floor.

"Piper! Wait! Please!" Dominic's voice echoed up the stairs behind her. "You don't understand."

Oh, she understood well enough. She had to get upstairs. She had to call the cops.

She had to find Charlotte.

Her feet pounded up the stairs. Just three more steps and she'd be at the top.

A gunshot sounded behind her.

Dominic yelped.

His desperate scream was filled with such pain, it sent shivers through her body.

Then his voice fell silent.

She turned back. Dominic was lying on the floor in the basement now. Blood pooled beneath him.

A figure stood over him, his face hidden in the shadows.

"Hello, darling." A cold voice rasped from the darkness. "You really shouldn't have hit your friend like that. He was only trying to save you and his family. Wouldn't want all those precious little nieces and nephews to have something terrible happen to them on Christmas Day." Dark chuckles poured like ice water over her skin. "I told him I'd let you all live if he followed my instructions and did what I say. Not that I was ever going to let him go alive. Not after what he did."

The sledgehammer tightened in her grasp. She took a step backward up another step. Candlelight was flicking in the living room. Dim and faint. "You're Alpha?" Her feet were now just two steps from the top. "You were the cruel, mean, controlling boyfriend that both Charlotte and Trisha wanted so desperately to get away from. You terrified Charlotte, so much that she wouldn't even go to the cops. She had no family and you were paying her rent and tuition. She thought she could steal something valuable enough to gain her freedom or buy her way to a new life. But you wouldn't let her go, would you? You followed her here. You spied on her and Dominic."

"Stop it!" he bellowed up the stairs toward her. "He has no right to try to take my love from me!"

"But Charlotte got away, didn't she?" Her feet slid back up another step.

A floorboard creaked in the darkness behind her.

Someone else was there in The Downs, behind her in the darkness.

Lord, as much as I wish Benjamin was here, I also hope he's still far, far away and in safety.

"Stop right there. Or I will hurt you." Alpha stepped forward slowly into the light. She saw two well-polished shoes. Tailored tweed pants. A cane.

Piper's free hand rose to her lips. *Tobias.*

The arrogant, delusional man who wrote books about warfare and torture, who in one moment would spout random things out of context and had confused both Trisha and Piper with university students, but in another was lucid enough to spin long, creative stories. He now stood in the tiny pocket of light at the bottom of the basement stairs, a gun in his outstretched hand, still smoking from shooting Dominic.

Ever since Kodiak had first attacked her by the barn it had almost felt like she was stuck in a time loop. Charlotte had come to The Downs six years ago. Yet, Alpha seemed to think she was there now.

What if, in Alpha's mind, it was still six years ago?

All this time she'd foolishly presumed Alpha had to be some young heartthrob to hold such sway over both Charlotte and Trisha. And not just because she'd thought Alpha, not Dominic, was the man Uncle Des had seen Charlotte kissing in the woods six years ago. *It's all about thinking like a predator, Piper.* Now she could imagine how a well-spoken, well-connected man might have sounded as the online suitor and financial benefactor to a vulnerable young woman so many years his junior.

"Surprised I see." A self-satisfied smirk curled at his lips, like a magician too proud of a conjuring trick. A chuckle rumbled in the back of his throat. "Oh, you'll be amazed what you can get a person to do for you if only you know how to motivate them properly. Charlotte and Trisha were all alone in the world and needed caring for. But a disappointing number of people are easy to control by nothing but a very generous check."

Through the blood pounding in her head she heard another footstep behind her. Someone was waiting behind her, hiding, and all she could hear was the sound of their breath.

Benjamin, I have no reason to believe you'd be here. But if you are, signal me somehow. Tell me what I can do to help you save us both.

Her voice rose. "But you failed, didn't you? Charlotte ran into the arms of another man. She came up with a plan to get away from you. Did you catch up with her before or after she destroyed my living room looking for the speakeasy?"

His smirk turned to a grimace.

"Let me guess," she said. "You found her and hurt her, but she got away and you lost her in the house. You tore up The Downs looking for her, but she was gone."

If what Piper had guessed from reading those hidden blueprints was true, she could even forgive Charlotte for tearing down the tree and destroying the nativity. Pain and fear made people do desperate things.

Her hands tightened on the sledgehammer. She picked it up like a baseball bat. He might still have a gun pointed at her face, but just one good swing was all she'd need and then he'd be down. She backed up onto the last step, reaching the main floor. A hand brushed against her back in the darkness.

Benjamin?

Then a hand clamped her throat from behind, choking the air from her lungs. The other grabbed the sledgehammer and yanked her arm hard behind her back. Her wide eyes stared in horror at the crude bear tattoo on his wrist.

No. Benjamin was hours away celebrating happily with friends and family.

It was Kodiak.

Tobias laughed as Kodiak slowly wrenched her arm harder and harder until the sledgehammer fell with a reverberating thud.

Lord, don't let them get away with this. No matter what happens to me, may this monster get caught before he hurts one more woman.

She shook her head, forcing words out as the fingers on her throat slowly grew tighter. "I'm not one of those vulnerable women you can control, manipulate and scare into silence."

"Oh, but, Charlotte, you are." Tobias stepped closer, one step at a time, with an exaggerated, dramatic flair, until he reached the top. "You think brown hair and a pair of glasses could fool me?"

Help me, Lord! He's lost his mind.

Kodiak's grip tightened until the pain forced Piper down onto her knees. Whimpering and helpless, she felt Kodiak tilt her toward him like an animal exposing her neck for the kill. Alpha leaned his face in toward hers until she had no choice but to look in his wild, delusional eyes. "You will never leave me again, Charlotte. I was too kind to you before. But this time I will hurt you. I will break you. Until I make sure you'll never leave."

Chapter Seventeen

The sound of Piper crying out in pain stabbed Benjamin like a knife. He crouched low on the second-floor landing, and watched as Kodiak forced Piper down to her knees. The beat of his heart roared inside him like an ocean wave.

It was now or never. Either he was going to save Piper or die trying.

He crept to the top of the stairs. Then froze. The stairs leading from the second-floor balcony to the living room were gone, nothing but a pile of smashed boards and timber. If he'd been walking faster and not paying attention, he'd have fallen right through to the floor below. *Now what?*

Jump the wrong way and he could break both his legs. Chairs and tables were pressed up still against the walls. The room below was dark and empty except for candles flickering theatrically on the dining room table. No wonder he hadn't been able to see any light through the window. An agonizing breath filled his lungs as he watched Tobias lean toward Piper as Kodiak's grip kept her firmly kneeling there in front of him.

But her eyes shot upward toward the balcony. Was she praying? Did she know he was there?

"Don't you remember?" Tobias's voice echoed through the darkness. "I'm quite the expert in knowing how to hurt a woman so she isn't anywhere near dead, but wishes that she was. Apparently I was all too kind to you."

Then he strode into the living room and spread his arms like a maestro conducting a hidden symphony. Kodiak wrenched Piper's head back and forth so her gaze followed his employer's movements.

"From now on, you do not speak unless I direct you to." His voice rose as if he was addressing a full lecture hall. "Nod, Charlotte, to show you heard me."

She didn't move. Tobias snapped his fingers. Piper gritted her teeth as Kodiak forced her head up and down in a nodding motion.

"Oh, you think you're so strong, don't you?" Tobias's eyes grew cold. He nodded to Kodiak. "Break her arm."

Benjamin couldn't wait one second more. He leaped. His feet hit the back of an armchair just long enough to break his fall, before throwing himself at Kodiak. Out of the corner of his eye he could see Piper slam her elbow back into Kodiak's face and scramble from his grasp.

Kodiak swore in pain and lunged after her. But Benjamin got to him first. His fist flew, catching Kodiak in the jaw and sending him sprawling backward onto the floor. The vicious thug-for-hire leaped to his feet. A knife flashed in his hand. He lunged at Benjamin, with the glint in his eye of a man prepared to kill. Benjamin raised his arm and blocked the blow with one strong movement. Then he forced the attacker's arm down with so much speed that Kodiak's weapon landed deep in his own leg. Kodiak grunted, falling on his injured leg.

"Enough!" Tobias shouted. "Stop right this second! Nobody fights without my permission."

Yeah, that wasn't about to work on Kodiak right now, Benjamin thought, no matter how much Tobias was paying him.

From the corner of his eye, Benjamin saw Kodiak vault at him, landing on top of him. He grabbed Benjamin by the throat and began to squeeze. For a moment he could feel unconsciousness begin to overtake his mind. But this time he wasn't about to go under. He leveled a swift, decisive blow to Kodiak's jaw, followed by a second one that knocked the thug unconscious.

Benjamin climbed to his feet. One down.

Just a delusional madman to go.

"I said stop! Hands up. Or she will die!"

He turned. Tobias had Piper by the hair. Her dark mane was wrapped around one fist, while the other pressed a gun between her eyes.

"Hands up! Now! You think you can take Charlotte away from me?" Tobias's eyes bulged as he nudged Piper's face with the gun. Compliant, Benjamin lifted his hands. The man had completely lost his mind. "Charlotte is mine. Forever. Aren't you, Charlotte? You think she'd ever want a stupid, uneducated thug like you when she could have a real man taking care of her? A man like me?"

Piper's eyes met Benjamin's for one agonizing second. A prayer whispered across her lips. Then her eyes turned to her captor. She met his gaze without flinching.

"You found her here six years ago and you hurt her, didn't you?" Piper said. "Then you went home and got on with your life, finding and hurting other women, all while the memory of what you'd done to her haunted the edges of your rapidly failing mind. But when you saw in the paper that The Downs was about to be renovated, at least part of you worried your dirty little secret might come to light. So, you manipulated people into finding out what had happened to Charlotte. How frightened you must have been. Knowing your mind was slipping. Knowing you couldn't quite remember." She leaned closer, ignoring the gun, until her face was inches from his. "Having fleeting, painful, panicked moments, remembering just what you'd done to the woman you claimed to love, having them bashing up brick and tearing up rooms looking for her. Her dead body."

"Liar!" Tobias's outstretched hand flew toward her face. But she was too quick. Taking advantage of the momentary distraction, Piper broke free. She ducked under his arm and ran for the corner of the room.

That was the moment Benjamin was waiting for. He leaped forward, like a professional tackle. Tobias's weapon fired, seconds before it flew from his hands and clattered into the darkness. Benjamin knocked the would-be alpha to the ground.

But the cry of pain that echoed behind him filled his heart with the sinking knowledge he'd been too late.

The bullet had found its mark.

Piper had been shot.

He turned. "Piper!"

She was down on the ground, pulling herself toward the fireplace. Blood seeped from her pant leg.

"Go!" She grabbed the Christmas tree he'd made for her and used it to pull herself to her feet. "Take care of him. It's just a graze. I'll be okay."

"You really think you can escape and outsmart me this time?" Tobias crawled over to the table. "You think I wasn't prepared? I tried to warn you. I'm the master of booby traps and snares. I've locked all the doors, Charlotte. I've destroyed the stairs. I've hidden explosives at the exits and wired the windows so if you try to escape you'll die."

His eyes were wild, his gestures manic. He wiped blood from his face, then swept a candle up off the table and waved it over the woodpile that once was the stairs. Then he dropped it in.

"You think I just broke your generator to keep you in the dark? I wanted the fuel to start a fire to smoke you out if you didn't come to me. You can fight me until your energy fails. But trust me, there is no exit I haven't thought of and no contingency I haven't planned for."

But you never planned to face a man like me.

And Piper's no Charlotte.

Smoke billowed and flames flickered from the woodpile that had once been the stairs.

Benjamin spun toward Piper. She'd snapped off a hockey stick from the makeshift tree and slid it under her elbow as a crutch. She hobbled toward the fireplace.

"Find a way out!" Benjamin called. "Whatever it takes. Don't wait for me."

"You aren't going anywhere!" Blood poured from Tobias's chin. He pulled the small World War I grenade from his belt loop and waved it like a bone in front of a dog. "A warrior is always willing to die in battle and I will fight you with my dying breath."

Benjamin looked around. Fire rose from the pile of broken stairs. Flames raced up the long, lacy curtains and spread along the second-story balcony. Had Tobias really barricaded all the exits? Were there really booby traps and explosives? Could he risk it?

"Tobias, tell me how we get out of here! None of us needs to die here."

"He's a coward!" Piper shouted. "I suspect that grenade isn't even real. Even if it is, he doesn't have the courage to throw it!"

Benjamin had also presumed it was fake when he'd seen Tobias with it at breakfast yesterday. But what on earth was she doing, taunting a madman who might be holding something explosive?

"Go on!" Piper banged the end of her hockey stick on the floor. "If you think I'm Charlotte and you really want to prove I should fear you, throw it at me!"

Tobias snarled, pulled the pin and lobbed the grenade. Piper caught it in the air with the hockey stick, slapped it to the ground and sent it spinning into the fireplace.

Benjamin threw himself behind the sofa as he heard Piper call out his name.

Her next words were cut off in a rush of falling debris and a scream that seemed to echo from all directions.

A gaping hole in the floor now lay where the fireplace had been.

Piper was gone.

Chapter Eighteen

"**P**iper!" Benjamin ran for the hole that was once a fireplace. He looked down into the darkness. "Are you all right?"

"I'm okay. I just lost my balance." Piper's voice floated up from the hole in the floor. "There seems to be a room down here. But I can't get back up. It must be a fifteen-foot drop."

"Stand back. I'm coming to get you."

Tobias was half sitting and half lying beside the table. Flames climbed the curtains behind him and smoke billowed around him. The second-story balcony was now alight. Tobias pulled a tiny pistol from his ankle and struggled to load it with bullets. "We will fight to the death, you and I. It will be a warrior's death and an honorable end to my life."

Benjamin shook his head in disgust. "There is no honor in murder. You can die if you want to die. I'd rather live."

He grabbed the remains of the Christmas tree,

clipped the windup flashlight to his belt and wound the string of lights around his hand as a makeshift rappel rope to slow his decent.

He slid backward into the hole.

Darkness filled his eyes. Cold damp air seemed to press up against him His feet hit cold stone and he struggled to maintain his balance. Then soft hands slid over his chest.

"Benjamin."

He felt Piper before he saw her. Her face pressed against his chest, then he lifted her head and his lips found hers in a kiss.

He slid one arm around her waist and felt her weight fall into his arms. "Are you hurt?"

"A bit. But I'm okay."

The flashlight whirred to life in his hands. They were standing in a wide cellar. Dusty bottles of amber liquid filled racks by the wall. The remains of a body lay on a bench by the wall, clad in a university jacket and sweatshirt.

Charlotte.

"Charlotte found the speakeasy, and we found her." A choke caught in Piper's throat. Benjamin's arm tightened around her waist and held her close to him. "She must have been so desperate to get away from him she was willing to rob me if that's what it took."

In her mind she created the scenario Charlotte must have faced years ago. "Tobias tracked her to The Downs and attacked her. She crawled in here hoping to hide and escape. She might have even been hoping that Dominic would decipher the star and find her. She probably didn't realize her wounds were fatal until it was too late. I think Tobias suspected she'd found the speakeasy and died here, but didn't know how to find it himself. Then when he read that we were planning to renovate the bed-and-breakfast, he panicked and realized her body might still be found, and there might be evidence on her that would point back to him." She shivered. "Maybe there still is."

She sat back against the crumbling wall. Gently, Benjamin used his knife to slit the bottom of her jeans from heel to calf. Then he tore a strip off the bottom of his sweatshirt and used it to bind Piper's leg wound. Thankfully, it looked as if the bullet had merely grazed her. "Can you walk?"

"Yeah. I think so."

But still, as he helped her to her feet, the wince that escaped from her lips and how deeply she leaned into his shoulder told him that it hurt her to stand. Burning and broken floorboards tumbled through the hole behind them bringing the fire with it. It probably wouldn't be too long before the entire floor above collapsed in. There was a lot of wood down here, not to mention flammable liquid.

He scanned the darkness for a way out and found a small opening on the far side of the room. It looked like a tunnel.

"Come on." He strengthened his grasp on her shoulders. "We've got to get out of here."

Her eyes met his. "Where's Harry?"

"He'll be okay. I left him in my truck with plenty of blankets and the door open, so he can jump out if he needed to. But The Downs is on fire. Once the flames reach down here, with all these bottles of bootleg liquor, the place will explode."

Her arm slid around Benjamin's waist. They ran.

The tunnel was dark and sloped downhill so steeply they could barely see. Walls pressed in on every side. The smell of smoke chased after them. Then they could hear the pop of bottles exploding as the fire reached the speakeasy. They kept running, until the ground sloped down so steeply they lost their footing and went into a slide.

Right into a solid brick wall.

They were trapped.

Panic thudded in Piper's chest.

The air wouldn't last forever and there was no way back. No, they couldn't die trapped here in the ground like this.

Help us, Lord. Show us the way out.

Benjamin shone the windup light in all directions. Above them he saw a shaft. He pressed the flashlight into her hands. "I'm going to try climbing. You going to be okay?"

She nodded and leaned against the hockey-stick crutch. "Yeah, go ahead."

He started climbing, finding holes and ledges for his fingers and toes in the brick. Then he stopped. "There are some loose bricks up here. But I need something to dig them out with."

She braced herself against the wall and passed up

the hockey stick. "Here, use this. It's not going to be much use to me if we can't get out of here."

She waited, breathing through the pain, as he started digging at the bricks with a piece of broken hockey stick. Then a dim light shone through the cracks.

"Thank You, God!" Benjamin shouted an echo of the prayer filling her heart.

The hole grew larger. Then soft white snow fell in toward them.

"Where are we?" she called.

"The barn. I'm pretty glad I smashed my truck into your chimney now. I think I might have busted us an exit."

He hopped down, grabbed Piper around the waist and gently lifted her up until she could crawl out into the snow. Then he crawled through after her and stood. They were beside the remains of the barn, back where Benjamin had saved her from Kodiak two days ago.

The sun was beginning to rise over the tops of the trees.

It was Christmas morning.

Benjamin lifted her up off the ground and into the shelter of his arms.

She slid her arms inside his coat and felt the warmth of his chest. "Thank you for coming back for me."

"There's nowhere else I'd rather be." The scruff of his cheek brushed her face. Then she felt his lips on hers, kissing her deeply.

Smoke billowed through the snow above them. Emergency sirens filled the air and relief filled her chest. Someone must have seen the smoke and called the fire department. She prayed the heavy snow would keep the fire from spreading while the firefighters did their work.

Benjamin carried her through the trees, up toward the house, holding her to his chest. She lay her head on his shoulder, safe in his arms.

Lost in her thoughts she noticed the sirens had stopped. Another sound took over the air.

Voices singing.

"The thrill of hope. The weary world rejoices."

It was as if an entire choir was singing carols.

"Can you hear that?"

"Yeah." His head shook in wonder "It's unreal."

"For yonder breaks a new and glorious morn..."

They followed the sound up the hill. Once they'd passed the tree line they saw the top of The Downs. The roof had caved, the turrets had fallen. But every nook and cranny of the building was covered in shimmering ice, as water blasted from the firefighters' hoses. A frozen castle, it was the most beautiful, surreal sight she'd ever seen.

One of the firefighters ran toward them. "Let me take her."

Benjamin held her close. "No, we're good. Just point me to the paramedics."

He directed them around the front of the house.

"Did you manage to pull anyone else from the house?" Piper asked.

The firefighter nodded. "Three men. They're on their way to the hospital now."

"Please mention to the paramedics that the overweight, middle-aged gentleman seems to be suffering from some kind of mental breakdown," Benjamin said. "He's violent but he's not in his right mind and seems to be trapped in the past."

They kept walking. Piper leaned her head into the crook of Benjamin's neck.

"I know he hurt you terribly and murdered Charlotte," he said, "but Tobias is still a very sick man. I hope the justice he faces is still mingled with some mercy."

Piper kissed his cheek. "I know, and I adore that about you."

Lord, have mercy on them all.

They walked around the front of the house. Then she saw the carolers. Dozens of them were milling about in The Downs parking lot behind the emergency vehicles and police tape, singing carols and holding candles. They poured mugs of hot cocoa and coffee, and passed around muffins as they linked arms. Praying. Singing. Watching. Waiting.

The sun had risen on Christmas morning. And the community had brought Christmas to The Downs.

"It's Piper!" One voice rose from the crowd. "Thank You, Lord!"

"Aunt Cass!"

Her aunt was sitting in a folding chair behind the line of police tape, beside the ambulances, Harry cuddled at her feet and Uncle Des by her side. Benjamin ran toward them. He dropped gently down to one knee beside Aunt Cass, holding Piper to his chest, and she felt her aunt's and uncle's arms slide around her.

"You're hurt," her uncle said.

"Nothing serious. A bullet grazed me. But Benjamin bound it. I'll be okay." She glanced back at the shimmering pile of wood that was once her aunt and uncle's home. "I'm just sorry we couldn't save The Downs."

"Sir." Benjamin was by Uncle Des's side. "I have a boat. It's not much. But if I can find a buyer for it, it might be enough to help give you a head start to getting back on your feet."

Piper's hands grabbed his. "No, Benjamin. Don't. That boat is your dream. You've been saving for it your entire life. You can't give it up for me. I won't let you."

His finger ran down along the side of her face and curled under the back of her neck. "But I love you and I don't want you to lose your home."

"I love you, too," Piper said, "and I don't want you to lose your boat."

Uncle Des smiled. "Thank you for the offer, Benjamin. But whatever we do with The Downs now, it won't involve robbing anyone of their dreams."

Then the old man's eyes turned to Piper. "Your aunt and I had a very long talk last night after you left, mostly about our own dreams and the promises we made to each other. Your aunt Cass gave up her home in England to follow me here. I think it's about time I make good on my promise to take her back home. We don't know what shape that's going to take, but now that The Downs is gone it really feels like the dream we thought we were chasing here isn't going to happen. We'll take a hard look at our finances, see what happens with insurance, contact some of your aunt's friends and family, and try to move back. Now, before you argue, there are good doctors and hospitals in England, too, just like there are here, plus there's less snow to get around so that will help."

Aunt Cass and Uncle Des were going to move across the ocean at their age? With their health problems?

But any doubt Piper had in her mind was quelled when she saw her uncle take her aunt's hand and watched the joy dance in their eyes. The elderly couple bent toward each other in a kiss like the one they'd shared thousands of times before.

Benjamin picked Piper back up in his arms again and started carrying her toward the paramedics, Harry trotting along by his side. Benjamin's mouth brushed over her hair. "I want our love to be like theirs."

So do I.

"But wait." She squeezed his arm. Benjamin stopped. "If my uncle and aunt move to southern England, I'm going with them. There's nothing keeping me here in Canada. It'll be a huge adventure for them." An exciting once actually. She'd finally be able to see the country where she'd been born. "But they're still going to need my help. If they move, I'm going, too."

"I know." He bent his head toward hers until their foreheads touched. "Fortunately, pet laws being what they are, you should be able to take Harry with you no problem. I'm sure he'll learn to bark with a British accent in no time."

"But what about us?" She closed her eyes and breathed him in. "England isn't Canada, but it's still not Australia."

"Nope, it's not." Benjamin laughed. "It's a whole lot colder and lot farther north. I don't know right this very second how we're going to make this work. But I know with my whole heart that I want to. Now that I know I love you and that you love me, I promise I will do whatever it takes to find a way for us to have a chance at spending our lives together. That's all I have to give you this Christmas—the promise that no matter what, I will find a way."

"That's the best Christmas gift you could give me."

Light snow fell down around them and carols filled the air as Piper brought her lips up to his.

"Merry Christmas, Piper."

"Merry Christmas, Benjamin," she whispered back.

Epilogue

A late-August sunrise danced on the dark gray water of the English Channel. Piper's footsteps picked slowly over the smooth stones of the shoreline. A light chill brushed off the early-morning waters. Still, she kicked her sandals off and ran barefoot down the marina's maze of docks. Harry's paws thudded down the wood behind her. She reached the end of an empty slip and sat. Her legs hung over the edge, her feet brushing just above the gentle waves. Her eyes stared out over the expanse of water to the hazy outline of France on the opposite shores. She slipped her phone out of her pocket and turned it on.

For someone who'd never been a fan of getting up early in the morning, it was funny how quickly this had become her favorite time of day. As Benjamin's global sailing trip had him crossing time zones, several hours ahead of her, they'd agreed that whenever he was able to find a phone he'd call her at six o'clock in the morning her time.

Harry stretched out on the dock beside her. Golden rays of sunlight danced along the water. The clock passed six. Her phone didn't ring. She sighed. It had been nine days since Benjamin had been able to make the phone call. Six days since he'd even sent an email.

She opened the email program on her phone to write to him. But instead her eyes ran over the list of emails they'd exchanged in the almost eight months since they'd said goodbye. Her emails had all been so long and chatty, full of news about the sale of the remains of The Downs to a historical society, the ups and downs of her aunt's health journey, the criminal charges filed against Tobias, Gavin, Trisha and Cody Aliston, aka "Kodiak," reconciling her friendship with Dominic as he recovered in the hospital, and finally the huge, exciting adventure of helping her uncle and aunt move overseas to start their new lives.

A sailboat shimmered on the horizon, cutting between her and the rising sun. Her fingers scrolled through screen after screen of the words she'd poured out over the months to Benjamin. Her chest ached.

Yes, she knew he'd never been much of a letter writer. He wasn't much for talking on the phone, either. But while his trip around the world might be bringing him closer to England, these past few months had felt as if he was drifting further and further away.

The boat on the horizon grew closer until she could make out the logo on the sails. It was nothing but a small blue-and-white daytrip boat from a boating tour company down the shore in Brighton. They'd better not be heading for the small marina; they'd have a hard time finding a free place to dock.

Her eyes rose to the sky as it lightened above her.

Lord, was I wrong to think that Benjamin and I could have a future together? I trust his heart. I believe in him. And yet, it's been eight months since The Downs burned down and we're no closer to being together.

Voices were shouting back and forth on the boat. The small craft grew closer. Harry leaped to his feet and barked.

"Shush!" She stood, grabbed his collar with one hand and steered them both down the dock. But the dog braced his legs and stood his ground. She pulled a leash from her pocket and clipped it onto his collar. "Come on. Time for breakfast."

"Piper!"

Her name echoed behind her on the morning air. She turned. A strong figure stood tall in the boat, waving his arms above his head.

She dropped the leash.

He dove off the boat. Strong arms cut swiftly through the water toward her. As he came closer, morning rays of sunlight fell on the full wet beard, dazzling smile and eyes that shone even brighter than the first light of morning.

"Benjamin!" Joy filled her chest, filling her eyes with tears and her mouth with laughter.

He reached her. Two strong hands gripped the dock and then he pulled himself up onto it and stood in front of her, water streaming down his body. She threw her arms around him, anyway. Felt his strong arms pull her tight toward her. Tilted her face toward him and let his mouth find hers in the kiss her heart had ached to feel for eight long months. Then he pulled back and she felt the warmth of his gaze on her face.

"What are you doing here? Where's your boat?"

"I landed in Brighton late last night. My boat's docked there. I'm sorry for not calling, but I didn't want to wake you. A friend of mine gave me a ride over this morning. He's also agreed to give me a job." His hand brushed over the back of her hair. "I'm sorry, baby. I got you soaked."

"I'll dry." She laughed. "You're the one who jumped off a boat."

"I couldn't see a place to dock and this couldn't wait a second longer." He reached into his pocket and pulled out a small waterproof container, the kind boaters kept their valuables in. The clear plastic box seemed to glitter in his hands like a block of ice. Her heart leaped in her chest.

He knelt on the dock in front of her, as a slender band of diamonds and gold tumbled out into his palm. "When we said goodbye at Christmas, I promised I'd find a way to spend my life with you. And I've missed you every day, with every breath since then. I thought I'd just finish my voyage first, and that all this could wait until I'd made it once around the world. But I can't wait any longer. There's no adventure worth having without you beside me. So, I'm dropping anchor. Here. Now. With you."

But she grabbed his outstretched hand with both of hers before a marriage proposal could pass his lips.

Her knees dropped down to the wood until they were kneeling face-to-face. "Wait. What about your boat, your life, your dream?"

"I'll run short boating trips around the British Isles and France. Then, whenever you're ready—no matter how many years it takes—we'll lift anchor, and you and I can sail the world together." The smooth circle of the engagement ring pressed into the skin between their palms. "You are worth waiting for."

Her lips trembled. But she forced them still and took a deep breath.

Everything inside her was bursting to say yes to the question he had yet to ask. Her heart ached to just fall deep into his arms and to stay there forever. Yes, her uncle and aunt were in a better place now, living with a cousin of her aunt's who was a retired nurse. With no business to run, they didn't need her living with them full-time and could probably even go without her for a couple of days at a time.

But still. Was he sure?

Was she?

They'd had so many months apart and too many goodbyes already. Could she trust that this time he'd stay?

"My aunt still doesn't have a firm diagnosis," she said. "They're renting a place from family. I'm just working part-time. I don't know how long you'd need to stay anchored for. Are you sure you want to risk your whole future on me?"

"My beloved." Benjamin brushed her hair from her face. "I took the biggest risk of my life when I walked across the store floor to talk to you a year ago, because I knew the moment our eyes met that my heart was going to fall into your hands." He pulled the ring out from between their clasped hands. "Please, marry me, Piper. Be my best friend and my partner in this life. Share all my adventures with me and I'll share yours with you. No matter what the future brings."

A question echoed deep and sincere in the blue of his eyes, aching for an answer.

A look she knew she could trust.

Peace filled her heart. "Yes. Of course I will. Yes!"

He slid the ring on her finger. Her arms flew around his neck, so fast it sent her glasses tumbling off her face and clattering onto the dock. She closed her eyes as his lips found hers again. And the light of the morning sun brushed over them, filling their bodies with warmth.

* * * * *

*Witness Robyn Lowry doesn't remember the crime she
witnessed—but someone wants her dead.
Keeping Robyn alive long enough to testify is
US marshal Slade Brooks's hardest mission*

Read on for a sneak peek at
Hiding His Holiday Witness *by Laura Scott,*
available November 2021 from Love Inspired Suspense.

Robyn thrashed helplessly in the river current, her body
numb from the twin assaults of shock and the ice-cold
water.

Gasping for air, she managed to keep her head above
the water for several minutes and strained to listen. She'd
heard two gunshots moments before Slade had gently
pushed her over the ridge, but now there was only the
rushing sound of water.

Did that mean they were safe? She had no idea.

And where was Slade? She tried to turn in a circle, but
the river was moving too fast for her to take more than a
quick sweeping glance around to look for him.

She knew she couldn't stay in the water for much
longer. With renewed determination, Robyn angled
toward the shore.

Up ahead was a large tree branch hanging over the
water. With herculean effort, she reached up and snagged
the branch. She used every last bit of strength she
possessed to pull herself up and out of the water.

Her feet found the ground, and she emerged from the river to sprawl on the grassy embankment.

"Slade!" Panic clawed up her throat, threatening to strangle her.

She didn't know who she was or who was after her. She couldn't do this alone.

"Robyn!" The sound of her name made her want to weep with relief.

A splash caught her eye, and she saw a dark shadow getting out of the water about twenty yards from where she lay.

"Robyn, I'm so glad I found you. Let's get into the cover of some brush, okay?" Slade's voice was near her ear. "We want to stay hidden from view."

Because of the gunshots.

With Slade's help, she stood, and together they moved away from the river into the wooded area.

"Are you going to start a fire?"

"Not yet. I don't want to draw undue attention if someone is out there looking for us."

"For us? Or me?"

He hesitated, then said, "I'm not leaving you alone, Robyn. We're going to stick together from here on out."

Until when? Her memory had returned? And what if it didn't?

Don't miss
Hiding His Holiday Witness *by Laura Scott,*
available November 2021 wherever
Love Inspired Suspense books and ebooks are sold.

LoveInspired.com

LISEXP1021

LOVE INSPIRED

Stories to uplift and inspire

Fall in love with Love Inspired—
inspirational and uplifting stories of faith
and hope. Find strength and comfort in
the bonds of friendship and community.
Revel in the warmth of possibility and the
promise of new beginnings.

Sign up for the Love Inspired newsletter
at **LoveInspired.com** to be the first
to find out about upcoming titles,
special promotions and exclusive content.

CONNECT WITH US AT: